Innocent or Guilty?

A. M. Taylor lives and writes in London. When not making up stories, she writes copy for a living and can most often be found drinking coffee, watching Netflix, and trying to keep up with a never ending TBR pile. She's been obsessed with mysteries ever since Nancy Drew first walked into her life and would probably have attempted to become a private detective at some point, if only it didn't involve actually having to talk to people. She has a cat called Domino, ambitions of owning a dog one day, and is as obsessed with *My Favorite Murder* as you probably are.

Also by A. M. Taylor

Forget Me Not

Innocent or Guilty?

A. M. TAYLOR

OneMoreChapter

One More Chapter
an imprint of HarperCollins*Publishers* Ltd
1 London Bridge Street
London SE1 9GF

www.harpercollins.co.uk

This paperback edition 2019

First published in Great Britain in ebook format
by HarperCollins*Publishers* 2019

A catalogue record for this book
is available from the British Library

ISBN: 978-0-00-831294-7

This novel is entirely a work of fiction.
The names, characters and incidents portrayed in it are
the work of the author's imagination. Any resemblance to
actual persons, living or dead, events or localities is
entirely coincidental.

Set in Minion by
Palimpsest Book Production Limited, Falkirk, Stirlingshire

Printed and bound in the UK by CPI Group (UK) Ltd, Croydon CR0 4YY

For my parents

1

THEN

They find the body on a Sunday.

He didn't return home the night before, which isn't unheard of, but when he doesn't make it back in time for church and he still isn't home by the time they return, the family begins to worry. His mother rings the police and they tell her to sit tight, while his father calls his brother and gathers up a few of the boy's friends to set up a search party.

He's lying in the woods.

He has been all night.

He's face down in the mud. There's blood on the side and the back of his head, matting down his hair, pressing it to his skull. It's a friend who finds him, calling out for the boy's dad when he does so, the father running wildly towards him, pushing him out of the way, slipping in the mud.

He makes the mistake of moving him. Grabbing him by the shoulders to shake him awake in desperation. When he pulls his hands away they're covered in blood and as the stories soon will go, the father screams, grief curdling at his throat. The police are called again and this time they come, sirens wailing on the damp air, a parent's desperate call. Friends and family are pushed to the side lines, forced to watch as the routines of a crime scene establish themselves and the detectives take statements, waiting for the medical examiner to arrive.

The boy's uncle is sent back to the house with a female police officer in tow to break the news to the mother. Neighbors will go on to tell other neighbors about how she answers the door, arm outstretched, finger pointing at her brother-in-law's broken face as she shouts "No, no, no, no, no," over and over and over again, until the female police officer wraps her arms around the older woman's shaking shoulders and draws her inside her own home.

Word spreads, text messages sent, phone calls answered, whispers met by gasps, grimaces of shock followed by the promise of tears.

Tyler Washington is dead they're saying.

Murdered.

Found in the woods with his skull bashed in.

Less than a week later my twin brother is arrested.

My brother was born eleven minutes and 37 seconds after me. It was an easy delivery for twins apparently, or so our mom always told us. We were her second pregnancy, and we practically slipped right out; she and Dad barely making it to the hospital before I made my appearance. I came screaming into the world, face red and pink and white, covered in blood and placenta, all of it quickly wiped away to make me clean. Ethan slipped out silently though; maybe I was taking up all the oxygen in the room. In the womb. But Mom says the nurse just gave him a little slap on his small round bottom and he joined me in my new-to-the-world screams.

Twins.

Mom says she was terrified to begin with. Not just of how much more work and effort was involved but with how different we were from our sister Georgia. We took up twice the space, twice the time, twice the breast milk, twice the effort, but we were also strangely self-sufficient she'd tell us. She felt superfluous, she said. Our older sister Georgia had needed her, wanted her, all the time. We needed her occasionally, and wanted only each other. But that was a long time ago and by the time Ethan is arrested we barely speak to one another. Sometimes, I like to tell myself that it's because we don't need to; we already know what the other is thinking. But it's not like that. We shared a womb, shared a life and then suddenly, we split. Into two different people and the difference was what we needed to make us two different people. Otherwise we'd have just spent the rest of our lives as 'the twins'.

But instead what happened was that Ethan became my twin. I was Olivia, and Ethan was 'Olivia's twin'.

Until the Sunday when Tyler's body is found.

Until the Friday, just under a week later when Ethan is arrested for Tyler Washington's murder, and I become, forever, irrevocably, impossibly 'Ethan Hall's twin sister'.

2

"There's no way she did it," Matt said, "no fucking way."

"Why?" I asked, "Because she's a cute girl you wanna screw?"

Matt's pale face pinkened ever so slightly, those promising rosy spots deepening on the apple of his cheeks. He avoided my gaze when he said, "No, man. She's just so … small. And quiet. She's not the type."

"It's never the type in these situations though, is it?" Daniel said, voice creamy and languorous, sliding his eyes towards me, glowing in the artificially lit room. It was dark outside already, the blank slate of a grey Oregon afternoon overcrowding the room, so we'd had to turn the ugly strip lights on even though it wasn't yet four in the afternoon. We'd been in the same room for hours, lunch detritus littering the table, the air pungent with uneaten sandwiches and cold coffee. Tempers and nerves were starting to fray, impatience climbing the walls. I loved this part though; when it felt like anything could happen, like there was no way we could ever lose, like justice wasn't a pendulum that could sway either way but a judge's righteous gavel just waiting to be knocked on wood, the sound echoing around the room.

4

We were doing background research on the firm's newest client Reid Murphy, and the man she'd been accused of almost killing, James Asher, who was currently in a coma on an intensive care ward on the other side of the city. Murphy was 22 and looked even younger, so young you'd ask if her parents were home if she answered her own front door. And Matt was right; she was small and quiet, scared to death in my opinion, not that my opinion really mattered here. All of it would help though; the jury bench packed full of people like my colleagues who thought a girl like Reid Murphy couldn't ever possibly hurt a man so badly she put him in a coma. But I'd seen something in the un-seeing stare of her eyes, the unwavering gaze, and I wasn't so sure. Anyone's capable of anything in my opinion. Again, not that it mattered, not that my opinion counted for anything; we were here to prove she was innocent whether she was or not.

We'd reached the ropiest part of the day, when we'd all been there too long: lunch had been eaten and we'd all start thinking about dinner soon, but for now it was the lull and the dip of late afternoon. Distraction roaring in, heads up, eyes darting between me and Matt, opinions readied to be lobbed across the conference room table. I looked across to Daniel, and could see that his eyes were dancing, like always, ready to tease and tickle, the facetious little quirk to his eyebrows getting more and more pronounced.

Daniel caught my eye and widened his, about to say something, mouth opening to a cartoonish 'o' when his phone began to vibrate and his forehead creased. He made the sign for 'one moment' at me, holding his finger in the air, and the groans began before he was even out the door. "You better be coming straight back, Koh!" Matt called after him, the glass door closing noiselessly on Daniel's retreating back. "That better have been some medical results," Matt continued to grumble, and I thought, not for the first time, about how quickly we'd all become exactly who and what the firm's partners wanted us to become. Snipping and sniping and picking each other off, one by one. It was all happy and good natured until someone looked as though they weren't pulling their weight, and suddenly the jabs had real force behind them and judgment started to crash the party. The best of friends, right up until we weren't.

Daniel's departure dampened the mood and a weight settled over the room. Instead of punchy and worked up, we fell into resigned lethargy, bending our heads down again, hard at work. Daniel was gone a while though, and my eyes had started to swim, desperate for more caffeine when he eventually came back. No one said anything to him when he did, but he was waiting for me when we finally left the conference room several hours later. He had been sat closest to the door and I furthest from it, so everyone filed out ahead of me, Daniel leaning against the hallway wall, waiting. "What's going on?" I asked, shouldering my bag, adjusting my jacket. He had a look on his face I couldn't quite decipher, maybe it was anticipation.

"That phone call was from my friend Ray, you know, the one who works on that podcast?"

"The true crime podcast? Why, was he asking for your help?" We might have only been first year associates, but we were working for one of the biggest criminal defense law firms in Portland, so a true crime podcast producer coming to Daniel for his expertise or opinion wasn't completely outside the realm of possibilities.

"No, he's here in Portland, with the host, Kat."

"Are they working on a Portland case?" I asked, interest creeping into my voice despite myself.

"Maybe, yeah. I told them about you. And Ethan. They're thinking about doing his case."

I couldn't say anything for a second, my mouth suddenly dry. When I eventually managed to speak it came out as a croak, "What?"

"Yeah, I emailed him about it ages ago, but they were just wrapping up the last season and wanted to do a little research, look around a little before deciding on their next topic." He was bouncing on the balls of his feet, his face lively, animated; eyebrows up by his hairline, mouth grinning and winning.

"Why did you email him in the first place, though? I didn't ask you to do that," I said, my mouth still dry, desperate for a drink.

"No, I know. Do I need your permission for everything?"

"When it comes to my fucking family, yeah you do."

Daniel's body stopped moving, his never-ending energy finally brought to a standstill. "Liv, come on, what's the problem here? This is a good thing. It could be *really* good; the first case they worked on the sentence got overturned, and the guy from the second season? He's just filed for a retrial, and finally got his request granted after years of trying."

My hands went up to the strap of my bag, fiddling with it, the weight suddenly uncomfortable on my shoulder. I didn't meet Daniel's eye when I said, "It's just not your place. What were you thinking? How could you do this and not tell me?"

"I'm telling you now," he said, the words expelled on a massive exhale of breath. "Plus, it's not as if it's all set in stone yet. Kat wants to meet you and Ethan, get to know you and the case a little better."

"What?" I said again, this time in a snap, "Me *and* Ethan?"

"Yeah, they like to work on cases where they can have the involvement of the family and a close relationship with the subject. You've listened to the podcast, you know that."

I shook my head, but once again I couldn't say anything, my mind a blank trap. Daniel reached out and put his hand on my shoulder, it was warm and heavy like it always was, a tiny reverberation thrumming through me as he said in a low voice, "Look, I've said we'll meet them for a drink at Blue Plate, and that's all it has to be if you want. A no-strings after work drink with an old friend of mine. That's it."

I knew that wouldn't be it, but I finally looked him in the eye, and even though I knew exactly what he was doing, the calm, convincing tone, the comforting touch, I nodded my head and

7

agreed to something that made the pit of my stomach scramble and lurch.

Blue Plate was busy and I couldn't see my roommate Samira anywhere. Probably she was back in the kitchen, prepping the desserts that helped make the restaurant so popular. The ma tre d' greeted me and Daniel with familiarity and gave us a corner seat in one of their coveted forest green leather booths. Being roommates with the pastry chef had its perks. Ray and Kat hadn't arrived yet, and this bothered me. I hadn't wanted to come after all, hadn't even known it was happening until roughly twenty minutes ago, and now here I was waiting on a couple of strangers. The restaurant was moodily lit, glittering candles, spherical sconces emitting a gas like low glow. The couple at the table right in front of us were on a first or second date, and to the left a large party had gathered to celebrate a birthday. The birthday girl had balloons tied to the back of her chair and the party's laughter spilled out over the whole restaurant, people turning to look. I fiddled with my cutlery, the table all laid up for us to eat although we hadn't ordered any food yet – just wine. I jiggled my legs up and down under the table, Daniel eventually moving his hand to my left knee to still it.

"What is wrong with you?" he said while pouring me a glass of wine. There wasn't any accusation in his voice; he was practically laughing and he gave me a sidelong look that seemed to say 'who are you?'

"I'm nervous," I answered.

"I guess I've never seen you nervous."

"I guess not."

"You don't have to worry, Liv. They're not banking on this for their next season, I'm pretty sure they've got other options, so if you don't want to do it, you don't want to do it."

"You think I should though," I said, taking a large gulp of wine, wishing there was bread on the table for me to bite down on.

Daniel shrugged, "I just think … what have you got to lose?"

8

I looked at him, wondering. I guess he would think that.

"Hey," he said suddenly, breaking eye contact with me, and moving to stand up although the table stopped him from doing so properly, so he was kind of crouching, hovering over the table, waving an arm in the air, "there they are! Ray! Over here, man." He was waving them towards us, ushering with his long, outstretched arm, and I watched as two people walked towards us, weaving their way around tables and chairs.

Ray was shorter than I'd expected, but then everyone is normally shorter than I expected. Kat, meanwhile – for I had to assume this was Kat – was over six feet tall, wearing a mustard yellow shearling biker jacket that matched the wrap she had on her head hiding her hair. Underneath the jacket, she was wearing a black and dark green leopard print jumpsuit, and her shoes were stacked high, not that she needed the extra height, chunky soled Chelsea boots protecting her feet from the rain outside. She smiled amiably at us both as introductions were made. I reached my hand across the table to shake hers, and her smile grew wider, "Hi, Olivia. It's really nice to meet you." Her voice was low and throaty, a little scratched, and immediately familiar after hours of listening to her on the podcast.

I nodded in response, and felt my throat constrict. Daniel had to nudge me a little to remind me to speak and I was relieved my voice came out sounding normal when I said, "Yeah, you too. Both of you," I added, taking in Ray as well. "I'm a big fan of the podcast."

"Oh, you listen? I wasn't sure after speaking to Danny about it," Ray said.

I raised my eyebrows at the 'Danny', but nodded again, "No, I listen. I just didn't ever expect to be the subject of it."

Kat and Ray shared a small look and Kat said, "Well, we haven't decided on the topic for our third season yet, to be honest. And it would really be Ethan rather than you that was the subject ..." she finished with a grin, stretching her hand out to take the glass of wine Daniel had just poured for her.

"Oh, I know it wouldn't be me," I said, taking a deep breath, "I just meant … this was hard for my whole family, you know? It's not just Ethan, although obviously it's his story. He is the one in prison, after all."

Kat raised both her eyebrows at me and nodded slowly. "Do you think you'd be able to get your family to talk with us? If we moved forward with Ethan's story?"

I licked my lips, trying to stop myself from biting at them. "Maybe, I don't know. Probably Georgia, my sister, but even then I'm not completely sure."

"But, they do believe he's innocent, right? Like you do?" Kat asked.

And there it was; Ethan's innocence, dropping into the room like a rock through water.

"Yes," I said eventually, but it was so long since I'd talked to my family about Ethan and his innocence, I wasn't completely sure whether I'd just told a lie or not.

3

THEN

The room changes the moment the judge says the word, 'guilty'. I watch Ethan's shoulders stiffen, his entire body braced. We were told to expect this, and yet still, somehow, I didn't. Didn't think the system could get it this wrong. Ethan's long, slim body is completely still; he hasn't moved, but his lawyer is next to him, arm slung around his shoulders, and I wish I could hear what he's saying but I can't. Ethan still doesn't move. Doesn't make to reply to his lawyer, doesn't look as though he's ever going to move again, until suddenly he does. He's forced to; the bailiff is attaching his handcuffs again, taking him away.

He turns then, finally, and even though Mom calls out his name, her voice cracking the room in two, he looks straight at me, our identical eyes catching. We're the same height. He's not all that tall for a guy, but for a girl I am, and so we're eye to eye. Mom reaches up to him, pulling him into a hug before they take him away, and Dad has to pull her from him, letting my older sister, Georgia in for a hug too, and then clapping Ethan's shoulder. Dad says something I don't hear, and Ethan is swaying slightly in the push and pull, arms and hands outstretched towards him, taking, taking, taking. And still he hasn't taken his eyes off mine. Finally we hug, for the first time in years it feels like, and of course it's only one sided because he's already in chains, but before he's pulled away again I say, "I'll make this right, okay? I promise."

He nods at me, as if it's all understood, a done deal, as if he knows that, somehow, someday, I'll get him out of this, out of prison, even though I have no idea how, and wish that he'd tell me. Mom and Georgia are crying, albeit quietly, as Ethan is led away, and when I turn to look at Dad, he's dumbfounded, his face a mask of stupefied tragedy like I've never seen it before. I want to reach out to all of them, to be pulled back into their orbit, but I feel detached from them now, a satellite circling them, no longer a part of the home planet. Mom and Georgia look so similar huddled together, the same size and shape, small and compact, shoulder to shoulder. Ethan and I always took after Dad more, and when I look at him now I wonder if I'm seeing my twin in thirty years' time, face crumpled and destroyed by sudden loss, transfixed by a horror no one ever saw coming. And then I make a decision, putting my arms around them all, pulling them towards me, pulling them into my own tilted orbit; the strange, circling satellite, and like that we walk out of the courtroom together.

4

NOW

"Did you ever doubt him?" Kat asked, swirling the wine in her glass around so it shone in the candlelight. "Did you ever think he might have done it?"

"No," I said.

"Really?" She said, her head pulled back in surprise, her voice going up. "Not even once?"

"We shared a womb. It breeds a certain amount of trust."

"So, you guys are like, really close?"

I took a sip of wine, licking my lips after, "We weren't when it all happened ... when Tyler died, we hadn't been close for years, not since we were nine, ten."

"Why?"

I shrugged, trying to think back that far. It had all seemed so important then. "We were just really different. We still are."

"But you're close now?" Kat was leaning forward, her arms resting on the table. It felt casual, but it wasn't and I wondered for a second if she was recording the whole thing.

"It's a little difficult to be close when there's an entire prison system between you, but yeah, I guess you'd say we were close."

"I'd really like to meet him. To go and see him, but I don't think he'll see me without you there."

"What makes you say that?" I asked, my palms beginning to itch.

"Because that's what he told me."

"You've spoken to him already?" I asked with a sideways glance at Daniel. He was drinking from his glass of wine and didn't seem to notice.

"Yeah, of course. I wouldn't be here unless I had done. Look, Olivia," she said, rearranging herself in her seat, settling in for something, "you can't take this lightly. We go all in on a subject and a case when we research it. We want the truth and we want some kind of resolution, and it can be really painful and uncomfortable for a lot of people, even the innocent and the victims. If we do this, we're going to be dredging up your whole family's past. Yours, Ethan's, pretty much everyone who was involved in the investigation. So, you have to know what you're getting yourself into. And Ethan really has to know, because it's going to affect him the most. I need to see it in his eyes that he understands everything that we're going to do in the process of making this podcast, otherwise it's not going to happen. I need that from you too."

The birthday party was still roaring with delight at the table next to us, and the couple on the date had descended into distractingly awkward and prolonged silences. Waiters and waitresses were passing our table constantly, eyeing up our rapidly depleting carafe of wine with professional interest, stopping to drop by some dinner menus. But it was as if the four of us, hell the two of us – Kat and I – were all alone in that din. She was staring at me with such intensity, my natural inclination was to look away, but I couldn't. She demanded attention. I reached for the stem of my wine glass, needing something to touch, something to do, and finally I shrugged, feigning a kind of natural indifference I felt a million miles from, and said, "Of course."

"Okay," Kat said, suffusing that one word with a sense of boundless relief and animation, and leaning back in her seat with a wide grin before reaching over to pick up one of the menus that had been left for us, "So, what's good here?"

I sank back in my own seat, mirroring her and said nonchalantly, "Here? It's all good." But it was a nonchalance I didn't feel – does anyone ever feel truly nonchalant? – and when I picked up the menu to see what was on offer tonight, I felt like I'd set something in motion that I'd never be able to stop. I wasn't used to feeling so out of control. Ever since Ethan had been arrested, I'd done everything I could to maximize the sense of control I had over my life, and that of my twin brother's. It was the whole reason I'd gone to law school, the reason I'd stayed in Oregon, so close to a home that had so thoroughly rejected me and my family; I was going to clear his name. But I'd never imagined doing it this way, with microphones and journalists, and a whole audience watching. Or listening, at least. So, why did I? Maybe it was Daniel's luminous eyes staring so expectantly at me, as bright as a child's; or maybe it was Kat's, hard, dark and defiant, the face of true tenacity. Or maybe it was the thought of Ethan's, so similar to mine – identical in fact – staring at me in horror and disbelief, an unasked, pleading question hidden within them on the day he was pronounced guilty. I knew that he'd given up thinking that anyone, least of all me, would be able to get him out of there by now. I'd gone to college for him, surprised everyone and got into law school for him, and yet I still hadn't been able to do the thing that really mattered, and have him exonerated. Or maybe I said yes to the podcast, because I'd finally figured out that control was an illusion; a net the size of the world trying to catch just one single butterfly. And that chaos always managed to creep in, flap its wings, and change everything forever.

So, we ordered dinner, a bright pink beetroot risotto with bright white beads of goat cheese melting into it for Kat who

15

turned out to be vegetarian, a shared beef bourguignon for Daniel and Ray who most certainly were not, and a cedar plank salmon for me. By the time we were ready for dessert, the restaurant had quieted to a lull, the birthday party having moved on to a bar, the flaccid date disbanded in near-silence, and my roommate Samira came out to join us, bringing more desserts than we'd ordered with her.

"You have to try the apple, cheddar and caramel pie," she declared, skootching in next to me on the bench, "all anyone's ordered tonight is the chocolate freakin' torte."

"Well, if you didn't make it so freakin' delicious maybe they wouldn't order it so much," I said.

"I'm not going to argue with you there, all I'm saying is it's a crying shame that only four people so far have tasted this sensational delight. It's served with rosemary ice cream for Christ's sake," Samira said.

I took one of the servings of pie from her and introduced her to Kat and Ray. "*Shadow of a Doubt*?" she said, her eyes widening, "Man, this is an honor. I do my best pastry making listening to you guys."

It was Samira who had got me listening to *Shadow of a Doubt* in the first place. She'd told me about it before Daniel had even realized he'd gone to college with the often referred to, but rarely heard producer, 'Ray'. *Shadow of a Doubt* had been my introduction to true crime podcasts, and now I listened to them constantly, voraciously, omnivorously. Funny ones, sentimental ones, sincere ones, straight down the line ones. At first I'd thought I'd be too close to it to enjoy any of them. Both as a lawyer and as my brother's sister. But it turns out the opposite was true; I loved them just as much as anyone did. And boy, did everyone seem to; our collective blood lust undimmed since Jack the Ripper stalked the streets and sold out newspapers, and the Victorians realized just how much murder sells.

"Are you sure about this?" Samira asked as she looped her

arm through mine and we walked home together. Daniel had left with Kat and Ray, his face silly and drunk, eyes alight when Ray had mentioned something about their hotel bar. It was a Friday night, but the neighborhood was crisp and quiet as we walked. All it took was a sudden left turn, and the lights and sounds of restaurants, bars and coffee shops transformed into rows of quiet houses, buttoned up against the early fall evening.

"Why are you asking? I thought you loved *Shadow of a Doubt*."

"I do, and don't get me wrong, I am thrilled to have just met the great Kat Thomas, and mysterious Ray Mackenzie in person, believe me. But come on, it's going to be a whole different thing, actually *being* on the podcast."

"Yeah, I know."

"I mean, you did change your last name just to stop people knowing you were Ethan Hall's sister. This is kind of going to blow that little charade right over."

I laughed, the sound getting lost on the wind; Samira was always coming up with sayings and aphorisms that weren't quite right, that she'd plucked straight from the air in front of her. "I know that."

"Yeah, I guess you do."

"Anyway, it's all a moot point until Ethan agrees to it."

We walked along in silence for a while, our house coming into view, the streetlight that stood sentry outside it turning the red of the cherry tree's leaves almost neon in the night. "Do you think he will?" Samira asked.

"I think he'll think he doesn't have a choice," I said, although as we ascended the steps to the front porch, I had no idea if that was true or not.

"And what about your family? Kat said she'd want them to be involved right? You really think they'd be cool with that?"

I sighed, thinking about my parents and sister, all three of whom, as much as they loved Ethan, preferred to pretend that none of the nasty business of ten years ago had ever happened.

"I don't know," I said, sliding my key into the lock, "I'm seeing them for dinner on Sunday though, so I guess I'll find out then."

* * *

"Keys, wallets, all personal effects in the trays to your left, and then step through, please ma'am."

It was just like being at the airport, except instead of boundless freedom and flight on the other side of security, there was the complete opposite. I went through the motions without comment, Kat right behind me, free of her recording equipment and her producer, Ray, as only two of us were allowed during visiting hours at a time. This part of any visit was always the strangest. When Ethan was right in front of me, and I could see his face, hear his voice, I could almost forget where we were, and when I wasn't there, the reality of it was dimmed, but this in-between part reinforced that reality all too clearly. I'd expected to have to talk Kat through the rigors and rigmarole of prison visitations, but realized that she must have done plenty of prison visits in the past for the first two seasons of *Shadow of a Doubt*. Her face was blank and mild, although her eyes retained their alert liveliness, and she was unfailingly polite to everyone we came into contact with.

Ethan was already in place when we walked into the visitor's room. Gone were the days when I had to talk to him through bullet proof plastic and a telephone handset. Good behavior had seen his privileges expand, and now we could sit around a round, concrete table, curved benches fucking up our backs. The windows were high in there, taller than any human and the room had the same artificial lighting of any institution; harsh and unforgiving. Ethan watched us walk across the room towards him, his eyes trained on Kat. He didn't look at me at all until after I'd introduced them and they'd awkwardly shaken hands. He looked tired and thin, but then he always looked tired and

18

thin, so I tried to look for ways in which he looked different to normal, certain that something was off. It took me a little while to realize, but finally I got it; his eyes. They were alight and alive in a way I hadn't seen in years. That was why it had taken me so long to figure out; because it had been so long since I'd seen him like this. He looked excited. He looked awake.

Kat had got out her notebook and pencil she'd been allowed to bring in with her and was making note of the date, time and place in grey lead.

"What's your show called again?" Ethan asked.

"*Shadow of a Doubt*," Kat said.

"And it's an online only thing? Like YouTube?"

"It's a podcast. It's audio only. Most people listen from their phones. Obviously, we have a website though, where we post updates, and sometimes transcripts or other artefacts that listeners can read for a deeper understanding and experience."

Ethan's brow furrowed, the light leaving his eyes a little. "But people really listen?"

"Yeah, they really listen," Kat said.

"They average about 250,000 downloads per episode," I added, Kat turning to me in surprise. "I looked it up last night," I said, shrugging.

"And that's a lot?" Ethan asked.

"That's a whole lot," I assured him. They had a TV in the rec room, and there was internet access from some ancient computers, but sometimes it was hard to truly fathom just how far the prison, and therefore the prisoners, lagged behind the rest of the world. Ethan lived in a time warp where the word 'Netflix' meant DVDs arriving by mail, and Instagram nothing at all. It always brought me up short in conversations with him; he hadn't even joined Facebook before being imprisoned, that's how long ten years was in the 21st century. To someone raised on the viewing figures of *Friends* or *CSI*, 250,000 people must have sounded inconsequential.

"Okay," Ethan said slowly, turning his attention back to Kat, "so, what's the point of your show? Are you going to prove I'm innocent, somehow?"

Kat took a deep breath and shifted in her seat so she was sitting up a little straighter. She was wearing the same yellow head wrap she'd been wearing the night before, a deep yellow color, almost gold, but the rest of her outfit was grey and black, in contrast to the colorful get-up I'd seen her in at the restaurant. "We never set out to prove if someone is innocent or guilty," she said, "that would mean we were starting from a hypothesis and that's definitively what we do not do. In both the cases we've worked on before there was strong indication that there had been a miscarriage of justice, and I think we've been able to help shed light on that, and maybe even bring about some real change. But really this is about figuring out what happened and why there's still doubt hovering over any one case."

She spoke like she did on the show, in full, thoughtful sentences that sounded as if they might have been written beforehand, but in this case clearly weren't. Maybe it was the way she always sounded – it was certainly how she'd come across last night, but I found myself wondering what she'd sounded like before she started podcasting, or when she was two bottles of wine in and sloppy and drunk.

"And is this going to be on the podcast?" Ethan asked, motioning between the two of them to indicate he meant their current interaction.

"No. They wouldn't let me bring my cellphone or any recording equipment in, so I'm not recording this. I'll take notes though, and if we decide to go ahead with the show – all of us – then what I'll probably do is describe this initial interview to the audience. Does that all sound okay to you?"

"Okay. So, how will you actually interview me, then?" Ethan asked, looking puzzled.

"Probably over the phone. If you give your consent, that is.

We wouldn't be able to keep coming back and forth from here anyway," Kat said.

"Right, okay," Ethan said, although I thought I could detect a tremor of uncertainty as he glanced over at me.

"Okay, so. Tell me about Tyler," Kat said and my stomach rolled over. I hadn't expected her to ask about him, although why not, I'm not sure.

"Tyler?" Ethan asked, his eyes locked on mine.

"Yeah. You must have known him, right?"

"We both did," Ethan replied, his gaze returning to Kat.

5

THEN

The judge calls for closing arguments and I turn instinctively
to the jury. I've been studying them, searching their faces for
weeks now, scouring for anything, any little thing, that gives
their sympathies away, and I'm still none the wiser. Any time
one of them shifts in their seat, sighs from bodily discontent, or
shrugs a shoulder, my eyes swivel to them like the search beam
of a lighthouse. But they all sit up a little straighter now, their
attention trained on the prosecutor; they like him, I realize, or
maybe they're just relieved to see light at the end of this tunnel,
a way home and a way out. At least for them.

"Tyler Washington was eighteen when he died, his whole life
ahead of him," the prosecutor begins and I think, despite myself,
here we go. It's not that I don't feel bad for him, or for his family,
but this is the way every statement about Tyler Washington, from
the very first news article, to his obituary, to the opening statements of the trial, have begun. At first they stopped me short;
dead at eighteen, a life cut so very, very short, but it's been almost
a year now and hearing the same sentences over and over has
worn me down. The jury is listening though, alert, not quite

jaded. Only one juror is sitting slightly slumped in her seat. She's young, the youngest on the jury by quite some margin, and as I stare at her, her eyes flick from the prosecutor, straight to me. As if she could feel me watching her. She has sullen, hooded eyes and the look of someone who doesn't spend much time outdoors, which is unusual around here. I wonder if she went to the same high school as Tyler, as all of us, maybe a few years ahead, and then I realize that the prosecutor is still talking and I'm missing the whole thing.

"It wasn't just that Tyler was class president and captain of the basketball team, or even that his mother is mayor of this city. It's that his teachers described him as 'charming' and 'cheeky', his friends would call on him to help move furniture, to drive them out to a new climbing spot, to lend them money even, and he'd invariably say yes. His peers knew him as friendly and affable, even caring and kind and his family relied on him for cheer and quick wit, even in trying times. 'He always seemed to have a smile on his face', his former vice principal said. In comparison, people have very little to say about the defendant. Ethan Hall doesn't stir up happy memories, or a long list of complimentary adjectives. At school he was a loner, and if he hadn't killed Tyler Washington, his peers say they barely would have remembered he even attended Twin Rivers High with them."

Ethan's shoulders have stiffened; I'm watching them. This is the same shit Ethan's lived with most of his life, and for most of that time I was part of it, I helped fuel it. I wonder if we weren't twins it would have happened differently. If Ethan would have blended in to the background more if it wasn't for me, constantly calling attention to myself. But we're so different it was constantly remarked upon; the cheerleader and the loner who somehow once shared a womb. So far, this is nothing compared to what's been written in newspapers and discussed on TV screens, or even what was shouted at him in the hallways of our high school, way back before any of this happened, but the prosecutor's just laying the ground work. There's more to come.

"When Tyler Washington left his friend's house that night, do you think there could have been any way he thought he might not make it home? No. Of course not. That's not a thought that ever crosses an eighteen-year-old's mind. At eighteen, you are invulnerable, indestructible, immortal. But Tyler wasn't any of those things. All he was doing was trying to save time, to cut a couple corners and get home through the woods a little quicker. But Ethan Hall had other ideas. We may never know if Ethan followed Tyler into those woods with the intention of killing his former classmate, but let's focus on the things we do know. Ethan had been hanging out that night at his friend Kevin Lawrence's house, just a twenty-five-minute bike ride away from where Tyler was at Jessica Heng's house. So, when he left Kevin's house he would have entered the woods at almost exactly the time Tyler Washington is believed to have died. Remember that the medical examiner estimated and testified to the fact that Tyler most likely died between 1:45 and 2:45 on the morning of Sunday August 24, and that Kevin Lawrence has stated that Hall had left his home somewhere between two and two thirty a.m.. Did Ethan watch Tyler enter the woods and seize on an opportunity, or did he happen upon him and the two get into a fight, as the defendant admitted to in a confession he has since recanted?

"Ethan Hall is not to be trusted. His refusal to stand by his initial confession and plead guilty to this crime proves that. Don't be confused by his quiet demeanor and slight frame. Ethan may not be the strapping basketball player Tyler was, but he trained as a fencer for much of his young life, and as we heard in witness testimony from a fencing expert, this kind of training could easily give him the advantage, even in a fight against a larger man."

I knew it wouldn't take long before the fencing came up. It's been over four years since Ethan did any seriously and yet here we are, talking about how it's possible he might have killed someone based on the fact he used to be able to point an unusually thin

24

sword in the right direction. The prosecutor has been standing in front of the jury bench the whole time, attention focused on them, impassioned words underlined by hand movements and gesticulations, but now he turns to Ethan and his demeanor changes. Ethan's does too. His shoulders fold in on themselves, he shifts lower in his chair, shrinking. It makes me want to grab him and pull him up, force him to sit straight, to look ahead, to face these accusations with both eyes wide open. But there's nothing I can do, and I can see in the way most of the jury members look at him, that they think this shrinking, this shirking, makes him look guilty.

"And what then, of motive?" the prosecutor asks, the words puncturing the room. He's still looking at Ethan, as if he'll get out of his seat and answer the question directly, but then, smooth as butter, his attention shifts back to the jury and he leaves Ethan alone.

"Tyler was the golden boy, liked – loved even – by all, as I've already mentioned. Who could possibly want to hurt – to kill – him in this savage, unprovoked way?"

6

"Tyler was ..." Ethan, trailed off, leaving the air blank.

"Tyler was kind of a dick," I finished for him, "especially to Ethan."

"And that's what they focused on, right? In the trial? That you had cause to kill him because he'd been bullying you for so long?"

Ethan swallowed, not looking at either of us, not making eye contact. "Yeah, 'bullying' makes it sound kind of ... I dunno, after school special. Ha," he interjected himself suddenly, "I guess it all was."

"Tyler was *that* kid, *the* guy. Every school has one, right? The person everyone looks up to and emulates and yet also basically hates?" I said.

"Sure, I know the guy you're talking about," Kat said, "I know the girl too. Safe to say none of us here were that person."

"Well, actually, Olivia kind of was," Ethan said.

"I wasn't – not really. I mean, I was no Tyler Washington, that's for sure."

Ethan raised both his eyebrows at me and then turned to Kat, "Olivia was popular. Like, pop-u-lar," he reiterated, sounding out every syllable. There was something in his voice that sounded

26

teasing, light, and yet I detected the edge of it too. I always could.

"Oh, so you and Tyler were actually friends then?" Kat asked. "You were close?"

I swallowed, pushing something down, away. "We were friends, sure, but we weren't close. We were in the same group."

Kat nodded, scribbling something down in her notebook and I resisted the urge to lean forward and read over her shoulder. "So, if we go ahead with all this, how would you feel about the fact that I'll be talking to people who were close to Tyler too? Who might have a slightly different opinion of him than you do?" she asked Ethan.

Ethan didn't answer for a while and I watched a cloud pass over his eyes before he said, "You really think they'll be willing to talk to you?"

"I hope so. Otherwise this might not happen at all."

"I don't know. What do you think, Liv?" Ethan asked, turning his gaze on me.

I shrugged, leaning against the table, looking between him and Kat, "There's two sides to every story, right?"

Except I didn't really believe that. There weren't two sides to every story; there was more like eight, and most of the time all eight sides existed inside just one person.

"Do you mind if I talk to my sister in private?" Ethan asked after a while. Visiting hours were coming to a close and there was new movement in the room. Family members were saying goodbye to one another once again, the guards paying even closer attention when anyone got up, especially if there was physical contact involved.

"Sure," Kat said, "I'll meet you outside," she directed at me.

"What's up?" I asked once she was out of ear shot.

"I just wanted to make sure you were really okay with this."

"Me? Why? I'm the one who brought her here."

"I just – I'm trusting you on this. I haven't listened to the show,

I don't even really get what it is, what their angle is, if they have one, who their audience is. It's all Greek to me."

"I think it's a good idea," I said, nodding emphatically.

"Have you spoken to Mom and Dad about it yet?"

"No ... that's on tomorrow's to-do list."

"They might not be so sure."

"I know."

There was a pause, not long, but loaded, as Ethan looked straight at me. "If you're okay with it, I'm okay with it," he said very slowly.

"This can't be my decision," I said, shaking my head. "All of this will affect you more than anyone."

"Maybe. Maybe not."

"What do you mean?" I asked, leaning across the table, trying to read the furrowed lines of his forehead.

"Just that we live in different worlds. I don't know that a podcast will change anything in here."

I leaned back, watching him still. "You don't think this will work. You don't think anything will change."

"It's hard to imagine change from inside here. Nothing ever changes. The faces do maybe, but then eventually, we all start to look the same anyway."

I stared around the room, looking at the faces of Ethan's fellow inmates, realizing how remarkably true his words were. We were running out of time though. The guards were hustling prisoners back towards their cells, and there were fewer and fewer visitors in the room. The room was losing its warmth; what little there was of it in the first place, and suddenly I felt a desperate urgency.

"You know I've done everything I can on my own, right?" I asked, leaning towards Ethan once more, "I've written to the Oregon Innocence Project every year since you were arrested."

Ethan nodded, his eyes boring into mine, holding fast. "I know that, Olivia. What I don't know is how some radio show is going to change my situation."

"Podcast," I said, reflexively.

"Podcast, sorry. But you know what I'm saying, don't you? You were there, you remember what it was like. The closing of the ranks in town, the accusations. I can't imagine it going any other way, even now, ten years later. Kat said they were after the truth, and I respect that. I'm just … not sure anyone will ever know the truth about Tyler Washington. Except for the people who were there."

* * *

"Mom? Dad?" I called, opening the door to my parents' house with the key they still insisted on me having. I'd tried knocking already but to no avail. I walked through the hallway and down towards the kitchen, where I could normally find one or the other of them, but the house was still and quiet. The rain had let up that morning, peeling back a faded blue sky of a Sunday and I wasn't surprised at all when I spotted them both outside in the yard, the back door open a little, pushing back and forth in the light September wind as they enjoyed the thin rays of the sun. "Mom!" I called again, and this time her head shot up from the flower bed she was working on and she called back, "Georgia?"

I walked out onto the back porch and waved at Dad sitting in his favorite lawn chair, before realizing his eyes were closed and he was deep in a nap. "Oh, Liv," Mom said, standing up, a little unsteady on her feet and brushing her hands on the fabric of her pants as she walked towards me. "I wasn't expecting you yet, sweetheart," she said as she pulled me into a hug.

"I messaged you last night, you didn't get it?" Mom let go of me and shook her head, squinting at me, even though the sun was hardly bright out here. "You lose your glasses again?"

"I can't find them anywhere, sweetie, they've disappeared forever this time, I'm afraid."

"And that's why you haven't read my message?"

"My little detective," Mom said, squeezing my shoulder and walking with me back towards the house. "Anyway, it's nice to see you. I thought you might be little too busy for dinner tonight. You have a big new case to work on, don't you?"

"I do, but I have something else I wanted to talk to you about."

"Uh oh."

Even though neither Georgia nor I lived at home anymore, Sunday night suppers remained a fairly regular tradition in our family. When we were growing up it was often the only time all five of us would sit down to eat together in the week, and after Ethan went to prison and we all moved away from Twin Rivers, they continued on as a familial touchstone. We all loved to cook, but my mom and Georgia were by far and away the best chefs in the family. So, it wasn't unusual for us all to gather together like this, it wasn't even that unusual for me to turn up unexpectedly on a Sunday night with the expectation of being fed; I'd spent plenty of weekends in law school, working my brain into disarray, just trying to keep up and catch up, and sometimes the only way to maintain a semblance of sanity was to keep Sunday nights sacred and to have a member of my family cook for me. I never failed to think of Ethan and the endless numbers of meals he must have eaten in prison; barely distinguishable ingredients swallowed down at speed, while trying to avoid whatever prison politics were being played out in the canteen that day or week or month. There were times during this whole ordeal when I was so, so sure that Ethan's arrest and prosecution were going to pull our family apart, leave us looking nothing like the family we were before. But over time the four of us managed to stitch ourselves back together, and sometimes I found myself wondering what we would all look like if Ethan was sat at the table too, and I scared myself by thinking that we might all have become closer without him.

We didn't sit down until much later, not until Georgia had arrived, her arms full of the fresh vegetables she'd been harvesting at her community garden all day. Mom was a landscape gardener and all the green fingers and thumbs had been inherited by Georgia, completely bypassing me. Ethan had them too, although I doubted they got much use in prison.

"So, you guys know what a podcast is, right?" I asked, Georgia shooting me a look that said *duh*, as well as *where are you going with this*, while Mom put down her fork to grab a glass of wine before saying,

"Yes, we have managed to figure out what they are, thank you darling."

"Cool, have you listened to *Shadow of a Doubt* at all?"

"Which one's that?" Dad asked.

"It's true crime," Georgia said, "right, Liv?"

Dad groaned and rolled his eyes towards me, "Not all that true crime nonsense again, I thought you'd got that out of your system years ago. Hasn't your brother's troubles taught you anything?" I'd been something of a true crime junkie growing up; inhaling episodes of *Forensic Files* the way most people watched *Friends*. I even used to fall asleep to them.

"This is different. It's not just going over what happened, they actually investigate and they've even led to retrials, and sentences being overturned." I realized that I was taking on the role Daniel had played on Friday night, convincing my parents of the podcast's validity, persuading them towards my view.

"Okay, so what? You want us to listen to this podcast?" Mom asked, looking a little bemused. "Or are you going to start working for them instead of Coleridge and White?"

"No, I'm not leaving my job. But they're interested in covering Ethan's case for their new season. And I think it's a good idea. And so does Ethan."

I watched as my parents shared a look. A zipped up, private communique that I'd witnessed a thousand times before, and yet still didn't really know how to decipher. "You've spoken to Ethan about this already?" Georgia asked.

"Yeah, I went to visit him yesterday with the host, Kat."

Both my parents put down their cutlery at the same time, their gazes now firmly locked on me, "That's not – he thinks it's a good idea?" Mom asked, a tremor of worry lining her voice.

"Yeah, well I'm still not sure he quite gets what a big deal the podcast actually is, but yeah, he's on board."

"I'm surprised at you, Olivia," Dad said, his voice firm and low, "you know what this kind of attention can cause. We can't go through all that again."

"I know, and I thought about that, believe me. But this could really change things, Dad. It's not just about attention, it could potentially change the outcome. Look," I said, picking up my phone and googling the name of the first case *Shadow of a Doubt* had covered, Warren Kincaid, "this guy had filed for appeal three times before the podcast started investigating his case. Now he's been acquitted."

Dad took the phone from me, squinting down at the screen. He didn't say anything for a while, taking his time reading through the article before removing his reading glasses and passing a hand across his face. His shoulders were slumped, exhausted. "I just don't know, Liv. I'm surprised you even think this is a good idea. You're the one who changed her name, after all."

"I know, I know. I just … I've done everything I can think of to help him. I've filed for retrials, I've contacted the Innocence Project every year for almost ten years, I even went to *law school* for Christ's sake, but he's still in there, and I genuinely think this could change that."

"It's certainly impressive, this Warren Kincaid story," Dad said, picking up the phone again and waving it around. "Very different case, though."

"They're all different cases, Dad," I said.

"Would we have to be involved?" Mom asked, her eyes on me as they had been this whole time.

"Not if you didn't want to," I said with a small sigh, "Kat wants

32

as many participants involved as possible, and obviously as Ethan's family we'd help with perspective and giving the show legitimacy, but I spoke to her about it earlier, and she says she's okay with it just being me and Ethan. It's not ideal obviously – really what they'd want is to interview all three of you, as well as me, but I think they'd still be interested in going forward with Ethan's case, even if you didn't agree to interviews. I don't think Ethan will give the go-ahead until you gave it your blessing though. What do you think Georgia? You've been pretty quiet."

Georgia was listlessly twisting her fork through some spaghetti squash and didn't look up when she said, "I don't know. I'd have to think about it."

I let the discussion turn to less controversial topics and waited until both of us were getting ready to leave before questioning my older sister. "So, you hate it right? The podcast?" I asked, while pulling on my coat.

Georgia rolled her eyes, "I don't hate it. I actually like the podcast – I've listened to it before. I just think maybe you've forgotten what it was like ten years ago. I don't want to go through all that again, I really don't want Mom and Dad to go through it all again, and I don't think you do really either. Do you?"

"No of course not, but we'd be more in control this time. Plus we'd know what to expect, how to prepare for it."

"We wouldn't be more in control," Georgia said, shaking her head, "you think that now, but all it takes is a few Reddit threads, an article in BuzzFeed and the whole thing has run away from us. And I don't know about you, but I don't ever want to wake up with pig's blood on my porch again."

33

7

THEN

We're three weeks into the trial, and despite everything, the end seems to be in sight. It has felt interminable, these twenty days, each one longer than the last, an entire lifetime rolled up into three weeks. But this is the last day of witness testimonies, and then there will be closing arguments, and then the jury will be told to deliberate on whether or not they think my twin brother is guilty of murder. My chest tightens as I think of it, and I force myself to get out of bed. Every time I wake up now, I think of where Ethan is waking up, and the sheer force of the guilt that he is there, and I am here, propels me out of bed.

The day is bright, clear, crisp. Morning sunshine streaming through my window as I draw the curtains open. It's the kind of day you want to drink in, to bathe in, sunlight warming skin, cool air burnishing the edges. There are sounds of activity coming from downstairs, my parents already up and about. Mom has stopped sleeping, spending nights holed up in the den, reading over documents, poring over anything and everything that might help out Ethan's case. Her eyes have become bloodshot, and her skin pale. She hasn't been in the garden in months. Weeds grow in her vegetable patch, choking the life out of formerly lovingly cared for plants and flowers. Heading downstairs I almost slip on the hardwood floor as a strangled scream comes from the hallway, setting me off running. A loud "FUCK!" follows the scream, followed by a sob of frustration and a slam of the front door.

"Do you know what they've done?" Georgia screams at me as I get downstairs, her face an abstract painting of red and white blotches, her eyes wide and wild with anger. "There's blood on the fucking porch, Olivia, BLOOD. How can people be so fucking disgusting." She rushes through the hallway, back to the kitchen where Mom is waiting, pulling her into a hug and I watch as my normally calm, quiet older sister shakes with rage in our mother's arms. Walking away from them I open the front door, always needing to see something to believe it. The whole front porch is covered in a thin slick of bright red blood. In some places, it has run so thin it looks pink against the white of the wooden boards. The sun bounces off it, this glittering red pool of accusation and for a reason I can't quite fathom, I crouch down to stick my finger in it. The blood on my finger glows up at me malevolently, practically neon, and I stand up too quickly, suddenly feeling lightheaded.

I wash my hands in the downstairs bathroom before heading back into the kitchen to silently grab the mop and bucket. I push blood away from me, watching it spill over the edge of the porch, fertilizing the green, green grass below, and then I wash it all away with water. Every so often I feel eyes on me and look up to stare back at whoever is staring at me. Across the street ten-year-old Billy Strong, who I have spent half his life babysitting, watches me the longest, but he's not the only one. I wonder which of our neighbors did this, which of my friends potentially. The nausea that rippled through me when I first saw the blood disappears as I clean it all away. The firm feeling of the mop handle gripped in my hands reassures me, and as the blood tumbles to the ground beneath the porch I watch it disappear into the earth with satisfaction. In certain light, a slight pink tinge stains the white porch, but I have made this mess disappear, I have solved a problem, however small, and I decide I like how that feels.

I make coffee and breakfast for my family, preparing us all for the day ahead. We drive over to the courthouse in silence, unable to listen to the radio in case they report on my brother's trial, and too distracted to pick and choose between music. As we pull into the car park, I yell at Dad to stop but I'm too late and the bucket of blood sloshes its way all across the windshield, with a sickening sound. I strain out of my seatbelt to see who it is, and my stomach rolls over when I recognize the face of Hunter Farley, one of Tyler's best friends and someone I've spent count-less hours with at lunch tables and movie theatres and parties.

"MURDERER!" someone shouts as I get out of the car, my heart shuddering to a near stop in terror, before pulling myself together, putting my mask back on and grabbing Georgia's hand so that we can walk up the courthouse steps together. On the other side of those doors to the courthouse is the Mayor and her family, waiting for us to arrive as they have done every day since the trial began. Every day they have stared us down as we walk past them and into the court room. Burning their own version of justice into our skin and the back of our heads as they follow our every move.

But what I'm really bracing myself for on the other side of those doors is Ethan. Because every day that we walk through those doors holds the potential to be the last that we see him as he really is, as Ethan Hall, twin, brother, son, rather than Ethan Hall, convicted murderer. I take a deep breath and hear and feel Georgia do the same as we push the heavy wooden doors open at the same time and confront those waiting eyes.

NOW

The following week dragged, long days and longer nights at work stopping me from seeing much of either my family or Kat and Ray to talk about the podcast. In stolen minutes I managed to arrange with Kat to meet them in Twin Rivers on Saturday. They were already there, setting up shop and making a camp for themselves in the small city where my brother had been convicted of murder. I hadn't been back to Twin Rivers in years. Not since my parents sold up and moved, as soon as they possibly could, to the outskirts of Portland. And now that I was facing down the reality of having to physically go back and confront my family's past and my brother's present, Friday had come around all too quickly.

I let out a sigh of exhaustion, and Karen Powers, the second chair on Reid Murphy's case, and my boss, shot me a caustic look. Karen Powers didn't sigh or yawn. She didn't ever give the sense that she was as physically fallible as that. "We keeping you from your bed, Kitson?" she asked archly and I felt burning red begin to creep up from underneath my shirt collar. Kitson was the name I'd taken when I applied for law school. 'Hall' was a common enough surname, but when combined with my first name, not to mention my face and its uncanny similarity to my twin brother's, it was a name I no longer wanted to be burdened with. Sometimes it felt like a betrayal. Of Ethan, of myself, of my family in general. Other times it just felt like what I had to do to get through the day.

"No, I'm fine," I said.

"Good, well why don't you run along and get us all some coffees just to stave off that evident exhaustion you're feeling."

With a nod I left the room, catching Daniel's eye who smiled back at me sympathetically, as I did so. By the time I returned to the conference room, jobs that would take all evening and probably all night had been delegated and I was left with the least interesting; babysitting the defendant, Reid Murphy. Reid had been released on bail, and the whole week had been dedicated to preparing her for taking the witness stand. It's fairly unusual for defendants to take the stand, but Karen liked to lean into controversial situations and had made what I thought was the fairly shrewd observation that Reid was likely to elicit sympathy from the jury more than anything else. There was a reason everyone on the team but me seemed to think she was innocent. Small and slight, with wide watery blue eyes, and mousey brown hair, she didn't look like she could hurt a fly, let alone almost kill a man. Quiet dropped over the room once everybody else had left, taking the coffees I'd retrieved with them. Reid stared down at the table, or possibly at her thumbs, the skin around her nails bitten and ripped to ribbons, while I sat in the corner by a large window that was slowly being plastered with rain. I scrolled through my phone, switching between email, Twitter and Instagram while drinking my coffee, and was largely ignoring Reid when suddenly she spoke, her voice quiet at first but getting stronger.

"You don't believe me, do you?"

I looked up from my phone slowly, eyes meeting hers almost involuntarily. "I don't have to believe you, Reid. I'm your lawyer not your mother confessor."

Her face pinched together a little, skin losing color. "I just thought you of all people would get it. Would believe me."

"What do you mean, 'me of all people'?" I demanded, back straightening in my chair, legs uncrossing, both feet planted on the ground.

"You're Olivia Hall, right? Ethan Hall's sister? I just figured you'd get it, what with everything you and your family went through?"

I could feel my muscles tightening, clenching, almost against my will, and I forced myself to relax, lean back again, and maintain eye contact. "Why would you say that?" I asked.

"Well, you are Olivia Hall, aren't you? I thought I recognized you, but then everyone kept calling you Kitson."

"I changed my name," I said, finally answering her question.

"I knew it," she said, this time quietly again. "You look exactly the same."

"Well, not exactly the same," I said, mildly affronted. "Ethan's jaw is much stronger."

"No, not as Ethan. As you did in high school."

Something pulled at my stomach, something hard, sudden and strong; the same thing that always warned me when I was about to walk into something I should probably walk away from. "High school? You're from Twin Rivers?"

"Yeah."

"But you're too young for us to have been in high school at the same time," I said. Reid was just 22, making her six years younger than me.

She nodded, agreeing with me, "Yeah, but my sister was the grade below you. Spencer. You came by our house a few times, and I always had to go watch the basketball games because she was a cheerleader. Like you."

I remembered Spencer. She'd been keen, a little clingy even, desperate to be part of the squad, always making sure she was at every single party. I hadn't been her biggest fan, but she was nice enough I supposed. "You're Spencer's little sister? Wow, that's so weird. Where is she now?"

"Twin Rivers still. She's a teacher there," she said quickly, clearly not here for me to reminisce vicariously about her older sister. "You know he totally deserved it, right?" She said this in a rush, her words picking up speed as if she'd been revving up to this all along and suddenly taken her foot off the gas.

"My brother?" I asked, a slight cold sweat pricking at my back.

"No, not your brother. I don't care if your brother did it or not. Tyler Washington. He totally had it coming."

I looked at her carefully, trying to work out what she was saying. Sympathy for Tyler Washington was practically universal; I'd never heard anyone say anything like what Reid had just said. "What do you mean by that?" I asked finally.

"He was an asshole."

I sank back into my chair, disappointed. "Not all assholes deserve to be killed, Reid."

"No, but he did." She took a deep breath and swallowed, her gaze holding mine right where it was.

"What on earth would make you say that?" I asked sharply.

I felt pinned by her eyes as she said forcefully, "I just don't think he was a good person."

"And what could you possibly have known about that?" I asked, "You didn't know him, did you? You couldn't have known what kind of a person Tyler was."

"I didn't, but my sister did, and she said he was just … awful. She said your whole group was full of kind of shitty people."

"Oh really?" I said, taken aback, "Because that's not how I remember it at all. From what I remember Spencer was desperate to be our friend."

I watched as Reid's expression changed, as her posture grew more rigid, as she seemed to tighten up within herself. Shutting down and zipping herself up.

"Was James Asher an awful person too?" I asked lightly, looking

40

down at my phone again in the hopes that she'd think I wasn't too bothered about how she answered.

"Yes," she said, her voice so firm and strong, so direct, that I was forced to look back up at her. Something in her eyes shifted and a little light crept in. She smiled, however small, and nodded at me. "Yes. He was a terrible person."

* * *

When I'd left Portland, the morning had been low and grey, the sky practically within reach as it hovered over the earth, but the sun had cracked the sky wide open, just as the car rolled into the city of Twin Rivers, and Daniel had claimed it as a good omen. I hadn't intended to let Daniel join me on this trip, but he'd dropped by early that morning, and had teamed up with my roommate, Samira to convince me I needed the support.

Checking into the B&B I'd booked earlier in the week, Daniel proceeded to amuse himself by pretending we were there for a romantic getaway, while I messaged Kat to find out where she and Ray had got to by then. They were staying in a motel closer to the edge of town to save a bit on money, so we arranged to meet at one of the many breweries that dotted the town.

"This is nice," Daniel said. He'd been waiting for me out on the porch while I visited our en-suite bathroom.

"You did choose it," I said drily. I'd been about to book in at the same motel as Kat and Ray when Daniel intervened on my behalf, pointing out that I had a bit more money to spare than a couple of investigative podcasters, and I was beginning to wonder if he'd been intending to join me all along. What I hadn't told him when I booked it was how close the B&B was to my old neighborhood. We were a few streets over from my childhood home, but really, Tyler had died mere minutes from here, and standing on that front porch set something on edge. The B&B could have been my house, the street it was on could have been my street; luckily it couldn't have been ten years ago. Far too much had changed.

We walked to the brewery in milky sunlight, Daniel excitedly pointing out landmarks of my former life to me. At one point we crossed over the top of my old street, and I hesitated, looking up at the street sign, exactly as it once was: there was no evidence of previous heartache, no indication that this was somewhere I and my entire family had run from. As I walked next to Daniel, it simply became a pleasant Oregon town, currently basking in some surprising autumnal sunshine.

Kat and Ray were already there when we got to the brewery. Huddled together at the end of a long table they looked a little conspicuous, heads bent towards each other, talking intensely, a private world for two. But Ray jumped up immediately when he spotted us, speed walking over to clap Daniel on the back and join us at the bar.

"Is day drinking really the best way to kick off an investigative podcast?" I asked as we joined Kat, orders in hand.

Ray laughed, a round little chuckle, "Well, not normally no, but during some of our research this week, we found out that one of the witnesses at the trial works here now, so we thought we'd scope it out."

My hand stopped in mid-air as I raised my beer to my lips. "Who?" I asked.

"Cole Sampson," Kat said. "You knew him, right? He's the general manager and head brewer here now."

"Cole?" I said, shifting in my seat, looking around me at the large, semi-industrial room, sure that he must have suddenly appeared as if from nowhere. "Yeah, I knew him. We used to date." 'Date' didn't really cover what Cole and I were together, and 'I knew him' was a pretty poor way of describing what he once meant to me, but I wasn't about to get into that in the middle of a busy brewery he apparently worked in. I'd experienced most of the significant 'firsts' in a teenager's life with Cole, and that included my first major betrayal.

"Wow, that's great," Kat was saying, blissfully unaware of the cord tightening inside me. "Do you think you could reach out to him, see if he'd be willing to do an interview? We've been coming up against a little resistance when it comes to people talking."

"Yeah, I'm not surprised. My brother is hardly this town's favorite topic, unless it involves dragging his name through the mud."

"But Cole would be up for it right? If he testified for your brother?" Kat asked.

"Cole? No. He was a witness for the prosecution," I said slowly.

"Wait, what?" Kat looked stricken, embarrassed by her error and she opened up her laptop with practiced ease, swiping through various documents before coming to the right one. "Oh, right. He testified the same day as Jessica Heng and Nick Green. I guess I got confused when you said you guys dated."

I raised an eyebrow, "Well, it was a pretty big part of why we broke up."

9

THEN

"Mr Sampson," the prosecutor says, Cole's eyes snapping to his, locking in, "you were in attendance at the party Tyler Washington was at on the night he died, is that correct?"

"That's correct, sir," Cole says, keeping his eyes on the prosecutor, his face serious, earnest.

"And you saw Mr Washington leave the party?"

"Yes, I saw him as he was leaving."

"And could you state for the record when this was?"

"It was around two o'clock, I think. I can't remember exactly, but it was definitely around then. Could've been a bit before, could've been a bit after, but definitely around two."

"On the morning of Sunday August 24?"

"That's right."

"Was he alone at that point?"

"Yeah, he was alone. I didn't see anyone leave with him."

"And where were you exactly when you saw Mr Washington leaving? Were you still in the house yourself?"

"No, I was out on the porch. The front porch."

"And from here you could watch Mr Washington leave and

walk down the street towards the entrance to the woods?"

"Yeah. There's a little shortcut down there by the high school that everyone uses, and you can still see it pretty easily from Jessica's porch."

"And you saw him walk into the woods from your vantage point?"

"Yes, definitely."

"And was anyone else with him at that point, when he entered the woods?"

"No, but a little while later I looked back around and saw someone on a bike go into the woods right in the same place Tyler had."

"And you recognized that person as being Ethan Hall?"

"Yes, sir."

"How could you be sure?"

"Well, I was pretty sure I recognized him anyway, as it really wasn't that far, but he also rides a bike that has black and bright orange striping that's pretty distinctive. I don't know anyone else with that kind of bike."

"And how much time had passed since you witnessed Mr Washington leaving the party and entering the woods?"

"I can't be sure because it's not like I checked the time or anything, but probably between ten and fifteen minutes."

"So, that would make it about two ten, two fifteen a.m.?"

"I'd say so, yes, sir," Cole says with a sharp nod of his head, and I wonder where all this sudden deference has come from.

"And do you think the two parties involved could have arranged to meet in the woods?" Curtis asks.

"Objection," Ethan's attorney calls, jumping to attention, "calls for speculation on the witness's part."

"Sustained," the judge intones, eyes on the prosecutor, "please keep to the facts, Mr Curtis."

"Yes, Your Honor. My apologies." He places his hand over his heart as he says this, false sincerity leeching from him, before turning back to Cole.

"Did you see either Mr Hall or Mr Washington come back out of the woods at all, Mr Sampson?"

"No, but I went back inside to the party not too long after that. Also, they were both heading in the same direction, towards Winward Road, so there's no reason why either of them would've come back to Hillier Street."

"And you yourself didn't then enter the woods later that night? Or morning rather?"

"No, I live in the other direction, so I just walked back along my usual route."

"Thank you, Mr Sampson. I have no further questions."

I hold my breath as the judge asks Ethan's defense attorney if he'd like to question the witness, but he declines, and I can't help but release a sigh of relief as he does so. Just watching Cole up there, taking the stand against my brother sets my teeth on edge.

I hear the voice in my ear, sweet and slow like honey, feel hands against my skin, hot and frantic, the not-so-artful addition of pressure, a knee between my thighs, pushing them apart. I shut my eyes against the court room scene, trying to push the memory away and out, shame cascading through me as I dig my fingernails into the palms of my hands forcing a new feeling. It's just a memory I tell myself, it can't hurt me here. It's not Cole who's on trial; it's not even me. It's Ethan. I open my eyes again, and Cole is gone from the witness box. He's back in his spot across the aisle on the other side of the courtroom; like I'm here for the groom and he's here for the bride. He's safe back there though, and so am I. As long as he's out of my eyeline I don't have to see him and don't have to think about him. I train my eyes again on the back of Ethan's head, reminding myself why I'm here, and whose life, exactly, is on the line.

10

NOW

"Olivia?" someone said. And even with the doubt and surprise lacing their voice, there was still something unmistakable, something achingly familiar about it.

Cole Sampson.

I turned around in my seat to see him standing there in coveralls, dark brown eyes full of confusion, arms full of empty crates.

"Hey, Cole," I said, slipping on an old voice I barely recognized; bright, breezy, barely aware of herself.

Cole was having trouble keeping hold of his stack of crates while processing my presence in his brewery tap room, and Daniel jumped up just as the stack was about to fall, taking a few out of Cole's arms, relieving his load. Cole's gaze swerved to him quickly and he gave a nod of thanks just as Daniel said chirpily, "Let me help you out here, man."

"Uh, thanks … thank you," Cole said, clearly still wrapping his head around what was going on. "Olivia, what the hell are you doing here?"

Easy lies, little white ones used to lubricate awkward social situations, slid through my mind, a whole pantheon of them,

47

but in the end I decided the truth was probably the easiest of all. "This is Kat Thomas, and Ray Mackenzie," I said gesturing to them behind me, "they're doing a podcast on my brother's case."

"Your brother's case?" Cole said, eyes suddenly twice their normal size, "you mean Tyler's murder, right? You couldn't possibly be here to try and exonerate your brother."

"Ethan didn't kill Tyler, Cole. He's serving a sentence he doesn't deserve."

Cole shook his head, his eyes not leaving mine. "Unbelievable. This is unbelievable. *You're* unbelievable. Do you have any idea how long it's taken people to get over his death, and now you're coming back here to drag it all back up again. Morgan still gets nightmares, did you know that? She hasn't been back in those woods since."

"Morgan?" I said, summoning up a picture of Tyler's pretty older sister.

"Yeah, we're ... we, uh –" Cole trailed off, his gaze finally pulling away from mine as he shifted from foot to foot.

"Oh. You're together now. You and Morgan. Wow."

"Who's Morgan?" Daniel asked, and I was surprised to find him still there, standing next to me, his arms almost as full as Cole's with empty crates. The tap room had dwindled down to me and Cole for a minute as I crashed my way through long lost memories, but Daniel's voice brought me back to the present. Cole gave him a look that said he wasn't going to bother answering his question and proceeded to clumsily retrieve the crates Daniel had previously taken from him. I only sat down again once Cole had left – without saying another word to any of us – and proceeded to tell the others who Morgan was.

"She older or younger?" Kat asked.

"Older. Just by a year. She took it hard," I said.

"Well, her brother did die, Liv," Daniel said in a low voice, as if he had to remind me.

"I'd like to talk to her," Kat continued, "but I guess you're not

48

the best person to put me in touch with her."

I shook my head, "I wouldn't even know where to begin with Morgan. The same goes for pretty much everyone else in this town."

Kat and Ray shared a look that was worth an entire sentence. "Yeah, I'm starting to pick up on that," Kat said, "having you around might be more of a hindrance than a help."

"Is that going to be a problem?" I asked, and Kat gave me a quizzical look. "I mean, will it affect your decision on whether or not you do Ethan's story for the next season?"

"Oh," Kat said, taking a sip of her beer and then placing it carefully back on the table between us again. "We're definitely doing Ethan's case, don't worry about that. I was just hoping you might be able to help grease the wheels a little bit, but it looks as though we'll have to go with a different tactic. We're obviously not about to record anything with Cole, so how about we go somewhere a bit quieter and get some intro stuff with you on tape, and then we can take it from there? We might find that it's easier getting on with things with you back in Portland, but we may as well get an interview with you while you're here, right?"

In some ways, this was exactly what I wanted to hear. I didn't want to be here, not really. I felt safest, and most myself in Portland, but I also didn't want to just leave Kat and Ray here on their own, here where the story could be told any way they wanted, any way the town wanted it to be told. If they stayed here without me, I felt sure something would go wrong and the story would get mangled, led astray again, and Ethan would stay stuck in prison.

"Okay," I said, nodding slowly, and taking a long pull on my beer so that when I put it back down, it was practically drained. "Can I just ask ... what made you decide to definitely do Ethan's story? You didn't seem so sure back in Portland."

Kat raised both her eyebrows at me, and then I watched as her whole face tightened into a strange grimace. "It's hard to explain what draws us to a story and what doesn't ... it's just a feeling, I guess? That something's wrong? We can't be sure what we're going to find here, but the fact that we filed a request for the police files over a week ago, and we still haven't got them ... Well, that tells us there's probably something in those files they don't want us to see."

I nodded, able to follow Kat's logic. But really, all my attention was on the thought of those old police files. Of what was in them, of what they revealed, of what long held secrets they might hide inside.

Back at the B&B I watched as Ray set up the equipment, and Kat looked over her notes. I was starting to regret the beer: my brain felt on the verge of fuzzy, my blood a little too warm, and my heart was beating a little too loud, a little too fast. I swallowed, thinking of all the interview requests my family and I had refused ten years ago. What was I doing, agreeing to this? I licked my lips, so sure they were beginning to crack open, they felt so dry, and Kat silently handed me a large glass of water. I swallowed it down, almost desperately, and when I looked over to thank her, she smiled.

"It's normal to be nervous, Olivia. Just take a few deep breaths and try to forget about the microphones."

I looked pointedly at the microphone Ray was at that moment setting up in front of me, and Kat laughed. "Well, I did say *try* to forget."

* * *

Extract from transcript of Season 3 Episode 1 of *Shadow of a Doubt*:

Ethan Hall: If I'd taken the plea, and pled guilty to manslaughter, I'd be getting out right about now. I think about that all the time.

But I couldn't do it. I couldn't admit to killing someone when I hadn't done it, not even accidentally.

It's weird – how many people do you think have perjured themselves just to take a plea? To be sure of a lighter sentence? Our justice system is … it just doesn't work. It doesn't work. And I'm testament to that.

Kat Thomas [voiceover]: And it's this system that put Ethan Hall behind bars for a crime he claims he didn't commit that we're about to investigate.

I'm Kat Thomas, you're listening to Switchblade Media, and this is the third season of *Shadow of a Doubt*.

Musical interlude with snippets of dialogue overlaid between Kat Thomas, Ethan Hall, Kevin Lawrence, Morgan Washington and Olivia Hall as well as news caster announcements.

KT [continued]: Ten years ago, on August 24, in the city of Twin Rivers in Oregon, 18-year-old Tyler Washington was found dead in the woods that surround the town. Son of the mayor, captain of the basketball team, and set to start college in Southern California in just a few short weeks, Tyler's death shocked not just his many friends, and his loving family, but the town itself, and even the entire state. His death didn't remain a mystery for long however, as less than a week later, Ethan Hall, a classmate of the dead teen was arrested for Tyler's murder. Prior to arrest, Hall had been interviewed without an attorney present for almost seven hours and during this time confessed to his classmate's murder, only to recant and plead not-guilty.

51

If there's anyone who knows the ins and outs of Ethan Hall's case, it's his twin sister Olivia. Olivia now works under a different name at a law firm in Portland, a career she says she felt called to after her twin was – she believes – wrongly imprisoned.

Olivia Hall: I just think the system failed him at every turn. I remember thinking, the whole time during his trial and even before that – the trial didn't actually take place until almost a year after Tyler was killed – something has to happen. Something has to happen, something new has to come to light, because surely he's not going to be convicted of this.

KT: But nothing ever did.

OH: No. And it's not like he didn't have the resources and support, you know? His defense attorney was a friend of our father, we were there for him the entire time, but it just shows how easy it can be for appearances to dictate beliefs.

KT: What do you mean by that?

OH: Just that Ethan was something of an easy mark. He was different from everyone else in town, he didn't have many friends.

KT: You weren't particularly close at the time of his arrest, were you?

OH: No. We spent most of high school not talking to each other.

KT: Do you regret that now?

OH: I don't know. It's hard to say … we're much closer now. Closer in some ways than we've ever been, but I like to think that would have happened as we got older anyway. As a teenager you're stuck in this weird dichotomy where you're constantly trying to figure out who exactly you are, while simultaneously trying to figure out how to fit in. You want to be different, and special, and to stand out, but you also want to be part of the crowd. Ethan never had any of that, to be fair. I'm talking about me more than anything. Ethan was always just so distinctly … Ethan, and teenagers don't always respond all that well to people who are actually being themselves, you know? I do think as we got older we would've figured out a way to be friends again, though. Even without all this.

KT: But it's fair to say your brother's arrest and conviction threw you back together? Made you closer?

OH: Yeah, I guess it's kind of ironic, right? We've become closer even though, physically, we're separated.

KT: So, Tyler's death, Ethan's arrest – it really did change your life, didn't it?

[pause]

OH: Yeah, there's no doubt about it. It definitely did.

KT: Do you think you would've become a lawyer if it hadn't been for your brother's case?

OH [laughs]: Definitely not. It wasn't even on my radar. I didn't even have a major picked out at that point, I don't think, but pre-law definitely wouldn't have been on the shortlist.

KT: And at the same time that your brother was arrested, you were also dealing with the death of a friend. Because, and this is kind of a weird twist of fate – you were good friends with Tyler weren't you?

OH: We were friends, yes. I … I don't know if I'd describe us as 'good friends'. He was best friends with my boyfriend at the time, and we hung out a lot, but kind of just in that way you do as a big group of friends and acquaintances when you're a teenager, you know? I never spent any time with him, just him and me. It never would've even occurred to me. We weren't calling each other up to go to the movies together, or anything, let's say.

KT: And it was your boyfriend Cole, who found Tyler's body that morning, right?

OH: I actually think it was their friend, Nick. Nick Green. The three of them – Tyler, Cole, and Nick – were all very close, and from what I can remember, Tyler's parents called both Cole and Nick up that morning to see if he was with either of them – they used to end up spending the night at each other's houses all the time. But he wasn't, and they all got a little worried, so they went out to look for him. Nick, and Cole, and Tyler's dad and uncle. But it was Nick who actually … actually spotted him first, and told the others. I'm pretty sure.

KT: It sounds like you remember that morning pretty well, Olivia.

OH: I do. It's impossible not to. You're not likely to ever forget the moment your best friend calls you up to tell you your friend has been found dead, and that he's probably been murdered.

KT: And was it around this time that your friends started distancing themselves from you?

OH: Yes. Well ... no, not immediately, I guess. It was a very strange, strained time, that whole week. It already had this surreal quality to it, because we were all getting ready to leave for college. And then, suddenly Tyler was dead, and my brother was arrested, and all of that ... all of that just disappeared. And because I stuck by my brother, and refused to believe he could've killed Tyler, I ended up losing all my friends too.

KT: That must've been difficult.

OH [quietly]: Yeah. It was tough. I don't like to talk about it much – except to my therapist – because so many people have had it so much worse. Tyler's family lost him, and my brother is in jail for something he didn't do, so falling out with your high school friends and breaking up with your boyfriend kind of pales in comparison, but it was definitely a hard time. For a lot of reasons.

KT: And what about media attention? Did the case generate much?

OH: It did, yeah, although it was mostly local, and a few state-wide news stories. But it was enough. More than enough. Tyler was the mayor's son, so within Twin Rivers at least, he and his family were pretty high profile, which impacted the media coverage, as well as the ... attitude and atmosphere. Towards Ethan. And us. His family.

KT: In a case like this, with quite a lot of media coverage – some would say biased media coverage – as well as the inherent bias within the city against the defendant, I would expect the court to decide to bring in jurors from outside. Did they do that at all?

OH: I think at one point they were going to, but in the end, they decided not to.

KT: Do you know why?

OH: I honestly couldn't tell you. Knowing what I know now, I think it was a pretty extraordinary decision.

KT: And you've never wavered in your belief in your twin?

OH: Never. He's innocent, I know it.

KT: If he is innocent, then that means whoever did kill Tyler Washington is still out in the open, living their life, possibly still in Twin Rivers, while your brother sits behind bars. Do you ever think about that, about who did actually kill Tyler?

OH: I think about it all the time. I go to bed thinking about it, I wake up thinking about it, I have nightmares about it. But, and this is going to sound so incredibly selfish: My main concern is with getting Ethan out of prison. Getting him a retrial, having him exonerated, clearing his name. I can't tell you who killed him, but if there's one thing I'm sure of it's that Ethan Hall did not kill Tyler Washington.

11

THEN

Ethan's lawyer is done questioning Kevin, and the judge asks the prosecutor if he'd like to cross-examine the witness.

Unsurprisingly, he does and as he stands up from his chair, buttoning up his suit jacket as he does so, he says to Kevin, "What exactly is your relationship to the defendant, Mr Lawrence?"

"We're friends?" Kevin says, giving the prosecutor a quizzical look.

"You don't sound completely sure of your answer, Mr Lawrence."

"No, I mean we are friends. I just … we're not related or anything."

"No, but you have known one another for quite some time have you not?"

"Since kindergarten, yeah."

"And would you describe yourself as Mr Hall's best friend?"

"Yeah, I suppose so."

"You suppose?"

"I've never really thought about it, if I'm honest," Kevin says shrugging, "I guess he's my best friend. He's kind of my only friend."

"And vice versa?"

"Yeah."

"And as established in your conversation with my esteemed colleague just now, you were with him on the night of the incident in question, August 23 and the early morning of August 24?"

"Yeah, he was at my place."

"Your parents' house?"

"Yeah, sorry, my parents' house."

"And what were you doing there?"

Kevin shrugs again, his signature move. If Kevin has ever been bothered by anything in his life, he has never let anyone know it. The phrase 'water off a duck's back' was invented for him. I once overheard our moms talking about how little both their sons had cried growing up, and whereas Mom had worried constantly about Ethan's lack of lungpower, Kevin's mom had said he didn't seem to ever cry because he was too busy laughing. At the time, this had sounded a little creepy to me, but now watching him on the witness stand I can easily see how his good-natured languorousness could put you at ease. "We weren't really doing anything," he says, "we were just chilling, you know? Hanging out?"

"And was it just the two of you?"

"Yeah."

"So, you didn't attend Jessica Heng's party that night at all?"

"No."

"Why not?"

"Well, we weren't invited."

There's a ripple of movement, a shifting reaction from the other side of the courtroom when he says this. Jessica Heng and her friends bristling at this mild accusation, despite the fact that Kevin doesn't look or sound bothered by it at all. I've spent my life carving a space for myself at the very center of things, but Ethan's never been bothered by any of it, and Kevin even less so. His tone is even, indifferent, and he leans back in his chair, looking more relaxed than anyone else who has taken the stand up to this point. I look over at the jury to try and gauge their reaction to Kevin, but their faces are a wash of boredom. They have already been here so long.

"Now, Mr Lawrence, as we've just heard from your testimony, you claim Mr Hall left your parents' house at between two fifteen and two thirty in the morning, but in your initial statement to the police you told them Mr Hall had left your house by two a.m."

"Yeah, but I wasn't completely sure. I said it was around two, two thirty."

"Oh, so now you're saying you can't be sure?"

"I think it was just before two thirty, but I know I said it was more like two a.m. at first, so I'm just saying I can't be one hundred percent sure."

"If you weren't sure then, and you aren't sure now about what time Mr Hall left, where did the two or two thirty am time frame come from?"

"I figure he was gone by two thirty because I know I went online for a while, and when I logged off it was about three a.m."

"And how long do you think you were online for, before you logged off?"

"It was like twenty to thirty mins max, which is why I think maybe Ethan left a little later, more like two thirty."

"What was it exactly you were doing? Online, I mean."

"I was just on AIM."

"And by AIM you mean AOL instant messenger?"

"Yes."

"So, you were messaging with someone?"

"Yeah," Kevin says, and for the first time he looks a little unsure of himself, a little worried.

"Who was it you were messaging with?"

"Just a friend," Kevin says, shuffling in his seat, shifting his eyes suddenly to the jury bench and back again.

"A friend? I thought you said you didn't have many – or any – friends, apart from Mr Hall?"

"At school, yeah, but this was someone I know outside of school."

"Is this person your boyfriend, Mr Lawrence?"

"What?"

"Is this – Caleb Donovan – who you were messaging on that night, your boyfriend?"

"No – I – I'm not … with anyone," Kevin says, stricken, almost speechless.

"Because we have a record of those messages and not only do they indicate that you and Mr Donovan know one another intimately, but they're also time stamped."

"Objection!" Ethan's lawyer finally calls, getting to his feet. "The witness's sexuality and relationship status has nothing to do with the trial, and these messages haven't been entered into evidence."

"I have them right here, Your Honor," the prosecutor continues smoothly, unruffled. He picks up a file from where it's been waiting this whole time, and walks it over to the judge's bench. "And they clearly show that Mr Lawrence had finished … messaging with Mr Donovan, and logged off by 2:47 in the morning, indicating that if he had been online for around thirty minutes as he claims, then Mr Hall would have left the Lawrence home before two fifteen in the morning, leaving him plenty of time to meet the victim in the woods and kill him before getting home just before three in the morning."

Kevin starts speaking rapidly, filling up the silence that has fallen over the courtroom, "I might not have been online for as long as thirty minutes though, like I said, it might've only been twenty minutes, maybe even less time, I'm not sure. We'd been smoking and I might have –"

The judge holds up his hand, interrupting Kevin's hurried speech, indicating he should stop talking. Taking the file from the prosecutor, the judge peers down at both the prosecutor and the defense attorney with bored equilibrium, while flipping the file open, paging through the thin document, before finally looking up. "Your objection is overruled, Mr Castle," he says to Ethan's lawyer. "While I agree that the witness's sexuality and relationship history has little to do with the proceedings here, these records clearly show that his online interaction with this Caleb Donovan had ended by 2:47am."

"The defense hasn't had the opportunity to examine this evidence, Your Honor, and we demand a recess in which to do so. Why didn't the prosecution enter this into evidence before the trial?"

"It's only just come to light, Your Honor," the prosecutor says.

"That's all well and good," Castle interjects, "but if you have the conclusion of the message stream between Mr Donovan and Mr Lawrence, surely you also have proof of when the AIM conversation started between the two of them, and we can put this all to rest."

"The defense raises a fair point, Mr Curtis," the judge says, "I don't see any indication here of when this conversation started or what time it was initiated. Do you have the start the of these messages?"

"I don't believe we do," Curtis says, staring up at the judge.

"Well, either you enter the AOL Instant Messenger conversation in its entirety into evidence, with time stamps for both the beginning and the end of the conversation between Mr Lawrence and Mr Donovan, or you do not enter it into evidence at all," the judge says.

I watch Curtis shuffle in front of the judge and say something to him that no one watching can here.

"In that case," the judge says, voice ricocheting around the courtroom, "I have to ask the jury to disregard this evidence, and to ask them not take it into consideration during any future deliberations."

I turn to the jury, trying to decipher what they make of this, but it's impossible. Just as it will almost certainly be impossible for them to 'disregard' anything they hear in court throughout this trial, whether the judge asks them to or not.

61

12

NOW

"That was great, Olivia," Kat said, when the interview was over, and she'd finally turned the 'record' button off.

"Does that mean you'll let me hang around for a little bit longer?" I asked, making my tone as light as possible. The interview had been draining: I hadn't spoken about Ethan's case, or the night of Tyler's murder so much in such a long time, and the experience was enervating. I wanted to crawl into bed and sleep for several hours, but I wasn't about to let Kat and Ray know that.

Kat gave me a small smile and glanced over at Ray. "You can hang around as long as you want, Olivia, I just think maybe you should give us a list of the people in town who won't be so happy to see you," she said, with an arch in her voice that let me know she was only half-joking.

"To be honest, it might be simpler and faster if I gave you a list with the people who would be happy to see me," I shot back.

Lying over on the bed, Daniel gave a shout of laughter that made me jump. I'd practically forgotten he was there. "Typical Liv," he said, smiling at me.

"You make enemies wherever you go, or something, Olivia?" Ray asked.

"It does sometimes feel like that, yeah," I said. "But I can think of at least one person who might be happy to see me. Or if not happy, then at least, not outright hostile."

"Who?" Ray asked, looking as skeptical as he sounded.

"Kevin Lawrence. He was my brother's best friend. Still is."

I'd been a little surprised to find Kevin still living in Twin Rivers, but there he was, languorous smile still in place as he slowly recognized me as I walked towards him in the outdoor equipment shop he was now working at. I knew he was still in contact with Ethan – that they wrote to each other, and that Kevin had visited him – but I hadn't seen him since I left town.

"Man, this is wild," he said as I approached him behind the counter, "I'd forgotten how similar you both look. It's like looking at Ethan."

"Thanks, Kevin. I always love it when people say I look like a man."

"You know what I mean. You must get it all the time," he said, laughing while rolling his eyes.

"Too much."

"I'll bet. So, how are you Olivia Hall?"

"Never better."

He lifted one skeptical eyebrow and let out a puff of air, "Sure. Haven't seen you back here in about nine years, but you've never been better. Are you here about the podcast?"

"Yeah, did Ethan tell you already?"

"Yeah, he asked if I'd get involved and I said yes. Thought the host would be getting in touch first though, not you."

I explained that Kat and Ray were busy elsewhere, but that they'd left me to approach Kevin about consenting to an interview. Kevin nodded his head energetically, "Definitely. Anything to help Ethan out."

"Can I ask you something?" I asked, lowering my voice and glancing around the shop as I did so. It was hardly busy, but there were a few customers in there, browsing the racks of climbing and camping gear, the rows of outdoor clothing.

"Sure."

"Why did you stay? How did you stay? Everyone here believes my brother is guilty, how do you just live with that?"

Kevin shrugged, "It doesn't come up as much as you probably think it does. It's been a long time, Olivia. And this is my home. Why should I leave?"

I wasn't sure it had been all that long, although I was willing to bet it had felt twice as long for Ethan. Being back in Twin Rivers was beginning to make time fold in on itself; all of a sudden ten years felt like nothing, felt like it could've been yesterday, but seeing familiar faces aged by the years made them seem even longer. "So, you're not universally hated and vilified?" I asked.

"Not exactly, no. Going on this podcast is hardly going to help though, is it." He didn't phrase it as a question, as if he already knew the damage he was going to be doing to himself, and was willing to accept it.

"How have you always been so sure?" I asked, my fingers worrying at the packet of a Clif Bar that was part of a display to tempt hungry shoppers paying for their chosen purchases.

"Because I know he didn't do it. There's no way Ethan could kill someone. Why? Haven't you always been sure he was innocent?"

"Well, yeah, but I shared a womb with the guy. You didn't have to believe he was innocent. I did."

"You might have shared a womb with him, Olivia, but I'm the one who actually knew him. He was always so surprised you believed him."

"He was?" I asked.

"Yeah, he thought maybe it was guilt."

"Guilt?" I said, unable to stop the stretch and strain of my voice.

"Because you were such good friends with Tyler and that

crowd. I think Ethan just assumed you'd stick with them, when it came down to it."

"Well, not when it came to murder," I said, and Kevin raised both his eyebrows.

"I guess not. Blood really is thicker than water, huh?"

I thought suddenly of that pig's blood on our porch, the bucket of blood thrown over the windshield of my father's car; thick, viscous and vicious dripping to the ground in malevolent accusation. Shaking off the lightheadedness that shivered through me, I nodded at Kevin before making arrangements with him to record an interview once his shift was over that afternoon.

* * *

Extract from transcript of Season 3 Episode 1 of *Shadow of a Doubt* [continued]:

Kat Thomas [voiceover]: It's not hard finding people willing to talk about Ethan Hall in Twin Rivers. What is hard is finding someone willing to talk about him, not only on the record, but in positive terms. Kevin Lawrence was, and probably still is, Ethan's best friend. They grew up together and even now, Kevin is one of the few people who visits Ethan in prison who isn't related to him. He was also a defense witness during the trial for Tyler's murder, but his conflicting testimony ended up hindering, rather than helping his friend's case.

So, have the intervening ten years changed Kevin's mind about the case, or does he still believe the wrong person was locked up for Tyler Washington's murder?

Kevin Lawrence: Absolutely. I absolutely believe Ethan is innocent.

KT: What is it that convinced you?

KL: I didn't really ever need to be convinced. Anyone who knows Ethan, knows he's incapable of killing someone. Of murder. The problem was that no one here really knew him.

KT: So, you think the police and the prosecution were able to take advantage of the fact that Ethan didn't have many friends or allies in town?

KL: Definitely. And not just that. He was up against a town institution, you know? It wasn't just that Tyler was this super popular guy, his mom was the mayor. She still is. Talk about power and influence.

KT: The longer we've spent in Twin Rivers, the more it's become apparent just how influential his family was and is. We've filed request after request for the investigation files, but so far they've all been blocked, and I'm beginning to think that's all coming from the mayor's office.

KL: I wouldn't be surprised by that at all. And that's how it all felt at the time too, you know? There was so much pressure on the police to wrap up the murder investigation that they just pinned it on the first guy they found. I always felt like Ethan was just in the wrong place at the wrong time.

KT: Can we talk about that for a second, because during the trial you were brought as a witness for the defense because you could place him at your parents' house until around 2:30am. This timing was really important because Tyler's time of death was given as between 1:45 and 2:45am, so if he was still with you at 2:30, then he wouldn't have been able to kill him.

KL: Yeah, that's right.

KT: But that all fell apart when the prosecution revealed evidence that contradicted your timeline of events.

KL: Yeah.

KT: Your initial statement to the police also stated that you thought Ethan had left your house by 2am, which would have meant he didn't have an alibi right in the middle of the time of death window.

KL: Yea-ah.

KT: So, did you lie at any point during the investigation and trial, Kevin?

KL: No. My statement to the police was actually that I thought Ethan had left between 2 and 2:30 in the morning. I wasn't sure because I hadn't been paying really close attention, but that's the time I gave, and apparently they just put it down as 2am.

KT: What was it that made you change it from 'between 2 and 2:30' to 2:30am?

KL: Well, it wasn't precisely 2:30am. I think it was probably a bit before that, but not much. Basically, I remembered going to bed at like, 3, but I knew that was only about a half hour after Ethan left.

KT: So, what about the record of the messages between you and Caleb Donovan the prosecution produced at the trial?

KL [**sighs**]: Man, all that stuff was just … you know they only had the end of the message thread?

[pause]

But they didn't have the beginning of the message thread from that night, which if they had would have been at about 2:20am, around when Ethan left. That whole conversation on AIM lasted about ten or fifteen minutes.

KT: In court, you said you the AIM conversation lasted thirty minutes.

KL: I did? Well, maybe I'm remembering wrong, or maybe I was wrong back then. Honestly, you try remembering a conversation you had online with someone ten years ago, and see how easy it is to remember how long it lasted. Maybe at the trial I was referring to how long I'd been online, rather than how long Caleb and I had been chatting? I don't know. I can't remember exactly.

KT: So, you didn't lie and change your statement about when he left your house, in order to provide him with a better alibi?

KL: No. I know that's what people said and what a lot of people still believe, but genuinely I didn't. People don't understand what it's like when you're being questioned by police. Especially in a murder investigation when someone's dead, and another person's whole life hangs in the balance. Plus they brought me in for questioning a few days after Tyler was actually killed, so it was all a little bit hazy by then anyway. You're always working with an approximation of what happened, because you're only human, and you're

68

under pressure and your memory is fallible, but then the police term it as 'evidence' or whatever, and suddenly you may as well have carved that statement into a tablet of stone. So, then when you re-think something, or come to a realization, or just have a little more time to think about something, you're branded at best as unreliable and at worst a liar, and suddenly your witness testimony is worthless.

* * *

"Thanks Kevin, that was great," Kat said, removing her head-phones and indicating Kevin could do the same.

"When will all this be released?" Kevin asked, and I thought I could hear a slight strain of concern in his voice. As if his conversation with Kat had finally made what he was doing sink in.

Kat exchanged a look with Ray, another of their private, impen-etrable moments I couldn't hope to decipher, and said, "We're going to start releasing episodes from next week. We like to get as much research done as possible in the weeks leading up to recording, but then we prefer to record week by week. So the story can change and develop as we go along."

Kevin swallowed deeply, nodding his head and his gaze flicked over to me, meeting my eyes. "And do you think you'll use this interview in the first episode?"

"Probably, yes. We've already recorded a little introductory interview with Olivia today, and we'll have one with Ethan in there too, of course."

We were recording in Kevin's kitchen, countertops gleaming white, the window above the sink revealing a small but well-tended yard, the walls painted a deep, rich blue. Kevin and Kat were talking still, comparing notes of visiting Ethan in prison, and I stood up suddenly, my chair almost toppling over behind me as I did so. Ray reached out a hand to stop it from falling and he gave me a quizzical look as I marched over to the sink, staring out of the pretty window as I washed my hands in bone chilling water. "You okay, Liv?" Kevin asked as I leaned down to splash my face and I made an indecipherable noise, before turning off the tap and turning around to face the others.

"Yeah, fine, just suddenly a bit hot," I said, red warmth creeping up my neck.

Kat wasn't paying too much attention, looking around at the kitchen instead. "This isn't your parents' place, is it Kevin?" she said.

"No. They still live on their farm, just outside of town."

Kat nodded, her face scrunched in concentration, cogs whirring inside. "Could you take us to see it? And maybe walk us through the route Ethan would have taken that night?"

Kevin shrugged, his eyes meeting mine for a second before flicking back to Kat, "Sure, why not?"

Kevin's parents' farm backed up right to the woods that surrounded the south-eastern corner of the city. Sitting on three acres of land, the Lawrence family had apple orchards I'd spent my childhood running through. Our mothers had been friends for years, bonding over green fingers and the desire to watch things grow, and up until the age of ten or eleven, I'd spent almost as much time here as Ethan. The farmhouse was weathered now, peeling yellow paint and lopsided porch railings, when all those years ago they'd looked sunshiny and new. I hadn't been there in almost two decades and it forced the same sense of disjointed familiarity that being back in Twin Rivers did. An almost-there, but not-quite feeling; one I didn't want to get too comfortable with.

"So, this is it," Kevin said, eyes squinting in the thin sunshine.

"It's a long way from the road," Ray pointed out.

"Yeah, the driveway's about a quarter mile long alone."

"So, how long would it have taken Ethan to cycle back home from here?" Kat asked.

Kevin tilted his head to the side, "Well, he didn't take the road. He never did. See, if you cycled back through the woods using the footpaths, it cut the journey time way down. I did it everyday to school too, and Ethan – and Olivia's – house was just on the other side of the school."

Kat looked to me and I nodded in confirmation. "Going on the roads, it would probably take at least 40 minutes, but the woods meant it only took about 20, 25 minutes," Kevin clarified.

"Even in bad weather?" Ray asked, "with mud or whatever?"

Kevin just shrugged, "Yeah."

Kat turned towards Ray and said in a low voice, "It would be great if we could get hold of a bike, do the trip ourselves ..."

Ray nodded thoughtfully while Kevin let out a shot of laughter, "You want a bike, we've got about 20. Come on," he said, striding off towards one of the farm's outbuildings, beckoning us with a wave to follow him.

The red doors creaked open, stiff and in need of some WD40, letting out a puff of dusty air as they did so. Inside was dimly lit by daylight creeping in at the wooden slats and through the now-open doorway, dust motes newly lit by the afternoon sun swirling in our pathway. It was a treasure trove of broken down, barely used machinery. Not just push bikes but quad bikes, about five different types of lawn mower, several tractors, and somewhere right at the back, I knew there was an ancient decommissioned fire truck. Kevin didn't have any siblings to share this bounty with, but his dad had inherited the farm years ago, and with it this barn full of semi-useful objects.

"Take your pick," Kevin said expansively, extending his arms out beside him to take in the entirety of the barn.

Ray let out a low whistle and Kat said, "Well, someone could be on an episode of hoarders."

Kevin laughed, pulling one of the bikes towards him as he did so.

There wasn't an official path leading into the woods from the

Lawrence farm, but one had been formed there over the years, well-worn and walked over, tire tracks marking the way. The day darkened as soon as we were under the cover of the trees, light filtering through in patches and golden-hued columns. It took just two minutes to reach the public foot and cycle path that Ethan would have turned left on that night, and many nights before.

"He seriously rode this way at night?" Ray called a little breathlessly to Kevin who was leading the way.

"Yeah. He did it all the time."

"It would be pitch black, though right?" Ray asked.

"He had good lights on his bike, and a headlamp," Kevin clarified. "Plus, he knew it like the back of his hand. Could've done it in his sleep."

"What about Tyler?" Kat asked, "Would this path lead to his house, too?"

There was a short pause that was filled with the heavy sound of our breathing, the crunch of the path under our bike tires, and thick rustle of leaves in the wind, animals in the undergrowth, birds in the trees. "He lived on the other side of town," I said, explaining how 10th street bisected the town, with Tyler's house on one side, and my family's and Kevin's on the other.

"So, there's no reason he would've been in the woods?" Kat asked.

"Not really," Kevin said.

"In the trial, they said he was taking a shortcut home though," Kat said, breath catching, "like Ethan."

"Yeah, but that never really made sense to me," Kevin explained. "I've never been able to figure out why Tyler would've been in those parts of the woods that night, to be honest."

There was silence again as we approached the road, and Kevin pulled up to a stop. "So, this is the short cut Ethan probably took. You leave the woods here, and cycle straight up Hillier Street, past Jessica Heng's house, where the party was, and then into the woods again, right by the high school," he said, pointing ahead of him. "If you stay in the woods for this bit it takes twice as long navigating the trails, so he always cut through here."

"And so, this is where Cole Sampson would have witnessed Tyler going into the woods, shortly followed by Ethan?" Kat asked.

"At the other end, yeah," Kevin said, getting ready to take off on his bike again. We followed the route right past Jessica's old house, where I spent that last night before Tyler died. Someone else lived there now, different cars in the driveway, the outside painted a different color. I stared up at the windows of the first floor while we rode by, as if the ghost of my teenage past might be there, but all I saw was the fluttering of pale pink drapes. Jessica had lived just a few blocks from the high school, and it took us mere minutes to get there, Kevin up ahead, flying past the entrance and going right to the back where the street trailed off into the woods. This had been my route to and from school every day, walking past stoners and slackers, loners and young lovers who sought out the coverage and seclusion the woods easily provided.

"Will you show us where Tyler was found?" Kat called, her voice echoing in the chamber of cedar trees.

It didn't take too long before Kevin slowed to a stop once again, scanning the area with a searching look on his face. "He was found somewhere round here, I think," he said by way of explanation. "I couldn't tell you for sure."

"Olivia?" Kat said, "Do you know?"

There were trees as far as the eye could see, trunks thick, leaves an everlasting green. It was hard to believe we were just a few minutes from busy streets, a bustling high school. If you listened hard enough you could hear the gentle rush of Cedar Creek, and then, further away, the growing roar of Hood River. It seemed darker than it should have been, a temporary twilight falling over the footpath, and I looked up; through the canopy of leaves the sky had started to turn grey, and with my face upturned I felt a drop of rain land on my cheek. "Olivia?" Kat said again, bringing me back.

I looked around us, and shook my head, "I don't know the exact spot, either. But it was probably around here. We're still a few minutes from my old house."

By the time we reached the house, the 20 or 25-minute bike ride Kevin had predicted had taken much longer due to all our stopping, and Kat and Ray were saying they wanted to try it again with no stops this time. Maybe even under the cover of darkness, just to be sure. "And we need to go back to Jessica Heng's old house," Kat said, "I want to see if you could actually identify anyone going into the woods from that far away. I wasn't sure I'd be able to –" Ray started to say something and Kat held up her hand, as if she knew exactly what was coming, "*With* my glasses on I mean."

But my attention had been caught by something just a few houses down the street. I narrowed my eyes, not sure I could really believe them, because standing out on a porch, just three houses away from where I'd grown up, were Cole Sampson and Morgan Washington.

And they were watching us.

13

THEN

It's the first day of Ethan's trial, the air heavy and slow with heat, summer wafting in through my open window as I dress. My legs and arms shake as I worry over what to wear. Is a dress too much? Is a suit too formal? Eventually I settle on a dark blue jersey maxi dress I would normally wear to the beach, but with a brown leather belt cinching it at the waist, it somehow looks okay. My hands tremble as I do up the belt, fingers sticky and stiff. I have no idea what I'm doing.

But no one does. That's what I soon realize. I can't rely on my older sister, or even my parents to lead the way now. Neither of my parents could ever have imagined finding themselves in a situation like this. My dad is a city planner, my mom a landscape gardener. They see life through a series of plans and blueprints, one stage leading to the next, leading to the next. You prepare the soil, you plant at the right time, you water the ground, and whatever you put in there, you grow. But they could never have planned for any of this. Nothing about their lives up until this point, up until the morning the police knocked heavily on our front door, could have left them with even a hint that their only son was going to be arrested for murder. They did everything right, prepared us all perfectly for the world that was waiting for us, but they failed to take into account the blurred or broken line on a blueprint that eventually led to ruin and chaos; the weeds running rampant in the garden; the woodworm condemning the house to rot. So, when we get to the steps of the courthouse, the sidewalk and street packed with journalists, photographers, reporters and cameramen, I lead the way. It's as if I can feel my parents' inability to believe any of this is happening, and instead of scaring me, it bolsters me somehow. Because someone has to go in there and show Ethan they believe him, and that everything's going to be okay.

But I'm not prepared for the other side of the courthouse door. I thought this would be the worst of it – the reporters and the onlookers, the rubberneckers and the muckrakers, but I couldn't be more wrong, because on the other side of the door is Mayor Washington and her family. Her husband stands by her side, arm clamped around her shoulders, and in front of them is their daughter Morgan, my former friend and cheer captain, just one year older than both me and Tyler. I don't expect anyone to say anything; I don't know what I would say, what any of my family would say, so I can't imagine what any member of Tyler's family would say either.

But apparently my imagination isn't quite up to scratch, because before I realize what's happening, Mom is edging away from our family huddle, and taking a few steps towards the Washingtons, her mouth open to speak. But the sound that comes out is strangled and all wrong, and the Mayor just gives her a withering, disgusted look, her mouth drawn into a hard, straight line while Morgan says, "Don't you dare come a single step closer, you murderous bitch."

But her voice is thin and tinny, when I know from hours of cheerleading practice with her, that it's normally hard and strong, as cheerful and confident as it is forceful. And for some reason, it makes my mind go clear, a glorious blank sheet of water roaring through it, and even though I have no idea what I'm doing or why, I walk over to Morgan and pull her into a hug, whispering into her ear as I do so, "I'm so, so sorry," and that's when I finally let myself cry, and that's when her body collapses and the shudder of her sobs join mine.

14

NOW

Kat was unable to resist striding over there, Ray a few steps behind her, muttering something about not having their recording equipment. I watched as Kat introduced herself to Morgan, but Morgan just stood there, arms crossed against her chest as she listened to Kat, while every few seconds her gaze flicked directly to mine. Despite having seen and talked to me just hours earlier, Cole's eyes didn't land on me once.

He was sat on a wooden bench, one leg crossed over the other, a bottle of beer in hand as he watched the interaction between Kat and Morgan. Clouds had scudded over the sky, but it was late in the day now, evening strolling in, and the combination of sunset and clouds turned the world yellow, meaning Cole was squinting as he watched his girlfriend talk to Kat. Morgan was gesticulating, her face twisting and turning, and I wished I could hear what they were saying, but I felt rooted to the ground, stuck in place. Morgan kept bringing one hand to her stomach, every couple of seconds or so, and my eyes instantly flicked to Cole, trying to read his face, figure out if what I was thinking could possibly be true.

"Is she pregnant?" I asked, turning to Kevin all of a sudden.

Kevin looked from me over to where Morgan stood on her porch, staring down at Kat and Ray who were talking full force at her now, giving her the pitch. "Don't know. Why?"

"She just keeps ... touching her stomach, I thought maybe ..." but I couldn't finish the sentence, and Kevin just shrugged and said lightly,

"Maybe she just had a really big burrito."

"Thank you, Kevin. You don't think maybe you could take this a tiny bit more seriously?"

Kevin made a face at me and sighed, "What would it matter anyway, Liv? If Morgan is pregnant, so what. What's it to you? Or Ethan? Or the podcast?"

"Nothing, it's nothing to me," I said stoutly, turning away from him, "I was just curious." And then after a beat I couldn't help asking, "They're not married though, right? Just dating?"

Kevin laughed, the sound running down the road and catching up to Kat, Ray, Cole and Morgan who all turned to look at us at the same time. "You worried about them having a baby out of wedlock, Liv?" He asked, still laughing. But when I didn't immediately answer, he said, "No, they're not married. They do live together though. So, a bit more serious than 'dating'."

Ray was strolling back towards us now, telling us that Morgan had miraculously agreed to an interview so he was going to go back and get their recording equipment from Kevin's if that was okay? Kevin agreed and the two of them hopped on their bikes again, about to speed off when I said, "Can I stay? For the interview?"

Ray turned back to me, looking over his shoulder, eyes catching the eerie, watery yellow sunlight as they shifted over towards Cole and Morgan's house, where Kat was following the two of them inside. "Um, I don't think that's the best idea."

"Why? Did Morgan say something?"

"No, it's not that. I just don't think Kat would be cool with it.

It might influence the interview, stop Morgan from saying certain things. You get that, right?"

I looked over towards the house. All three of them had disappeared inside now, and my gaze was drawn instead, inexorably, towards my old house. It had been repainted, and was now a cornflower blue with a bright white trim, whereas my mom had always insisted on keeping it all white when we lived there. When wisteria draped itself over the porch railings and trim, roses grew up the side, and alliums lined the pathway. I looked up to the second floor window I'd spent so much of my life looking out of, but just like with Jessica Heng's house, it wasn't ghostly figures I saw there, but the faint outlines of a desk pushed up to the window and a chair no one was sitting in. I said goodbye to Kevin and Ray and got back on my bike, pedaling back towards the B&B where Daniel was waiting for me.

"One or both of us is going to have to head back to work tomorrow," Daniel said as soon as I opened the door to our room. The floor and coffee table were littered with papers Daniel had brought with him, but it was the phone in his hand that my eyes were drawn to.

"Why?" I said, "it's Sunday tomorrow." It wasn't unusual for us to work weekends, of course, especially not during a big case, but it was still fairly early days with Reid Murphy's case, and the all-nighters and long weekends didn't usually begin until we were a lot closer to the trial.

"Reid's just been charged with murder. James Asher died late last night."

"Holy shit," I said, the breath drawn right out of me.

"Yeah. That was Colin I just spoke to, Karen's demanding all hands on deck from tomorrow."

I looked behind me, towards the doorway I'd just walked through, as if, if I hadn't come through that door, this wouldn't have happened, and I wouldn't have had to deal with the push-pull that was currently tugging away inside me. But that was wishful thinking, because Daniel would've called me regardless, telling me this news, and potentially cutting short this trip to Twin Rivers.

"You can stay," he said now. "Stay until tomorrow evening at least, I'll cover for you tomorrow."

"You drove me out here, remember?" I said, frustration finding its way through my words. If he hadn't insisted on coming with me, I'd have my own car here, and I wouldn't be obliged to travel back to Portland so soon. I could've just pretended I'd never heard this news, and stayed here until Monday. But Reid's charge being upped from attempted murder to murder really did change things, and I couldn't help thinking about the conversation we'd had just the day before, and how much her life had now changed in the intervening 24-hours.

"How did you leave things with Kat and Ray?" Daniel asked, ignoring my petulance.

"They're interviewing Morgan, Tyler's older sister, literally as we speak."

"You didn't want to hang around for that?" Daniel asked, confusion creasing his forehead.

"They wouldn't let me," I said.

But they did let me listen to the recording later that evening, when both Kat and Ray came over for a drink.

* * *

Extract from transcript of Season 3 Episode 2 of *Shadow of a Doubt*:

Kat Thomas [voiceover]: If you listen carefully, the names Ethan Hall and Tyler Washington are still everywhere in Twin Rivers. Tyler may have died, and Ethan been convicted nine years ago, but the wounds are still so fresh they have barely begun to heal. It's years later and while Ethan serves his sentence in the state penitentiary hundreds of miles away, Twin Rivers is still peopled by the players who were most severely affected by Tyler's murder.

The Hall family may have long since stopped walking its streets, but Tyler's classmates now teach in the very same high school they all attended, work in the bars and breweries they used to try to sneak into without being carded, manage the sporting goods stores they all bought their climbing gear from. His mother, Maria, is still mayor of Twin Rivers. She took a leave of absence for a while after her son died, but just a couple of years after Ethan was convicted of the murder of Tyler Washington, Maria was standing for election again. And she won.

I reach out to the mayor in hopes that she will want to talk to me about her son, but City Hall keeps her busy and I'm given the brush off by more than one assistant or employee. It takes a trip to one of Twin Rivers' many craft breweries before we begin to really get anywhere. The head brewer at Two Sails Brewery is Cole Sampson who was not only a good friend of Tyler Washington, but is now also the boyfriend of Washington's older sister Morgan. Morgan won't speak to us and neither will he, we're told when we first approach Sampson, but fast forward a couple of hours, and a recce of the town brings us face to face with Morgan. And despite what her boyfriend told us just hours earlier, it seems she's ready to talk about her brother, wants to shed light on who Tyler Washington really was.

In the following interview with Morgan you'll sometimes hear interjections from Sampson who didn't want to go on record and therefore wasn't miked up for audio. My and Morgan's microphones were still able to pick up his words, however, and you can, for the most part, understand what he is saying.

KT [to Morgan Washington]: Morgan what made you decide to talk to us today?

[brief pause with the sound of chairs moving and paper being rustled]

MW: I heard you were talking to Olivia Hall and I wanted to make sure you didn't get a totally biased view of my brother. That if you were going to make this podcast, that you had all the facts, not just the ones she and her brother would tell you.

KT: Were you friends with either Ethan or Olivia Hall?

MW: [laughs] Ethan Hall? Hell, no. No one was friends with Ethan Hall, not even his sister, that's the real irony in all this. But Olivia? Sure, yeah. We were friends. We were both on the cheerleading squad, we spent a lot of time together. I thought I knew her.

KT: What do you mean by that?

MW: Just that you find out who your friends really are when you lose somebody.

KT: You couldn't really have expected her to have accused her own brother of murder, though could you? They're twins, what were the chances of her not standing by him?

[brief pause]

MW: Yeah, maybe. Maybe you have a point. But they weren't close, they never were. That's the weird thing. Ethan was a burnout and a loser and a weirdo. He had one friend, they never went anywhere or did anything, you'd never see them at parties or anything. But Olivia was cool, you know. She hung out with all the right people, wore the right clothes, said all the right things. She was one of us. Even when people would say things about Ethan she wouldn't do anything. Sometimes she'd even join in. Like, I cannot stress this enough – *they were not friends*. If they didn't look so similar you wouldn't think they were even related, let alone twins. So, yeah, when this all happened it was just weird to see her on the other side of things, to see where her loyalties really lay.

Cole Sampson [muffled]: It felt like a betrayal.

MW: Yeah! Yeah, it was totally a betrayal. Her brother killed my brother and then she stabbed me in the back just to make matters even worse.

KT: You don't think that maybe it would have been a bigger betrayal for her not to stand by her brother? By her family?

[pause]

MW [sighs]: Maybe. Maybe you're right about that. And I guess now, with time, I can see that. But at the time, it didn't feel like that.

KT: Have you ever doubted that Ethan Hall killed your brother, Morgan?

MW: No! No way, uh-uh. He did it, he totally did it. Cole practically saw it happen, so.

CS [**muffled**]: I saw them both go into the woods, I didn't see it happen.

MW [**quickly**]: Same thing.

KT: You said that Ethan was known as a burnout and a weirdo in school. How did he get that kind of reputation?

[pause]

MW: I don't know if I should say.

KT: Why?

MW: Well, I mean I know he's in prison and everything but it kind of involved some illegal stuff.

KT: What kind of stuff?

MW: He was basically the main drug dealer for our whole high school. The weirdest thing about Ethan was that it wasn't like he was dumb, you know? Everyone always said how smart he was, but he was stupid enough to become a smalltime drug dealer, so you tell me how much of a genius he was.

KT: Was he ever arrested for dealing drugs, do you know?

MW: No, I don't think so.

KT: So maybe he was a bit smart. To not get arrested.

[pause]

MW: Well maybe. I've never thought about it that way.

KT: And if he was never actually arrested for dealing, then isn't this all conjecture?

MW: It's not conjecture. I'm telling you it's not conjecture.

KT: It could easily just have been a rumor though, right?

MW: No way was it a rumor, nuh-uh. Everyone knew about him, I'm telling you, *everyone*.

[muffled audio from Cole Sampson]

MW: I wasn't going to say anymore! [muffled inaudible conversation between MW and CS]

KT: Morgan? How did you know Ethan Hall dealt drugs?

MW [sighs]: How do you think?

[brief pause]

KT: Right.

MW: So, yeah. I knew. Everyone knew.

KT: Did your brother ever buy drugs from Ethan do you know?

MW: Yeah, he definitely did. Definitely.

[Muffled audio from CS]

What? Fine! I won't say anymore.

KT: Morgan? Could he and Ethan have been meeting up for an exchange that night do you think?

[pause]

MW: Ye-es. That's what I've always thought. Obviously Ethan denied they had arranged to meet up at all, but why would you believe a convicted murderer?

* * *

"So, the drugs," Kat said, ripping a piece of sourdough in two and spreading it with a thick layer of miso infused butter. "Did you know about it?"

We were sat in the front window of a popular neighborhood restaurant in Twin Rivers that was the current talk of the Oregon restaurant scene. Daniel was planning to leave after dinner, back to Portland and our office for a morning meeting the next day that he was somehow going to supply me with an excuse for. We were thinking stomach flu.

I shrugged, taking a sip of wine, "Yeah, I knew."

Kat raised both her eyebrows at me and let out an exasperated sigh, "And you didn't think maybe you should tell me about it?"

"I wasn't really thinking. It never came up in the arrest or trial, so it didn't really seem relevant."

"Yeah, why didn't it come up at trial? That seems so weird to me," Ray said, turning in his chair toward Daniel, "you'd totally bring that up at trial, right?"

"As a defense attorney, absolutely not. I'd be hoping to God it wouldn't turn up in disclosure, and thanking every star I could remember the name of when the prosecution didn't seem to have a clue," Daniel said.

"Would Ethan's lawyer have known about the dealing?" Kat asked me.

Again, all I could do was shrug, "I don't know. Not unless Ethan specifically told him. He'd never been arrested before, so it's not like he had a record."

"We need to get in touch with him," Kat said, drumming her fingers on the table.

"Who, Ethan?"

"No, his lawyer. Would you have his contact info?"

"It's Robert Castle. I think he's still here in town," I said, watching as Ray picked up his phone and started googling.

"Yeah, he's right downtown, not far from here. Closed this weekend, but I'll call on Monday," Ray said to Kat who nodded in response.

"I'm just so confused about prosecution not bringing it up at trial," Kat said, musingly. "You'd think that would be a gold mine, the smoking gun, right?"

I nodded, taking another sip of wine, taking my time answering. "Tyler's family were very into image. Especially his mom. If they'd admitted that Tyler took drugs, and that was why he might potentially have been meeting up with my brother, then that wouldn't have looked good for them. At all."

"Yeah, but come on. This is Oregon, everybody smokes weed, that couldn't have been that big a deal?"

"Maybe not, but it wasn't just weed," I said, shifting in my seat.

"So? Are you going to tell me what else he was dealing, Olivia? This is all pretty crucial information."

I met Daniel's eye for a second, suddenly wishing that we'd both decided to go back to Portland that evening, rather than stick around for dinner, for this.

"I think probably it's better if you spoke to Ethan about all this," I said at last.

15

THEN

It's May 4, I'm turning nineteen, and it's the first time I've ever celebrated my birthday without my twin brother. Not that you could really call it a celebration. The day is grey and overcast, the sky hanging low over everything, and I try to think back to a year ago, to what we were doing as we turned eighteen, but I can't quite get there.

I would have had two celebrations, just like I had done since we were fourteen or thereabouts. We always did something as a family, just the five of us, but when I started making friends with people other than my twin, I wanted to celebrate with them too. To begin with Ethan would be there too; it would be weird if he wasn't right? But as we got older, it became weirder when he was there. He wasn't friends with any of my friends, didn't make an effort with them, didn't care if they liked him or not. Didn't seem to care that they laughed at him behind his back, and forced me to do the same. So, eventually I started having birthday parties without him, as if he didn't exist, as if I wasn't someone's twin at all.

This is different though. I'm not going to be spending the day with the family, and the evening with my friends. Because our family is missing a crucial part, and my friends are no longer my friends. Georgia has come home from Portland of course, and Mom is baking a cake, but only because we're visiting Ethan in prison later. If we didn't have that lined up, this day – my birthday, *our* birthday – would have come and gone with no recognition at all.

We can only go in two at a time, so Mom and Dad head into the visiting room first, and then Georgia and I tag in after.

"Happy Birthday, sis," Ethan says to me as we sit down.

"The same to you," I say.

"I hear Mom's cake got confiscated," Ethan says.

"Yeah, it was your favorite too. Coffee and walnut."

"She should've made your favorite, I could've told her they wouldn't let her bring a cake in to me."

I shrug, "I like coffee and walnut. Plus, she needed to make it."

Ethan stares right at me, and I wonder what he's thinking. We used to tell ourselves we knew what the other one was thinking, but those days are long gone now, and I can't even remember if we really could, or if it was all an act. Finally, he says, "Nineteen years on this earth. Who would've thought we'd be celebrating here."

"Ethan," Georgia says, reaching towards him almost involuntarily, "you're not going to stay here, you know that right? There's no way you're going to be convicted. It's preposterous."

"Oh, I don't know," Ethan says lightly, "I really didn't like that Tyler kid much."

"Ethan," Georgia says warningly, sounding so much like Mom, Ethan's eyes find mine and we both smirk.

"Have you heard from Kevin at all?" I ask.

"Yeah," Ethan says nodding, "he's been around."

"Cool. Well, in that case, you officially have more friends than me now," I say.

Ethan laughs, a short, sharp bark. "Yet another turn of events we couldn't have seen coming."

I feel rather than see Georgia stiffen next to me. Her voice is constricted and tightly controlled, as if she's trying not to cry when she says, "Why are you guys making jokes like this? I don't get it. None of this is fucking funny."

"It's a little funny," Ethan says, looking at her with the sideways slash of a grin on his face.

"Ethan," she says again, and again he laughs.

"Georgia, it's fine, calm down. It's just the way we deal with things, you know that," I say, placating her.

But she shakes her head roughly and stares between the two of us, taking us in one by one. I feel a shot of wonder tear through me, wondering what she really thinks of us, wondering what she makes of having twins for siblings, wondering what it was like for her growing up with the two of us. Two people who look so similar staring right back at her every day. It used to shock even me sometimes when we were younger. I'd see myself in the mirror and think 'there's Ethan,' or I'd see him walking down the hallway a few steps ahead of me in school, or across the lunch hall waiting in line for food, and think 'what am I doing over there?'. I guess that was why I did it. Why I pulled away, why I made new friends, why I carved out a space for myself with a group of people who would never choose to spend time with Ethan Hall. For all the good that's done.

Because here we are. Back to where we began. Just me and Ethan and the rest of the world, still not quite getting it.

Ethan's smiling at Georgia now, the grin turned down a few watts. "It's our birthday, Georgia, let us have our fun. We can't talk about all this all the time, can we?"

Georgia looks around at the room as if to say, *look at where we are*, but then she closes her eyes briefly and says, "Okay, fine. You guys have your jokes. I'll just sit here worrying about everything."

"Don't worry," Ethan says, "this time next year, we'll be cutting cake and making jokes at home. All of us. I promise."

I stare at him, watching the movement of his face, the flicker of his eyes and I think, *he's good*. Because if I wasn't me, and he wasn't him, I'd believe him.

16

NOW

It was late by the time we finished dinner, and I was yawning as the white beams of Daniel's car headlights swept across me, Kat and Ray. But Kat and Ray were talking about heading back to Kevin's parents' place, seemingly tireless, completely indefatigable. All I wanted was to go back to that B&B and crawl into bed, but I was still annoyed I'd missed out on being there for the interview with Morgan earlier, so I asked if I could join them.

"Yeah, that would be good actually," Kat said, looking down at her phone as she spoke, tapping out a message to Kevin. "You'll know the woods better than us, right?"

"It's been a while, but I used to know them pretty well, yeah."

"As well as Ethan did?" Ray asked.

"Probably. Obviously he'd know the route back from Kevin's better than me as he did it more often, but we both used to use them as short cuts all the time."

"Okay, Kevin's going to meet us there," Kat said, looking up from her phone, "he'll bring some extra bike lights for us."

I nodded, thinking about the woods in the dark, which could go from as soft as velvet to sharp and threatening in the blink of an eye. It had been years since I'd tramped my way through them at night, and as we stood at the edge with Kevin, kitting out our borrowed bikes with the same kind of lighting Ethan would've had on the night Tyler died, I couldn't believe I used to do this all the time. I stared into the damp thickness, the rich green of the forest earlier in the day turned to a stifling black; there wasn't any sunshine to filter through anymore to help soften and soothe the threat of nature. This wasn't wilderness, of course, nothing like that. It was tamed and lived in, its wild edges rounded out by city planning and city life, foot paths and bike trails well signposted, with yet more signs reminding dog walkers to keep their pets on a leash, and to take their shit with them, thank you. But none of that was obvious at night, and I took a second to wonder at the power of teenage invincibility to scrub all that fear out and replace it with naïve bravado.

"You want to lead the way again?" Kat asked Kevin, who'd decided to join us.

"Sure," Kevin said, nodding.

"But no stopping. And try and go as fast as Ethan would've gone." She checked the time on her phone, and turned to Ray. "Eleven twenty-three p.m. You sure you don't think we should wait and do it at the same time Ethan would've been doing it?"

Ray shrugged, his gaze shifting to the wavering outlines of the trees leading the way into the woods. "I don't think it's necessary. We'll time it exactly, and it's as dark now as it would've been then."

"Okay," Kat said, throwing her right leg over the bike, and settling onto the saddle. The light attached to her handlebars sent out a milk white beam which shook and shivered as she maneuvered herself. "Everything recording?" she asked Ray, who nodded a 'yes' in response.

We were all miked up with tiny microphones, attached to the collars of our sweatshirts and jackets, while Ray had a larger

93

microphone attached to his backpack, so that he could pick up the sounds of the woods and anything else that might make itself known on the trip.

Kevin set off first, then Kat, Ray, and lastly me, bringing up the rear. Our lights bobbed and weaved as the sound of our breathing filled the dark air of the woods. Short, sharp pants gave way to deeper, more labored breaths as Kevin sped up ahead, standing up in the seat of his bike to avoid rocky earth, fallen branches, raised roots. Kevin was easily the fittest and fastest of all four of us, but I was starting to regret going last. I ran three miles every day come rain or shine, even longer on the weekends. Judging by their performances, Kat and Ray's fitness regimes were hindered by days on the road, and long nights researching and recording their podcast. It took more effort for me to keep my pace down, than it would have done to keep up with Kevin. I was concentrating so much on the actual cycling that it took me by surprise when Kevin raised his arm and shouted back to the rest of us that we were about to pass out of the woods and onto the street where Jessica Heng had once lived.

"Thirteen minutes so far!" Ray shouted back to no one in particular. Then, as we past Jessica's old house, porch light burning, windows all dark, he shouted again, "Sixteen minutes!"

We were going faster than I'd anticipated; when we'd done the same journey earlier in the day, all the stops and starts had made Ethan's ride seem so much longer. We whooshed past the school in convoy, its hulking black mass haunted in the black night, and then we were heading back into the woods again. The path was a little clearer here, thanks to years of wear from the sneakers and boots of teenagers, cutting class and taking short cuts home. At the same point we'd stopped earlier that day, Kevin held up his arm and pointed further into the woods, shouting back so Ray and I could hear, "This is about where Tyler was found."

"Twenty minutes now!" Ray shouted in response.

A few minutes later, all four of us pulled to a stop outside my old house, and Ray whipped out his phone again, stopping the stopwatch. "Twenty-six minutes and 38 seconds," he said.

Kat looked over to Kevin, "You said you thought it would take 20, 25 minutes from yours, right?"

"Yup. Almost bang on. Plus Ethan would've known that path even better back then, than I do now, so it might've been a little faster."

Kat shared a look with Ray and then, shaking her head as she turned back to me and Kevin said, "That still puts him in the woods at the time of Tyler's death though. Even if he left at 2:20, 2:25, as you think Kevin, that means he would've been getting home at about 2:45am maybe. And Tyler's death was given as between 2 and 3 in the morning."

"1:45 and 2:45 in the morning," I corrected, "and I know he was home before 3am because I saw him before going to bed that night."

"Okay," Kat said slowly, her face thoughtful in the darkness, "so, I guess with Ethan definitely being in the woods during that time period, the reasoning becomes that he just wouldn't have had time to kill Tyler and get home by the time you saw him. Right, Olivia?"

"Yeah."

Kat nodded her head, "Okay. But wouldn't he have seen the body? From the track? His tire marks were found less than ten feet from Tyler, right? So, wouldn't he at least have seen him lying there? Why didn't he stop?"

Ray stared back the way we'd just come, back into the thick black knot of trees, dense and deep and said, "I don't know Kat. I don't know about you, but I was just concentrating on the path ahead, maybe he genuinely wouldn't – or couldn't – have been able to see Tyler?"

Kat let out a long heavy breath, folding her mouth into a thin, straight line before she said, "Looks like we're going back in. Make sure you're recording all this, Ray. It'll make a good addition to the second episode of the podcast, I reckon."

Extract from transcript of Season 3 Episode 2 of *Shadow of a Doubt* [continued]:

Kat Thomas [sound of branches snapping, leaves crunching, heavy footsteps and deep breathing]: Okay, it's round here, right?

Kevin Lawrence: Yeah, just over there.

KT: You think this is roughly ten feet away?

KL: Pfft, it's hard to tell but yeah, about that.

KT: Ray, will you go over there?

Ray Mackenzie: You want me to lie down too?

KT: Just stay standing for now and we'll see how we get on.

[sound of RM walking away; rustle of leaves, branches, footsteps and then quiet]

KT: Okay, now we'll all turn our lights off, then face the direction Ethan would've been going in and then I'll turn just my bike light on.

[pause]

KT [quietly]: Can you see him?

Olivia Hall: No.

KL: Yeah, me neither.

KT [shouting]: Ray?!

RM: Yep?

KT: Wave a hand or something.

[pause]

KT: Okay, yeah, I saw that. Did you guys see that?

OH: Yeah, but only because he was moving and I knew where to look.

KT: Yeah, I know. Do you think it would be excessive to try cycling past as Ethan would've been?

KT [voiceover]: I could see even less when I was cycling past. It wasn't just that it was totally dark, with only the narrow beam of my bike light, but cycling in the dark, over rough track rather than road requires even more concentration than usual. I probably wasn't even going at the speed Ethan would've been cycling at, which would have made the possibility of him spotting Tyler's body lying just 10 feet away even more unlikely.

Ethan never denied being in the woods during the time period Tyler was thought to have died. A witness had him entering the woods somewhere between 2 and 2:30 in the morning, and his sister, Olivia had always maintained that she'd seen him back at home just before 3am. But 25 minutes doesn't give him much time to leave Kevin's, cycle through the woods, and kill Tyler. Unless of course someone, somewhere is wrong. Or lying.

And what if, as Morgan said in her interview, Ethan had gone through the woods with the express purpose of meeting someone – of meeting her brother in fact? When Morgan brought up the possibility of Tyler and Ethan meeting up for some kind of drug deal, I wasn't just mildly surprised, I was blindsided. Because I've spoken to Ethan a few times now, and he's never mentioned these allegations against him regarding drugs. I've also spent hours reading all the coverage of his trial, and it isn't brought up once. This seems strange to me, because although the prosecution had enough circumstantial, witness and even forensic evidence to place Ethan at the scene of the crime, there never seemed to be much indication of motive.

Tyler was presented as the golden boy at trial, as undeserving as you could possibly be of the kind of grisly death he met with. But conversations with classmates of both his and Ethan's, as well as Morgan have revealed a slightly different side to Tyler. Not just a recreational drug user, but something of a bully and a ringleader as well. If Ethan was a known drug dealer, and if Tyler not only bought from him, but spent much of the school day pushing Ethan around and putting him down for whatever reason, what if Ethan did finally snap? Wouldn't that make for a motive?

Ethan Hall: No way man, that's not how any of that worked out.

KT: So, you didn't deal drugs in high school.

EH: Uhhh. Yeah, I guess I did. For a while yeah. I never really thought of it as dealing though. It wasn't some big outfit. It started out with study drugs, and then I started growing my own pot and people would come to me knowing they could get it from me easily.

KT: And the police had no idea about this?

EH: No.

KT: But everyone at school did?

EH: Sure. I dunno, I never really considered myself a dealer, you know? I just grew the stuff and then I'd sell it on. It was more of a co-op [short laugh].

Kat Thomas [voiceover]: It's probably worth pointing out here, that although Oregon is now known as being a pro-cannabis state, it's actually only been legal to buy, use, and sell marijuana recreationally here since 2015. So, when we talk about Ethan growing, selling and using pot in high school, it was still very much illegal in 2008.

KT: How did you get into growing it?

EH: I kind of just love growing stuff. Always have. It's my mom's fault really, she's the gardener. She always had a little patch of weed growing somewhere when we were growing up, and one day I just took a cutting, took it over to Kevin's house and eventually we had enough to grow this big patch.

KT: Where was it?

EH: He won't love me for telling you this, but we grew it on Kevin's place because of his parents' farm you know, which is so big we knew they'd never find it. So, that's where it was. There's probably still some there to be honest.

KT: Tyler's sister Morgan maintains that you were going to meet with Tyler on the night he was murdered.

EH: You mean for drugs?

KT: Yes.

EH: No, no way. I can kind of see why she'd say that, why she might think it, but Tyler had stopped coming to me for anything by then. It had been over a year since he'd hit me up for anything.

KT: Did he ever buy anything other than weed from you?

EH: Oh yeah, sure. I kind of got into selling Adderall which I'd had a prescription for since I was like, 12, but I didn't think I needed to take as much anymore. He bought from me a couple of times, but so did almost everyone.

KT: But not recently? I mean before he was killed?

EH: Uh, no. Like I said, Tyler really hadn't bought anything from me in over a year. I wasn't bothered about it, though. Anything that kept me as far away from Tyler Washington as possible was good by me.

KT: Why was that?

EH: The guy was just kind of an asshole. He was a user. He was probably one of the only people I sold weed to who could easily afford it you know? And yet he was always the one promising to pay me later, and then never doing it.

KT: Did he owe you money?

EH: Yeah, probably at the time. From months before. I didn't really keep track or keep count. I was kind of a crappy drug dealer if you could call me one at all.

KT: But don't you think that could count as motive? If he owed you money?

[pause]

EH [sighing]: I can see how someone might think that. Look, I'm just trying to be as honest as possible here, okay? As straightforward as possible, so yeah, it might sound like motive, but really, honestly, at the time I probably wasn't even aware of whether or not Tyler owed me money. If he did, it wouldn't have been for a lot because I didn't charge much, and it would have been from upwards of a year ago, so I probably would've forgotten all about it by then.

[pause]

I didn't hold grudges back then, you know? He was an asshole and he owed me a bit of money, but I honestly didn't really spend much time thinking about Tyler Washington.

KT: So you think he'd found another dealer?

EH: Yeah, I assume so.

KT: And, if you had to guess at who Tyler's new dealer was, who would it be?

EH: Oh, I wouldn't even have to guess.

KT: So, you know for sure?

EH: Sure, yeah. Everyone knew.

KT: Who was it?

EH: Nick Green.

KT [voiceover]: I recognize the name Nick Green immediately because, as I mentioned earlier in the episode, we've spent a considerable amount of time reaching out to Mayor Washington over the past week. Most of the calls we've made, and emails we've sent have been answered by her assistant Natalie, but there was one instance when we were directed to her Chief of Staff.

His name? You guessed it: Nick Green.

Oh, and he also happens to have been the person to find Tyler's body on the morning of August 24, 2008.

17

THEN

It's the day of Ethan's preliminary hearing. The day we'll find out just how big the case is against him, just how hard and long this fight is going to be. I'm finding it hard to believe we've even arrived at this point; I keep thinking the charges are about to be dropped, the case reopened with a different suspect, but Twin Rivers PD are convinced Ethan's guilty, and so is the DA. And now, we'll finally find out what it is they have against him.

It's six months since Ethan was arrested, since Tyler died. I try to remember what I was doing six months ago but can't make sense of it. Six months ago, it was summer. Six months ago, the sun still felt like warm butter melting on your skin, Tyler was still alive, and my brother was still at home. Six months ago, to the day, I was down at the gorge with Cole, Jess, Nick and half a dozen other people, and yes, with Tyler. He'd grabbed me round my waist at one point, pulled me through the donut hole of my inner tube and I'd felt like I was about to drown, rising to the surface, gasping for air, shouting his name, hitting him around the side of his head in protest.

I have no idea where Ethan was, what he was doing that day.

The courtroom is stuffy and overbearing, the heat overpowering. There's not as many people here as I was expecting, though; just family and a few friends. On the other side of the room, sitting behind the prosecutor who is shuffling papers, about to convince the judge of his case, are Cole, Jess, Nick, and everyone else who was down at the gorge with us that day. None of them meet my eye, or even look at me; I don't exist now, and I wonder if I should be grateful for that, because having their attention would be so much worse. Ethan is sat next to his lawyer, Robert Castle, his hair cut short, ears sticking out at the top, making him look younger, even more vulnerable than usual. I wonder whose idea that was, if it was a calculated move on Castle's part to make Ethan look even less like a murderer than he already does, or if perhaps it was all Ethan's idea. The main doors swing open and everyone turns to see who's arriving late as Kevin walks through them with his mom, and they come to join us on our side of the room; two more people to swell our ranks.

I'm sat between Georgia and Dad, so close that I can hear, feel and smell their breath, but I feel completely alone, detached. There's a part of me that, instead of sitting back here, safe among my family on an uncomfortable wooden bench, is sat up there with Ethan, about to have my life changed forever. If I cut my hair and shaved my head, we'd look identical, I think to myself, imagining our roles reversed; me up there, and him back here. Would he be feeling like this too? Is this simply what happens when one twin breaks away so definitively there's no turning back?

The judge enters the room and we all rise as demanded. When we leave this room, we'll know exactly what it is Ethan is supposed to have done.

"Please state your full name for the court, ma'am," Prosecutor Curtis says to the too-young looking forensic investigator who has just taken the stand.

"Kellyanne Wimpole," the woman responds, shifting in her seat almost imperceptibly.

"And Ms Wimpole, you're an investigator in the Portland Metropolitan Forensic Laboratory?"

"Yes, that's right."

"And how long have you worked there?"

"Just over a year."

"Had you worked with Twin Rivers Police Department before being asked to lend your services in this case?"

"I hadn't personally, no, but the department often consults for police departments in the area surrounding Portland."

"And at what point did you arrive on the scene, Ms Wimpole?"

"As I understand it, the body was found a little before noon on Sunday August 24, police arrived and secured the scene approximately 18 minutes later, and were in contact with the lab by 12:45. I arrived on the scene just over an hour later, so by 2pm."

"And were you assigned this case by a superior?"

"I was the investigator on call that weekend, so I was assigned the case by default. I was actually at home when the call came in."

"Had the scene been well secured by the time you got there, in your opinion?"

"Given the circumstances of the body's discovery, I was impressed by how well the Twin Rivers Police Department had managed to secure it, yes, but because of the mud from the rain the night before, there was definitely an element of the scene having been compromised, both by the civilians who had found the body, and by the police department themselves. But due to the inclement weather, this was to be expected."

"And was it you who found and identified the tire tracks in question?" Curtis asks, holding up the photo of a bike tread mark, pressing itself deeply into rich brown mud, which is why Wimpole is here.

"I was alerted to the presence of the tire tread marks by one of the officers first on the scene, Officer Michelle Barnes. Both

Detective Rawes and I thought it was more than worth taking an impression as well as the usual photograph."

"And can you tell us how far from the body, exactly, the tire treads were found?"

"It was less than ten feet. Approximately nine feet ten inches."

"Nine foot ten. That's not far is it?" Curtis muses to Wimpole, but this is a rhetorical question, and Curtis turns from her to the judge and clarifies, "No, in fact, it's approximately two middle schoolers stood on top of one another." Curtis turns back to the investigator from Portland and continues, "Ms Wimpole, how did you connect this tire tread mark to the defendant, Ethan Hall?" Here, the prosecutor gestures towards my brother, Ethan's shoulders and back stiffening as the entire courtroom follows the direction of Curtis's arm and all eyes fall on Ethan.

"In the end, it was pretty simple. The police already had two witnesses, Cole Sampson and Nick Green I believe, who were able to place Mr Hall, and his bike, in the woods around the time the victim was killed, and we were able to gain a warrant for the bike. From there, it was just a case of comparing impressions from those found at the scene, and those from Mr Hall's bike."

"And it was a match?"

"Yes. One hundred percent, it was a match."

106

18

NOW

"I'm not sure it's such a good idea that I'm here, actually," I said, looking around. We were sat in the waiting area of the mayor's office in City Hall, waiting to hear if Nick Green was willing to see us or not. I was betting not.

"Why?" Kat asked, "You were friends with Nick, weren't you?"

"Yeah, but …"

"But what?" Kat said.

"Well, I can't imagine he'll want to see me any more than Cole or Morgan did."

Kat made a face, tilting her head to the left and fixing me with a penetrating stare. "But you didn't used to date Nick, and you also aren't related to the person accused of killing his brother … what can Nick Green have against you?"

"Believe me," I said, drumming my fingers against the armrest of my chair, "I'm sure he'll have thought of something."

It wasn't just the thought of seeing Nick that was making me nervous. I also wasn't exactly comfortable with the idea that Maria Washington, Tyler's mother, was on the other side of the doors that had a nice, shiny brass nameplate with the word 'Mayor'

107

emblazoned across it. I hadn't seen her since the day of Ethan's sentencing, almost nine years ago, and I couldn't begin to imagine the reaction she might have to find me waiting in her office for her. Nick was one thing, but I definitely wasn't ready to confront Maria Washington yet.

"Olivia Hall," a deep voice said suddenly, drawing me from my thoughts. My fingers stopped their incessant drumming and I looked up into Nick Green's face. It took a second for me to recognize him fully. His sandy hair had got darker, there was carefully thought about scruff dusting the bottom half of his face, and he was wearing a dark blue suit, crisp white shirt undone and loose at the collar.

"Nick," I said, standing up to hold out my hand for him to shake. He raised one eyebrow, almost imperceptibly, smiled tightly and shook it.

"The prom queen herself, Miss Olivia Hall. To what do we owe this great honor?" he said. I took a deep breath and introduced him to Kat and Ray, who had both stood up when he appeared. Explaining about the podcast, I watched Nick's face closely, trying to find the boy I'd known, and failing.

I'd been surprised to hear that Nick worked in politics now; that he worked for the Mayor. That certainly wasn't the track he'd been going down in high school. But people change, and they grow up, and sometimes they manage to get their act together. This was different though. I'd recognized Cole immediately, and I don't just mean physically. He was still there, the person I'd known, the person I'd shared a childhood and an adolescence with. Nick seemed to have taken on a completely new identity; if he reminded me of anyone, it was Tyler, and the thought of that made me shiver involuntarily.

"An interview?" Nick said, talking to Kat and shaking his head. "No, I don't think so. That would be impossible," turning to me he said, "Have you lost your mind, Olivia? You do realize that the mother of the boy your brother killed is on the other side of that door, and you've come here asking me, and potentially even her to go on a *podcast* about it?"

I looked at Kat for a second, trying to weigh up the best approach with just one glance, and took a big breath, "I know it's a lot to ask, Nick. And really, I never thought the mayor would agree to be interviewed anyway. But you were there that night. You found the body. You found Tyler that morning, and I really think that's an important thing to have on the podcast."

Nick shook his head, keeping his eyes on mine as red slowly crept its way up his neck, under his fashionable beard and pinched at the tips of his ears. I'd forgotten this about him; that his anger and frustration, annoyance and embarrassment was so easily written across his face. So that was one thing that hadn't changed about him, I guess.

"You don't care about that, you don't care about Tyler. Don't pretend that you do. This is all about your brother, and your crazy insistence that he didn't kill Tyler, when we all know that he did."

"Nick, if I could just say something –" Kat said, but Nick wouldn't let her finish.

"Your twin brother killed someone, Olivia, and you've never been able to face up to that, and you know what? I'm sorry, I really am. It must be hard, to know your own twin is able to do that. But just because you've managed to convince two strangers to take up your fight, doesn't mean I have to pay them any kind of respect or attention. It's still lies, whether it's coming out of your mouth, or being spewed on a podcast."

"Nick, if I could just say something here," Kat said again, trying to regain her footing in the conversation, "this podcast isn't about proving Ethan's innocence. It might seem that way to you, because we turned up here with Olivia, but it's really not. We think, that somewhere along the way, there may have been a miscarriage of justice, and it's possible that the wrong person was arrested and convicted of Tyler's murder. But we're also open to the idea that everything is exactly as it appears to be. Of course, from our point of view, that makes for a slightly less interesting and exciting season of the podcast, but we will never twist a story to fit our aims. We always go where the story leads. Where the truth lies."

"Well if you're listening to Olivia Hall, you're not going to be getting the truth," Nick shot back.

"Nick, if that's your opinion, if that's your truth, then we want to hear it," Kat said, urgency pumping through her voice, as she took a tiny step towards him. She was almost as tall as him, and I swear it was this, as much as anything, that finally forced Nick to look her in the eye.

"I don't have a truth, or a story to tell. My story is the same one that got Olivia's brother arrested and convicted in the first place. In my case, the truth and the story are the same thing. I can't speak for Olivia, of course." Nick said, breaking eye contact with Kat, and once more focusing his gaze on me.

"So, you don't have a response to Ethan Hall's accusation that you were selling drugs throughout high school?" Kat asked. She had lowered her voice so that no one else in the room would be able to hear: there were two assistants sitting at their desks who had been paying avid attention to the conversation, ever since Nick had joined us.

Nick went still, and took so long in answering that I wasn't sure he'd even heard Kat. But the red on his face deepened, and he rolled his lips into a thin flat line, before saying, "I have no idea what you're talking about. And if I were you, I'd think long and hard before taking a convicted murderer at his word."

The assistant sat outside the mayor's office door then gave an almost imperceptible tilt of her head, and Nick held up his hand at us, before walking over to confer. We had been dismissed.

"I'm sorry," I said to Kat and Ray, as we exited City Hall. "You guys should try approaching him further down the line, when I'm not around."

It was sunny again and I put on a pair of oversized sunglasses, the big frames and dark lenses allowing me an anonymity I hadn't yet had while being back in town. We were only a few blocks down from the police station, and if we walked another ten or so blocks west we'd get to the court house. Twin Rivers was either a very small city or a big town, depending on your perspective, but whichever way you looked at it, it was really just a village. Maybe you didn't know everyone by name, but you saw the same faces every day, said hello to neighbors in the street, made conversation with your barista and bartender. It was just like anywhere else in the world then; so much smaller than you thought, but with so much more bubbling up beneath the surface, just waiting to boil over.

"You really think he'd agree to come on the podcast if you weren't there?" Ray asked.

"I don't know," I said shrugging, "but I have a feeling he'll be listening to the show once you start airing it, and then he might change his mind. He's not going to want the whole town, let alone the rest of the world, thinking he used to deal drugs. You saw him in there, he's a million miles from handing out MDMA at parties. He's going to want to protect that."

Neither Kat nor Ray responded immediately, and for a few seconds, all I could hear was the sound of our feet on the sidewalk and disjointed puffs of our breathing. "Here's the thing, Olivia," Kat said at last, "I'm not sure I fully believe he used to hand out MDMA at parties. He's right: all we have so far is Ethan telling us Nick used to sell drugs, and I don't think that's enough. We have to think about where accusations like this can lead."

"He could sue us for slander," Ray said, putting it more bluntly.

"Is there anyone else you can think of who'd be willing to corroborate Ethan's statements? Aside from you?" Kat asked.

Just about everyone I'd gone to high school with had either bought drugs, or been given them by Nick Green at some point, but that wasn't what Kat was asking. Twin Rivers hadn't been split down the middle when Tyler died, and Ethan was arrested;

no one except my family had been willing to say that the police had got it wrong, and that the wrong person had been arrested. I had no friends left in this town – they'd abandoned me years ago, when I'd decided I couldn't let my brother go to prison for a crime he didn't commit. So, there was no one I could turn to now, to ask for a favor, to help me help my brother. When I told Kat and Ray this I could feel their disappointment as easily as I could see it. Worrying that they were beginning to think this story was more trouble than it was worth, or worse, that there was nothing here to report on in the first place, I suggested going to see Ethan's defense lawyer, Robert Castle.

Castle was an old family friend. He and my father had grown up together in Twin Rivers, and both had come back in their late twenties, and early thirties to raise their families and establish their careers. It had seemed only natural at the time for Dad to turn to him in Ethan's hour of need. I had never questioned his appointment as Ethan's lawyer when we were younger. Now though, with age and more experience of the law, I'd begun to realize what a sizeable mistake it might have been to allow Castle to represent my twin. He was a criminal lawyer, sure, and he'd represented accused murderers before, but that had all been years ago, at the beginning of his career. By the time Tyler Washington died, and Ethan was arrested, Castle's time was mostly taken up with white collar crime and drug offences. He had never been the primary on a murder case.

Should my parents have hired someone else to represent Ethan? I'd spent many nights lying awake wondering if they should've done, and even more when I'd met my boss Karen Powers, thinking about how different Ethan's life could've been if we'd had a lawyer like Karen on our side. But changing the past has never been an option. Not for anyone. All we can do is attempt to keep making the right decisions in the present, and pray they're not the decisions that will lead to countless sleepless nights in the future. So, I wasn't exactly brimming with optimism when I suggested making an unscheduled stop at Castle's home. But I knew at the very least that he'd have all his old files on the case. And while we were waiting on the police to release their files, Castle's would be a whole lot better than nothing.

"So, I'm happy to give you all my files on the case, but it's not going to be as comprehensive as the police files you're looking for. I always suspected the prosecution might've held something back in discovery," Castle said.

We were sitting at his kitchen table, bathed in Sunday sunlight. When we'd arrived, he'd been in his backyard reading, a beagle snoozing at his feet as his wife lounged nearby with a glass of rosé in her hand. I'd watched as Kat and Ray had shared another, impenetrable look, although this time I think I got it; it was such a cliché, we'd moved onto pastiche. Despite my suspicions that he hadn't been up to the job of adequately defending my brother, I still liked Castle. I always had. Even making the decision to represent Ethan had taken a certain amount of courage and integrity; he must have known how the trial was going to go down, at least in the town and in the media, considering the victim was the son of the city's mayor.

"Do you have them here?" Kat asked, sitting forward on the very edge of her seat.

Castle cleared his throat, his face clear, open and deceptively young looking considering his actual age. "No, they're back at the office. You can swing by tomorrow, or we can head over there now, if you're desperate. It's not far," he said.

I exchanged a look with both Kat and Ray, and answered for all of us, "We'll take them now, if that's okay?"

"Of course, of course," he said, raising his arms, palms facing me, as if in surrender.

"Before we go though," I said, "I was wondering if you knew that Nick Green was now the mayor's Chief of Staff?"

Kat had been about to get up when I spoke, but I felt her

113

still now, turning her attention towards me, trying to figure out where I was going.

"Nick Green?" Castle said, "Yes, I'm aware. He's been working for Washington for a while now. Wasn't he very close friends with Tyler?"

"Yes, they were. I was just wondering ... before Tyler was killed, did you ever have to represent Nick for any drugs charges?"

Castle shook his head at me. A cloud had scudded across the sun, and his face was doused in shadow now, making him look sad somehow. "Nick Green? No, not that I can remember. I don't remember ever coming across him, until Ethan's trial. Why'd you ask?"

"He used to sell drugs in high school. But I couldn't remember if he'd ever been arrested for it or not. I figured with your job, you might have been called in to represent him, if he ever had done."

Castle shook his head again and said, "But what would that have to do with Ethan's case anyway?"

"We spoke to Morgan Washington, Tyler's older sister, yesterday and she claimed that, even though it was never mentioned at trial, she'd always thought that Tyler might have been going to meet Ethan to buy drugs, as Ethan was known as something of a low level dealer," Kat explained.

Castle raised both his eyebrows and settled back in his chair, "Yes, I remember Ethan warning me at the time that rumors such as that might crop up. I was surprised they didn't, in all honesty."

"He told you?" I asked.

"Yes, he did. I told him I didn't want any nasty surprises. Of course, the real surprise was that it didn't come up at all. I was sure they were going to attempt to destroy his credibility that way."

"Why do you think they didn't?" Kat said.

"I couldn't tell you. Ethan had never been arrested before though, so it could just be that all they had was hearsay regarding his involvement with the drugs, and they realized that was a less than desirable way to go with their argument." Castle glanced

114

over at me, eyes narrowing as he did so. "I'm guessing that's the problem here too? All you have is hearsay that Nick used to sell drugs too?"

"So far we only have Ethan's word for it," Kat answered.

"And mine," I added, although the look Kat gave me indicated that that was hardly any better.

"Well, I'll have a dig around, talk to some old colleagues and contacts, and see if I can come up with anything," Castle offered, "but I'm not hopeful."

"What's your relationship with Detective Rawes like?" Kat asked, "He was the lead investigator, right? I'd really love to get an interview with him, but we're being stonewalled by everyone at the police department at the moment. Any good word you could put in would be really appreciated."

Castle sighed, and hung his head for just a second before raising it again. "Well, for starters, he's Chief of Police now. He was promoted a good few years ago. I can approach him about it, of course, but I doubt it'll do much good. We're civil – we've known each other for decades – but the relationship between law enforcement and criminal defense attorneys is often rocky. Not to mention the fact that Ethan's case *made* Rawes. He wouldn't be where he is without the success of that case."

"Success," I said blankly, staring at Castle.

"Yes, well ... success for him. Obviously it wasn't quite such a success for me. Or Ethan."

"So, you don't think Rawes would be willing to speak on record with us?" Kat asked.

"I would be very surprised if he did," Castle said.

I couldn't stop thinking about what Castle had said about Rawes's success as I headed home to Portland that evening. My trip back to Twin Rivers had been brief, but my time away from it felt anything but; if anything, the past ten years were beginning to feel even longer than they actually were. With Rawes now Chief of Police, and Nick acting as the mayor's Chief of Staff, not to mention Cole and Morgan's relationship, it felt as though everything hinged on the night Tyler had died, and the day, a week later, my brother was arrested. I'd never had any trouble recognizing the impact Tyler's murder had had on me, my brother, and the rest of my family but I was beginning to realize just how myopic my view had been: living away from Twin Rivers, I hadn't ever stopped to think about how the city, and all the people I'd grown up with would have changed without me. It was stupid really; selfish. But finding out the man responsible for arresting Ethan was now the head of the police department had made my head spin, and I wasn't quite able to put my finger on why.

19

THEN

"Ethan. Ethan, honey, just think about this for a second, are you sure you want to turn this down?" Mom is reaching across the table, not just her hands, but her whole body leaning forward, stretched, bending towards him, as if it's not just her voice that's pleading, but her body too.

But Ethan just shakes his head. His face is impassive, and he's barely made a move since we all entered the room, but I think I can see something in his eyes, something like fear. But then he speaks, and I realize that he's about to cry, his voice trembling in the exact same way mine does when I'm right there, on the edge, tipping forward and tripping over. "How can you ask me that, Mom?" he says, and that's when I get it; he's not just afraid, he feels betrayed. "I'd be saying I was guilty. I'd be *pleading guilty*. And I didn't do this. I did not kill Tyler Washington."

"I know that, honey, I do. But just think, please. If you take the plea, admit to manslaughter, you could be out in ten years. We have no idea what way it might go if you go to trial, right, Robert?" Mom says, turning now to Ethan's attorney, Robert Castle.

117

"Right. All we know is that we'll definitely be looking at murder. Whether they go for first or second degree, I still don't know," Castle says.

Ethan shakes his head again, his face set and stony, lips practically pouting in defiance, and for a second I'm taken back ten, fifteen years, to us as children, as toddlers, staring into a face just like mine as it was about to let loose and wail. Except Ethan never did wail and tantrum the way I did, so what, or who am I remembering?

"What are his chances like at trial, Robert?" Dad is saying now.

Castle looks between all five of us, faces upturned, and I wonder what he sees there. Hope? Desperation? The fine line that divides and blurs the two until they're one and the same? He sighs and rubs a hand over his mouth before answering, "All they have really is circumstantial evidence, as far as I'm aware. Witnesses placing him at the scene, the bike track, the miniscule blood splatter on his jeans. For me that's nowhere near enough to convict, and it's still on them to provide the burden of proof. We haven't even had the preliminary trial, remember. This is just an arraignment. If Ethan pleads not guilty, then we've got a long way to go before we even get to trial. It's a marathon, not a sprint. Just remember that."

"But you would recommend taking the plea. Right?" Georgia's voice is low and hollow, but it's the first time she's spoken since she, Mom, Dad and I entered the room, so everyone automatically turns towards her.

"I can only offer counsel, Georgia," Castle says. "Ultimately, the decision has to be your brother's."

"Liv, come on, say something," Georgia says, turning to me, "you can't think going to trial is a good idea?"

Her face is stretched and tired, her skin pale and yet blotchy, the dark circles under her eyes somehow even more pronounced in this harsh strip lighting. But it's not her I'm looking at when I say, "But he didn't do it, Georgia. Ethan didn't kill Tyler, and we can't ask him to say he did just because we're scared no one else will believe him."

My eyes are locked on Ethan's and he nods, as if that's that. We file out of the room, back out into the glare of the courthouse hallways, and back into the courtroom, where Ethan will stand up in front of everyone there and declare himself not guilty of the crime of murdering Tyler Washington.

20

NOW

The morning after I got back from Twin Rivers, I was awake at three a.m., and out running by four. I'd had insomnia for years after Ethan was arrested, but I thought I'd got it under control recently, and certainly hadn't been subject to a three a.m. wake-up call in a while. It was cold and dark as I pulled the front door quietly behind me, stretching my legs on the porch before setting off, the sound of my Nikes slapping the wet sidewalk the only soundtrack. The streets were lined in red, yellow, and gold, the trees doing their annual thing of showing off while the air felt delightfully crisp and clear, with none of the chill that would soon begin to creep into everything. Soon, pumpkins and gourds would appear on porches and stoops, wreaths of autumnal leaves and produce would adorn front doors, welcoming guests. But for now, it was the middle of the night, and it was just me pounding the sidewalk, slipping on leaves, running from the same thing that had been chasing me ever since Tyler Washington died and Ethan got arrested.

Back home, I showered and dressed, feeding my cat, Jellybean when she followed me down to the kitchen to make my own breakfast. Samira walked in, sleepy faced and tying the cord of her threadbare bathrobe, as I was making myself a bowl of oatmeal.

"You're back," she said, giving me a one-armed shoulder hug from behind as she walked past me to the coffee machine. "How was it? Was it as terrible as you thought it was going to be?"

"It was definitely weird. Everything's different, but exactly the same, you know?"

"Well, that's home for you, right?" Samira said, raising her eyebrows as she settled in at the breakfast bar with me. "Always exactly how you remember it, but never as you left it." Samira was from Anaheim, land of Mickey Mouse ears, rollercoaster screams, and Santa Ana Winds, and always claimed that the only way anyone could get her to move back would be in a body bag.

I didn't say anything for a minute, and Samira squinted at me over the rim of her coffee mug, and said, "You didn't sleep last night, did you?" I'd lived with her for so long that Samira was almost as well acquainted with my insomnia as I was.

I shook my head. "Awake at three. Brilliant way to start the week, huh?" I took another long sip of coffee and finally said, "My ex is now living with Tyler's older sister, Morgan. And I'm pretty sure she's pregnant."

I watched Samira's eyes widen, as she choked back a bolt of laughter. "I'm sorry," she said, gasping a little, "it's not funny. I know it's really serious … but seriously? Your ex and Tyler's sister are having a baby?"

"I think so," I said.

"Your ex – that's Cole, right?" Samira asked, while taking a spoon from the cutlery drawer and helping herself to my leftover oatmeal.

"Yeah," I said. I'd told Samira about Cole and Twin Rivers years ago. We'd been friends since freshman year of college, back when I'd still been using Hall as my last name, and before Samira had dropped out to pursue baking as her profession.

"Didn't you think at one point that he might have had something to do with it?" she said.

I straightened up in my seat and reached for my mug of coffee again, but my jerky movements got the better of me and I ended up spilling the dregs of my coffee everywhere. "With killing Tyler? Cole?" Getting up to grab a cloth to clean it all up I said, "No, I never thought that. I thought he might have been wrong about what time it was when he saw – or thought he saw – my brother going into the woods, but I don't know."

"Wrong or lying," Samira said, her eyes on me as I wiped away coffee.

There'd always been something of a question mark hanging over Cole, of course. I hadn't exactly been surprised when he hadn't stuck by me and my family after Ethan was arrested – Tyler was one of his oldest, closest friends after all – but it had still been a punch to the gut to see him take the witness stand against my own twin. To provide the supposed 'proof' that Ethan had killed Tyler. But had he lied? That was another proposition entirely; something beyond loyalty, something more like malice. And if he was lying, who was he lying for?

* * *

Daniel was waiting for me when I arrived at work, even though I was early. He looked tired, his normally smooth skin a little sallow, his mouth, which was so often turned up on one side in a knowing smile, downturned and drawn.

"What's up?" I asked as I neared him, "you look terrible."

"Thank you. We've been here all night."

"You're kidding?" I looked at my watch – it was three minutes to seven. "What could possibly have been so important it required a Sunday night all-nighter?"

"Reid tried to kill herself," Daniel said blankly, and it took a couple of seconds for what he'd said to sink in.

"Where is she?" I managed to finally croak out, "is she ok?"

"She's in the hospital. The doctors say she's doing fine,

considering," Daniel said, strain tightening his normally loose, languorous voice.

"How ... how did she do it? *Try* to do it," I corrected, just in time.

"We don't actually know. Obviously, the doctors aren't releasing information to anyone but family. Karen's over at the hospital now, but ... she wants you over there."

"Me? Why?" I asked, and this time it was strain tightening my voice.

"Apparently, Reid's sister is there with her. And she won't talk to anyone but you."

"Spencer?" I said, thinking back to the conversation I'd had with Reid on Friday evening. It seemed so, so long ago.

"Yeah, you know her, right? Went to school with her?"

I nodded, but my mind had drifted, jumping from Reid, to Spencer, to Tyler, to Ethan. It all felt too much, too much coincidence, too much like fate, and yet nothing really made sense. It had only just hit me, how strange it was that Reid Murphy's case should tie me to it, and to Twin Rivers so tightly. How was it possible that the biggest case I'd worked on yet was defending someone from the same town as me? How was it possible that I'd gone to high school with her sister, cheered on the same squad, gone to the same parties? It felt like the world was laughing at me, and I'd never really enjoyed being laughed at. Something pricked at me, a needling thought that had been stirring its way through my mind ever since I'd first driven back into Twin Rivers; that I'd brought this on myself, by going back, opening up old wounds, rubbing salt in them. I'd said 'boo' to the ghost of my past, and now that ghost was trying to scare me right back.

"You want me to come with you?" Daniel asked, "to the hospital?" he added, when I failed to respond.

"No," I said, shaking my head, taking in his tired face once again, "you go home. Get some rest. I can handle this."

Reid had been transferred to a private room by the time I got there. I was surprised by the relative speed of her transfer out of the ER, but when I saw the police officers standing outside her door, I understood. She had been scheduled to have another pre-trial release hearing that very morning. With the charges against her being changed from attempted murder to murder, there was no way she'd be making bail now. The police presence was mandatory. Oregon hardly ever released suspects accused of murder before trial – my family and I had found that out the hard way – but that went double when the suspect was a suicide risk.

"What a mess," my boss Karen said, sidling up beside me in the corridor outside Reid's room, and passing me a cup of coffee. Karen Powers was an unnamed partner in the firm, and although she was only the second chair on this case, really she was in charge. Paul Coleridge, the first chair, would only really take over once we were actually in court and he could get up on the stage he so loved, and so loved him back.

"I don't understand. She's a smart girl, she must've realized how much worse she was making things for herself by doing this."

"She tried to kill herself, Olivia. She didn't think she'd be around to deal with it," Karen said.

"But why?"

Karen sighed and looked away from me, her bright blue eyes trained on the door where two uniformed police officers stood guard. "Because she killed someone, Olivia. She killed someone, and she feels terrible about it."

"You really think she did it?" I asked, because I hadn't yet been able to tell what Karen made of Reid Murphy and her innocence or guilt, but this seemed pretty clear.

"I think there isn't a chance in hell a jury won't convict her now. Not after this." Karen took a sip of her coffee and made a face, "Ugh should've gone to Stumptown before I came here. Anyway. There's more. That's why I asked you here."

"More? How?"

And what could it possibly have to do with me?

124

21

THEN

"This is a collect call from an inmate at Multnomah County Jail, do you accept the charges?"

"Ethan?" I say, a question in my voice despite the fact that there's only one person it could possibly be.

"Olivia, hey," Ethan says, although it doesn't sound like Ethan at all.

"Everything okay?" I ask, even though I know it's not, not really, and it's a stupid question to keep asking.

"I heard Dad got a new job," he says, not answering my question, which I can hardly blame him for.

"How'd you hear that?" I ask perplexed.

"Georgia."

"Right, yeah. He doesn't start 'til next month, but I think he's relieved. Bit weird for him to still be working at City Hall when, well, y'know."

"Yeah, I know, Liv. I'm living it."

"Sorry."

"Not your fault."

There's a pause I don't know how to fill and then I say, "They're thinking of putting the house on the market too."

"Good. That's good. They should get out of there. Georgia told me about the car."

We'd woken up a few weeks ago to the sound of the car alarm, the whining call of an automobile in distress, and every single one of the windows in Dad's car broken and shattered. Lights in houses up and down the street had all switched on, as Dad went out there to shut the alarm off, but no one ventured out of their houses, onto their porches to see what was going on, whether or not they could help. I'd gone out too, stood on the path leading to our house, looking out across at the pitch black entrance to the woods, just a few steps away and felt rather than saw more eyes there, watching.

"I've told them we can't leave until the trial's over," I say to Ethan.

"What? No, Liv. That's crazy. It's driving Mom mad living there, I can tell. Just move out, it's fine."

"How's it going in there?" I ask, changing the subject, "I mean really?"

"How d'you think it's going, Liv?" Ethan says. "It's fucking shit, and fucking scary," and here his voice drops to a whispered hiss, and I imagine him leaning away from whoever's standing next to him, trying and failing to have a private conversation. Castle initially petitioned for Ethan to be kept in a juvenile detention center as he only turned eighteen recently, but he was pessimistic about his success, and he was right to be so: there was no way the judge was going to go soft of Ethan, not with the mayor breathing down his neck. So, instead Ethan was the youngest person currently being held in the County Jail system, and I was trying hard not to think too much about what that really meant. "Oh, and the food fucking sucks. Is that enough detail for you? Because it's about all I've got, right now."

"Sorry," I say again. "I just feel like I should at least ask, you know? I don't know what else to say to you really."

"Tell me what's going on with you. Georgia says you got a

job?" Ethan says and I can't tell if what I can hear in his voice is strain or laughter.

"Yeah, just at this coffee shop. It's like almost a two hour drive round trip, but at least no one knows who I am, so it's whatever."

"You must be spending almost as much on gas as you're earning, Liv."

"Yeah," I say, "I must be."

"What's the point?"

"Gives me something to do. And there's no way I'd be able to get a job anywhere in town. Not that I'd want to," I say.

"Are you still being given a hard time?" Ethan asks and I can't help but laugh at his choice of words. He's the one doing hard time, after all.

"It's calmed down now. Cole and Jess, and pretty much everyone have all gone off to college now, so it's just me left pretty much. There's still some kids who'll shout something or other whenever they see me, but it's nothing I can't handle."

"I know you can handle yourself," Ethan says.

"Right."

"Really it should be you in here," he says with a faint laugh that makes my heart lurch, "You've always been the one with the fighting spirit."

"What's that supposed to mean?" I ask.

"Just that you know how to claw your way to the top."

"I don't know if I should take that as a compliment or not," I say.

"Take it however you want. I'm not sure I meant it as a compliment."

I'm silent for a second or two, digesting Ethan's words, but then he says, "Hey, I think my time's up. Better say goodbye."

"Okay. Bye. I love you."

Ethan lets out a shock of laughter, and then says, "Yeah, okay. Love you too."

22

NOW

"What is this?" I asked as Spencer handed me an iPhone 5.

"It's Reid's old cell phone. She changed her number, all her account details, completely left social media, but it still wasn't enough."

Reid's old iPhone felt heavy in my hand, and I looked from it to Karen, trying to add things up as quickly as possible. But my brain was overworked and sluggish. Karen's eyes narrowed as they met mine and she too looked down at the iPhone. She was getting there faster than I was. Reid's parents were in Reid's room with her, so it was just the three of us in the family waiting room. There was an unnatural hush, and no windows, making it feel almost womb-like, as if we should have been whispering instead of talking out loud.

"He was stalking her. Harassing her?" Karen said. "James Asher."

Spencer nodded silently. She sat down suddenly, as if her legs had gone from underneath her. She was pale and white, dark circles under her eyes which looked blank and hollow. "You okay?" I asked, sitting down next to her. "You want a coffee? Or water? Something to eat?"

She shook her head, looking as if she was powering through a wave of nausea. "No. I'm fine. I just need you to look through all that stuff, okay?"

"But – but what is it?" I asked, still with the weight of that phone in my right hand.

"It's evidence. That he was stalking her, harassing her. That he wouldn't leave her alone."

"Where did it come from, Spencer?" Karen asked, her voice low but direct in the quiet room.

"It was next to her when … when my mom found her. She must've had it hidden somewhere or something. I think she'd been going through all the messages right before … right before she took the pills."

Before handing us the phone, Spencer had told us that Reid had overdosed on Klonopin, a drug Reid had been taking on-and-off since high school when she'd started having debilitating anxiety and panic attacks. Since then she'd clearly somehow managed to stockpile enough of it to overdose with.

"Did you know about any of this?" I asked, "the stalking I mean?"

"I knew she was having some problems with this guy. With James Asher. They met at work, and then went out for like a month, maybe? But then she broke it off, and he wouldn't let it go."

"Shit," Karen said, and both Spencer and I turned to stare at her.

"Sorry, but it was bad enough that Reid and Asher had been in a relationship, but now we know he was stalking and harassing her, we have an actual motive for the murder."

"I know this doesn't look good, but there's no way Reid could have killed him," Spencer said, shaking her head. "I mean, just physically? She's tiny. And she's not … she's not a violent, angry person. Or, maybe she is but it's all directed inside, you know? Look at what she's done, where we are – she'd hurt herself before she hurt anyone else."

"Regardless, we're obliged to turn that over to the police," Karen said bluntly, nodding at the phone in my hand. I widened my eyes at her in surprise, and she added, "We'll get everything we need off it first, don't worry, but it's an ongoing investigation, and we'll be charged with obstruction if we don't admit it into evidence."

Karen took the phone back to the office with her and I was left with Spencer in the waiting room. I still wasn't completely sure why she'd asked me to be there as well. Maybe she just needed to see a familiar face while processing this new information.

"None of this looks good for her, does it?" Spencer said, not meeting my eye. "I know she couldn't have killed him, but I almost didn't show you the phone because I was so worried about how guilty it might make her look. But then I decided that the world deserved to know what kind of person James Asher was. I've seen and heard the way people still talk about Tyler Washington, like he hung the fucking moon, when really he just did and said and took whatever he wanted. I can't bear the thought of Reid going to prison for this, and I still can't really believe she could've killed him, but if she did do it, I kind of get it, you know?"

I'd sat down next to her when she'd started talking, and she finally looked up to meet my eyes, laying her hand flat on my right arm. It was warm, sweaty, and heavy but strangely comforting as well, and I swallowed something down before nodding and saying, "Yeah. I kind of get it too."

I hadn't seen any of the messages or evidence Spencer said was on that phone she'd found yet, but when I eventually did see it, I'd understand even more. Understand Reid's fear and desperation, her shame and distress, that feeling that there was no way out, nowhere for her to go, nowhere to find safety and peace.

"And I think I get you now, too," Spencer said quietly, eyes piercing mine as a cold shiver ran through me.

"What do you mean?" I said, my voice scratchy and raw. I really needed a glass of water.

"Why you're doing this podcast, why you're so determined to get your brother out of prison." I hadn't seen Spencer in years, but as soon as I'd walked into the waiting room she'd told me she'd already heard all about the podcast. She still lived in Twin Rivers, and word had got around apparently. I'd recognized her as soon as I saw her – I'd completely forgotten about her until Reid reminded me of her on Friday, of course, but Spencer looked exactly the same, sounded exactly the same, acted exactly the same. But then I remembered what Reid had said about Spencer thinking Tyler and every one of my friends back in high school were 'awful', and I wondered what she was hiding. What she really thought of me, despite her warm reaction when I'd reintroduced myself.

"You really had no idea Asher had been harassing her like he had?" I asked eventually.

Spencer shook her head sadly. "Reid's never been particularly open about things. She's painfully shy, had anxiety and panic attacks her whole life. I was really worried about her moving to Portland, but she'd got this great job offer, and seemed to be really enjoying it, and then Asher came along, and it all went to shit."

Reid was an IT specialist, was something of a computer genius by the sound of things and I knew that even though she'd dropped out of college at some point, she'd still managed to find work at one of Portland's biggest hospitals in their IT department. James Asher had been her manager, almost a decade older than her, and a whole lot bigger. I had to agree that the idea of tiny Reid managing to overpower Asher was farfetched, but I'd seen enough to know what a scared, terrified woman, desperate to survive could do. And the fact that there was a history of harassment changed things.

"It doesn't really matter if she's guilty or not," I said, "we'll do everything we can to protect her regardless."

"You really think that?" Spencer said, something flashing across her face.

"Of course. This is the best criminal defense team in Portland. And Karen Powers is the most determined woman I know. She'll get a not-guilty verdict if it's the last thing she does." I was trying to reassure Spencer, give her the hope she needed to help get her and her sister through the next few months, because if there was one thing I really did know, it was that Spencer, Reid, and the whole Murphy family were going to need every shred and shard of hope they could muster to get through all this.

"No, I don't mean that. I know you guys are good. I mean, do you really think it doesn't matter? If she did it or not? If she … if she killed someone?"

"Not to me," I said, standing up and wandering over to the vending machine, pretending to take a look at what was on offer. It was a paltry selection of choices, but that didn't stop me from rooting around in my purse for some change, and popping enough in for a bag of Skittles. When I turned back around to Spencer to offer her the bag, she shook her head and continued to stare at me. As though if she stared long and hard enough, she could see right through me. "I'm a lawyer, Spencer," I said with a sigh, "it kind of goes with the job not to worry about guilt and innocence."

"How can you say that when at the same time, you're still fighting to prove your brother's innocence? Of course it matters. You've said all this time that the wrong person went to prison in your brother's case, and the same thing could happen here, with Reid, and you're really going to stand there and tell me it *doesn't matter*?"

"You're right, I'm sorry. I misspoke. Of course it matters. I'm just saying, regardless of what anyone on Reid's defense team actually thinks, we'll fight for her as though she were innocent."

"But she is innocent," Spencer said, the words turning into a strangled cry as they caught in her throat. Her face, so pale before, was now a picture of red and white frustration, and I was worried the tears making her eyes shine so vividly in the low light, were about to fall down her face.

I fingered the lime green packet of Skittles I'd just bought, feeling the shape of the candy through the plastic, worrying at them as if they were a stress ball. "Can you really be one hundred percent sure of that?" I asked, staring down at the packet in my hands, unable to meet Spencer's tear struck gaze.

"Can you really be one hundred percent sure that Ethan is innocent?" Spencer asked. Her voice was low and steady now, and somehow that made it even more cutting. I looked back up at her just as my phone started to ring. I didn't answer it immediately, my eyes glued to Spencer's, which were a mix of fear and fury. But then she just made a disgusted, 'pick it up' gesture with her hand, and so I pressed the green button. I was expecting it to be the office, and had barely managed to say 'hello', when I was shocked by the familiar but unexpected voice at the other end.

"Cole? Why are you calling me?" I asked, giving Spencer the sign for 'give me a minute', and slipping out of the room. The bright lights of the hospital corridor surprised me after the low, almost orange-hued light of the waiting room, and I blinked into them as Cole replied.

"Call off your fucking Sarah Koenig-wannabes, okay Olivia? This has all gone far enough."

"Kat and Ray would be in Twin Rivers even without me being involved, Cole. What makes you think I have any control over them?" I said.

"Oh please. This shit has Olivia Hall written all over it. Trying to re-write history so it makes you look better, just trying to keep up those appearances, huh Liv?"

I let out a laugh, and the short bark of it echoed down and around the surprisingly quiet hallway. "Me, trying to re-write history? Are you kidding? Tell me, Cole, was there any part of Tyler you actually recognized during the trial?"

"So, he wasn't perfect, who cares. He's dead, Liv. Murdered. Isn't that enough? Why do you want to drag his name through the mud? And why now? Shit, do you have any idea what this is doing to Morgan?"

"She agreed to go on the podcast. Don't act as if she didn't know what she was doing. And if I'm not mistaken, you were

133

right there with her, giving her your 'permission', or whatever."

"I wasn't giving her my permission, I was trying to protect her."

"Because you've always been so good at that," I said sharply, the words out of my mouth before I could stop them.

"Are we really going to get into this now?" Cole said, and I could hear the set of his jaw, practically see the vein pulsing in his neck.

"Morgan's her own woman, Cole. I'm sure she can be trusted to make the decisions that make the most sense for her. Even if you don't like or understand it," I said finally, deciding to focus on the present, rather than the past.

"It's not as simple as that," he said with a sigh, before adding, "she's pregnant."

The flush of victory rushed through me, because I'd guessed right, but then, almost imperceptibly, I felt a weight in my heart get just one ounce heavier. "Wow," I said, instead, trying to ignore whatever mixed up feelings were getting even more mixed up inside me. "Congratulations."

"Thank you," he said gruffly, begrudgingly. "But look, what I'm trying to say is that it's not just Morgan you're dealing with – it's the baby, and it's me, and the rest of her family, and she just doesn't need this kind of crap right now, okay? She doesn't know what she's doing, what she's getting herself into. Neither do you."

I let out a long heavy breath, suddenly feeling the weight of the day. And it wasn't even nine a.m. "I can't stop your girlfriend from going on a podcast, Cole. And by the sounds of it, neither can you."

"You can stop your friends from constantly asking Morgan for interviews, can't you? Aren't you the one in control here, isn't that exactly how you like it?" His voice had turned nasty, young sounding, and bullying, and I flashed back to high school when it seemed like everyone sounded like that; wheedling and needling, pushing and pulling right where it hurt, finding the softest, weakest spot and going right for it. It nauseated me to think I'd ever sounded like that too, but I knew that I had, and that sometimes my voice had been the loudest of all.

I rolled my neck, trying to get the strain out of it, trying to focus on anything else. "I can't stop them from doing anything, Cole, it's their podcast, not mine, and frankly I wouldn't even if I could. You know Cole, I'm not doing this out of revenge, as you seem to think. I'm doing this because my brother has been in prison for a murder he didn't commit for almost a decade now. And the thing is, I think you know that. I think you know he didn't kill Tyler. That you've always known."

"I don't know anything, Olivia," he said slowly, "I only know what I've been told," and then he hung up, leaving me alone in the spartan brightness of the hospital corridor to wonder what, exactly, he meant by that.

Everyone was busy poring over printed off messages from Reid's old cell phone by the time I got back to the office. I helped myself to a coffee and a banana, staring longingly at the empty box of donuts that the team had already eaten their way through.

"Hey," Daniel said, sidling up next to me, gently placing a hand on the small of my back that, for some reason, made me jump, "you okay? How'd it all go?"

"It was fine, Reid was waking up when I left." I hadn't wanted to impose on the family, so I'd told Spencer to call me if she needed me, and drove back over to the office, fingers tapping out an unsteady rhythm on the steering wheel as I went over my phone conversation with Cole.

"This shit is out of control," Daniel said, nodding his head towards the conference room table where Reid's messages now littered it in paper form.

"It's bad?" I asked, taking a sip of my coffee.

"There's more than enough there that it would've been a snap for Reid to get a restraining order against Asher. I just don't understand why she didn't."

135

"It's not always that simple," I pointed out. "He was her boss, maybe she was worried she'd lose her job."

"I'd rather lose my job than live with what she was dealing with," Daniel said, shaking his head in disbelief.

"Well, not everyone has that luxury, Daniel. Maybe she needed her job, maybe she liked her job, maybe she didn't want to feel like she'd been run out of it."

Daniel held up his hands and sighed, "Fine, Liv, I don't want to argue with you. Just maybe take a look at these messages and see if you could've lived with it for so long without doing something about it. Without snapping," he added darkly.

"Oh, so now you think Reid could've killed Asher?" I asked.

Daniel puffed out his cheeks, widening his eyes as he let out a huge breath and said, "Let's just say I really wouldn't blame her if it turns out she did."

Hours later I was stood outside in the parking lot, yet another cup of coffee in hand, intermittent rain falling lightly on my face as I caught my breath, and tried, fruitlessly to clear my mind. Daniel hadn't been exaggerating about Asher's abusive messages. They were endless it seemed. Cruel, angry, entitled, vindictive, obsessive, nasty, dark, and endless. I could understand Reid's hopelessness, her need to do something about it. What I was busy trying to work out, was whether her breaking point had come before or after Asher died.

Deciding I needed something to distract me I pulled out my phone and rang Kat.

"Hey," she said on picking up, "how are you?"

"Not great. I could really do with hearing some good news."

"Well. I might have something to cheer you up. Three things actually," she said, her excitement turning her voice singsong and light.

"Really?"

"One, we're releasing the first episode tomorrow. It'll go up at nine a.m."

136

"Wow," I breathed. It was finally happening; the podcast was going to go out into the world, and once again everyone was going to be paying attention to Ethan Hall's story.

"Yeah, so I guess 'cheer you up' might not be the best words, but it's a move in the right direction. And what we're really hoping is that listeners might come forward if they know anything about the night Tyler died, or anything about the investigation in general," she said.

"That's good. That's enough for me right now."

"I said I had three things, remember. Don't you want to hear the rest?" Kat said, and I could practically hear her smile down the line.

"Hit me," I said.

"Well, we also managed to convince Morgan to do another interview. It didn't take all that much convincing, to be honest. We recorded it this morning. I just emailed you a recording of it, so you can listen to it a little early."

"Well, that explains a lot," I said, and went on to tell Kat about Cole's irate phone call.

"He's a little controlling, huh? Was he always like that?" Kat said in response.

I didn't answer immediately, and Kat had to say my name to bring me back to the conversation. "I don't know," I said finally, "it's hard to remember. Everything looks so different from where I'm standing. Maybe he was controlling, and I didn't realize it yet because I was eighteen. I just don't know."

"That's normal, Olivia. People change, memories change with them, time is an absolute mind fuck," Kat offered.

I let out a laugh that seemed to disappear on the moisture-filled air, "You're exactly right there. So, what was the third thing? You said there were three things to cheer me up."

"Right. Well … we found a copy of the transcript from Ethan's police interview in Castle's files."

"You did?" I asked, a little breathlessly, pressing my phone up against my ear until it hurt, as if that would change anything.

"Yeah, there's no tape or video recording though, which is weird because that's been a requirement for years now. Decades even. You know anything about that?"

"You'd have to ask Castle. It could've been a digital file maybe? Maybe it's on a hard drive somewhere," I said, mind suddenly racing with where and how we could get our hands on the video or audio recording of Ethan's so-called 'confession'. The confession had been given before Ethan had actually been arrested, and because he later retracted it, it wasn't ever used as evidence in court. Ethan always claimed that it hadn't been a confession at all; that he hadn't realized what he'd been saying, that he hadn't realized how serious the situation was, that he'd just been messing around. Of course the police, and the media – not to mention the Washington family – were able to handily manipulate his defense. What kind of monster jokes about murder after all? Especially when you're sat in a police department interview room just days after your former classmate has been found dead in the woods? Only a cold blooded killer could sit there laughing and lying, while Tyler Washington lay dead in the morgue, not even buried and properly mourned for yet.

But Kat had moved on, and was now asking me about making time for another interview for the podcast.

"I'd love a run down of that night from your perspective," she said, meaning the night Tyler died. "You were at the same party Tyler, Cole, and Nick were all at, right?"

"Yeah, I was there," I said, "I left a little earlier than everyone else, though."

"Why?"

"I think I'd just gotten my period and was feeling pretty bad, so I went home to bed. I'd already been home a while by the time Ethan got back."

I closed my eyes, leaning my head back against the brick wall, letting cool rain patter at my face, while I thought back to that night. It had rained then too, heavy and strong, putting a wrench in our plans to spend the night in Jessica's yard around her parents' fire pit, so we'd all squeezed into her kitchen and living room, occasionally spilling out onto the porch when the heat got too much, or someone wanted to smoke. I could smell it practically; the rain on late-summer earth, the hoppy, tanginess of bad, cheap beer, the sharp grunginess of sweat on skin, the tell-tale acrid waft of weed on the wind. I opened my eyes onto the parking lot in Portland I was currently standing in, reminding and reassuring myself I didn't have to go back; I never had to go back. But sometimes, to move forward, we have to go back, even if just a little, and I was worried I was going to get caught there, in the spiderweb of memories, and all the lies that had been told, and the loyalties that had been broken.

I listened to the interview recording with Morgan that Kat had sent me on the drive home later. It was strange to hear Morgan's voice, all those years later, filling up the air around me and surrounding me in the comfort of my own car. Out of everyone, she had changed the least, I thought. She sounded exactly as she always had, a strange combination of supreme confidence and uncertainty, a mixture that made her seem much younger than she actually was now.

* * *

Extract from transcript of Season 3 Episode 3 of *Shadow of a Doubt*:

Kat Thomas: Hi, Morgan, thanks so much for agreeing to come back on the show.

Morgan Washington: Yeah, well, if you're going to keep talking to Olivia and Ethan Hall, and Kevin Lawrence, and Ethan's friggin' defense attorney what else am I supposed to do?

KT: We'd love to have an even more balanced view of the case, to be honest, but there's definitely a little more reluctance to talk to us from Tyler's side of the story.

MW: Yeah, because Ethan's behind bars, justice was served, and the whole horrible nightmare has been over for a while now, so why bring it up? This is really, really painful for my family, you know? And the rest of the town. People loved Tyler, I just don't get why you're so determined to dredge all this back up.

KT: So, you don't think there's any chance your mother might talk to us one day?

[pause]

MW: No.

KT: You don't think she might have something to say about your brother's drug use? Does she know you've been talking to us about it?

MW: What are you talking about?

KT: Morgan, in our last interview you mentioned Tyler's recreational drug use, and that you thought he might have been in the woods that night to meet Ethan Hall because he was buying drugs from him.

MW: Oh, that. No, I was just talking you know? Throwing ideas out there. I don't know that for sure.

KT: I understand, but your family clearly tried quite hard to keep Tyler's drug use out of the trial, and out of the media, so how do you think your mom's going to react now, hearing you talk about it on a podcast?

[long pause]

MW: She doesn't listen to podcasts.

KT: Okay. So, she doesn't know you're talking to us about any of this?

[short pause]

MW: No.

KT: What about Nick Green?

MW: What about him?

KT: Are you friends with him?

MW: Sure, yeah. He's my boyfriend's best friend. He was close with Tyler too.

KT: And were you aware that he dealt drugs back in high school too?

[sound of movement, a chair scraping back along the floor]

MW: I don't – that's not. Why are you asking me about this?

KT: Because in our last interview you said you thought your brother might have been in that part of the woods to buy drugs from Ethan Hall. But Ethan claims not to have sold anything to Tyler in over a year at that point, so maybe

Tyler was meeting with Nick instead?

MW: You'd have to ask him that.

KT: We tried but he wouldn't agree to an interview with us.

MW: Well. That's hardly a surprise, is it?

KT: Did you ever buy drugs from Nick Green, Morgan?

MW: No. I can honestly say I never did.

KT: Ok. How about this – did you ever get drugs from Nick Green, regardless of whether or not you actually bought or paid for them?

[more sounds of movement in the background – another voice is heard but words are indecipherable]

MW [muffled, moving away from microphone]: I don't – I'm not answering that. Can we stop recording please?

23

THEN

I slam the door closed behind me, shaking rain from me as I do so.

"Honey?" my mom calls, suddenly appearing in the door to the den. "Where've you been?" she asks, her voice stretched and strained.

"Went for a walk," I say, and then motion at my damp clothing, "and paid the price."

Dad appears behind her in the doorway and they share a glance before Mom says, "You didn't … go to the funeral, did you? I know it was being held today."

I pause a second too long and Dad says, "Oh, Jesus Christ, Olivia that's just what we need," and wheels back into the den. He's taking long frustrated strides around the room, like a dog on a leash, desperate to be free.

Mom motions in at the den with her head, and says, "Come on honey, come sit down, I think we need to talk."

"I'm fine," I say curtly, but I follow her into the room anyway, taking a seat in my preferred armchair.

"No, you're not. And that's okay, I totally understand that, but your dad and I are a little worried, and we were wondering whether or not it might be better for you to head off to Eugene soon. We're not saying tomorrow, and the college administration has been very understanding so far about you delaying your entrance. But the add drop season will be over soon and you'll be behind before you even get there, if you're not careful."

I take a deep breath, and swing my legs up and underneath me. "I'm not going, Mom, I can't. You have to understand that, right? I can't just go off to college while Ethan is *in prison*."

My parents share a look again, worry and concern from my mom, consternation and frustration from Dad. "Olivia, you can't delay your life like this, Ethan wouldn't want that."

"He's not dead, Dad, we could just ask him what he wants," I say.

"Well, he certainly wouldn't say 'I want my twin sister to stay home and do nothing but worry about me until my trial,' I can tell you that much."

"Oh, is that what you're worried about? Me, sitting around at home doing nothing? Not making myself useful or making any money? I'll get a job, if that's what you're so worried about."

"Who would hire you?!" Dad roars into the room, color rising on his face and neck as Mom and I turn to stare at him in shock. "Sorry, sorry, I didn't mean … it's not about you, Liv, I just honestly don't think anyone in this town would hire a Hall at this point in time. It has become, almost impossible, for me to do my job at the moment, and I'm already in employment. Do you have any idea how many contracts your mother has lost since this all began?"

"What? How many? It's only been a few weeks, how many clients could've left you by now?" I ask.

"Not many. Yet. But it's enough to be worried about," Mom says. "But, look, honey, that's not what we wanted to talk to you about. Will you just think a little about college? I just don't think it's good for you to be here right now. Your friends …"

"Are not my friends anymore," I say.

"No, but you could make new friends, in a new city if you

144

wanted. God knows your father and I would jump at the chance to leave Twin Rivers right now, and you – well you actually have the chance to."

"Wait, you'd move and leave Ethan here? We can't do that," I say, sitting up straighter in my chair, staring at both of them, trying to figure them out. Ethan is being held in the County Jail while he waits for his trial, and even though we can't just drop in and see him anytime we want, it's a comfort to know that he's still just a short drive away. If Mom and Dad move us out of Twin Rivers, we could end up miles away from Ethan.

"We're not going to. We can't. Not right now at least," Mom says with a sigh, which doesn't ease my concerns any. In some ways, I've never really wanted to leave Twin Rivers, not really. Not like Ethan did. It's a world I know and understand, somewhere I used to feel safe and in control. But all that's gone now, and even though I can leave, I know I shouldn't. I made life in Twin Rivers for Ethan bad enough as it was, I can't just leave him here while I go off and do the one thing he's always wanted to do, and now maybe never can: escape.

"Look," Dad says with a sigh, finally sitting down, "if you don't want to start college right away, we understand, but could you at least think about starting classes after Christmas maybe?"

I look at him, look at Mom, and not for the first time, I wonder what they think of all this. Nothing in their lives has prepared them for having a son on trial for murder. They look tired, resigned, and I wonder how they've been sleeping, whether they've been sleeping at all. I am awake by three a.m. every morning now, come rain or shine; it doesn't matter if I go to sleep at ten at night, or one in the morning, by three a.m. I am wide awake, jarred back to earth from dreams I can't control. When I wake up I feel something between relief and fury, tears leaking from my eyes as they open, anger and fear swelling in my chest before I take a deep breath and force myself to confront the day and find comfort in my surroundings. Would these early morning wake up calls end if I move away, go to college? The thought stops me short for a second, as I consider it. But then I shake my head to myself. As long as Ethan is in prison, I can learn to cope with insomnia, the early hours stretching ahead of me like a sentence without end.

24

NOW

Extract of transcript of audio recording of the interview of Ethan Hall by Detective Rawes on Thursday August 28, 2008 at the Twin Rivers Police Department, Interview Room 1

Detective Rawes: So … you didn't see Tyler at all on the night of August 23? That's the story you're sticking to?

EH: I'm not 'sticking to' anything. That's the truth. I didn't see him. I hadn't seen him for ages in fact. We don't exactly make a point of seeing each other.

DR: Despite the fact he's friends with your twin sister?

EH: My sister and I don't spend much time together either.

DR: That's interesting.

EH: Is it?

DR: You'd think you'd be close as twins.

EH: You'd think. But we're not. I've always liked to buck trends.

DR: You like to be different, is that it? You like to be the anomaly?

EH: [sighs] I feel like you're trying to trap me here, but yes, I guess I do like to be different. Doesn't everybody?

DR: [laughs] Look around you kid, if everybody liked to be different, they wouldn't be so fucking similar.

EH: [laughs] Wow, Detective Rawes, I think you might have just made a pretty good point. Almost profound.

DR: Well, we're not here for profundity, we're here for Tyler Washington.

EH: RIP

DR: Mr Hall.

EH: Sorry.

DR: I just want you to talk me through this Ethan, because the eye witnesses I've spoken to– the very same people you saw hanging around outside Jessica Heng's house – they say that you followed Tyler into the woods, not ten minutes after him. So, how did you not see him? At all? Or hear anything? That's what I can't quite grasp.

EH: I don't know how I didn't see him. Unless they're mistaken about how long the time was between Tyler and me going into the woods. I mean, they were at a party, right? I know they were because that's where my sister had been, so, come on, they'd been drinking, they were probably maybe a little stoned … let's not pretend their memories are completely accurate.

DR: They all seem pretty sure.

EH: All?

DR: Yes, Ethan. All.

[pause]

So, here's what I'm thinking. You cycled into the woods shortly after Tyler wandered into them, and because you were on a bike and he was on foot, you caught up with him pretty quickly. Maybe he said something to you you didn't like – neither of you much liked each other, that much we know. And, as you say, he'd probably had quite a bit to drink so may have been feeling more antagonistic than usual. Maybe he even forced you to stop the bike and get off it. Maybe he even threw the first punch, I don't know. But what we do know, is that he had injuries that imply he got into some kind of fight or physical altercation, and that at some point he was on the receiving end of a blunt force trauma to the head.

Am I getting anywhere yet?

[pause]

EH: You've painted the scene very well.

149

DR: Haven't I?

EH: Yes, it's very imaginative of you. Honestly, I wouldn't have thought you'd have such a well-developed imagination, Detective.

DR: No imagination needed for this one son, it's all right there in front of me.

EH: [laughs] Really? You really think that?

DR: You don't care about any of this at all, do you? You think you're above it all.

EH: I'm not 'above it all', I just know I didn't kill Tyler Washington and that you're barking up the wrong tree. Hell, I'm pretty sure you're in the wrong fucking forest.

DR: [loudly] Do not curse at me, young man!

EH: [laughing] What? You were swearing earlier. I thought this was a safe space.

DR: This is not a safe fucking space, this is a police interview room.

EH: That sounds a little threatening, Detective. You should be careful.

DR: You should be careful, Mr Hall. Very, very careful if I were you. Because we have you in the woods at the same time as Tyler's murder, and we have witnesses placing you there – as well as your own admission – and we have your sister saying you didn't get home until just before three in the morning.

EH: Yeah, so if I didn't get home until almost three, then that means I probably left Kevin's at around two thirty.

DR: Except that we have witnesses saying you were cycling into the woods at two fifteen.

EH: Well, that's clearly just not true or accurate, because it wouldn't have taken me over forty-five minutes to get home from Kevin's.

DR: Unless something slowed you down.

EH: Oh what, like killing Tyler you mean?

DR: That would certainly take some time wouldn't it? But forty-five minutes, well, that gives you more than enough time to be waylaid by him – for whatever reason, we don't have to go into that right now – for the two of you to get into a fight, for you to kill him, whether accidentally or otherwise, and for you to hide or get rid of whatever it was that caused his fatal injury.

EH: If I got into a fight with Tyler Washington don't you think *I'd* have some injuries to show for it too?

DR: Well, it's been five days, Ethan, bruises fade, scratches heal.

EH: From a fight to the supposed death?

DR: There's nothing 'supposed' about Tyler's death, Ethan.

EH: That's not what I meant.

DR: I know what you meant. And I think you know what I mean.

EH: I can honestly say, I really don't. You clearly think I killed Tyler, but I don't know how many times I can tell you I didn't, before you start to believe me.

DR: I just think if you really were innocent, you'd be a lot more worried right now.

EH: Or maybe I'm not worried, because I am actually innocent? You ever think about it like that? I know you don't have anything on me, because I didn't do it, so, yeah, I'm not really worried.

DR: You should be, Ethan, you really should be. Aren't you even a little bit sorry, son? That someone you grew up with is dead?

EH: I didn't *grow up* with Tyler Washington. We went to the same school. That's it. And, as I've already pointed out, he was kind of a dick to me. So, yeah, I'm not saying I'm happy he's dead or anything, but I'm not going to sit here and cry crocodile tears over someone I barely knew, and didn't like.

DR: That strikes me as incredibly heartless. Don't you have any empathy? For his family, his friends? What about your sister? You say they were friends at least, so don't you have even a little sympathy for what she might be going through right now?

[long pause]

EH: I think I'd like a lawyer now.

DR: Oh, something I said struck a chord finally, huh?

EH: No. I'd just like a fucking lawyer, as I believe is my right as a US citizen.

DR: You get a lawyer now, and you know there's no way anyone's going to think you didn't kill him. How's that going to affect your family, Ethan? Your sisters, your parents?

EH: This is fucking bullshit, you know that right? I'm eighteen, I'm not fucking stupid, and I know I'm allowed to have a lawyer here with me. The only reason I haven't asked for one until now is because I would've thought anyone with half a brain cell would easily see that I didn't have anything to do with Tyler's murder, but now I'm starting to realize that you are actually stupid enough, or maybe just so fucking bad at your job, that you're going to go ahead and keep me here until I say that I did do it.

DR: I'm going to keep you here until you admit you killed Tyler, because you did kill him, Ethan.

EH: This is ridiculous! You cannot be serious about this. What do you have? You have me in the woods at the same time as Tyler, and *that is it*.

DR: There's no one else in the frame for this, Ethan, do you understand me? There are no other suspects.

[pause]

EH: Then get me a lawyer.

153

[long pause]

What do I have to do to get a fucking lawyer round here?!

DR: Calm down, son, this isn't the way to go about getting what you want.

EH: What I want is a lawyer and to go home, and for you to get back to doing your actual job rather than sitting there accusing me of killing someone I barely knew.

DR: I'll get you a lawyer … if you admit to what you did. Just admit you're guilty, and we'll see about getting you that lawyer you so desperately want, Ethan.

EH: Oh, that's it, I admit to killing Tyler, and I get a lawyer? That's all I have to do? As if it's some magic fucking wish from my twisted genie. I say I killed Tyler and I get to get out of here?

DR: So, you admit to killing Tyler in the early hours of August 24 2008?

EH: Yeah, fine, I admit it. Now get me a lawyer.

[pause]

DR: With pleasure, Mr Hall.

EH: We're back to Mr Hall now, are we?

[pause]

Detective? You know I wasn't being serious, right?

DR: Termination of interview with Ethan Hall at nine thirty-seven p.m. on Thursday August 28, 2008.

EH: Wait, what. I wasn't being ser –

END OF INTERVIEW

"Fuck," I said, after finishing reading the transcript. I was FaceTiming with Kat and Ray, and both their faces filled my laptop screen.

"You hadn't seen or heard it before?" Ray asked.

"Not all of it. The police released bits of it to the media, and the Chief of Police read parts of it out at the first press conference they held, right after Ethan was arrested. But they just cherry picked the bits that worked best for them, didn't they? This is nothing. They had literally nothing. Ethan's so-called confession was just him making a bad joke in a moment of frustration. Have you spoken to Castle about it at all?"

"We emailed him asking about a digital file like you suggested," Ray explained.

"And?" I said.

"There isn't one," Kat said.

Even through the computer screen, I could practically see the energy buzzing through both Kat and Ray. They were vibrating with barely contained excitement.

"So, there's no record of Ethan's interview and confession, other than this transcript?" I asked.

"That's right," Kat said.

"How is that possible? It was 2008, they must've had to record the interview? It was a state requirement by then," I said.

"It was recorded digitally, but then apparently the file got corrupted somehow, and so that's the only record of his interview," Ray said, leaning forward, a grin forming on his mouth, practically giddy with the breakthrough they'd made.

155

"Are you talking about Castle's version of the file, or the original police recording?" I asked.

"The original police recording. Apparently, they had, get this … a virus."

"You're kidding me," I said, feeling dulled and numbed by this revelation.

"Absolutely, one hundred percent, not kidding," Ray clarified, sharing a look with Kat.

"Do you know at what point in the investigation they got the supposed virus?" I asked.

"We're not sure, but it must have been fairly early on, because otherwise the audio file would have been shared with Castle, right?"

"Yeah, maybe," I said.

"But think about it," Kat said, "if anyone had got hold of a recording of this at any point – Castle, the media, anyone – they'd clearly hear Ethan's tone of voice, and realize he wasn't being serious. But read out the bits that help you make your case and, you can make it sound however you want."

"So, you think they purposefully lost it? Deleted it and then claimed they'd had a virus?" I asked.

Kat shrugged, but everything about her screamed 'yes'. "This is it," she said, looking at me, bright brown eyes practically lit up gold with energy and exhilaration. "This is the crack we dig into and make as wide as possible, until we prove Ethan didn't get the trial he deserved."

I noticed she didn't say 'prove Ethan was innocent,' but I tried not to dwell on it. *Shadow of a Doubt* wasn't about proving innocence, after all, it was about interrogating the idea that everyone got the 'free and fair trial' they were promised under the constitution. As Kat had routinely stated throughout the first two seasons of the podcast; the guilt or innocence of their subjects didn't interest them, what interested them was whether or not – beyond a shadow of a doubt – their guilt had been proven in a court of law. In another life, Kat might have been a lawyer, but I could also tell that it was the unraveling of a mystery that inspired and excited her. She might claim that it wasn't about 'whodunnit', but the truth was she wanted to know who killed Tyler Washington.

Whereas all I wanted was to prove it couldn't possibly have been my brother.

25

THEN

I've bought a bunch of flowers from the grocery store, the cellophane wrap tacky and noisy as I stand at the grave of someone I don't know, hovering over their death like a living specter. I glance at the headstone again: **Elizabeth McConnell, 1947-2001.** A beloved mother, grandmother, and sister apparently.

Sorry, Elizabeth, I think as I watch the too-big, too-black hearse creep into view, a flower garland spelling out his name gracing the top of Tyler's coffin.

It wasn't hard to find out the details of Tyler's funeral.

I wasn't invited, of course, but it was all over social media, and for whatever reason, no one's actually blocked me yet.

I didn't dare step foot inside the church for the service, but I figure there's nothing anyone can do if I'm just here in the cemetery. I got here early, and I've chosen a grave far enough away that hopefully no one will notice me, anyway. I could be anyone, just another anonymous mourner. I'm not dressed all in black as I'm not technically at a funeral, but I've dressed in muted tones, trying not to draw attention to myself, tucking my hair into the neck of my sweater so that it looks shorter than it is. Luckily, it's also turned chilly, so I'm wearing a navy beret I found in Georgia's room. Anything to aid in the disguise.

The mayor, her husband, and Morgan all get out of the long black car that followed the hearse through the cemetery. The mayor stands a little way apart from the rest of them, rigid and tall. Morgan and her father stand clutching one another, Morgan visibly crying into her father's shoulder. Suddenly, a column of people crests the hill leading to the Washingtons. Jess, Nick, Cole and several of our friends are all close to the front of the pack, and I recognize all their parents with them too. There's a group of Morgan's girlfriends, all of whom I know, who have taken the time to come home from college to say goodbye to her brother. And amid them, adults of various ages all dressed in coal black, ash grey, deepest navy. And then, way, way back, the reporters and photographers.

Maria notices the reporters just as I do, her head turning towards them as a flash goes off. Sandford removes himself from his daughter's arms, and places a hand on each of Maria's shoulders, leading her away and up towards where her son will be laid to rest. Someone's head flashes towards me, and I turn quickly to gaze at Elizabeth again. I wonder what Tyler's parents will have chosen to have engraved on his headstone; no words enough to accurately describe the mark Tyler's too-short life has left on those left behind. I take a breath and look back over at the large gathering of mourners. They're assembled around Tyler's grave now, but there, at the edge, someone is turned away from the group and looking right at me.

Cole.

I haven't spoken to him since the Tuesday after Tyler was found, almost two weeks ago. Four days later Ethan was arrested, and it was Cole's witness statement that helped make it happen. I've called and texted, Facebook messaged him, and even gone round to his house, but he refuses to see me, to speak to me. I can't help feeling like I'm the one who should be angry at him, ignoring him, but everything's so messy and tangled, so fucked up and fucked over I can't figure out who's done wrong to who. It's only been just over two weeks since Tyler died, but two weeks is all it's taken for me to be frozen out completely, relegated to saying goodbye to Tyler from a safe, anonymous distance.

My breath catches as Cole takes a step away from the mourners. A step towards me. But then he seems to think better of it, and just before he can turn away again, I crouch down in front of Elizabeth's grave, placing the cellophane-wrapped dahlias in front of it. I reach out and trace the lines of her name. I don't know why. Maybe I just need to touch something solid, and when I stand up again, Cole has turned away, and the congregation is concentrating hard.

I turn and walk away, newly empty-handed, and even though I swore I wouldn't, just as it starts to rain, I begin to cry.

Goodbye, I think, although to who, to what, I'm not quite sure. To Tyler? To Cole?

And then I realize: to all of them. To everything.

26

NOW

"Hey," I said softly, touching Reid's pale arm with just my finger-tips. She looked so fragile, a tiny figure hidden by hospital-issued blankets. Her face was a wash of pale, pallid skin, colorless lips textured with drying, dead skin, her under eyes purple, providing a livid flash in the too-bright hospital lighting.

"Thanks for coming," she rasped, and I tried not to balk at how different, how strange her voice sounded.

"Of course. What can I do for you?" I asked. Spencer had contacted me that morning to tell me Reid was asking to see me. It was five days since she'd first been admitted to the hospital, and although the doctors were saying she was going to be fine, I was trying to maintain my cool, to help keep Reid relaxed – if that was at all possible – while inside I cringed with nervous energy, watching in horror as a silent tear slipped from the side of Reid's eye, crawling down her cheek to her chin.

"Spencer says you've seen the phone?" she asked, her voice almost getting lost in the endless beeping of hospital machines. "You've seen all the messages?"

"Yes," I said.

She nodded silently, her gaze shifting from my face up toward the ceiling. I watched as she swallowed, twice, before she said, "It was worse than all that," she said eventually, "so much worse. I thought it was never going to end."

"Did he physically stalk you as well as harassing you online?" I asked.

"Yes. He'd find a way of always being wherever I was. I have … a pretty structured routine. I don't cope with new things all that easily; it was the only way I managed to cope with moving to Portland, starting a new job. I made it easy for him," she said softly, still staring up at the ceiling, unable to look at me.

"No," I said, taking her hand and squeezing it. It felt so light in mine, practically a child's hand, feather soft, and made of bird bones. "It wasn't your fault, Reid, what he did to you, he would've found a way, whatever your life was like."

She nodded again, but her face was immobile. I got the sense she was trying not to cry. "You wouldn't have put up with it though, would you?" she asked, her words staggered, a strangled staccato as she breathed through tears.

"What?" I said.

"I just can't stop thinking about if I'd just told someone what he was doing, if I'd gone to the police, gone to anyone, told work, but I just couldn't."

"Why didn't you?" I asked, because Daniel had been right when he'd said Reid had been in possession of more than enough evidence to get a restraining order out against Asher.

"I was scared," she said simply. "Scared that if I did that, he'd kill me." I sucked in a breath of too-clean, bleached out hospital air. "I'm weak," she said, and this time her voice had gained strength. It was the strongest she'd sounded the entire conversation, and it was because she was berating and blaming herself. My body stiffened in reaction, gripping her small hand a little too tight, as my heart began to drum a too-heavy beat in my chest.

"Reid, no. Don't say that, you've withstood a lot more than most people have. That's strength."

She turned to me finally, disbelief in her eyes and then she said, her voice back to a whisper again, "I wish I had killed him. I wish I'd had the strength to kill him, instead of trying to kill myself."

Her eyes were holding mine now, pinning them and I swallowed, unsure of what to say. I tried to imagine what my therapist might say to Reid, or even my mother, or my sister Georgia. But I couldn't bring anything to mind so, instead I said, "You really didn't do it, then?"

"I thought you didn't care, that you were my lawyer, not my mother confessor."

"I care about you, Reid," I said, and I realized that that was true. Seeing her sent something through me that I wasn't at all sure of. I realized that no matter how much we want it, no matter how often we strive and reach for it, objectivity was a lie. Maybe it was the simple fact that it was Reid; someone I had a connection to, someone from home, someone who knew me, or at least knew of me, before Tyler Washington forced me to change my name. But I didn't think that was all it was.

I could spend the rest of my life representing any Tom, Dick, and Harry, telling myself it didn't matter whether they were innocent or not, trying to remain neutral, impartial, but it did matter.

"Do you think there were other girls?" I asked. Her eyebrows drew together in confusion, so I elaborated, "Other girls he may have stalked or been obsessed with?"

"I don't know," she said, suddenly looking even more exhausted. I hadn't thought it was possible, but it was.

"Okay. That's fine," I said. I squeezed her hand again before letting go, "You just concentrate on getting better, okay? And we'll concentrate on getting you out of all this."

I let go of her hand and picked up my coat and bag from the chair next to her bed, getting ready to go but before I could leave the room she said, "There was someone, when I just moved to Portland."

"Okay," I said, turning back to look at her.

"I was … it was when I was still dating James," she said. She looked sick saying the words, pushing them out of her as though they were poison. "She tried to warn me about him, told me to be careful. I thought she was … I don't know, jealous maybe?"

"Was it someone at work?" I asked.

"No. It was a bartender at the bar we always went to. I didn't think anything of it at the time, the fact that we always went to the same place; I have my routines, he has his, I thought. But I think maybe he'd been going there for her the whole time."

"What was the bar?" I asked.

"Tin Man's," she said dully. "It's close to where he lived."

"And do you remember her name?"

"No. She never introduced herself. She always seemed a little nervous when we were there though. She was tall, about your height maybe. And she had dark hair, almost black. Blue eyes."

"Okay," I said. "I'll check it out."

Daniel was in the waiting room, right where I'd left him, raising his eyebrows at me as I walked towards him. "You heard of a bar called Tin Man's?" I asked, taking the empty seat next to him.

His forehead creased as he said, "Tin Man's? No. Lemme look it up." There was a pause while Daniel searched the name of the bar. "Looks like it's in Laurelhurst."

"That makes sense, I guess. Not far from the hospital they both worked at. Reid said it was near his house too."

"Whose house?" Daniel asked, and I explained about Asher, and the bar and the bartender. "So, I guess we're taking a trip to Laurelhurst, huh?" he said.

The bar didn't open until noon, so we grabbed coffee and a bite to eat in a café opposite, waiting for Tin Man's to open its doors. "Hey," I said, nudging Daniel with my elbow. We were sat in the window, and Daniel had begun to drop off a little, his eyelids winking in a soporific dance. "Check it out, tall, dark hair, can't tell from here but maybe blue eyes. That could be our girl." She was taking a delivery, standing just outside the doorway with her arms crossed against her chest, keeping watch as the delivery guy wheeled in crate after crate of bottled beers. She was dressed all in black, tight jeans tucked into Timberlands, a black t-shirt with white writing I couldn't decipher from across the street. As we got closer I realized it said, "*The husband did it*" in gothic script. Daniel turned to raise his eyebrows at me in amusement, just as I did the same.

"Hi," I said to the girl, "I'm Olivia Kitson, this is Daniel Koh, we work for Coleridge, White and Associates."

"So?" she said in response.

"We're representing Reid Murphy," I said, hoping she'd been following the news and would know who and what I was talking about.

"Oh," she said, her eyes widening. Bingo. "You better come inside, I guess."

It was dark inside the bar. That daytime bar-dark that always feels wrong somehow, no matter how many times someone exhorts that it's 'five o'clock somewhere'. "You're here about James Asher?" she asked with a sigh as she sailed around behind the bar, and indicated that we should take a seat at a barstool of our own choosing.

"You knew him?" I asked.

She placed a glass on the bar, poured three fingers of whisky out, downed it swiftly and said, "For my sins. I'm Rachel, by the way. Rachel Grey."

"How did you know James Asher, Rachel?" Daniel asked.

Rachel shrugged and raised her arms, indicating the bar was to blame. "From here. He was a regular. A very regular regular. For a while at least."

"I spoke to Reid this morning, and she said someone who worked here – she didn't know their name, but gave a description

165

that sounded a lot like you – warned her about Asher. Does that sound right?" I said.

"Yeah, that sounds about right. I never knew Reid's name, but I recognized her immediately from her photo on the news."

"Why did you warn her about Asher? What were you warning her about?"

Rachel stared down into her empty glass for a beat. Passing a hand over her face she took in a deep breath and said, "It started out innocent enough, you know? We have tons of regulars, almost all of them men, who come in her three, four times a week, some every day even. That's just bars, right? James didn't seem any different from the other guys that come in here all the time, except that he was younger and a little more charming. He had a thing for me, that was obvious. He'd make sure he was here for my shifts, didn't bother coming in at all if he knew I wasn't working that night. We went out twice. Went to the movies, that kind of thing. He dropped me off at home both times, I didn't invite him in. But. He knew where I lived." She sucked in a breath, and looked at me askance. "Do either of you want a drink? I hate drinking alone," she said, pouring out another whisky and drinking it, albeit a bit more slowly this time.

"We're working," I pointed out.

"So am I," she said with a bitter laugh.

"How about you give me a Coke in a little glass, and we'll pretend there's some rum in it," Daniel said good naturedly, making Rachel smile. She poured me one too, and we each took a sip from our respective glasses before Rachel took up her tale again.

"He'd friended me on Facebook ages ago, but then he started following me on Instagram, Twitter, Snapchat, everything. He had my phone number and he'd text me all the time. Multiple times a day, and that's on top of commenting on everything I posted on Facebook or put on Insta."

"You said you only went on a couple of dates," I said, "What did he do when you told him you didn't want to go out with him again?"

Rachel licked her lips, swallowed, eyes darting around the dark, empty bar. "It wasn't as bad as you'd think. He seemed to understand, you know? But then everything just ramped up. The online stuff, especially. And then I started seeing him outside my apartment. He'd follow me home from the bar, saying he just wanted to make sure I got back safely. But then I'd see him there, in his car, later in the day when I woke up. Part of me was just like … why aren't you at work? I didn't understand how he even had the time to be everywhere I was, and I figured he'd back off eventually, get bored or whatever."

"And did he?" I asked.

"Yeah. But that's when he started bringing Reid round."

"Do you think it was to make you … jealous?" Daniel asked.

Rachel shrugged, "Who knows why it was, but there was just something about her. She looked so young, and seemed so much more … vulnerable. It was like, maybe I'd been too strong, or too resistant to him or something, so he went for someone more vulnerable? That's how it seemed to me at least."

"What did she say when you warned her off Asher?" Daniel asked, "What was her reaction?"

"She seemed scared, kinda, but not of him. She just seemed really taken aback that I'd even talked to her. Panicked. They never came in again after that," Rachel said.

"And did you ever tell anyone about Asher? About what he did to you?" I asked. I knew she hadn't reported anything to the police because it would have come up already in our research on Asher, but I found it hard to believe Rachel would've kept this all to herself.

"Yeah, I told a bunch of people. Told my manager here, and the owner. Told all the girls that worked here, a bunch of my friends, my brothers. Not my mom though. She would've freaked," she said with a raised eyebrow.

"And the last time you saw Asher?" I asked.

Rachel sighed and sucked down the last of her whisky. "Would've been that night, I guess. When I spoke to Reid. Like I said, they never came back after that."

"What do you think?" Daniel asked, buckling up his seatbelt, and slipping the key into the ignition of his car.

"I think she's the polar opposite of Reid," I said, staring at the bar still.

"Yeah, weird right? You'd think someone like Asher would have a type. I reckon she might be onto something about him preying on someone more vulnerable with Reid."

"It definitely seems possible," I said. Neither of us said anything as Daniel pulled out of his parking space, and the car glided down the street, away from the bar, and back towards downtown. We were stopped at a red light when I said, "I reckon she could've taken him."

"What?" Daniel said, turning towards me with alarm.

"I think we should get the firm's investigator to look into her movements the weekend Asher was attacked."

Daniel was quiet for a while, his eyes on the road, but eventually he said, "Yeah, okay. No stone unturned, right?"

27

THEN

It's 72 hours since Ethan was arrested, and if we lived in just about any other state in the country, we'd be on our way to his bail hearing right about now.

Ethan's lawyer is sat in the den with the four of us. I can't help noticing that Mom, Georgia, and I have taken the seats we usually occupy, me in the tattered, corduroy armchair Mom's had since her college days, Georgia at the end of the patterned couch that gives her the best view of the TV, and Mom at the other end of it, where she gets the best light for reading by. Only Dad is standing. Back against the wall, arms folded across his chest, face lined and heavy. Castle is sitting in the armchair across from me, another aged piece, but this time covered in the softest, butteriest leather. It's Ethan's spot, but where Ethan usually sits in it sideways, long legs stretched over the arms, Castle is sat forward, leaning towards the rest of us, hands steepled between his knees.

"So, there's a very strong chance he's going to be denied pre-trial release, okay?" Castle is saying, taking us all in, one by one. "He's been charged with murder, rather than manslaughter as we were hoping, and the state has the right to deny release in cases of murder."

"But he's never been arrested for anything before, he has no record, he's lived here his whole life, that's got to count for something, right?" Georgia asks.

Castle nods, "Yes, this is his first arrest, and if it was for anything other than murder, you'd be right, but I really can't see it going that way in Ethan's case," Castle says.

"Because of Mayor Washington," Dad says from his post by the entrance to the room. His voice is low, the words practically muttered, but we all hear him.

"David," Mom says to Dad on a sigh, not looking at him. "She just lost her son."

"And I'm about to lose mine," Dad says. These words are barely any louder than the last, but they cut through the room like the rough serrated edges of a knife. Raw and jagged. I turn to look at him and his eyes are boring into his own feet, head bowed in defeat. As a city planner, Dad knows Maria Washington, mayor of our city, mother of Tyler, better than any of us here, but more than that, he's more aware of the machinations of City Hall, of local government, of the imbalance of power involved not just in the State vs Ethan Hall, but the city of Twin Rivers vs Ethan Hall.

"David," Castle says to Dad, "I understand what you're going through here, but really, it's highly unusual in any situation for a murder suspect to be released pre-trial in Oregon."

"What happened to the presumption of innocence?" Dad splutters, finally looking up from his feet, pushing himself off from the wall.

"He'll just have to be innocent from jail, David, I'm sorry," Castle says, checking his watch as he does so and standing up.

"Robert –" Dad says, and I'm surprised to hear the anguish. My skin pricks, and I look down at my hands; they're trembling, and I hadn't even realized. I've never seen Dad like this before, he's always been so good in a crisis, so good at solving problems, seeing the bigger picture and the path that gets you there. But this is different. A different level of crisis, a whole problem he never imagined he'd come across in his life, and he's not prepared for it. Something flares inside of me and I look at Georgia, wondering what his reaction would be if it was one of us stuck in jail instead. It's not as if Dad's ever played favorites – I've always felt the closeness of Mom and Georgia, the invisible bond that ties them together – but I can't help wondering about the specificity of Dad having his only son taken away from him.

"We have to go," Castle says quietly, interrupting Dad while placing a hand on his back and leading him gently out of the room.

Mom and Georgia stand up. At some point they joined hands, and they're still joined now as I follow them out of the room, into the hallway, onto the porch, into the car, and finally, into the courthouse.

28

NOW

Kat and Ray were keen to record another interview that weekend. So, that Friday I drove back to my home town, this time without Daniel. I booked the same B&B as last time, and told Kat and Ray to meet me there on Saturday morning; my suite would be a much nicer place to record than their dingy motel room. They arrived just as I was eating breakfast in the dining room. There was no one else staying that weekend, and somehow Kat managed to charm the proprietor into making her and Ray breakfast too, so we were all eating pumpkin, poppy seed waffles, with a side of bacon for me and Ray and something made out of tempeh for Kat, all of it dripping in maple syrup.

"Mmm," Kat said through a forkful of food, "I think this is the best breakfast I've had in years. I freakin' love tempeh."

I caught Ray's eye and we both laughed, Kat sending a little huff in our direction. "How have you guys been getting on?" I asked.

Kat laid down her fork, chewing thoughtfully. "We need a way of getting to Nick," she said finally.

"Nick?" I said, pausing to take a sip of coffee, and thinking back to that night, so long ago. "I suppose you could try reaching out to Jess."

"Jessica Heng?" Kat said, through yet another mouthful of waffles. "It was her party you were all at that night, right?"

"Yeah. Plus, she and Nick used to go out, so even if she doesn't have anything useful for us, just knowing she's talked to us might change Nick's mind."

Kat and Ray exchanged a glance, and Kat nodded back at me, "Well, it's worth a shot. Why not? Are you still in touch with her?"

"Me? No. Definitely not. But I might know someone who is."

"You want me to get in touch with Jessica Heng for you?" Spencer asked, a tiny vertical line appearing between her eyebrows. We were sat in Celador, Twin Rivers' favorite wine bar with Kat and Ray. I was surprised to find that she was back in town, having expected her to be with Reid in Portland, but she explained that she'd just got back that afternoon; she'd already taken a week off work and needed the rest of the weekend to prepare for the school week ahead, and catch up on everything she'd missed.

"Yeah, are you still in contact?" I asked.

"I mean, yeah, I guess. 21st century contact, anyway. We're friends on Facebook and we follow each other on Instagram. I haven't called or texted her in years though," Spencer said.

I'd asked her about Reid when we'd arrived, and she'd said she was slowly on the mend. But getting better and being charged with murder seemed paradoxical, and I could tell Spencer was finding it difficult to concentrate on anything. I felt bad about pulling her away from her sister at a time like this, but Kat and Ray were good company and a great distraction if nothing else. She managed to loosen up and unwind a little as the evening wore on, and we all managed to get through a few more bottles of Sauvignon Blanc than we'd anticipated.

"So, you knew Olivia back in high school, huh?" Kat said loudly to Spencer when we were a few too many drinks in. "We heard she was quite the little queen bee."

Spencer's eyes widened and she nodded her head aggressively, "Oh yeah. She was *it*."

"It, huh? Well, we didn't know she was *it*," Kat said, grinning widely at me.

"Shut up," I said, "it was a long time ago."

"No, no, I wanna hear this. I wanna know all about mean girl Liv."

"Oh, she wasn't mean," Spencer said quickly, and I raised my eyebrows at her. "Okay, maybe she was a little mean," she amended with a laugh. "But you weren't like, a bitch."

"Everyone's a bitch sometimes," I said.

"Amen," Ray said, raising his glass at me.

"So, were you at the party that night? At Jessica's?" Kat asked Spencer.

"Mmhmm, yeah of course," Spencer said around the rim of her wine glass.

"You were?" I asked, turning to her on my bar stool, suddenly feeling a lot more sober. "I don't remember that."

"Well …" Spencer said, color picking at her neck and cheeks as her eyes slid away from mine.

"What?" I said.

"You were a little in your own world. You and all those guys. It was a little … impenetrable."

"Okay," I said slowly, swallowing deeply.

"That night was different though. It felt even more like your show."

"*My* show?" I said.

"Not you specifically, just all you guys. You'd all graduated, were about to go off to college, you seemed … golden, untouchable, but like there was something else going on, you know." Spencer took a long gulp of wine and shrugged, "Probably that's just hindsight talking. Knowing what happened after. It really felt like something was over, like it was ending, but I've never been able to figure

174

out if that's just because of what happened to Tyler, or if that's how it actually *felt*. Does that make any sense?" she said to Kat.

"Yeah, that makes total sense to me. Memory is our trickiest master," Kat said.

"Yeah," Spencer said with a deep sigh, staring at her fingers playing with the stem of her wineglass, "I've often thought that. There's a memorial for him at the school, you know? It's more like a shrine really. I have to walk past it every day. It makes me think that we never know anyone. Not really."

"That's what it makes you think?" I asked.

"Yeah," Spencer said slowly, raising her gaze to meet mine. "I mean, do you really think you can say that you actually knew Tyler Washington?" she said.

* * *

Extract from transcript of Season 3 Episode 4 of *Shadow of a Doubt:*

Kat Thomas [voiceover]: You will have heard the name Jessica Heng on earlier episodes a few times now. It was her house the party was held at the night Tyler Washington died. She was close friends with Olivia Hall, as well as Tyler himself, Cole Sampson, and Nick Green, with whom she was in an on-again-off-again relationship. In an earlier episode you heard us reenact the bike ride Ethan would have done the night he's accused of killing Tyler, and we rode right past what was once Jessica Heng's home. Now, we've managed to track her down, and she's agreed to talk to us about that night. We spoke to her over the phone from her home which is why the sound might not be as good as listeners to the podcast are used to.

KT: Hi Jessica, I really appreciate you talking to us today.

Jessica Heng: Yeah, no problem. I've listened to both seasons of your show so far.

KT: Oh, thank you. That means a lot.

JH: I was a little surprised to hear you were covering Ethan's case though. It didn't seem like the kind of thing you'd be interested in.

KT: Why's that?

JH: It's just such an open and shut case. He did it. He killed Tyler. There's no doubt in my mind. And there wasn't in the jury's either. It doesn't seem worth the effort, if I can be honest.

KT: You can most certainly be honest, Jessica, that's what we're looking for.

JH [laughs]: Yeah, I'll bet.

KT: So, I thought we could start with your party that night. We've already heard a lot about it, but it was at your house, right?

JH [lets out long breath]: Yeah, and boy do I wish I'd never had it [laughs]. Would've saved us all a lot of trouble, that's for sure.

KT: Did you get in trouble for holding the party?

JH: No, no. I mean, yes I did, but that's not what I meant. That paled in comparison to what happened to Tyler.

KT: What do you remember about that night, Jessica?

JH [sighs]: That's a hard question to answer, because it should be something I remember really clearly. It changed the course of my life, of all my friends' lives, it's the night one of my best friends died. But it was also a really long time ago, and I'd spent the entire night drinking, so I don't really know. I don't know how to answer that.

KT: But you testified in court Jessica, and now you're saying you can't really remember what happened at all?

JH: I mean I can't remember *now*. Years later.

KT: So, your memory of the night was fine when you testified in court almost a year after the events of the night in question?

JH: Yeah. Yeah, I guess. It must've been.

KT: You stated then that you saw Tyler leave at around two in the morning.

JH: Yeah, that sounds about right.

KT: Do you know why he was leaving?

JH: Why? Yeah, he was going on a beer run, I think.

KT: A beer run? At two in the morning? Where was he expecting to find someone selling beer to underage drinkers at two in the morning? I've checked around, and there aren't any liquor stores in Twin Rivers that stay open that late.

JH: I think he was going to go get some from someone else's house. Nick's maybe.

KT: Nick Green?

JH: Yeah.

KT: Did Nick go with Tyler to pick the beer up?

JH: I don't know. I don't think so.

KT: But why would *Tyler* go pick up this beer from Nick's house, if Nick was there too?

JH: I ... I don't know.

KT: Wouldn't it have made more sense for Nick to go get the beer? Or for him to at least have gone with Tyler to get it?

JH: Maybe yeah. But they were always in and out of each other's houses.

KT: Who, Nick and Tyler?

JH: Yeah.

KT: So, they were particularly close?

JH: Yeah, of course.

KT: Can you explain a little about what you mean by them being in and out of each other's houses?

178

JH: Just that … Tyler's house was really nice, but his parents were pretty strict, so when they wanted to party they'd be more likely to hang at Nick's, whose parents were hardly ever there, and were pretty … relaxed about everything. But if they were just chilling they'd be at Tyler's. He had this huge rec room, a swimming pool, that kind of thing.

KT: And you'd be with them too?

JH: Sometimes yeah, but not all the time.

KT: But do you really think it's likely that Tyler would have felt comfortable going over to Nick's house to get beer without him? Why wouldn't they have just gone together?

JH: I honestly can't remember. Maybe he couldn't find Nick?

KT: But Nick testified to seeing Tyler leave in the direction of the woods, and then seeing Ethan Hall cycle into the woods not long after.

JH: Right. Yeah. That's what happened.

KT: But why wouldn't Nick have gone with Tyler, Jessica? That's what I'm confused about.

JH: I don't know. Maybe he just couldn't be bothered.

KT: Did Nick have any reason to hurt Tyler? Was there any reason you can think of why Nick would be angry or upset with Tyler?

JH: No! God, no. They were like brothers.

KT: Brothers fight.

[pause]

JH: Yeah. Of course they do. I know that. And yeah, maybe Nick and Tyler had disagreements from time to time, but it was nothing serious. They always made up.

KT: Jessica, you've admitted to being in a relationship with Nick Green while in high school.

JH: Yeah. So?

KT: Did you know Nick was dealing drugs at the time?

[silence]

Jessica? You still with us?

JH: I'm not answering that.

[brief pause followed by sound of phone line going dead]

KT: Jessica? Jess? [to Ray] I think we lost her. She hung up.

* * *

I watched as Kat pressed the button to stop playing the recording of her interview with Jessica Heng. Nick didn't make a move. He was staring down at the rough wooden tabletop, arms resting on the table, elbows out, hands gripping each other.

"Nick?" Kat said gently, "I think it's really important you give yourself the opportunity to respond to this. It won't be aired for a couple of weeks, so there's still time to get your side of the story out there."

"My side of the story is already out there. I've told you this already, I've told you this a thousand times," Nick said, pushing the words out through his teeth. "It's the story I testified to in court, and it's the story that got Ethan Hall convicted of murder." He looked up, staring directly at me. We were in his kitchen, having finally convinced him to let us in. It had taken some doing, but I knew we had his attention as soon as I mentioned Jessica's name.

"Nick, we're at the point now, where we have several people either stating or implying that you were regularly selling drugs while in high school," Kat said.

"No, you have Olivia and Ethan Hall stating I used to sell drugs, and Jessica refusing to answer your ridiculous question."

"There's also Morgan," I said quietly.

"What?" Nick said, genuine shock written clearly across his face.

"We have an interview with Morgan, it'll be on this week's episode, where the implication is that Morgan knew you dealt drugs back in high school, and that you sold them to her brother. It will sound to the audience as though Cole is trying to keep her quiet, stopping her from revealing something she'll regret later, which will only serve to make you look more guilty," Kat said.

Nick looked right at me again, eyes flashing as he said, "This could ruin my life. Do you care about that at all, Olivia?"

"Maybe it deserves to be ruined," I said.

Kat spun around in her chair to face me, surprise and wariness in every line of her frown. She held out an arm to me, as if physically distancing me from her and the podcast, and said, "Okay, that's not helpful. Olivia, maybe you should take a back seat on this one, yeah?" turning back to Nick, she said, "We don't have an agenda, Nick. We might be here with Olivia, but all we're concerned about is getting to the truth, okay? Not Olivia's truth, not Ethan's truth, not even your truth, but *the* truth."

"Wow," Nick said drily, cynicism dripping from the word. "That really is an incredibly noble aim." He was talking to Kat, but his

181

eyes kept flicking to mine, and I couldn't quite figure out if it was in wariness, or in challenge.

"I think Nick has a much more casual relationship with the notion of 'the truth' than you do, Kat," I said, her head once again whipping around towards me, eyes narrowed in warning. But my eyes were locked on Nick, watching the pulse in his jaw pick up to a too-steady rhythm. "You know: as a budding, young politician."

Nick let out a bark of laughter that bounced off the walls of his kitchen, "Bit rich coming from you, isn't it, Liv?" he asked, his voice heavy with goading.

"Is it? Because I'm not the one sitting there lying about what really happened that night. I'm not the one sitting there claiming innocence and ignorance, when really I was there that night, threatening Tyler over the money he owed me." Everything in the room stilled as I spoke, Kat once again turning towards me slowly, shock in evidence all over her face at what I'd just said. That shock was mirrored in Nick, who was momentarily struck dumb until he shook himself out of it, and, taking advantage of Kat's attention being on me, rearranged his expression to one of contempt and derision.

"I have no idea what you're talking about," he said, "why would I have 'threatened' Tyler? Why would he have even owed me any money? Come on, we both know how rich his parents are and how ... not rich my parents were. You're clutching at straws, Olivia. Not a good look on you, I have to say."

"Because of the drugs, Nick," I said, too loudly in frustration, throwing my palms up in despair as I spoke. "Because you'd been covering for him for months, and whoever you owed that money to, was after you for it. Does any of this sound familiar at all?"

Nick shook his head and said, acid dripping slowly from his tongue, "That really is a very vivid imagination you have. It's a shame you don't put it to better use, Olivia. And with that outrageous accusation, I'm going to have to ask you all to leave. I'm not going to be accused of this in my own home. I'm sure you can understand," he said, turning to Kat and Ray, as if pleading to their better senses.

I watched Kat and Ray carefully, trying to figure out their reaction, what they were thinking. I knew that what I'd just accused Nick of had come out of nowhere for them. I'd never once hinted that I knew Tyler had owed Nick money at the time of his death. But I could see Kat's mind ticking over, everything slowly falling into place as she conceded to Nick that, yes, probably the interview should be terminated, and yes, we would happily leave his house. Neither of them said a word as we packed up and left, and even as we walked out to their van, they were silent, apparently deep in thought. It was only once Kat had slid into the driver's seat, turned the engine on and driven down the street, that she broke the stretched out silence and said, "Okay, Olivia. You've got a lot of explaining to do."

29

THEN

I wake to knocking on the front door, the knocks are coming thick and heavy handed, exactly in time to the beat of my own heart and for a second, I can't tell if it's someone at the door, or my own heart knocking at my chest, shouting me awake. "Police!" they call, and I think that I must still be dreaming. The police don't announce themselves like that in real life, only on TV, only in the movies. But then it comes again, loud, insistent and I sit up in bed, wide awake and inside a nightmare.

The knocking stops and I hear voices next, although much lower, murmurs. It's my dad at the door; Mom's voice is too high, too naturally loud for me not to know exactly what she's saying from two, three rooms away. There's a thudding along the hallway, soft, slippered feet making their way somewhere and I finally leave my bed, open my door and see Ethan standing there on the landing, right at the top of the stairs, watching. His face is calm, half asleep and he turns to look at me, shrugging as he hears my door wheeze open, the hinges forever in need of oiling.

"Ethan?" Dad's voice says then, floating up the stairs towards us.

"Yeah?" he answers, and there's a crack in it, a crater a mile wide I'm surprised to hear.

Following Ethan down the stairs I watch, heart pushing at my breastbone with increasing uncertainty, as my twin brother is arrested and read his rights.

"Olivia?" Ethan says turning to me, shock shot right through his eyes.

But I can't say anything; my throat is sticky and stuck from surprise, and I am pinned to the ground right where I'm standing, so I can't even move.

"What's going on?" Dad demands from somewhere. I'm barely aware of him anymore. The rest of the world has shimmered into soft-focus, my eyes trained exactly on Ethan who is staring at me, dumbfounded.

"Olivia," he says again. "Olivia, tell them. Tell them I barely knew Tyler. I had nothing to do with this, I swear to fucking God."

"He's right," I croak, voice scratching and smarting, "he didn't do this, he couldn't have. Why would Ethan kill Tyler Washington?"

"You're not doing yourself any favors, son," Detective Rawes says, holding onto Ethan by the shoulders, as if he's about to tear away. "I'd cool it with the swearing, if I were you."

"Detective please, you have to believe me," I say – or plead rather – sidling up to where he has Ethan in cuffs. "Ethan wouldn't kill Tyler. He has no reason to, they'd barely spoken to each other in years."

Rawes looks down on me, and I can see every crease and crinkle on his lined face. Every etching of disdain and condescension. But then his eyes alight on my right arm, where the very edge of the purplish rose of a bruise is blooming under the sleeve of my t-shirt. His eyes narrow as they meet mine, and my gaze, instinctively, flips to Ethan. When I look back at Rawes his narrowed eyes are on Ethan too as he gives his head a grim little shake, and tells Ethan it's time to go.

Mom is silently crying on the porch as we watch the unmarked police car ride stoically down the street. If I'd been expecting the screech of tires, and the wail of sirens, then I was disappointed. It doesn't stop the neighbors from looking on through windows, or from their driveways where they're washing cars and picking up the mail.

Dad is murmuring something comforting to Mom, but I can tell it's not working. I feel like I've stepped through a sliding door and into a parallel world, but I can't tell at what point I walked through the door, and whether or not we'll ever be able to turn back. So I just stand there, staring out at the street. The police car's disappeared now; Ethan's gone.

How will we ever get him back?

30

"Why didn't you tell us all this sooner?" Kat said, sounding breathless, urgent, and exasperated all at once. "This is huge, Olivia. Huge."

We were back at my B&B, sitting in the small den adjacent to the dining room where we'd all eaten breakfast just yesterday morning. I was the only guest that weekend, so we had the place to ourselves, although I'd had to ask the owner for a little privacy once she'd brought through a platter of lavender and earl grey shortcake, and a huge jug of homemade lemonade. Ray was happily making his way through his second shortcake while Kat and I studiously ignored them. I'd just finished telling them about the fight I'd overheard the night of the party while hiding in Jessica's bathroom. I'd been up there looking for a tampon of all things, when Tyler and Nick had burst into Jess's bedroom, arguing about money Tyler owed Nick. I couldn't remember exactly how much money it was that Nick had accused Tyler of owing, but I remembered it being a lot. So much that it had taken me by surprise; I'd known Tyler had become a more than prolific drug user by that point, but I had no idea just how bad it

187

had gotten. Nick, for his part, had sounded on the edge of utter despair; for Tyler it was nothing, of course. Nothing ever touched him, nothing even came close to touching him.

Not until what happened to him in the woods.

But Nick's fear over what might happen to him if he didn't get his money had been real, and his frustration at Tyler for not taking it more seriously, had been even more real. I'd just finished explaining all this to Kat and Ray and I was afraid that the contents of what I was telling them was getting lost in Kat's anger and astonishment that I could have kept it from them at all.

"I just don't get it, Olivia," Kat continued, shaking her head, "This is everything we've been looking for. Everything. You knew we were looking into Nick, you've known for ages, and you're just telling us now? Hell, I'm starting to wonder why you weren't the person to tell us he sold drugs in high school yourself? Why did we have to wait to hear about it from Morgan and Ethan?"

Taking a deep breath I leaned forward in my seat and said, "I don't know. I don't know why I didn't tell you immediately. About all of it. I guess I was trying to figure out what all this meant, and where I stood with you guys, how much I could trust you."

Kat's eyebrows shot up just as she let out a huge puff of air and held up her hands in disgust. "Don't you see that all this does, is make us question whether or not we can trust *you*?"

"It doesn't look great, Olivia," Ray said quietly around his piece of shortcake.

"This whole thing is a two way street, we've said that from the very beginning," Kat pointed out.

"I know, I know. I guess I've just ... I've been living with what happened that night, and the repercussions of it, for so long and really, I'm still dealing with how close I was to all of it."

"Yeah, well, maybe you're too close," Kat said.

"What?" I said.

"We like to have the involvement of the family, and friends if it's possible, of course we do, but we've never actively brought family members of subjects into the investigation before. Maybe it just doesn't work. Maybe this dynamic isn't working."

"You want me to take a step back."

"I want you to take several steps back," Kat said.

I looked over at Ray, but as ever, the two of them appeared to be in agreement. He smiled sadly at me, but I knew he thought Kat was right. "We'll still be interviewing you, still be talking to you, but it's probably for the best that you don't come along with us to interviews anymore, or help with research," he said. I nodded, not meeting either of their eyes, and felt a wrench in my stomach. I reached for a glass of lemonade, hoping it would help, but it was too sweet by half, and almost made me gag. "This is good for you though, too, right?" Ray continued. "Sounds like you've got loads on your plate at work right now, what with your current case and everything."

"Yeah," I said, nodding again, trying to get back on track, back in control. "Yeah, that's true. I really should be getting back to Portland anyway." I picked up my phone, as if a text or email might have appeared then and there demanding my presence back at work. I looked up in time to see Ray and Kat share the flicker of a glance and all of a sudden felt a pressing need to be home as soon as possible.

"Can I just ask you one more thing?" I said instead.

"Sure," Kat said magnanimously.

"What will you do next? With this information I mean? You saw Nick earlier. You put this on the podcast, and he'll just deny it."

"That's true," Kat mused, looking around the room as if for inspiration. "Did you tell the police any of what you just told us?" she asked suddenly.

"Yeah. All of it. In one of my interviews with them," I said, nodding furiously, still trying to claw back some credibility.

"One of?" Kat said.

"Yeah, there were a couple. All that first week after Tyler was found."

189

"Were these at home or at the police station, Olivia?" Ray asked.

"Umm, the first one was definitely at home. It was the afternoon they found him. They went round to all the houses in the area, asking if anyone had heard anything, that kind of thing. And then when I told them I knew Tyler and was friends with him, and had been at the party the night before, they told me I'd have to be questioned at the station. That was a couple days after he'd been found. Maybe Wednesday?"

"When did you tell them about the fight you heard between Nick and Tyler? Which interview was it?" Kat asked.

"I can't remember exactly, but I'm pretty sure I was at the station for that one."

"So, there'd be a recording, or at least a transcript of it?" Kat said.

"Should be, yeah."

"We really need to get our hands on the police file," Ray said, turning to Kat. "Castle's files just aren't enough anymore. It's clear now the prosecution held things back in discovery, because we haven't come across a single interview with Olivia yet."

Kat nodded, and turned her gaze on me. "There might be one last thing you can do for us, Olivia."

"Sure, anything," I said.

"Your boss. Karen Powers. Bit of a hot shot, right?"

"She knows how to get a job done," I said, a little surprised to hear that Kat knew who my boss was. I couldn't remember ever mentioning Karen's name.

"I'm thinking that a request for Ethan's files from someone like her might be a little more effective than a request from someone like us," Kat said, motioning between her and Ray.

I reached forward for one of the last remaining lavender shortcakes, and said, "Oh, yeah. I think that's something Karen could make happen."

Karen was only too happy to file a request with Multnomah County. Of course, I was the one who actually filled out all the paperwork, but it was her name, and the firm's reputation that meant Kat and Ray had their hands on the files within two weeks. I was desperate to see what was inside those files. It had become obvious by now that the prosecution team had held back evidence; aside from the fact that Castle's files had no mention of the interview I'd done with the police, there was the issue of the missing audio and video recordings of Ethan's police interview. And those were the things we knew of – who knew what else was in there. The thought made me nervous almost, the thought of everything that file could be hiding, and especially the thought that Kat and Ray would be uncovering it all without me. But the answer to Ethan's case was in there somewhere. That much I was sure of. I was just going to have to wait and find out what that answer was by listening to *Shadow of a Doubt*, along with the rest of the country. If Ethan could deal with it, then I could learn to too.

"Why is this the first I'm hearing about this?" he said down the line to me from prison. I'd just told him that I was being forced to take a step back from the podcast because I hadn't told Kat and Ray about the fight between Tyler and Nick that I'd overheard the night Tyler had been killed.

"I honestly thought you knew," I said, staring down at my own left hand, where my forefinger picked incessantly at the skin around my thumbnail. It was a nasty habit I thought I'd kicked years ago, but tended to rear its ugly head during times of stress and anxiety.

"How would I know, if you didn't tell me, Olivia? I'm not a mind reader."

"Well, I was under the impression that Castle knew, so I assumed he would've told you about it too. I had no idea my interview wasn't included in all the discovery files," I said.

"That still doesn't really explain why you didn't tell me. You could've told me at any time."

"When, Ethan? We weren't exactly on great speaking terms

191

at the time. I don't remember you coming back from the police station and telling me everything they'd asked you, and everything you'd said."

"Yeah," he said slowly, conceding my point, "I guess there was a lot we didn't tell each other back then."

"Right," I said, nodding, even though he couldn't possibly see that.

"But that's it, right? There's nothing else you need to tell me? No more nasty surprises?"

I paused for just a beat too long and Ethan said slowly, gently, "I'm just teasing, Liv. I know you're working your hardest on this."

"I am," I said, "although it still doesn't feel like enough."

"Well, I'm sure if you think of anything else you might be able to do to help me out in here, you'll do it."

"Ethan, is that a subtle hint to add more money to your commissary account?" I asked, trying to inject a little lightness into the conversation. For my efforts I received a small laugh and a change in the conversation topic as Ethan asked me about work, and I proceeded to tell him how busy we were with Reid's case.

Not so busy that over the ensuing two weeks my mind didn't stray to Twin Rivers once every two minutes of course. And certainly not so busy that I didn't stop waking, breath short and panting, body hot and sweating, by three o'clock every morning, but just about busy enough to stop me from crawling up the walls at least, while Kat and Ray continued to make the podcast without me.

Reid was set to be released from hospital soon, and we were busy preparing for her pre-trial release by arguing for her to be released into her parents' custody on bail. Making bail for murder in Oregon is almost impossible, and the fact was that Reid had already proved to be a danger to herself. Karen's plan was to argue that she certainly wouldn't get the care she needed while incarcerated, and could possibly be pushed further towards a complete mental health breakdown if she was forced to wait out her trial in the county jail. If she were kept under house arrest, however, and cared for by the two people who loved her most in the world, then maybe she'd get to trial in one piece. It was a longshot, but the judge had been known to be somewhat sympathetic in the past, and Karen was counting on Reid's recent medical records doing much of the hard work for us.

It had been just over three weeks since her attempted suicide, and I was on my way to the hospital to be there for her discharge. From the hospital we'd head straight to the courthouse. It was a long time to be kept in hospital, but it had been difficult to get a date set for her new pre-trial release hearing, and so she'd been kept in her private room with officers guarding her door day and night.

Getting into my car I realized that with everything going on, I'd forgotten it was Tuesday, which meant there was a new episode of *Shadow of a Doubt* out. I'd listened to all the episodes that had been released, of course, but this, the fourth episode, was the one I'd been waiting for. I knew it was going to include the phone interview Kat had done with Jessica, but it was also the first episode to be released since Kat and Ray had got the police files. Pressing on the ignition button, I paired my phone to the car's Bluetooth and pressed 'play' on Season 3, Episode 4 of *Shadow of a Doubt*.

* * *

Extract from transcript of Season 3 Episode 4 of *Shadow of a Doubt* [continued]:

Kat Thomas [voiceover]: It takes three requests, almost an entire month, and one giant favor for us to finally get our hands on the police file pertaining to Tyler Washington's murder, and Ethan Hall's arrest. File requests are supposed to be easy, especially when it comes to supposedly closed cases, and in most cases, a request is granted within a week, if not sooner. But we've been given the runaround ever since getting to Twin Rivers, and while we've had Ethan's defense lawyer's files to work with, they clearly don't tell the whole story.

You just heard me talking to Jessica Heng who refused to answer my question about whether or not Nick Green, her ex-boyfriend, was known for dealing drugs while they were still in high school. We've asked Morgan Washington this question too, and much like Jessica, rather than deny Nick's involvement in drugs, she too has been evasive. Now you're going to hear from Olivia Hall again. It's not her voice, but these are her words from her second interview with police after Tyler's body was found. The interview took place in the Twin Rivers Police Station on Wednesday August 27, just three days after Tyler's death. We weren't able to get hold of the official recording – apparently a computer virus corrupted all of the police station's digital files from that case. But we do have the transcript. Both Olivia's words, and those of Detective Rawes are being voiced by actors.

Detective Rawes: So, Olivia. It's Olivia Hall, right?

Olivia Hall: Right.

DR: You were in attendance at Jessica Heng's party the night of August 23, is that correct?

OH: Yeah, I was there.

DR: And what time did you leave the party?

OH: It was about one, one thirty I think. Pretty early.

DR: One thirty in the morning?

OH: One or one thirty, yeah.

DR: And did you see Tyler there at the party that night?

OH: Yeah. He was there.

DR: Do you remember when you last saw him?

OH: Before I left, you mean?

DR: That's right.

OH: Umm ...

[pause]

DR: Olivia?

OH: Just trying to think, sorry. I actually saw him right before I left, I think.

DR: So, that would have been around one thirty a.m.?

OH: One, one thirty. I can't remember exactly.

DR: And this was inside Jessica's house? Or outside?

[pause]

Olivia?

OH: Sorry, sorry. Everything's a little blurry from that night

... but I think it was inside. Yeah, yeah, it was definitely inside. I was using the bathroom and I overheard him having an argument with Nick.

DR: That would be Nick Green you're referring to?

OH: Yeah.

DR: Can you remember what they were arguing about?

OH: Money.

DR: Money? They were arguing about money? Huh.

OH: Yeah, Tyler owed Nick money, and Nick wanted him to repay it like, now. That night.

DR: Tyler owed Nick money? You're sure it wasn't the other way around?

OH: No, I'm sure. Nick said Tyler owed him like, three thousand dollars.

DR: That's a lot of money, Olivia. Are you sure that's how much was mentioned?

OH: Definitely, because I remember thinking 'woah, that's a lot of money.'

DR: Did you see either of them during this conversation or just hear them?

OH: I heard them. I was in Jessica's bathroom and they were in her bedroom.

196

DR: So, you didn't actually see either of them? You can't be sure that it was them talking?

OH: Oh, no, I'm sure. I'd recognize their voices anywhere, besides they said each other's names, so.

DR: Had you been drinking that night Olivia?

[short pause]

You won't get in trouble if you say yes. We're not here to arrest anyone for underage drinking.

OH: Yes. I'd been drinking.

DR: Is there a chance that you might have been confused over who was speaking when, and be mistaken over who owed who money?

OH: No. Like I said, they kept saying each other's names. Besides, I've known them both for years, I know the difference between their voices. Believe me, I was surprised Tyler owed Nick that much too, but … well …

DR: What? What is it?

OH [takes deep breath]: I don't really want to tell you this, because he's my friend, but Nick's been selling drugs for years, and Tyler's basically his biggest customer. When I heard he owed that much money, I kind of assumed maybe Nick had been letting him off the hook paying him for a while, you know, doing his buddy a favor or whatever, but everything had eventually caught up to him. You know?

DR: You're saying Nick Green is a drug dealer, and Tyler Washington is a drug user?

OH: Well – yeah.

DR: And that, according to the argument you heard them having on the night of Saturday August 23, Tyler owed Nick three thousand dollars?

OH: Yes.

DR: Okay. And so, after you heard this argument take place … Did you see either Tyler or Nick that night?

OH: I … hmm, I'm not sure. I waited 'til I heard them leave the bedroom as I didn't want them to know I was there, and then I basically went home. I'd just got my period and was having really bad cramps, so I said goodbye to Jess, and went home.

DR: And you didn't see either of them again, not as you were leaving the house or anything?

OH: Maybe in passing? But I didn't stop to talk or say 'bye' or anything like that. Like I said, I wasn't feeling good, I just wanted to get out of there.

DR: Okay, thank you Olivia.

OH: You think this could have anything to do with Tyler's murder? The money, I mean.

DR: We'll be sure to look into it. Thank you, Olivia.

* * *

The podcast episode came to an end just as I pulled into the hospital parking lot, and although I was keen to get upstairs to Reid's room and help her prepare for court later, I pulled my phone out of my bag to call Kat.

"Is there anything in the police file from Nick? From his interviews I mean? Did they even ask him about any of this?" I asked, after quickly getting through the pleasantries.

"Not that we've come across yet. We've found stuff from an interview he did on the Tuesday, but that would've been before you told them about the argument, because you didn't speak to the police until the Wednesday, right?" Kat said.

"Right."

"So that kind of makes sense, I guess. There's a hell of a lot to go through though, so I'm sure we'll come across something else. That can't be the only time they spoke to Nick." My left hand was resting on the steering wheel of my car, and I began to tap out an unsteady rhythm with my fingers. "Olivia?" Kat said, prompting me, "You still there?"

"Yeah, I'm just thinking. There must be someone else who knew about Nick dealing drugs, and would be willing to talk about it. Maybe even knew that Tyler owed him money."

"You're thinking the audience won't believe it just coming from you?"

"I'm thinking a judge would dismiss it as hearsay evidence in court. The prosecution would've known that, which is probably why they didn't submit it as evidence."

"It still should've been submitted to your brother's attorney in discovery though. Speaking of which, didn't you tell Castle about this interview while he was defending your brother? He might've figured out then that there were some major discrepancies," Kat said.

"I just assumed he knew already," I said, providing her with the same explanation I'd given Ethan, "It didn't occur to me that they'd be holding anything back. I didn't think I *had* to tell him."

"Yeah," Kat said with a sigh, "fair enough. And exactly why we decided to air the interview, actually. We're hoping it might make someone come forward or get in touch about Nick. There have to be other students from your school who bought drugs from him, but aren't mixed up in all this, right?"

"Right," I said, "although I won't be holding my breath on that front. He is Chief of Staff to the town's Mayor now, after all. Who's going to want to accuse him of having sold them a few pills back in the day?"

"You'd be surprised by what people are willing to get themselves mixed up with, Olivia," Kat said, "especially with the promise of a bit of exposure. Besides, the podcast will hopefully reach some people who remember Nick from school but no longer live in Twin Rivers. They might be a bit more forthcoming," Kat pointed out.

I agreed with her and we hung up. Where Nick was working these days, and in particular who he was working for, had become a bit of a sticking point. I wasn't sure Kat and Ray fully understood the significance of Nick working for his former best friend's mother, but the fact that he was the Mayor's most senior employee and advisor had me wondering about more than nepotism. How had he ended up there? And why? Tyler had been the class president; if he had lived, I could easily see him ending up in politics, just like his mom. But Nick? There was no way Nick was there out of some long held desire to work in politics. Which begged the question: why was he there?

Reid was asleep when I got to her room, and I looked around for someone – a doctor, a nurse, a family member – confused. She was being discharged today, going to court for her pre-trial hearing; she should've been up and about by now, showered, getting dressed. Awake, at least.

"Reid," I said quietly, gently pressing a hand into her small, bony shoulder.

"Olivia?" she said, even more quietly. Her voice sounded

faraway, weak. The last time I'd seen her, she'd seemed much better, much stronger than this at least. Her eyes had been bright, her cheeks a little rosy, even if she had for the most part, looked and sounded unbearably sad. Defeated.

"Are you okay?" I asked, "Has something happened?"

"Olivia," someone said sharply from the doorway behind me, and I turned to see Karen standing there. She motioned towards the hallway and I obediently followed her out of the room.

"What's going on?" I asked, "Reid looks like she's gotten worse. How's that possible?"

Karen shook her head once, twice. "She's fine. She's ... they gave her a sedative. She worked herself up into a state this morning. Worried about the pre-trial hearing."

"Shit. I was worried that might happen. So, what now? Can we put the hearing off?"

"It's been delayed until tomorrow, but I'm worried the same thing's just going to happen again, to be honest. She's in absolutely no state to be taken back into custody in my view," Karen said, with something like disgust filling out her voice.

"The judge will agree with you though, right?"

Karen shrugged, looking at me with narrowed eyes. "As a human being, I hope so. But it's just not protocol in this state to release anyone accused of murder on bail."

"I know, but, come on," I waved my arm back towards Reid's room, "this is hardly normal circumstances."

Karen nodded, agreeing with me, but just then Reid's parents turned into the corridor we were standing in, months of worry and concern weighing down every inch of their bodies. Karen told me to go wait with Reid while she talked to the Murphys and I was pleased to see Reid's eyes were fully open when I walked back in.

"Olivia," she said almost immediately, struggling to sit up in bed as she did so. I reached around her to plump up her pillows, and gently pulled her into an upright position, smoothing the pillowcases down before letting her rest her head back against them. "Olivia, you have to talk to Spencer," she said and I nodded.

"Okay, you want me to get her out here?" Spencer had been back in Twin Rivers for a few weeks now, only able to come back to Portland on weekends in order to sit by her younger sister's bedside.

"No, no," she said and even though her words seemed to be coming out of her too slowly, they also seemed rushed, urgent somehow. Like she was rolling something impossibly heavy downhill, and just couldn't quite pick up any momentum. "The podcast. You have to talk to her about the podcast."

"*Shadow of a Doubt*?" I asked. "You've been listening to it?"

"Yes … yeah." Reid stopped to swallow, pinching her eyes shut with exhaustion, and I reached for the beaker of water on her bedside table, raising it to her lips, and helping her drink it. She opened her eyes again once the water was gone. "Tyler," she said, "you have to talk to her about Tyler. About the night he was killed. She was at the party."

"I know, Reid. I've spoken to her about it before."

"No," she said firmly, "Make her tell you. She has to tell you."

But just then her parents and Karen walked in, still talking, and all their attention was turned on Reid, who continued to look helplessly up at me. Helpless but determined.

I asked Reid if she needed anything, and then when she told me she was fine, I told Karen I was going to get some coffee. I needed a few minutes for myself. Deciding I couldn't stomach the vending machine coffee that morning, I walked down to the hospital's cafeteria, where the coffee was twice as expensive and only marginally more drinkable. I sat down at one of the tables nearest the windows with it, hugging the warmth of the cup with both my hands, and stared out at the day. It was drizzling. A light rain that looked and felt like nothing, but would soak you through if you weren't careful. It had been like this for days, those last splintering rays of September sunshine well and truly gone. My phone started to vibrate on the table, and I picked it up, assuming it would be Karen calling me back to Reid's hospital room. But the screen glimmered with 'Unknown caller ID', and I pressed the 'accept' button.

"Hello?" I said.

"Olivia Hall," a voice said. It wasn't a question.

"Yes?"

"This is Maria Washington. Tyler's mother."

"Oh. Hello, Mrs Washington," I said, in as calm a voice as possible, trying to keep the tremble of shock out of it; she may have been on my mind almost constantly recently, but Mayor Maria Washington was still just about the last person I expected to be calling me.

"I'm calling to find out what I can do to stop you telling lies about my son," she said.

Her words pressed in on me and I watched the rain mist the window. A screaming ambulance pulled into the emergency entrance around the other side of the hospital. Inside the cafeteria, conversations seemed to happen only on mute; voices a low drone. Every now and then the shouted words of a hospital worker would break through, shattering the strange and surreal enforced calm with the everyday reality of their jobs.

"I've never lied about your son, Mrs Washington," I said, finally.

She heaved a sigh down the phone, "I think it's best that we speak about this in person, Olivia. When are you next coming to Twin Rivers?" something about the way she posed the question made me realize she was well aware I'd been back recently. Well aware of Kat and Ray, and the podcast.

"I wasn't planning on returning any time soon, I'm afraid," I said.

"This weekend," she said, "I know you have a busy job, but you can make some time for me this weekend, can't you?" when I didn't immediately answer she said, "I really would appreciate it, Olivia."

"This weekend," I said reluctantly.

"Good," she said smoothly, "I'll be in touch with further arrangements," and then she was gone.

31

THEN

Neither of us even hear the knock on the door when Dad comes into the room, a concerned look on his face. Ethan and I are sat in the darkened den, both slumped in our usual chairs, watching *Jurassic Park* because dinosaurs, Laura Dern, and Jeff Goldblum are the only things we can both agree on.

"Ethan," Dad says quietly, "the police are here to talk to you."

My heart thuds at the words 'the police', and I look over at my twin who looks as startled as I feel. "The police?" he asks, "why?"

"They want to ask you some questions about Tyler Washington's death."

"Tyler?" I say, sitting up in my chair, looking between Ethan and Dad, trying to make sense of things, "what's Ethan got to do with Tyler?"

"Nothing," Ethan shoots at me, eyes narrowed and darting between me and Dad.

"Come on son, I'm sure it's nothing to worry about. Just answer their questions, and tell the truth and you can't go wrong," Dad says. "Just like Liv did a few days ago, when she spoke to them. Right, Liv? It wasn't so bad, was it?"

I shake my head, looking from Dad to Ethan as I say, "Right, yeah. It was fine."

Ethan nods silently, Adam's apple bobbing as he swallows again and again. I follow the two of them out of the room, and watch as the plainclothes detective and uniformed officer introduce themselves to Ethan.

"Detective Rawes," the plainclothes guy says, reaching forward with a large, meaty hand to shake Ethan's considerably smaller one. "We have a witness statement that places you at the scene of the murder of Tyler Washington during the time period he's believed to have died. Can you confirm you were in Cedar Creek Woods between one forty-five and two forty-five on the morning of August 24?"

Ethan is stood in the hall with his hands in the pockets of his jeans, facing the police officers. For some reason though, he turns back to me, eyes wide, before looking back at Rawes and saying, "Uh, yeah, yeah, I was in the woods that night. I was cycling back from a friend's house. That's when he died, then? Saturday night?"

"And you were cycling in the woods during that time period?" Rawes prompts, ignoring Ethan's questions.

Ethan takes a deep breath and looks back at me again, "Yeah, I think so. I can't be sure what time I left Kevin's."

"This is Kevin Lawrence you're referring to?"

"Yes, sir," Ethan replies.

"You were definitely back by three," I say quietly from my perch in the doorway to the den, thinking that Ethan keeps looking at me for help or confirmation, "we saw each other before going to bed, remember?" All four of the men in the hallway turn at the sound of my voice, and Ethan shoots me a look I can't quite read.

"What's that, sorry?" Rawes demands.

I step forward and say, "I'm Olivia, Ethan's twin."

Rawes's face clears in recognition, and he nods, looking down at his notebook for a second and saying, "Ah, yes, Olivia Hall. I remember now. We had you down at the station a few days ago, didn't we? So, you're twins, huh?"

"Yeah," I say, sharing a look with Ethan who manages to look baffled, concerned, and amused all at once. "I saw Ethan as he was getting home that night. I'm pretty sure it was a little before three. Right, Ethan?"

"Yeah, that sounds right. I think I left Kevin's around two thirty maybe?" he says to the detective. "I can't be sure though. Kevin might remember better than me."

"We'll be sure to ask him," Rawes says, before switching gears. "The bike you were riding that night, is that a Trek black and orange model?"

"Yeah, that's my bike," Ethan says.

"Is it here anywhere?" Rawes says, looking around the hallway as if it might suddenly appear from nowhere.

"It's in the garage," Ethan says slowly.

"Could you show it to us please, Ethan?"

Ethan looks to Dad, and I can feel my heartbeat pick up inside my chest. Something's going on here, and as much as I want to step in and do something about it, there's nothing I can do to stop it. But Dad just nods back at Ethan, as if to say, 'go ahead', trusting his son, trusting the police, trusting the system because he's never been given any reason not to. I want to shout, 'what about a warrant', but I'm not in charge here, I'm not in control and so I just watch as Ethan leads the police officers out the front door and round the side to the garage, where his bike is, tires still caked in drying mud.

32

NOW

I drove out to Twin Rivers again that Friday night. It was sooner that I'd been expecting to return – in fact, when Kat asked me to take a step back from the podcast, I'd thought my return visits to my home town might be over, and frankly I'd been more than a little relieved about it. The intervening three weeks had been harder even than I'd expected though. Becoming a spectator and a listener to the podcast rather than an active participant had my eyes straining from looking on in ignorance; I wanted to be in on the action, not watching it from a distance. I was hoping that my meeting with Maria Washington on Saturday might help me get back in Kat and Ray's good books again, and therefore back in the fold. If it went well, she might even agree to a podcast interview.

But before all that could happen, I was due to see Spencer on Saturday morning. Reid's pre-trial release had gone better than expected, and Karen had managed to secure her bail under the terms that she be released into her parents' custody and placed under house arrest. They'd even agreed to let her serve out her house arrest at their family home back in Twin Rivers rather than her rental apartment in Portland. All in all, it had been a cause for celebration for the team, and had Karen walking on air for up to 48 hours. We'd gone for drinks on the Wednesday night, everyone well aware that there was still a hell of a lot of work to do, and probably drinking a little more than we should have because of it. I don't remember what number scotch she was on when Karen cornered me next to the women's bathrooms and asked me why I'd never asked her to represent my brother.

She'd jabbed me in the shoulder with her finger as she said, "I've seen the files, Kitson" – she was still calling me Kitson, even though she now knew my last name was actually Hall – "his defense was a mess. I'm sorry but it was. There was no physical evidence – none – and all this stuff about Washington and the drugs, how did that never come up? It's a joke." She'd shaken her head emphatically, stern blue eyes staring right into mine, "What's the point of all this, if you're not going to get him the representation he deserves, huh?"

"I can't afford you, Karen," I said, shouting over the music to make myself heard.

She gave me a sideways look, a shrug, and a bark of laughter before she said, "You could, but that's besides the point. You're just bad at asking for help, aren't you?"

I swallowed, and shrugged, my shoulders tight and rigid. "Maybe."

"No, you are. I can see it. It's why you went to law school, right? You thought you could do all this yourself, get your brother out of prison, clear his name. Do you even know how far-fetched an idea that is?" I shrugged again, and Karen laughed, continuing, "It's okay. We all like to be in control, I get it. But you're gonna need me on this, I'm sorry. You're just not ready."

I nodded, agreeing with her, assuming that she'd have forgotten all about it by the morning, but when I got into the office the next day, head pounding, no sleep, with a mouth that tasted like something had died in it, she pulled me into her office to reestablish her offer. An offer, as they say, I couldn't refuse. So now, with Reid safely under house arrest, and with a relatively free weekend ahead of her, Karen had promised me she was going to curl up on her living room couch, and go through everything in my brother's case. It shouldn't have filled me with as much unease as it did, but I told myself it was just because I wasn't comfortable with my boss knowing so much about me, about my brother, about my family. Because in the end, she was right; when this was all over, when the podcast was done, we were going to need her.

Spencer answered the door when I arrived, coffee mug in hand, long hair pulled back, eyes much brighter than I'd seen them since her sister was first arrested.

"Hey," she said, sounding surprised. "What are you doing here?"

"You didn't know I was coming? Reid asked me to drop by."

"No, I had no idea. I didn't even know you were in town."

"Really? Reid told me you had something to tell me. That's why she invited me here."

Spencer's forehead creased as she opened the door and ushered me into the hallway. Her parents' house had an almost identical layout to my old house, just two streets away. I could have been walking into my childhood home, the hardwood floor cool against my feet as I took my shoes off, the den just off to the right, the staircase leading upstairs to bedrooms and bathrooms, a dining room on the left as we walked down towards the kitchen at the very back of the house.

Spencer was busy pouring me coffee when Reid joined us. She didn't look happy exactly, but she did look lighter, as if a weight had been lifted from her. I let myself wonder for a second whether she was relieved her suicide attempt had failed or not, before quickly pushing it away.

"Olivia," she said, giving me a hug, "thanks for coming."

"It's no problem, Reid," I said and she smiled back at me, the first time I'd seen her smile in a long time. I'd been with her in court for her pre-trial release hearing on Wednesday, but I still couldn't help thinking about her in the hospital bed on Tuesday, when she'd been so out of it, and yet so agitated. I could still see the film of sweat on her forehead, hear the sound of her short, insistent, tired breaths, the stretched but almost swollen, slurred words of warning.

She looked between me and Spencer now, both of us sipping from our coffee, and said, her voice so heavy it sounded almost comically ominous, "I think we should go in to the den to talk."

I looked at Spencer and raised my eyebrows, but she looked just as, if not more confused than I felt. She hadn't been there on Tuesday after all, when Reid had just listened to the podcast and told me, repeatedly, to talk to her sister.

"Spencer," Reid said solemnly as we all sat down. "You have to tell Olivia about the night Tyler died. About everything."

I turned to look at Spencer, a hammering picking up in my chest, my stomach heavy and just beginning to tie itself up in knots. The den was dark. That unnatural darkness that comes from an overcast day, when you always think about turning the lights on but don't because it's early morning still, and it feels so wrong. It cast Spencer in shadows, turned her from something solid to smoke, her eyes downturned, her posture rigid.

"There's nothing to tell, Reid," Spencer said shortly through gritted teeth, "I'm sure Olivia knows everything there is to know about that night. Perhaps even more than I do." I was watching her closely, but she'd been looking at Reid as she spoke, turning only to me when she said, "Right?"

I felt as though she were pleading with me slightly. Asking me not to ask anymore of her than I already had done, but I tilted my head to look at her better, trying to see past the shadows of the too grey day, wishing either she or Reid had turned the lights on when we walked into the room. "I don't know. Do I?" I said.

She swallowed and flicked her gaze away from mine, staring off into the middle distance, her back straight and stiff even in the comfortable easy chair she was sitting in. "Spencer," I said, leaning forward in my chair, elbows on knees, reaching for her, "if you know anything about Tyler and Nick, then you have to tell me. You listened to the podcast this week, right?" Spencer nodded, still not looking at me, and I continued, "well, the thing is that my interview from ten years ago isn't going to stand up to too much scrutiny."

Spencer turned sharply towards me and said hoarsely, "You lied?"

"No. No, it was all true, it's just given who my brother is, the podcast audience are probably going to think I was just protecting Ethan or something, or at the very least that I could have been wrong about what I heard – you must have picked up on the way Rawes kept asking me whether I was sure it was Nick and Tyler's voices, right?" Spencer nodded again, "Well, if we had another witness that night who could speak to whether or not what I said was true or accurate, that would help out so much. It would corroborate what I was saying, and turn it from hearsay to an eyewitness account. And that wouldn't just be good for the podcast – it could help get Ethan out of prison, Spencer."

Spencer took a deep breath and let it out long, and slow. It seemed to fill the dimly lit room. "I did see Tyler and Nick fighting that night," she said finally. "But I don't know if it was about the money Tyler owed Nick. And they weren't the only ones involved."

"Who else was involved, Spencer?" I asked.

"Your ex. Cole," she said, looking directly at me.

"Spencer," Reid said, and there was something about the way she said it that made me turn to look at her. It was hard to read what was written on her face, what was loading down her words. She seemed incredibly sad, but maybe also disappointed, and there was also an element of pleading perhaps. She was asking her sister for something, but I had no idea what it was, and Spencer, who shook her head, holding up her hand to stop Reid from going on, wasn't willing to give it to her.

211

"I'll go on the podcast and talk about the fight, if you think that will help you out?" Spencer said to me.

"It will definitely help, yes," I said. "Why haven't you mentioned it before?"

Spencer shrugged, looking away from me and out of the window instead, "I didn't want to get mixed up in all this. The podcast. I appreciate what you're doing for your brother, Olivia, but I still live here, I teach the children who live here. I see their parents every day – some of them people we were at school with. Do you have any idea what it'll be like going into school the day after the episode I'm on airs? It'll be hell."

Reid had sunk back into her chair as we spoke, she was so small she almost disappeared into it. She was watching us both carefully, and even though I was pleased Spencer was agreeing to go on the podcast, I couldn't help thinking that there was something I was missing out on. An even bigger story Spencer hadn't been willing to tell me.

After giving Spencer Kat's number, I left them both in the den, telling them I'd see myself out, and just as I was closing the front door behind me I heard Reid say, "Why didn't you tell her, Spence? You could've told her everything."

And then Spencer saying, "You know I couldn't, Reid."

33

THEN

It's almost noon on Tuesday – two full days after Tyler was found dead in the woods – by the time Cole picks up the phone to me.

"Olivia," he says, his voice heavy.

"Cole, what the fuck? I've been calling you for days."

"I know, I'm sorry, my phone's a little fucked up at the moment, and then ... well, you know. Haven't really been in the mood to talk."

"Are you okay?" I ask.

"That seems like a pretty stupid question," he says.

"Yeah," I say, "yeah, it does. I just ... I haven't seen you since before he died. I wasn't sure –"

"Liv, let's not talk about it okay? Everything that went down that night let's just ... Tyler's gone. He's gone. Let's just pretend it never happened."

"Pretend it never happened," I say.

"Yeah."

"You mean Tyler isn't dead or that –"

"Liv, Christ, of course I don't mean let's pretend Tyler isn't dead, are you fucking crazy? I just don't want to talk to you about what happened that night, okay? It's all too much."

"Sorry. Look, Cole, all I was doing was calling to see if you were okay. You know, like a nice, kind, thoughtful person would? Like your girlfriend would."

"Girlfriend," Cole says dully, and I know what's about to happen, I just can't seem to stop it from happening.

"Yes. We are still together aren't we? I don't remember breaking up on Saturday night."

"I don't remember a lot about Saturday night," Cole says.

"What does that mean? You weren't that drunk when I left," I say, although I do remember him being drunker than I was.

"I guess there's just some things I'd rather forget, is what I really mean," Cole says pointedly, enunciating each word with a cold, hard clarity I don't recognize from him.

I take a deep breath. Swallow. "So, what does that mean exactly, are we –"

"Jesus Christ, Liv. Let's not do this right now. I don't have the energy to do this, to think about this. My best friend just died, can you just give me a little bit of a break?"

I stop saying what I'm about to say, and soften my voice, change my approach. "I just can't believe I'm never going to see him again. The last time I saw him – the last time I saw you – Jesus, you looked like you wanted to kill him," I say.

"What the fuck is that supposed to mean?" Cole asks sharply, his voice rising to an almost-shout.

"Nothing, God, I don't mean that. I just can't believe –" I take another big breath, let it out slowly, trying to modulate my voice, "I can't believe the last time I saw him it was like that, you know? It's not how I want to remember him."

"Well, then don't," Cole says shortly.

"Was that when you last saw him?" I ask, and I'm thinking of the texts Cole sent me once I'd already left the party.

"What?"

"What happened after I left? It looked like you two were about to get in a fight or something," I say.

214

"What? No. No, of course we didn't; Nick came out and calmed us both down, broke it up."

"Nick did?" I ask.

"Yeah, yeah, Nick." I don't say anything and after a few seconds Cole says, "Liv? I've gotta go. I'm actually at the police station."

"The police station?" I say, parroting him again.

"Yeah, I have to tell them about when I last saw Tyler, what time, if I saw anything, that kind of thing."

"Did you?" I ask, "Did you see anything?"

"I … It's all a bit of a blur, to be honest. I was pretty drunk, don't really know what I saw. I doubt I'll be much help." He's muttering now, barely even audible, but I hear someone say his name in the background and then there's rustling movement, furniture moving and he says, "Gotta go, Olivia. I'll … we'll speak soon. Bye."

But somehow I know we won't speak soon. That this could very well be the end, and when the call cuts out, I slowly move the phone away from my ear, the real world beginning to coalesce around me. I'm standing in the window of my room, looking out at the same view I've always looked out on. Opposite me a house almost identical to mine stands dark, while behind it, trees glower in the grey noonday gloom, standing sentry over secrets they refuse to give away.

34

NOW

I knocked on the front door of Maria Washington's home at exactly six-thirty that evening. I was supposed to see her that afternoon at her office, but she messaged me at the last minute, saying she'd been held up and could we meet at her house later? I couldn't help thinking about the last time I'd been to her office – or at least to City Hall. Did Nick Green's presence there have any bearing on her change in venue? If I'd been suspicious of this change, I definitely hadn't been surprised to hear she was working on a Saturday. Maria Washington was up for re-election in November, and was clearly very busy with her campaign.

It was her husband, Sandford, who answered the door.

"Ms Hall," he said, without a hint of welcome in either his voice or the insincere smile that stretched across his face. "My wife is in her study upstairs." He gestured towards the wide staircase that swept up towards a spacious landing, complete with ornate bookcases and wingback armchair that overlooked the foyer. It was the kind of set-up that was for show only and I wondered how long it had been since anyone took a book off those shelves, or sat in that chair to read.

"Go right at the top of the stairs, and it's the last door on your left," Sandford instructed me.

The house was completely silent apart from the sound of my feet falling on the hardwood floors. When I looked back down from the top of the stairs, Sandford was still standing by the front door, watching me go. He motioned to the right, as if to remind me, and I nodded, walking all the way to the end of the hallway and knocking on Maria Washington's study door.

"Come in," she said through the closed door, and I pushed it open to find her sat behind a large desk, head bent over whatever she was working on. She looked up briefly to acknowledge me and said, "Just give me a second here Olivia, please," and I watched as she scribbled in the margins of something with a heavy looking pen, before placing the cap on it, looking up at me once again, and removing her reading glasses.

"Hello, Olivia," she said finally, "It's been rather a long time, hasn't it?"

"Good evening, Mayor. And yes. It has."

"Nine years, I'd say?" she said, leaning back in her chair. It hadn't been offered to me, but I'd nevertheless sat down in the time it had taken her to finish up her marginalia.

"Almost nine and a half," I said, and I couldn't help thinking that both of us were playing a part. We hadn't seen each other since Ethan's sentencing hearing, when she had advocated for the longest sentence possible for second-degree murder, and the judge, in all his wisdom had granted it.

"If I'm honest with you, I never thought I'd see you again, but then this little podcast of yours popped up, and suddenly I'm being asked questions at pressers for my re-election about whether or not my son was a drug addict, and if he owed Nick Green – Nick Green of all people – three thousand fucking dollars."

Her voice was smooth, modulated, perfectly composed; she said the word 'fucking' the way a waiter might tell you that

217

night's specials. I raised my eyebrows in response and simply said, "Maybe they should be asking Nick Green that, instead."

"Why do you hate this family so much, Olivia?" she said smiling sharply at me.

"I don't," I said, slightly taken aback by her change in subject.

"You do, otherwise you wouldn't be doing this. Isn't it enough for you, that my son is dead?"

Cole had asked me this too, and it felt strange to hear his words in her voice. I suddenly remembered that I was talking to his mother-in-law – or as good as. Cole and Morgan might not have been married, but they were having a baby, and this woman was its grandmother. I couldn't imagine Cole as Maria's almost-son-in-law. I couldn't even really imagine her as a grandmother, although to be fair, she wasn't one yet. Maybe she'd lean into it. I wondered how she felt about Morgan settling down with Cole; the manager of a brewery, rather than a lawyer or doctor, a management consultant or COO, or whatever else she might have imagined for her daughter when she first went off to college. It had surprised me to find Morgan still in Twin Rivers when I returned, and I wondered if her presence here disappointed Maria at all. Or maybe it looked good for her; her daughter still a member of the community, Morgan's boyfriend the manager of a successful, local small business.

"You know I'm sorry for your loss, Mrs Washington," I said slowly, carefully, "I always have been. But the fact is my brother didn't kill your son, so I'm afraid your re-election campaign is just going to have to weather this patch of bad publicity."

The mayor closed her eyes slowly and said upon reopening them, "It took me a long time to come to terms with the fact that there was nothing I could do to bring Tyler back. That however much I didn't want to, I had to learn to live with it, and to move on. Maybe you should learn to do the same, Olivia."

I let her words sink into the room, to fill it up, and then, when I decided a decent enough amount of time had elapsed, I said,

"The difference is, that there is something I can do to bring my brother back, Mrs Washington."

I thought maybe she'd appreciate that; that really there wasn't too much separating our two positions. That all I wanted was the same thing she wanted; to bring my loved one home. But she just sighed, looked right at me and said, "You at least couldn't have waited until after my re-election?"

My head jerked back in surprise before I could stop it, "So, that's it? That's what you're really worried about here, how it might affect your career?" I asked, unable to keep the incredulity from my voice.

Maria just looked at me for a while before saying, "Of course that's not the only thing I'm worried about, but it does present some problems for me, yes, Olivia."

I settled back in my chair a bit, trying to appear comfortable, and folded my arms across my chest. "And is that what Nick's worried about too? How the podcast might damage your reputation before the election in November?"

"That's one of the things he's worried about, yes. He is paid to be worried for me, essentially."

"And why is that?" I asked.

"Well, he's my Chief of Staff ... it's in the job description." The mayor had picked up her Mont Blanc pen again, and was spinning it around in her right hand. If she thought it would make her appear more at ease, she was wrong.

"And why is he your Chief of Staff? Nick Green is a pretty surprising choice. A bit on the young side too, if you ask me."

Maria smiled at me, her wide mouth stretching lazily across her face as her eyes pierced through mine. "Well, it's a good thing I didn't ask you, isn't it?"

"But seriously, Mayor. Nick Green? Your son's best friend? You know he used to sell drugs, right?"

Maria Washington's body stilled, and the air around her seemed charged with energy. And that was how I knew she knew the truth

219

about Nick. Then she leaned back, mirroring my posture, and smiled again, this time with every tooth she had. I'm sure it was meant to be charming, affable, a little seductive, even, but all I could see was someone holding onto their mask a little too desperately.

"You may leave now, Olivia," she said at last, her eyes on me. "I think you've said quite enough."

I smiled back at her, gathering up my coat and bag, and said, getting up to leave, "I think you have too, Mayor."

"So, the investigator finally got back to us about the bartender, Rachel Grey," Daniel said, over the phone that night. He'd called as I was getting ready for bed, and I told him all about my meeting with the mayor before he'd moved onto what he'd really been calling me about.

"And?" I said.

"It looks like she did actually call the police about Asher a couple times, but never actually filed a report, or took out a restraining order."

"Like Reid," I said.

"Right. But," he said, and I loved the sound of that but, "she has two brothers, both living in Portland, both with records for affray, assault and battery, drunk and disorderly."

"Anything else?" I asked, sitting up in bed a little straighter, suddenly greedy for more.

"Asher was admitted to the hospital about six weeks before he was killed, he'd been attacked he said; a mugging. But when the doctors asked if he wanted them to call the police to file a report, he declined. This was about ten days after the last time Rachel called the police to file a complaint about him."

"You think Rachel filed the complaint – one of many – the police did nothing, or very little about it, she gets her brothers involved, they warn him off with a beating, and he doesn't want to involve the police in case they look a little too deeply into him, Rachel, etc.?" I said.

"Exactly."

"And then, maybe it happens again, Rachel knows the police won't do anything, she ropes in her brothers again, and this time they take it a step too far?"

"It's plausible," Daniel said. "It's a hell of a lot more plausible than tiny Reid Murphy, too scared to ever call the police on him, beating the shit out of James Asher."

"So, do we think Asher was stalking Rachel still, even while he was harassing Reid?" I asked.

Daniel was quiet for a bit, and I felt the soothing silence of the cozy B&B bedroom stretch and fold around me. "I've been thinking about this," he said slowly, "because it struck me as a little strange to begin with. Obsessions tend to be pretty narrowly focused, don't they? But what if Rachel was the real obsession, and Reid was the distraction to make her jealous, or make her think he'd moved on? Only he didn't know how to have a normal relationship with a woman, so it morphed into the same thing with Reid. But he couldn't stop with Rachel, because she was his original obsession."

"It's a theory," I said. "What does Karen think?"

"She's all over it. We're getting a second opinion on the post-mortem. Going to try to prove more than one person must have been present, and that Reid isn't physically capable of inflicting such wounds."

"Good. It helps that he was attacked closer to the bar where Rachel works than Reid's apartment."

I practically heard Daniel shrug down the line, as he said, "It was the park closest to his apartment, Liv."

"It all helps," I pointed out, before telling him I was feeling tired and needed to get some sleep.

I stayed sitting up in bed in that sleepy darkness for a while longer though. Thinking about Ethan and Reid, about how much easier it might end up proving Reid's innocence rather than Ethan's. It helped that an entire city didn't already believe her to be guilty, of course, but it was also true that Reid had way more motive to kill Asher than Ethan had ever had to kill Tyler. I thought about the Washingtons' wide foyer, the impressive driveway leading up to the front door, the sweeping staircase, and Maria's seductively comfortable study. Their entire life was about image, perception, power, appearances.

Tyler's careless attitude had been enabled by all those things Maria cared so deeply about, and yet that same attitude had, at times, threatened to take it all away. Tyler had the kind of comfortable confidence that only comes from unearned wealth, power, influence; he didn't know the hard work and the sacrifices that had to be made to earn those things in the first place, and so he always assumed there was nothing he could do that could take them away. But Maria knew. It wasn't as if she'd climbed to the top all by herself; her family was rich, that enormous Queen Anne they lived in had been theirs for generations. But I was sure there were more than a few footholds that had been pulled out from underneath her on her way to the summit, and even more that she'd had to dig in and build herself. How much of a threat had her eldest son been to her? And more importantly, how much of a threat had his death been to her?

I knocked on the door to Kat and Ray's motel room early the next morning. I felt like there was more to talk about than I'd been able to with Daniel last night, and Kat and Ray were the only people as invested in all this as I was.

Kat pulled the door open with a crash, wiping sleepily at her face as she looked out at me. "Hey," she croaked. "This is a bit early, isn't it?"

"Sorry. I've been awake for hours. Was wondering if you guys wanted to get some breakfast?"

"You couldn't have called? Or texted?"

"I wasn't sure you'd pick up. Or answer," I said.

Kat bumped her hip against the door jamb and kind of rolled

222

her eyes at me. "Come on, Olivia. It's not like that, and you know it."

"So, does that mean I can tempt you with pancakes?"

"Me, yeah, but you're gonna have to do without Ray Mackenzie for now."

"Why?" I asked, peering round her into the dim room, "where is he?"

She grinned slowly, letting it creep across her face, her eyes caught in early morning sunlight, "He's at Kevin's."

"Kevin Lawrence?" I said, widening my eyes at her.

"Yup."

For some reason we both started to laugh, and I said, "Well, that's nice. At least we know something good will have come out of all this."

Kat smiled a little ruefully at me then, and I left her to shower and get dressed while I went across the street to the IHOP and got us a table.

"So, Spencer said Cole was involved in this fight, too?" Kat asked, after I told her about my slightly odd interaction with Spencer and Reid the day before.

"Yes," I said.

"Do you think he would've been defending Tyler? Assuming Nick was after him for the money," Kat said.

I drummed my fingers on the table, giving myself time to think. "I don't know. It would depend who started it all. Cole's not a fighter, not really. Or at least he wasn't. And Nick … he sounded angry and frustrated about the money, but honestly if there was anyone in our group who started the fights, it was Tyler. I can easily imagine Nick bothering Tyler about the money, Tyler throwing the first punch, and Cole stepping in to defend Nick or help break the whole thing up."

Kat nodded before saying, "Have you ever read the post-mortem?" The change in subject surprised me but I shook my head, wondering where she was going. "The cause of death is given as blunt force trauma to the head, but he received multiple blows to his face, torso, and groin area. He was beaten up," Kat said bluntly.

"You think it could've been multiple assailants," I said slowly, marveling internally at the mirror image revelations of both Asher and Tyler's deaths.

Kat spread her palms wide, taking the whole table in. "If what Spencer says is true, it's not exactly a difficult conclusion to come to."

I nodded, "But then, if Cole was defending Tyler from an attack from Nick, wouldn't it make more sense if it was Nick who ended up lying in the woods?" I asked.

"Maybe Cole wasn't defending Tyler," Kat said, staring keenly at me.

I nodded again, swallowing hard, staring down into my coffee cup. "Cole might have had a reason to be mad at Tyler that night too," I said, finally looking up to meet Kat's level gaze. "He thought Tyler and I were hooking up."

35

THEN

I am not a morning person. No one in my family is.

So, it's not normal for me to be wide awake at six o'clock in the morning. Even less normal is that I don't feel as though I've slept a wink. My chest is heavy, a weight against my sweaty sheets which are a bundled mess around me. This isn't normal either. I am a sleeper. A good one. Just like the rest of my family. It comes easy and heavy, and if I ever have dreams, good or bad, I rarely remember them. Reaching to my side table I pick up my phone, once again checking the stream of messages I've been obsessively checking every few minutes, every hour, since they began. Jess, Nick, Cole, Nick, back to Jess again.

But not a single one from Tyler.

My mind keeps slipping back to last night. Cool air on hot bodies, hot hands on sweaty skin, shaky breaths and pumping heartbeats. I kick the sheets fully off me and walk over to the window. The rain's started up again, the sky a low, grey glower, but I pull the window open, desperate to relieve some of the heat that for some reason, won't leave my body. I take in shallow breaths, but my lungs seem to have shrunk in the night and I can't get enough air in. It pinches at my chest, needles and nudges it, a cruel tease when what I need is a great big, gulping lungful. My phone is still in my hand, slippy against my palm, and I think about messaging, checking to see if anyone's heard anything, but the group chat's been quiet for hours; everyone else is asleep, finally. I pull up Tyler's contact and think about calling him, but then think better of it. How would that look? Me calling at six o'clock in the morning on a Sunday. *Everything will be fine*, I think to myself, still standing at the window, letting the outside inside, letting the cool air wash through me.

I leave my room, stopping outside Ethan's closed door, listening, wondering if he's awake too, but there's nothing, so I shower, desperate to get this sweaty sheen off me, desperate to be clean, and then go downstairs, where I put a pot of coffee on and wait for the day to come. Bracing myself for whatever comes with it.

I'm still not ready though, when the call finally does come. Jess calls me around 12:30, when my family's awake, moving slowly around the kitchen, clearing away our breakfast. I feel more like myself by now, with coffee and pancakes, bacon, fruit and maple syrup inside me. With the familiar chatter and clatter of my family around me.

"Hey," I say on picking up, leaving the kitchen as I do.

"Have you heard?" she says breathlessly, her voice cracking a little.

"Heard what?"

"They found Tyler," she says.

"What do you mean? Was he at some girl's house?" I say tightly.

"No. Liv. He's dead. They just found his body. Nick just called me. He was the one who found him."

My body goes rigid, my mind blank. And then Ethan walks into the den where I'm sitting on the arm of my favorite chair and gives me a weird look as he flips the TV on.

"Liv? You there?" Jess's voice nudges me from down the line, waking me up again.

"Yeah," I croak, "I'm here. He's really dead?" Ethan's head whips around towards me, ignoring the TV, and his eyes – my eyes – bore into me.

"Murdered," Jess says on a whisper, barely able to say it, barely able to believe it. "They're saying he was murdered."

My throat constricts and contracts again, dry as a bone, desperate for water. I swallow heavily, the effort almost making me cough or retch, and say, "Murdered?"

Ethan's eyes are still clamped on mine, and they widen now, before slipping away, out of reach. The word sounds strange in my voice, feels strange in my mouth. It doesn't feel real, feels like something you hear on TV or in a movie, feels almost like a game we're playing, a role, but cold sweat pricks all up and down my skin and there's a dead weight in my stomach.

Because this isn't a game, it isn't TV or a movie. This is real.

36

NOW

"But you didn't see the fight at all?" Kat asked me.

She wasn't happy I'd held this back from her too, but she was at least pleased that it helped give credence and context to her theory that Tyler might have been attacked and killed by more than one person that night.

I shook my head. "Cole followed me out of the house, and Tyler followed him, but I left them to it. If there was going to be a fight at any point that night, it was going to be then though. If I had to guess," I said.

"How long had it been going on, between you and Tyler?" Kat asked.

"It wasn't like that," I said, staring down at the plate of pancakes that had finally arrived. "It was … I don't wanna talk about it, okay? It was all a really long time ago."

Kat raised an eyebrow at me, and sat back in her seat, arms crossed against her chest. "You're not making this easy for me, Olivia."

"I know. And I'm sorry. I guess I've just never really wanted to confront my part in all this."

Kat nodded, picking up her knife and fork to dig into her

chocolate chip pancakes. "I did warn you that our work might bring up things you weren't ready or willing to deal with."

"I know," I said quietly, wondering if I'd made the right decision, and how far back I'd have to go in order to make the right one.

I was getting myself a coffee to go from The Daily Grind before driving back to Portland when I realized I was standing in line behind someone I knew.

"Hey," I said, touching Spencer gently on the arm, but still managing to make her jump.

"Hey," she said, turning back to me and taking her earbuds out. She was in gym clothes, a fine film of sweat showing on her face.

"Of all the coffee shops in all the world," I said.

She smiled a little grimly at me and said, "Yeah, I didn't realize you were still in Twin Rivers."

"About to head back," I said, "I had a meeting with the mayor last night, and was catching up with Kat and Ray today."

Spencer had reached the front of the line now, and a young woman, her arms covered in tattoos, stood behind the counter, frowning and waiting to take her order. Spencer looked at her and then back at me, a line forming between her eyebrows as they pulled together, "Uh. A green go-getter smoothie, please," she said to the barista, and then to me, "You went to see Mayor Washington last night?"

"Yeah, why?" The barista was raising her eyebrows expectantly at me now, so I ordered and paid for a black Americano before following Spencer to the collection area.

"What did she say?" Spencer asked in a low voice, looking around the coffee shop as if to check no one could overhear us.

"What's going on, Spencer? What's this about?"

"I just don't think it's a good idea for you to be talking to the mayor," she said, reaching for her smoothie, and shoving a straw through the lid with more force than was strictly necessary.

"Why?" I asked.

"I don't think we should talk about it here," she said.

"Well, can we talk about it somewhere else?" I asked.

Spencer nodded, short and sharp, "Do you have time to come back to mine for a bit?" she asked.

I wasn't thinking straight, so when Spencer invited me back to hers, I'd been assuming she meant her parents'. But of course she didn't live with them anymore, and instead we just walked the few blocks to her ex-warehouse apartment building, over-looking the river.

The apartment had a vast open plan kitchen and living room, which, with its floor to ceiling windows was flooded with light, as we walked in and I followed her over to a large leather sectional.

"What's going on, Spencer?" I asked, sitting down at the other end of the couch from her, "Why couldn't we talk at the coffee shop?"

Spencer leaned forward and placed her almost empty smoothie cup on the coffee table in front of her. When she leaned back and looked at me she had a serious look on her face, eyes dark and concerned, forehead creased with worry-lines. "I think you should stay away from Mayor Washington ... she can make you do things you don't want to," she said very slowly.

"That's a little too cryptic for my taste, Spencer," I said.

She shook her head minutely, a tiny little movement that was more for her, than for me. "I can't tell you what I need to tell you, Olivia. Do you understand?"

"No. I don't."

"There are ... contracts involved."

At this I sat up straighter, "You mean an NDA?"

Spencer nodded again, very slowly, as if by moving slowly enough, it was though it wasn't happening. "Spencer, why did you sign a non-disclosure agreement with Mayor Washington? What was it about?"

She raised her eyebrows at me and let out a short bark of laughter, "I can't tell you that, can I?"

I closed my eyes, sighing as I said, "But you want to tell me, right? So, does that mean it's about the night Tyler died? About the fight with Cole and Nick?"

"No, but … but I think they all might have signed something then too. Agreed to something. For a payout," Spencer said.

I looked around me, frustration humming at my chest and hands, and I had to stand up to let it out, pacing up and down in front of Spencer's huge warehouse windows as she watched me. "A payout," I said eventually. "Did you get a payout too? Is that how you can afford this place?" As soon as we'd walked in, I'd wondered how she could afford it on a teacher's salary.

Spencer raised her eyebrows and nodded, "Bingo."

"But why?"

She closed her eyes and when she opened them again there was something like pain masking her face as she said, "I told you, I can't tell you that."

"We're going round in circles," I said, sitting down heavily on the couch next to her. "Is this what Reid wanted you to tell me about yesterday?"

"Yes. She thinks you should know."

"So, she knows what it is? The thing you can't talk about?"

"Yes."

"Did she sign an NDA too?" I asked.

"No. Just me."

"Well, if she didn't actually sign an NDA, then she could tell me … as long as you were okay with that?" I said.

Spencer's gaze drifted away from mine and I felt as though I was losing hold of a balloon string. I'd been trying to bring it in to land, but now, one false move, and it was floating up into the sky above me. "Spencer?" I said, reminding her I was still there.

"The contents of my NDA aren't important," she said suddenly, firmly, as if she'd just made that decision and was pleased with it. "And I definitely don't want you bringing Reid into any of this. She doesn't need that right now. I just thought you should know

231

that it's the kind of thing the mayor does. To protect herself. And her family."

"Okay, that's fair enough. I understand if you don't trust me enough to tell me about your NDA –"

"It's not that I don't trust you, Olivia, it's that I can't. I'd be in breach of contract, you know that."

"You're right. I do know that. I'm sorry. I guess what I don't get is why you think the mayor might have paid off Cole and Nick, or anyone else who was there that night? Who would she be protecting in that scenario?"

"I don't know the answer to that. I just know that when they found the body, they didn't call the police. They called the mayor."

"Right," I said, even though I wasn't sure that Spencer was sure of what she was talking about at this point, at all. "Nick found Tyler and then Mr Washington called the police, and they went around to the house to tell the mayor in person," I clarified.

"No. Nick did find Tyler, he and Cole both did, but it was on Saturday night, not Sunday. And they rang Mrs Washington first, rather than the police."

I shook my head, trying to dislodge something, make sense of what she was saying, because, right now, it really didn't make any sense at all. "Wait, you're saying Nick already knew Tyler was dead when he found him on the Sunday morning? And so did Tyler's mom when the police went to tell her? And Cole and Jess, and everyone else knew he was dead already too?" I was having trouble keeping up, and keeping everything straight in my mind. None of this made any sense, and yet something was beginning to click into place at the back of my mind. Something I could hold onto, and maybe even begin to make sense of.

"Yes," Spencer said, nodding emphatically.

"But how do you know all this?"

"I was there … you're going to think I'm terrible for this, but I left as soon as they got back from finding Tyler, and Nick said he was calling Mrs Washington. I didn't want her to see that I

232

was there, and no one had really noticed I was there in the first place, so I just ran home. Literally. I ran home."

"Why?"

Spencer shrugged, "I just didn't want to … complicate things. And I was worried what she might think if she saw me there."

"You mean, because of why you'd signed that NDA?" I asked. When Spencer nodded I decided I might have an idea as to why she'd been forced into silence. Why she'd taken a payoff. And why she wouldn't want Mayor Washington to see her there, in case she confused any of that with motive. I was about to ask her, when Spencer's phone began to ring, and she held the screen up towards me so I could see it was Reid calling.

"Sorry. I have to take this," she said, disappearing through a door I assumed led to her bedroom.

I took out my own phone, thinking that I really needed to message Kat. But instead of tapping out a text to her, I just sat there, my phone a solid weight in my hand, as my mind buzz-sawed with this news.

37

THEN

He's standing on the stairs, in the dark, when I open the door to the bathroom, and the creamy yellow light swamps us in a dreamy half-darkness.

"Did you just get home?" I ask, my voice hitching from the surprise of finding him there.

"Yeah. You took a shower? It's nearly three o'clock in the morning," Ethan says, sounding as equally surprised to find me there, as I am to see him.

I shake my head, "I know. I went to bed ages ago, but I couldn't sleep because of cramps, so I had a bath." Ethan nods a response and I peer at him through the almost-dark, "You get wet? It was pouring when I left Jess's."

"No, it must have stopped by the time I left Kevin's place."

"You've been at Kevin's?" I ask.

"Yeah."

"When d'you leave?"

Ethan squints at me through the half-darkness, "Twenty minutes ago, I guess? Twenty-five maybe?"

"You rode your bike?"

234

"Yeah. Why? What's with the third degree? When'd you get back?" he says, but his voice is mild now, almost amused.

"Little while ago. Georgia was still up. Well, actually, I'm pretty sure she was almost asleep, but she was still downstairs."

We stand staring at each other for a few minutes. It's the most we've spoken in weeks. Maybe even months. I shiver in my towel at the exact moment the sound of bed springs moving emanates from our parents' room. Ethan widens his eyes at me. We're eighteen, about to go to college, and past the point of curfews but neither of us particularly wants to be caught in the hallway at almost three o'clock in the morning.

"Better get to bed," Ethan says, making his way to his room.

I nod, and he opens the door to his room, flicking the light switch on and closing the door behind him almost simultaneously, so that I'm left standing there, shivering and alone, in the butter soft light of the bathroom.

38

"What I don't understand is why Mayor Washington would be part of the cover up of her own son's murder. It doesn't make any sense to me," Ethan said to me down the phone.

It was our weekly phone call – although they'd become biweekly over the past few weeks, as Kat and Ray's investigation intensified.

"I'm beginning to understand it, I think," I said slowly.

"Really? Please enlighten me."

"It's all got to do with the drug use. Maybe the money Tyler owed Nick too. She wouldn't want any of that to get out, but she also wouldn't want to be seen not to care who had killed her son. And there you were, cycling into the woods at just about the right time, without a care in the world."

"So, she lets the killer of her son walk free just to save face? To save her mayoral-ship? And then gives him a *job*?" Ethan's voice dripped with something close to disdain. Or maybe disgust. There was certainly some disbelief in there too.

"You don't think she'd do that?"

"It's a small city, Liv. This isn't *Boardwalk Empire*." I didn't say anything for a second or two, and Ethan jumped back in with, "So, you really think Nick might've killed Tyler?"

"I'm not saying that exactly ..." I said, trying to put all my thoughts in order, trying to rearrange my words properly, so that everything made sense.

"What about Cole?" Ethan asked.

"What about him?" I said.

"Well. He's obviously involved in some way. You ever think he might have had something to do with it? He did think you were sleeping with Tyler after all, right?" Ethan said all this matter-of-factly, parroting information I'd already given him, back to me.

"Cole didn't kill Tyler," I said, almost automatically.

"How can you be so certain, Liv?" Ethan asked, the words coming out of him slowly but surely. "Maybe you've just never allowed yourself to think about how Cole might be involved in all this?" Ethan said, and again it took me so long to reply he must've begun to wonder whether I was even still listening.

"Maybe," I said, reluctantly.

Ethan was forced to hang up not long after, and I found myself sat back in my kitchen in Portland. Rain pattered at the windows again, and the evening had crept into the room while Ethan and I talked, so that once the warmth of his voice was gone from the phone, I shivered with the chill of it. I got up, putting the kettle on for a cup of tea, and turning the lights on, creating a warm, well-lit womb in the well of autumnal darkness. The kettle whistled its 'I'm ready' tune and I pulled a mug down from the cupboard, pouring the hot water over a lemon ginger teabag. My throat had begun to betray me; too much work, too much travel, too many new revelations, and too many nights waking up at three a.m. had built up to the point where it felt as though there was barbed wire gripping at my esophagus every time I swallowed.

The front door suddenly banged open, and Samira called a loud hello while dropping her bag to the floor in the entryway.

She smiled at me, big and broad, as she walked into the kitchen, "You're home! I feel like I haven't seen you in *months*. Ugh," she said, pulling me into a hug, "you're too thin. Have you not been eating?"

"I'm sick," I said, weighing my words down with just enough fake self-pity so that she laughed as I leaned into her.

"Aw," she said, just as insincerely, as she broke free of my embrace. "You want me to cook dinner?"

"You've been cooking all day," I protested, although really, I did want her to cook dinner. It had been a while since I'd had one of Samira's homecooked meals. Hell, it had been a while since I'd had any homecooked meals.

"No, I've been *baking* all day. It's a whole different thing."

She shooed me into the living room, turning the TV on, and lighting some candles while I huddled under a blanket, relishing for a few minutes, the feeling of being taken care of. I switched the TV to Bravo, hoping for a little faux reality to help soothe the edges of my real, actual reality, but after less than thirty minutes I was pulling my laptop out of its case in the middle of an ad break, and opening up my email. Ignoring all the work-related emails, I headed straight for the new one, near the top, from Ray Mackenzie. He'd attached an audio file of their latest recording, including only a pair of emoji eyes in the body of the email.

* * *

Extract from transcript of Season 3 Episode 5 of *Shadow of a Doubt*:

Kat Thomas [voiceover]: How do you uncover a cover-up? How do you un-write a story that, for the last decade, has stood set in stone? How do you begin to pick out the characters and players who are key parts of the narrative, and others who are collateral damage, cast out to the margins,

238

watching from the sidelines? And finally, how do you figure out who wrote the damn thing in the first place, whose name should be on the front cover, rather than hiding behind a nom de plume?

Because that's what we're beginning to talk about here. If it sounds cryptic, that's because it has to. Because we've got as far as our third season without being sued, and we intend to keep it that way. But more on all that later. Right now, I'm going to play you a recording of the transcript from the first official interview the police did with Tyler Washington's mother on the afternoon of the day his body was found. As with the interview we played in the last episode, these are the words of Mayor Maria Washington, then Detective Rawes, and Officer Michelle Barnes but they are voiced by actors.

Michelle Barnes: Can I get you anything, Mrs Washington? Coffee, water, anything?

Maria Washington: Mayor.

MB: Sorry?

MW: It's Mayor Washington. And I'd like a cup of tea, if you have it.

MB: I …

Detective Rawes: We don't have tea I'm afraid, Maria. The coffee's pretty good though.

MW: No, thank you.

[sound of chair being pulled back, someone sitting down]

DR: Mayor, let me start by saying how very sorry we are for your loss. Tyler was a great kid.

MW: Thank you. Yes, he was.

DR: We just need you to talk us through last night and this morning, Sunday August 24.

MW: Well. We all had dinner together Saturday night. Myself, my husband, Morgan my eldest, and Tyler. I believe we sat down to eat at around seven p.m. I can't remember exactly, but Tyler would have left the house a couple of hours later. I'm not sure exactly when, but I do remember I had a phone call at nine which I took in my study, and he had already left by then. Sandford and I then watched television in the den until roughly eleven o'clock, when we went to bed. We weren't expecting Tyler back particularly early. We'd lifted his curfew when he turned eighteen.

MB: And your daughter, Morgan. Did she go to the same party as Tyler?

MW: I don't know. I don't believe so, though. She definitely went out, but they didn't leave together so I doubt they were headed to the same place.

DR: You don't know where your daughter was last night, Mayor?

MW: She turns twenty this year, Phil. I'm not allowed to ask any more.

DR: Okay. Can you talk us through this morning, when you realized Tyler hadn't returned home?

240

MW: Yes …

[short pause]

DR: Maria?

MW: Yes, I'm sorry. I'm just gathering my thoughts.

DR: Take your time.

MW: Thank you.

[brief pause filled with MW taking a deep breath]

I woke up at seven thirty a.m. as I always do on the weekends. I went downstairs to pour myself and my husband coffee, by which point he had joined me in the kitchen. After finishing my coffee, I dressed and went to use our home gym. It's in the basement. Next, we had breakfast. By this point it was nine, and Morgan was up too. She joined us for breakfast and we had scrambled eggs, sautéed spinach and sausage. Before sitting down to eat, I'd called up to Tyler to tell him breakfast was ready if he wanted it, but there was no response. I wasn't that surprised, but I had expected him to join us at some point. He often slinks in half way through a meal. Especially breakfast. I went upstairs after we'd finished to check on him. I saw that his bed hadn't been slept in, but that isn't unusual, so I texted him to ask where he was, and to let me know he was okay, and then the three of us got ready for church. We go every week.

[pause]

MB: Mayor …? Are you okay?

241

MW: I'm fine, Officer, thank you. Of course, Tyler didn't respond to my text, and so I called him after church, when he still hadn't appeared back at home, and then when it went straight to voicemail, I called a number of his friends, to find out where he was.

DR: Which friends were these, Mayor?

MW: Nick Green, Cole Sampson, Jessica Heng, whose party he'd been at. I believe that was it. But when none of them had heard from him, and hadn't seen him since he left the party, I began to worry. My husband and my daughter thought I was overreacting, but really, it was very unlike Tyler to not have at least messaged me or his father by then, and I knew it was too early to call the police – even if I am the Mayor, I don't want to be seen as wasting police time, or worse, being seen to get special or different treatment. So, Sandford, Nick, Cole, and Sandford's brother went out to look for him. And then, well … the next thing I knew you were showing up at my door Officer Barnes, with my brother-in-law Carson.

MB: Of course.

DR: And we know what happened from there. Mayor, do you know of anyone who might have wanted to hurt your son? Any enemies?

MW: Enemies? Phil, he was an eighteen-year-old boy. He'd just finished high school, he didn't have enemies.

DR: Not even at school? Maybe 'enemies' is the wrong word, Mayor, but what about other students he didn't get along with?

MW: Tyler was extremely popular Phil, you know that.

DR: I do know that, yes, of course, but … you know, popular kids have a tendency to make a couple enemies or two in the course of becoming popular. Was there anyone like that? Someone who might have resented Tyler for something, anything at all?

[pause]

MW: Well, there was a boy, but this was when they were much younger. Junior high I think it was. Tyler was going through … and I'm not proud of this at all, but he was going through something of an aggressive patch, asserting his dominance that kind of thing. But I can't see how that could possibly be related. It was years ago.

DR: Do you remember the boy's name? Was he still in school with Tyler?

MW: Yes, I hadn't heard much about him in recent years, but he graduated with Tyler this summer, and I know that because his twin sister had become quite good friends with Tyler in the meantime. Ironic really.

DR: Twins? So …?

MW: Yes, the Hall twins. She's called Olivia, I'm afraid I can't actually remember his. Terrible things, memories.

DR: Ethan Hall.

MW: Yes, that's it. Well done, Detective. But you can't really think this all goes back to some locker room roughhousing in seventh grade, do you?

MB: Bullying can leave quite a mark, Mayor.

MW: I wouldn't have called it bullying, Officer. Just boys being boys, really.

Kat Thomas [voiceover]: *'Just boys being boys'.* How many times have we all heard that? But Mayor Washington's lazy defense of her son's actions aren't the reason why I chose to play this interview for you. Because according to another witness that night – one who was never brought in for questioning – Mayor Maria Washington's account of the night her son died, and the morning his body was found, is false.

What you're going to hear now is an interview with this witness where we discuss what they saw the night of Jessica Heng's party, and how it disrupts the official narrative that was presented during the police investigation, and later at Ethan Hall's trial. While the witness initially offered to partake in this interview on the record, after discussing it, my producer Ray and I decided that it was simply too dangerous for them to do so. So their voice has been distorted, and the moments when I refer to them by name, have been bleeped out.

We understand that this might prompt you to question the veracity of the witness's testimony. Especially when you consider that they have kept quiet for so long. But you will just have to believe us when we say, they have their reasons for staying quiet, and that we're always going to put the safety of our sources above everything else.

Anonymous Witness: The party had been going for hours when the fight started up. I don't know what it was about exactly, but it started out on the street, outside Jessica's house.

KT: Can you remember about what time this was?

AW: It was just after one, I think. Everyone had had too much to drink by then. But I was still surprised to see a fight break out. Especially when I saw who it was who were fighting.

KT: Who was it, [bleeped out name]?

AW: It was Tyler, Nick … Nick Green, and Cole Sampson. They were all really close. You know, best friends, or whatever, so to see them actually have an all-out physical fight was pretty surprising. Eventually someone managed to get them to stop – Jess, I think – and everyone went back inside. They weren't so much physically fighting each other anymore, but there was a lot of shouting, pushing, you know.

KT: Can you remember what they were shouting at each other?

AW: None of it was particularly clear. They were all drunk. I do remember Nick shouting 'you owe me, man' a lot though.

KT: Who was that directed at? Tyler or Cole?

AW: Tyler. I can't remember how long it all went on for, but eventually Tyler left. Everyone calmed down a bit, people started leaving. But then, for some reason, Nick became obsessed with Tyler not having come back. I thought that was pretty weird, because it didn't seem like he was coming back. But Nick was really agitated, kept saying that Tyler should've been back by now.

KT: You can't remember why Nick was expecting Tyler to return? What exactly was he saying?

AW: He just kept saying 'he should've been back by now, he should've been back now'. He was very, very agitated by this point, constantly checking his phone, pacing around.

KT: And then what happened?

AW: Well, eventually Nick and Cole went out to look for him.

[brief pause]

And then, when they got back to the house, they said … they said they'd found Tyler.

KT: Dead?

AW: Yes.

KT: [bleeped out name], I'm confused. You're saying you were there when they came back from finding Tyler dead?

AW: Yes. There was hardly anyone left at the party by that point. I don't think they even knew I was still there. I'd actually fallen asleep in one of the rooms downstairs, and it was Nick and Cole coming back, shouting about Tyler that woke me up. I was really confused about what was going on – thought I was dreaming or something, but I could hear everything that was going on.

KT: You could hear everything that was going on? Do you mean you weren't actually in the room with them?

AW: No. I was next door. But I heard Jess say they should call the police. She was already crying at that point, but Nick just snapped at her and said 'We can't call the police,' and then he said he was going to call Tyler's mom, and when I heard him say that I kind of just slipped out of the house, and left. I ran home.

KT: And you were able to slip out the house without anyone noticing?

AW: Yes. They were all pretty preoccupied. I know it's awful. I should have stuck around, maybe even should've called the police myself, but ... I don't know. I was young and freaked out, and Tyler's mom was not someone I wanted to see right then.

KT: Why?

AW: Because she was – she still is – the mayor. It seemed crazy to me that Nick would want to call her instead of the police, but I guess he had his reasons. He was always really close with Tyler's family, so maybe he just thought Tyler's mom should find out what had happened before calling the police. But I don't know. It didn't really sound like that.

KT: Can you remember what sort of time this was?

[pause]

AW: I ... I can't be sure, but I think I was home by two forty-five in the morning. Or thereabouts. It was definitely before three.

KT: And how long would it have taken you to get home from Jessica Heng's house?

AW [sighs]: No longer than ten minutes. Especially as I was running. We lived pretty close together.

KT: So, Nick and Cole must have been in the woods, and found Tyler's body sometime before two thirty in the morning?

AW: Yes.

KT: And Ethan Hall was spotted cycling into the woods at roughly two fifteen in the morning.

AW: That's …

KT: That's what Nick Green and Cole Sampson testified to.

AW: I believe so yes.

KT: So, if what you say is true, and they went into the woods to try and find Tyler, and if what they say is true, and they saw Ethan cycling in the woods at around two fifteen a.m. wouldn't they all have seen each other in the woods?

AW: I … I don't know.

KT: So, when *did* Cole and Nick see Ethan, and did they lie about the timing to cover up the fact that they actually found Tyler that night?

* * *

Removing the AirPods from my ears, I took a deep breath and sank back into the comfort of the couch. The Anonymous Witness was Spencer of course. Kat had sent me a message the day before saying they'd finally had time to sit down with her, but were planning on distorting her voice. I hadn't been so sure about the choice: the whole point of getting her on the podcast had been to legitimize my claims of what happened that night between Tyler and Nick. But hearing her speak right after the transcript of the mayor's official statement to the police made me think Kat and Ray had made the right call. It would potentially be way too dangerous for Spencer otherwise.

But there was someone else on that recording who might be willing to help us, and I pulled up my browser, entering the name of the police officer who had been in the interview room with Detective Rawes when Mayor Washington was being questioned, Michelle Barnes. With a name like that it would have been an impossible search if I hadn't known the first place to start, but luckily I did. Like a lot of smaller police departments these days, Twin Rivers PD had a Facebook page where they posted positive things in the community, and occasionally asked for help in some of their investigations. I had to scroll back quite a long way before any mention or posting from Michelle turned up because, evidently, she'd left the department quite a few years ago, but then, there she was. I clicked through to her profile page, and although her profile was set to private I was able to see exactly where she'd moved to after leaving Twin Rivers. She was now a detective in the Portland Police Department. I smiled to myself, the smell of onion, garlic, ginger and turmeric wafting in from the kitchen as I opened up the Portland PD's website, noting down the exact precinct Michelle Barnes worked in, and writing a quick email to Kat and Ray.

Detective Michelle Barnes worked out of the Northeast Precinct, and I met Kat and Ray there after work the next day.

"Hi," I managed to croak out as I approached them on the precinct's steps.

Kat visibly recoiled from me, frowning as she said, "Are you sick?"

"Uh oh," Ray said, "Kat is wildly paranoid about getting sick while we're recording a season. You better keep your distance, Olivia."

"It's not that bad," I said, but even I could hear that it was. I sounded like I'd smoked a pack a day for the better part of the past three decades.

"Kat drinks this honey, lemon, ginger and turmeric concoction every night while we're making a season. Even if she's not sick," Ray said.

"It's preventative," Kat said slightly indignantly. "The secret is fresh ginger, fresh lemon, real honey. Fresh everything. None of that pre-made teabag crap."

"Yeah, okay, I'll get on that," I said, thinking of the sad little honey lemon tea I'd had the night before.

"And then, when I'm really ill I add cayenne," Kat offered.

"Shall we go inside?" I croaked, Kat and Ray both making a face at me as they nodded and I followed them into the police station.

Detective Barnes was busy when we asked for her, but we were told we could wait, all three of us taking a seat in the uncomfortable wooden chairs that lined the station's entryway. It was a cold evening, and as we sat there, the clock on the wall endlessly counting down the minutes, I wished I'd worn a warmer coat. It was forty-five minutes or so before she turned up. She walked in through the same door we'd come in earlier, chatting happily with her partner. The officer at the front desk pointed us out and said something I couldn't hear, and Michelle strolled over to us, both hands digging deep into her jean pockets.

She was in her late-thirties I guessed, light brown hair, brown eyes, and a wide mouth which was drawn into a frown as she approached us. "You wanted to talk to me?"

We all stood up at once, and she raised her eyebrows in amusement before Kat launched into our introductions.

"Oh, the podcast. Yeah, my brother told me about that. He's a fan. You're investigating Tyler Washington's murder, right?"

The episode with the recording of Barnes' interview with Mayor Washington and Detective Rawes hadn't been aired yet of course, but enough episodes had been put out by then that people were really talking. I realized that when Barnes had started speaking I'd expected her to sound as she did on the podcast recording, but of course, that had been voiced by an actor. "Look," Michelle continued after Kat confirmed we were looking into Tyler's murder, "My shift's about to end. I know you've been waiting a while already, but if you give me a few minutes we can do this someplace a bit more comfortable."

We went to a coffee shop across the street from the precinct. My throat was starting to close up again, so I stuck with tea, Kat following suit while Ray ordered his customary black coffee, and Michelle Barnes, surprising me somewhat, ordered a white chocolate mocha with extra whipped cream.

"It's my post-shift treat," she explained as she ordered it with a guilty looking grin. "I really shouldn't do it every day, but on a night like this …" We all assured her there was nothing wrong with a little self-care, and I picked out a table for us in a quiet corner.

"When did you leave Twin Rivers?" I asked as we all sat down.

"Oh, a while ago now. Not long after the Washington case actually, so almost ten years ago, I guess?" Michelle said.

"And you transferred straight here to Portland, or did you go somewhere else first?" Kat asked.

"No, I came straight here. It was an opportunity I couldn't pass up, and it came up at just the right time."

"Just the right time?" I asked, "what do you mean by that?"

Michelle had just taken a sip of her mocha and she had to wipe a smudge of thick cream from her upper lip before answering. "I got divorced. Needed a change."

"So, it didn't have anything to do with the investigation into Tyler Washington's death?" Kat asked quietly.

Michelle's eyes flicked to her, taking the podcast host in as she leaned back in her chair, one arm leaning on the back of her wooden chair, the other reaching out to her mug on the table. "I … no. No, not directly. But I'm not going to lie, I'd pretty much had it with Twin Rivers PD by then."

"Really?" Kat asked, "what does that mean, exactly?"

"What's the best way to phrase this? Policing in a big city like Portland compared to somewhere like Twin Rivers is … very different. It's harder, yes, in a lot of ways, but in other ways it's a lot less complicated. And by and large your colleagues are actually competent."

"Wow," Ray said, raising his eyebrows.

"What, too harsh?" Michelle asked with a short laugh. "I would've thought you'd love that."

"So, Detective Rawes – that is who you're referring to, right?" Kat asked.

"Among others. I can't say I thought all that much of the Chief of Police, either."

"Why?" I asked.

"I was asked to look the other way one too many times. Evidence went missing. Forms were fudged. Paperwork was as good as fictional in some cases."

"So, corruption," Kat said.

"Corruption, yeah. You could call it that. The problem was, they owed their jobs to the person who had put them there, and they knew it all too well. In bigger departments you're essentially more protected by how much further removed you are from the top brass and more importantly, the politicians. Cities the size of Twin Rivers are too small to give you that protection. You've got the mayor breathing down your neck in every investigation you do, because crime stats and creating safe neighborhoods is such a huge platform for politicians to win on. Now times that by a thousand when you're investigating the murder of your mayor's son. It's impossible," she said with a gentle shake of her head.

"Just to be clear, we're talking about Mayor Maria Washington here?" Kat clarified with Michelle nodding her confirmation.

"And what exactly, did the mayor ask you to do during the investigation into Tyler's murder?" I asked.

"I can't answer that," Michelle said slowly, and I could feel Kat and Ray practically deflate next to me. "I was only an officer then. All of my commands came from Rawes or the Chief, Fisher, but I can tell you that there were multiple occasions before he died when I'd bought Tyler in for something, and been told by one person or another to let him go. The first time it was the mayor herself, coming down to the station to pick him up ostensibly, and instead telling me he'd done nothing wrong. There was just a whole lot of looking the other way when it came to Tyler and his friends."

"His friends?" Kat asked, "Do you remember any of their names?" she continued, her gaze sliding my way, almost it seemed, against her will.

"Sure, Nick Green and Cole Sampson were the main culprits. Green specifically. He and Tyler were always together it seemed, and Green was ... well, I was pretty sure he was selling drugs to his class mates but I was never allowed to investigate it."

All three of us stiffened in excitement at Michelle's words. It wasn't that we hadn't heard any of this before; but now it was coming from a respected current Portland PD detective who had once worked for the Twin Rivers Police Department. Her accusation against Nick carried a lot more weight than mine, or Ethan's, or pretty much anyone else's.

"Michelle, would you be willing to go on record with any of this?" Kat asked, the urgency and desperation straining her normally radio-ready voice.

"Absolutely. I've never felt particularly good about leaving Twin Rivers PD. I wanted to of course. Believe me, I wanted to, but I was also aware that I was leaving the city to a police force that was more interested in protecting the people in charge, than its citizens," Michelle said.

As Kat started to make arrangements with Michelle to record a formal interview, I sat back, thinking about Nick. He wasn't a bad person, not really. At least not when I knew him. But he had always been very easily led. Especially by people with the last name of 'Washington'. Where Tyler had always been careless and carefree, someone who believed he could do anything and go anywhere, and never live to face the consequences, I always had the feeling that Nick was all too aware of his position in the world. Or at least, of his position in the social hierarchy of our school. He knew he owed everything to his friendship with Tyler, and Tyler's personal largesse. It wasn't just that being close to Tyler made him popular, got him girls, but being friends with Tyler had occasionally been the reason he had a roof over his head and food in his belly. And because Tyler was her son, that meant Nick also owed those things to Maria Washington. And now, there he was, working for her. Was he a substitute son for her in some way? And did she perform the same position for him that Tyler had done at school? A kind of personal protector who also provided a much larger platform for him than Nick could ever have hoped to scale on his own?

But that still didn't explain why he would call her, of all people, when they found Tyler's body lying in the woods in the middle of the night. There was something here I wasn't quite understanding, something I couldn't quite grasp, because to me, after everything the Washingtons had done for Nick, you'd think Maria would be the last person he'd want to call at a time like that. Of course, we didn't know for sure that Nick had even placed that call, or that the mayor had turned up. Spencer had left the party too early to see whether or not Maria Washington had actually put in an appearance, and I doubted anyone else there that night would be willing to tell us.

39

THEN

I don't expect anyone to still be up when I get home, but there's a light on in the den still, and when I poke my head round the door, there's Georgia stretched out on the couch, a blanket draped over her. The TV's still on, with the volume turned way down, and in the bottom right hand corner I can see the words *Deadly Women* on the screen.

"Hey," I say softly and she jerks up from the couch like a mummy rising from the dead in a B-movie.

"Jesus, you scared the shit out of me," she says wiping her eyes, "think I was half asleep. What time is it?"

"About one fifteen," I say, sitting down in my favorite armchair.

"Kinda early to be getting home from your wild party isn't it?" she says.

"Cramps," I say shortly, "feel like shit."

"Ah, sorry. You know I've been there," she says and I nod. "Is that all that's wrong? You look … angry."

"Yeah, well, PMS makes me angry," I say, placing a hand heavily over my abdomen, "plus I'm soaking wet, and I got in a fight with Cole."

"There it is," Georgia says, smiling, "what did you fight about?"

"It doesn't matter. I don't want to talk about it," I say, just as my phone buzzes with a text.

"Cole?" Georgia asks as I open it and nod. "What's he saying?"

"Just telling me I should go back to the party. Which isn't gonna happen," I say, looking down at my wet clothes, beginning to feel the cold seep into my skin.

"Yeah, no way," Georgia says. She's sitting up properly now, folding up the blanket, and turning the TV off. "I'm heading to bed, you staying down here?"

"No, I'll come up with you," I say, just as my phone buzzes again. I ignore it for now, switching off the light as I leave the room, but my phone continues to vibrate with messages as I trail Georgia up the stairs, and she lets out a disgusted sound before saying, "Will you just answer him? It's gonna drive me crazy if all I can hear from the next room is your phone vibrating."

"Yeah, yeah," I say, going into my bedroom and waving her goodnight.

Turning on the bedside lamp, I check my phone one last time. The most recent message from Cole says:

I just really need to see you, I can't get my head straight.

The familiarity of my bedroom surrounds me, like a warm cocoon, and I glance outside where it's still raining. I can see the path into the woods from here; it wouldn't take long for me to get back to Jess's, to make up with Cole, to salvage the night and to make all this right. But that doesn't make the prospect of going back out there any more inviting. As if on cue – as if in protest – my abdomen clenches, tight as a fist, and my ovaries punch and squirm, pushing out at the fleshy walls of my body.

I look down at my screen, which has faded to black again, and back out at the night, before taking a breath and tapping out my reply.

40

NOW

I called in sick to work the next day, which even though I was actually heading back to Twin Rivers to join Kat and Ray at the mayor's campaign rally, wasn't a complete lie. I was feeling worse than ever, my nose constantly streaming, my head banging against a brick wall any time I moved. My constant and consistent three a.m. wake up calls weren't helping any either. But it felt like we were really getting somewhere finally. What had started out as a drip, drip, drip of information, suddenly felt more like a torrent. Michelle Barnes was already lined up for a recorded interview once we all returned to Portland, but for now it was time to see what Twin Rivers' current and hopeful mayor had to say for herself.

"Feels a bit weird going to a political rally in a brewery," Ray said as I got out of my car and joined him and Kat at theirs, where he was busy unpacking his recording equipment. There was plenty of local media at the event, so we weren't going to stand out too much at least.

"Two Sails is a local success story," I said while blowing my nose as Kat gave me a withering look. "Plus she gets to parade

257

around her perfect pregnant daughter and soon-to-be son-in-law, right?" I added with a shrug.

"Still feels like an odd choice to me," Ray said.

All I could think looking up at the brewery's handsome brick walls was that this was their home turf. A haze of sunshine washed over the city but there was a bite in the air that let us know October was nearly over, and November was right around the corner. We followed the crowd into the brewery, Ray turning on his microphone so he could pick up background noise for atmosphere. I looked around, scanning for familiar faces, spotting Morgan and Cole almost immediately where they were standing next to the empty stage where bands usually played. I kept looking, sure that Nick must be there too, but unable to find him in the crowd. Maybe he was backstage, prepping his boss for the big speech.

Eventually the mayor came on stage, after being introduced by her beloved daughter Morgan who – and I'm pretty sure I wasn't imagining this – looked practically aglow.

"Four years ago I stood on this very same stage and asked the crowd assembled here whether or not you would consider having me as your mayor again," Washington began, "I promised better community engagement, a downtown you actually wanted to spend time in, schools you'd be proud to say your kids attended, and lower crime rates. Since then, Two Sails Brewery has gone from strength to strength, with award winning beers, their own bottles in stores across Portland, and a reputation as one of the state's best craft breweries. Two Sails, like Twin Rivers is a success story, and one that, together we can be proud of. This brewery is no longer the exception, but the rule. Twin Rivers is full of businesses owned not by huge conglomerates and faceless CEOs we only ever hear about in the news, but by you. The people who live here, and love here, and call Twin Rivers home. Just a few blocks from here are apartment buildings that used to be empty warehouses, attracting not just vermin and unclaimed garbage, but crime and vagrancy. Now, those former warehouses are homes, and those streets are communities where you'll find a Farmer's Market held every Sunday. And that's not all. Our schools are some of the best in the state, producing students who aren't just high achievers, but who are happy. Yes, some of you might have laughed and rolled your eyes at my introduction of a Bhutan-style 'happiness index' four years ago, but results have shown that our children are happier and healthier than ever, something most of you here know I am particularly dedicated to. It was losing my own son, after all, that made me see how much more there is for us to do when it comes to making our children safe, and secure. To not only ensure they survive high school, but that they thrive."

I turned to Kat and Ray, wanting to make sure Ray was getting all this, but Kat just pointed a little way ahead of us, where I spotted him weaving through the crowd, "He wanted to get a little closer," Kat explained under her breath, "make sure we don't miss anything."

"It's impressive," I said, and Kat shot me a look. But it was. If I didn't know what I did about Maria Washington, I'd probably be voting for four more years of her too. There was such a fine line between what we presented to the world and who we really were. The veneer was so thin, so exceptionally fragile, even more so than ever these days, and yet it still managed to fool people. Maybe, the truth was that we didn't want to admit we all saw the veneer, because we were all so busy maintaining our own fragile outer casing. Who wants to think about how they're being fooled when they're probably, on some level, also doing the fooling? We lived in a hall-of-mirrors world now; we were just far too distracted by our own reflections to do anything about it. It was then I finally saw Nick. He was stood a little way back from the small stage, away, apart from the crowd. I caught his eye, and rather than immediately look away, he held my gaze for a beat, giving me a small, impossible to read smile as he did so.

Maria was still talking, Nick's gaze flicking to the mayor up on the stage and then back to me, before heading towards one of the brewery's back exits. I nudged Kat next to me, indicating that I was going to follow Nick, and found him out in the parking lot, gazing up into the watery sunshine with his eyes closed. There was a travel mug of coffee in his hand with *Washington 2018* emblazoned across it, and he took a gulp from it as I called out his name. When he turned round to look at me, he didn't seem at all surprised that I'd followed him.

"For ten years I didn't see hide or hair of you, Olivia Hall, and now you're everywhere I fucking look. I enjoyed those years, you know. They were nice and quiet."

"Why'd you call the mayor that night, Nick?" I asked, dispensing with the pleasantries. "Why not the police?"

"I thought she deserved to know her son was dead."

"You know I know that's not the answer. Why didn't you call the police once you'd called her?"

"You'd have to ask her that," Nick said through his teeth.

"We're planning to," I said, and he met my eye again, this time laughter filling his as he shook his head and said,

"Good luck with that, Liv."

"I just don't get it, Nick," I said, moving closer to him as I dropped my voice, "help me understand, please. Why would you call her after finding Tyler, instead of immediately calling the police? Did you … did you feel like you owed her or something?" I asked, thinking of all the time Nick had spent at the Washington's house while we were all still in school, thinking of what Michelle Barnes had said about being constantly asked to look the other way whenever Tyler or any of his friends were picked up for anything. Thinking of who he currently worked for. She was inside the brewery still, working the crowd, making promises. Reading out words that, for all I knew, Nick himself had written.

Nick let out a bark of harsh laughter that rang around the empty parking lot like a shot. "Owe her? No, Olivia, you've got this all wrong. She owed me."

"What could she possibly owe you, Nick?" I asked, my voice a low hiss of urgency that turned into an embarrassingly ragged cough. Nick waited for me to finish before answering.

"Three thousand fucking dollars," he said bluntly, before turning on his heel and heading back into the brewery.

* * *

Extract from transcript of Season 3 Episode 5 of *Shadow of a Doubt* [continued]:

Kat Thomas [voiceover]: The brewery is filling up fast by the time we get there. A crowd has gathered despite the fact that it's 4 o'clock on a weekday afternoon. Mayor Washington has been an incredibly popular and effective mayor over the years. Both when she was voted in over ten years ago for her first term, and then again four years ago when she decided to stand for election once again. When we ask members of the gathered crowd their opinion of her, there is nothing but gushing praise.

Woman's voice: Oh, she's wonderful. I can't imagine ever having another mayor. She does exactly what she says she's going to do, which is what I like best about her, but there's also this real warmth to her. You know she runs a clinic every week when members of the public can go to her to make a complaint or what have you? She's very hands-on, you just know she really cares.

Young girl's voice: She built us a new playground, that's why I like her.

Man's voice: She's not like most politicians, and believe me, I've seen a few in my day. The first time around I thought she

261

was maybe a little too slick, one of those political operators who just promises, promises, promises, and then delivers on nothing. But after everything with her son you can really see her for who she is. The fact that even after all that she'd want to come back and serve her community and city says everything.

[background crowd noises, music, and chatter, Mayor Washington's voice rises over the crowd]

Mayor Washington: Just a few months after becoming your mayor for the second time I promoted Philip Rawes to Chief of Police and since then crime rates have gone down by 7%, with property crime down by an incredible 30% [cheers from the crowd]. Just as I knew he would, he has led the way with cracking down on crimes both big and small, but has also developed important community led initiatives alongside my office, which has seen the city's faith in its police force grow by 45%. Twin Rivers is a small city, a close knit community, and I know all too well how much a crime, of any kind, can rock its foundations. I think we can be proud though, of how we have pushed through as a community to a brighter, safer future. I know I am proud to stand here as your mayor, and I know I wouldn't be here, as a mayor, as a mother, as a fellow citizen of this city, if it wasn't for your support.

[cheers and clapping from crowd]

I want to thank you for being here, thank you for believing in me, thank you for voting for me four years ago, and thank you for voting for me again this November!

[cheers from crowd as speech ends]

[sound of chatter and movement, footfall and scrambling]

KT: Mrs Mayor! Mayor! Mayor Washington I just have a few questions for you.

Male voice [gruff]: She's not taking any questions at this time.

KT [out of breath]: Mayor Washington, is it true that you knew your son Tyler was dead before the police were called to the scene on Sunday August 24 2008?

Mayor Washington [muffled, barely audible]: What?

Male voice: That's enough, step aside please.

KT: Mayor, will you answer the question? Did you know Tyler had died before the police were called?

MW [muffled]: Nick, what's going on?

KT: Can you just tell us about that night? August 23?

Nick Green (Male voice): That's enough now. Step aside. She's not taking questions.

KT: Mayor!

NG: That's it, let me see that –

[scrambling sounds as recording is shut off]

"That's it?" I asked, "That's all you managed to get?"

We were back in the parking lot now, the rally over, the mayor bundled into a car and driven safely away. From what I could tell, Nick had walked away from me, and right back into the brewery just in time to pull Maria away from Kat and Ray's questions.

Kat sighed and squinted into the setting sun. "I wasn't really expecting her to give us any good answers, to be honest, Olivia. I just wanted her to know we were there. Watching."

I nodded my head, indicating I understood her line of thinking, but there was a tight feeling in my chest I couldn't entirely put down to my current ill-health. We were so close. I knew it. But we were never going to get anywhere if we couldn't get any closer to the mayor.

I said goodbye to Kat and Ray and drove home to Portland, feeling so awful that I just wanted to crawl into bed. But when I got home, I found Daniel sitting alone in the living room, waiting for me.

"What are you doing here?" I croaked as Daniel startled and looked up from the file he was reading.

"Samira let me in. I brought you soup," he said pointedly.

"Oh," I said, collapsing onto the sofa next to him. My back, neck, and shoulders ached, a dull, exhausting pain that radiated all the way down to my knees. I'd coughed the whole drive home and my throat felt red raw, the effort of speaking just a bit too much for me. "I was in Twin Rivers," I said.

"I know, Samira told me. Why didn't you let me know?"

"Didn't want you to have to lie for me. Plausible deniability."

Daniel managed to sigh and laugh at practically the same time. "It's probably cold by now, but I could warm up that soup if you want?" he said softly.

The soup was a chicken pho that Daniel had doused with sriracha and chili oil, telling me the spices would flush out my cold. I'd turned the TV on while Daniel was in the kitchen, but the volume was at a low, comforting murmur, the characters of *Brooklyn Nine-Nine* trading zingers as I told him what I'd been getting up to in Twin Rivers in between slurps of soup.

"Three thousand dollars?" he said, his forehead creasing slightly in the low light of the room, "why would she help cover up a murder for three thousand dollars?"

"I don't know. I'm not sure it's about the money for her anyway. Money's never been an issue for her. I think it was about reputation and appearances," I said before my words gave way to another coughing fit. Daniel gave me a sympathetic look, and passed me my glass of water.

"You know we've found another medical examiner Karen's happy with to offer a second opinion on Asher's autopsy?" Daniel said.

"Yeah ..."

"Well, why not use her for Tyler too? If you think it was Nick and Cole who did this, we might be able to prove it was two attackers, rather than one."

I took another long drink of water, gathering my thoughts and taking my time, before I said, "But I don't know that it was Nick and Cole. I'm just not sure if the timeline fits with that. Would they have had time between leaving Jess's house and coming back to ... to finish the job?"

"You can't completely trust Spencer's timeline of events, Liv. It was ten years ago, on top of which, she'd been drinking and there was a lot going on ... more time could've elapsed than she realized, or remembers."

"That's true," I said thickly.

"God, you do sound terrible," Daniel said robustly as I gave him what I hoped was a deadly look, but probably ended up a lot more helpless than I'd intended, as he smiled back at me, removing the bowl of soup from my hands, and said, "maybe you should get some sleep."

Speaking to Ethan on Sunday, I could practically feel him fizzing down the line as he told me about his meeting with Karen the day before.

"She thinks we have a real chance at a retrial, Liv, it's amazing. Apparently it's all to do with that interview you did with the police when you told them about the argument between Tyler and Nick, so I've decided I can't be angry with you for not telling me about that anymore."

I laughed, letting his energy and optimism infect me, if only for a few seconds, "You were angry with me?" I asked.

"Well, yeah," he said slowly, "that was a pretty big thing not to have told me."

"We've been over this, Ethan, we weren't really talking back then."

"And ten years have gone by, and you've had plenty of opportunity to tell me about it," Ethan pointed out.

I took a deep breath, steadying myself. Navigating my relationship with Ethan still sometimes took me by surprise. It could feel like a high wire act at times; finding that careful balance where we both felt comfortable, both felt at home, despite the fact that so much had changed, and nothing could ever be the same. I hadn't known my brother when he went to prison, not really. We hadn't spoken other than to trade barbs and insults, for almost eight years. I'd traded my most important relationship – that with my twin – for a place at a school canteen table and I could never take that trade back. The worst thing was, I wasn't sure Ethan even really resented me for it; he'd been baffled, amused, and probably a little contemptuous of my efforts to be as popular as possible at the time, but he cared so little about those things, that now it barely came up. We'd found a groove and a rhythm that worked for us since then, though. Maybe it was a little disjointed, maybe it was a little off, but it did at least work. And then sometimes, Ethan would say something that had me questioning everything. He was right: I could have told him at any time between then and now about that fight between Tyler and Nick on the night Tyler died. It might not have made a lot of difference at the time, but it would've been a step in the right direction, a step towards an openness and honesty that had been so sorely lacking in our relationship when we were teenagers.

But the reality was, and I hated to admit this, I still viewed life as a trade. If I'd given that one thing away, what else might I have been giving away? There was a part of me that knew, no matter how hard I tried, no matter what I did, nothing could make up for what had happened to Ethan and so these small tidbits of information paled in comparison and got lost in all the other secrets, all the guilt, and every other thing we'd lost in the midst of growing up, and growing apart.

"What did you think of Karen?" I asked, changing the subject, hoping to get on firmer ground.

"I had no idea lawyers could be so cool," Ethan said without a hint of sarcasm.

I laughed, "Well, great, I'll try not to take that as an insult. She is pretty cool, I guess."

"She's just so … impressive, you know?" Ethan said.

"Ethan, is that a small crush I detect?"

"Well, I have been pretty starved for female attention from anyone other than women I'm related to," he said.

"Fair enough."

"Although," and here he lowered his voice, "I've started to get some pretty weird letters ever since the podcast started airing. There's a 37-year-old woman in Idaho who wants to marry me."

"You're joking," I said through laughter.

"Not even. Totally, one hundred percent, telling the truth. One of them was from someone in Australia. I've gone global, Olivia."

"If only you were someone who craved outside affirmation," I said.

"It's not exactly affirmation they're offering me, Liv," he pointed out. "It's weird, actually," he continued after a short pause, "they don't care that I'm innocent, you know? I mean, some of the stuff I've got is really nice; people have been listening and paying attention to the podcast and can clearly see that something went wrong. But some of them, they just … I don't know how to put it. It makes my skin crawl thinking about all these people who think I could've actually killed someone. Who believe I did, and don't even seem to care that someone lost their life … Do you ever think about Tyler?"

"Yes," I said, after a short pause, "of course I do."

"Of course. He was your friend after all."

"It's all become a bit twisted since then, but yeah, for a while there, he was my friend," I said.

"Do you miss him?" he asked, taking me so much by surprise that my heart bumped in response, knocking at my chest.

"I don't know that I could say that I miss him," I said slowly, measuring out my words, carefully trying to find the right ones. "It's more like I wish none of this had ever happened. That I could erase that whole night from existence."

41

THEN

"I'm leaving," I say quietly in Jess's ear. But it's too quiet apparently because she keeps talking to Hunter, both their faces wide with grins, voices loud enough to shatter glass over the insistent pump of the music.

"Jess," I say again, turning her towards me.

Her eyes bug and she smiles even wider. "Liv!" she shouts, swaying slightly, "where you been?"

"I'm going home," I say, and her eyebrows pull together as her grin turns to a confused frown and she begins to shake her head.

"No way girl, it's early still. What's going on?"

"Nothing … just cramps, you know? Feeling like shit," I say, pulling a face and laying a hand over my stomach.

Jess sighs, deflating slightly but she pulls me into an unsteady hug, and says, "Fine. You go home. I'll call you in the morning."

I smile ruefully at her, wondering what kind of state she'll be in in the morning, whether she'll even be able to remember me leaving, promising to call. I pick up my discarded belongings; jacket, sweater, bag, and leave the house as unobtrusively as possible. No one else notices that I'm getting ready to leave, but that's the way I want it. I'm almost out the door when I hear Cole shout my name. He's at the top of the stairs, watching me go, but I just shake my head at him, pulling the door closed behind me as he calls my name again.

He catches up with me halfway down the road. Pulling on my arm and turning me towards him.

"Olivia. What's going on?" The rain is heavy and it's plastering his hair to his face, his t-shirt to his chest. I pull my jacket tighter round me, grateful for its warmth as I watch goosebumps rise on his bare arms in the glow of the streetlight.

"Nothing," I say, "I'm just not feeling good. Need to be in bed."

"I saw you with him," he says breathlessly, eyes dark in the night, boring into mine.

I shake my head, "It's not what you think, Cole," I say tightly, the words almost getting stuck in my throat.

"And what do I think, Olivia? You always seem to know better than me," Cole says, voice rising against the hammer of rain.

"It's just … he was … we're not –" I stammer, Cole's eyes widening in disbelief as I do so; I don't stammer.

"So, you're not cheating on me with Tyler Washington?" he demands, interrupting my ineffectual stream.

"No! No, I'm not. I promise." I begin to shiver and shake, pulling my arms tight against my chest. Cole takes a step back, looking at me like he doesn't believe me, like he doesn't know me. Something catches my attention out of the corner of my eye and I turn to look back at Jess's house. There's someone out on the porch, watching us.

Tyler.

Cole turns to look too, and realizing who it is, I hear him mutter, "Son of a bitch," at the same moment that I begin to walk hurriedly down the street, towards the woods, and back home.

"Olivia," Cole says again, this time more sharply, as he chases me down the street, spinning me around to face him, pulling me closer to him than I expected, his face bearing down on me so that I can taste the beer on his breath. "I saw you," he says harshly, "I saw you up there with him, so don't fucking lie to me, okay?"

"It's not what you think," I say again, but this just seems to frustrate him even more.

"What do I think, Olivia?" he roars, and I try to take a step back but he won't let me, hand gripping tight around my arm.

"He ..." I look back to the porch, where the outline of a figure still stands.

He's watching.

"He came on to me, okay? I was trying to get rid of him when you came upstairs."

"It didn't look like you were trying very hard," Cole says, the words like missiles going off inside my head.

I look down at his hand, knuckles white in the streetlight, gripping onto my arm, and something snaps because I spit out, "What, you mean like I'm not trying very hard to get away from you right now?"

Cole's eyes dart to mine, looking like I've electrocuted him, but he doesn't let go. At least not immediately. "I just want to go home, Cole," I say, "can we talk about this tomorrow instead?"

"Cole, man, just let it go, it was nothing," a voice says close to us and I jerk my head to see Tyler standing just a few feet behind Cole.

Cole's hand finally drops from my arm and he turns slowly to look at Tyler. He's perfectly still as he says, "You need to walk away Tyler. Right the fuck now."

I don't wait to hear Tyler's response. I don't want to see how any of this turns out. I turn on my heel and walk as quickly as I can down the street, heading home the fastest way possible, past the high school, and through the woods. They're both shouting my name as tarmac changes to gravel, and gravel to muddy earth beneath my feet, and I leave the streetlight-lit night behind and slip into the velvet darkness of the woods.

42

NOW

Karen found me in the bathroom at work on Tuesday morning, applying concealer to my under-eyes and the zits which had popped up along my jaw line, crawling their way down my neck like a stress-rash.

"Kitson," she said, in her usual brusque manner, as she emerged from a bathroom stall and began to wash her hands. I caught her eye in the mirror and she grimaced, "Something stressing you out, huh, Olivia? Now, what could that possibly be," she said lightly.

"Ha ha. You're starting to sound like my sister," I said.

"Speaking of your siblings. I went to see Ethan on Saturday". She let out a long, loud breath and shook her head, watching me closely in the mirror, "Wooooow, I was not prepared for how similar the two of you look. I'd seen photos of course, but seeing it in person is something else."

"Yeah," I said, "we get that a lot."

Karen shook her head again, dipping her hands under the air dryer and shouting over the noise of it blasting her hands dry to be heard, "He's a nice man, Olivia. He seems freakishly well adjusted for someone who's been in prison for a decade for a crime they didn't commit."

The dryer stopped abruptly and I nodded, "He's a better person than me, that's for sure." Karen furrowed her brow at me, and I scrambled to explain, "I see a therapist every week, am on three different types of medication, and still can't manage to get a good night's sleep. And there he is, in prison, with a smile on his face every time I see him. I just can't figure out why he isn't more angry, more bitter."

"Maybe he's just figured out that that doesn't serve him."

"Maybe," I said, raising my eyebrows at her response.

Karen cocked her head towards the door, indicating I should follow her, and we left the restroom together. "How's Reid getting on at home? You been in touch with her at all?"

Reid and I were in almost daily contact by that point, so I nodded and said, "Yeah, she's so much better. It's tough still, obviously, but she seems much more secure. She feels safe there."

"That's good. I have a feeling she's tougher than any of us are giving her credit for, but I'm still relieved to know she's being looked after."

"Hey, Daniel mentioned you'd found another medical examiner to give a second opinion on Asher's cause of death, right?"

Karen nodded, "Hayley Potter, yeah. We've used her before. Should be getting the results any day now."

"That's great," I said, "really great."

"Yeah, actually, I was thinking of having her look over Tyler Washington's autopsy report. It's starting to sound as if he might actually been attacked by more than one person, right? Like Asher."

"Yeah," I said, swallowing, "yeah, that's right."

"Well, I'll get her on it, then."

Kat called me later that day, when I was finally getting ready to leave work.

"Hey," I said, on picking up, shoving my phone in between my ear and shoulder as I stuffed some files into my bag and watched Daniel do the same from across the room.

"Hey, so we had like a billion downloads of the podcast today, and a listener has actually written in about the NDA Spencer signed," Kat said, her voice hushed but excited.

"What?"

"A woman emailed us about the NDA. Today's episode was the one with the mayor's interview recording, and then Spencer talking anonymously about the night Tyler died, and how she thinks Nick called the mayor to tell her Tyler was dead already."

"Okay," I said, my mind tired and sluggish, and not quite keeping up with Kat's breathless excitement.

"So, right at the end, Spencer says she'd signed an NDA with the mayor, and that she thinks the mayor might have tried the same approach with Nick and Cole et cetera. And now it's looking like this woman – whoever she is – might have signed one at some point too. I guess the mayor just hands them out like campaign buttons at this point."

I laughed, but it sounded hoarse and cracked, "Do you have any idea who it could be? The person who sent the email?" I was busy scrolling through the names of the girls I went to high school with, trying to figure out who this could possibly be. The name I kept ending up on was Jessica Heng, but after her interview with Kat on the podcast, I doubted she'd come forward with any more information, even anonymously.

"No. Ray thinks she set up the email address she's using just to contact us, but we're going to try and arrange a meeting with her."

"That's great, Kat. But …"

"What?" She sounded tinny and far away all of a sudden, and I thought about how much of my life was now marked by disembodied voices floating out of unremarkable speakers. Ethan's prison phone calls, constant updates from Kat and Ray, weekly podcast episodes. Daniel caught my eye from across the room, indicating that he was ready to leave and I nodded in response.

"I'm just wondering about the usefulness of another anonymous source at this point, that's all. If she's not willing to go on record, is this really going to help much?" I said.

"I know, and you're right, it probably wouldn't be all that useful. But I'm hoping we can convince her to go on record with her real name. Plus, we've got an interview scheduled with Detective Michelle Barnes for next week's episode too," Kat said.

Just then my phone elicited a few short beeps and I pulled it away from my ear to see who was calling me. "Kat, I'm gonna have to go," I said. "The mayor is calling me."

Kat issued me with a completely sincere 'good luck', and I switched calls to Maria Washington. "Mayor Washington," I said in my smoothest, most lawyer-like voice, "what can I do for you?" Daniel's head turned sharply towards me as I spoke and I motioned with my arms to indicate that I'd follow him out of the office.

There was a full, almost heavy silence for a second or two before the mayor spoke, and when she did every word was a bullet locked and loaded, her finger steady on the trigger as she spoke, "Ms Hall, I warned you to leave me out of this podcast. I am seriously contemplating taking out a cease and desist order."

"It's not my podcast, Mrs Washington. If you have a problem with its contents, it really would be better to take it up with either Kat Thomas, or Ray Mackenzie."

"They wouldn't be here if it wasn't for you, Olivia, and I want them gone." I was following Daniel through the halogen-lit hallways of our office building, lights blinking out in offices all around us, the stifling heat of the central heating system clinging to me. Still, the sound of her voice, rich and sonorous and yet sharp as a blade was able to take me right back to her home office. The full bookshelves, comfortable chairs, the forest green of the painted walls imitating the evergreen view outside her window.

"I don't know what to tell you, Mayor. If you really want to take out a cease and desist order, there's nothing I can do to stop you, but in all honesty I'm not sure it would deter Kat or Ray, and if you did then attempt to sue them, I can't imagine you'd ever win. Have they tried to talk to you anywhere other than at a public event?" I asked, referring to the aborted interview at the mayor's campaign event at Two Sails Brewery.

"You know they haven't," she said.

"Maybe you'd feel better about the whole thing if you just spoke to them," I said, "if you gave them your side of the story. It would give you an element of control over where the story takes them," I offered, knowing full well she wouldn't bite.

"What exactly do you take me for, Olivia? No, of course I'm not going to be recorded talking about the murder of my son on a two-bit podcast that's determined to besmirch his name even further."

Something in me snapped then and when I next spoke, my voice seemed to come out in a low, ragged rumble. Daniel turned to look at me in surprise in the elevator as we glided smoothly down to the underground parking lot. "You have a lot of nerve talking about besmirching people's names, Maria. That's all you and your family have ever tried to do to Ethan. And I know you know he didn't do it. He couldn't have. Because you were there, weren't you? You were there, in that forest, covering up for Nick Green as your son lay dead, and you know full well they'd already found his body before Ethan ever rode his bike through –"

Daniel suddenly snatched the phone out my hand, shaking his head as he pressed the end call button and stared down at me hard.

"What are you doing?" I practically shouted.

"That's not the way to do this, Olivia," he said. "You won't get anywhere with those kinds of accusations. You need to be methodical about it. Build up evidence, make a case, not give into the emotions of it."

I pulled my phone out of his grip just as the doors dinged

276

open, and I stalked out, leaving him trailing behind as I headed resolutely to my car.

"Shall I meet you at the restaurant?" he called after me.

"No," I said, not turning around as I threw my bag into the backseat of my car and opened the driver door. "I'm going home."

He didn't say anything, but he was only parked two cars over so I could still feel him watching me. "I'm beat," I said, finally looking over at him, "I just want an early night."

"Yeah, okay. That's probably for the best," he said, nodding along to his own words, agreeing with himself, and I had to clamp my jaw down to stop from saying something I might regret.

But I didn't go home. Instead I drove back out to Twin Rivers, arriving in my hometown just before eleven p.m. It was too late to book in to my usual B&B, so I pulled up into the forecourt of Kat and Ray's motel, the neon vacancy sign lit up in the night air. The receptionist handed over the keys after I'd handed over my credit card, and I parked in front of room eleven, the door wheezing open with a stale puff of air. It was a king room, brown carpet and brown comforter, with wooden siding. The most modern thing in the room was the flat-screen TV that sat propped on top of a dresser.

I hadn't told Kat yet that I was coming, so I sent her a What's App, half hoping that she'd reply saying she and Ray were just a few doors away, and to come right over. The room was lonely and cold, and I wondered why I had thought this was a good idea, why I wasn't at home, tucked up in my own bed, getting the sleep I so desperately needed.

I took a shower while I waited for Kat to reply, warming myself up, but when she still hadn't got back to me as I was toweling myself off, I instead climbed into the gym kit I kept in the trunk of my car and got into bed wearing too-tight leggings and a moisture-wicking t-shirt.

I woke up at two twenty in the morning, something about the

room, and being back in Twin Rivers shortening the length of my too-short sleep even further. There was a message from Kat on my phone, apologizing for her delay in replying, and telling me she and Ray would meet me for breakfast in town tomorrow. The lights in the motel car park glowed orange through the brown fabric of the drapes, and I watched, eyes heavy as every so often shadows passed across in time to the sound of a car going by. Eventually I got up, pulling socks and sneakers on, and grabbing my trench coat and car keys before locking up behind me and getting back into my car.

The motel was on the other side of town to my parents' old house. Driving away from the highway, and the further into the city I got, the quieter and quieter the streets became. It was gone three a.m. now, on a Tuesday night in October, the fact that it was Halloween the next day in evidence just about everywhere. The city was dripping with fake spiderwebs, bats flying across the windows of shops and cafes, and as I drove into my old neighborhood, driveways, paths, and porches were lined with pumpkins and gourds. I told myself I didn't know where I was going until I was stopped outside the high school, dark and ominous in the October night. The sound of the car door slamming shut behind me echoed through the air, and I checked my phone for battery, making sure I had enough charge to use the flashlight.

Concrete gave way to gravel under my sneakers as I walked past the school, and then to the mushy softness of mulched up autumn leaves as I left the track behind and walked into the woods. The weak beam of my cell phone flashlight was only able to show me what was right in front of me, while all around the trees shivered, the woods fluttered, and my heart set to hammering in my chest.

I remembered walking here as a teenager, feeling utterly beyond reproach, beyond fear, beyond anything that could reach out and catch me in the dark. Now though, the night sank deep into my bones, told me it was dangerous, told me I was foolish for being there. But I kept going.

It took me fifteen minutes to get out to the other side, streetlights greeting me on the street where I'd lived, their warm glow the color of home. Every single house was dark, not a single light on anywhere, not even a porch light. They were as decked out for Halloween as the rest of the city was; a huge spider clung to the driveway gates of one house, a ghost fell from the porch of another, and I wondered how different it would all feel tomorrow, on Halloween night, with children and teenagers ravaging the neighborhood, parties possibly going on somewhere until who knew when.

I stared at the blank windows of my old house and wondered again what I was doing there; it was one thing to wake up at two twenty a.m., it was another thing entirely to leave the comfort of your bed and skulk around other people's houses.

Shivering, I turned back to take the path through the woods again, back to my car, but it seemed to have got darker somehow. My eyes should have become better adjusted to the dark by then, but it was inching towards dawn, and the night was getting darker before letting the light back in. A breeze picked up, sending the leaves rustling and shivers down my arms and spine. I turned back towards the street and started to jog. It was a longer way back to my car, but if I ran it wouldn't feel half as bad. And besides, I was already wearing exercise clothes.

I was breathing heavily but steadily by the time I turned onto 10th Street, which cut a line through Twin Rivers and was one of the busiest streets in the city. A car drove past me and I started, the slow, gentle whoosh of it beside me making me jump. I concentrated on the sound of my feet on the sidewalk, the steady beat, the in and out of my long breaths, staring dead ahead of me as I did so. I did this every day at home in Portland. It wasn't so different to be doing it out here, was it? But then I heard another car coming up behind me. The engine slowed, and my heartbeat picked up as I increased my speed. But it's not as if I could outrun a car – even a slowly rolling one – and

I forced myself to turn and look, facing it head on. The face I saw peering out across the empty passenger seat and right at me made me stumble, feet tripping up over each other, as I pulled up short. Nick's eyes widened in recognition and, after idling at the sidewalk for what felt like forever with our eyes locked on one another, he gunned the engine and sped off down the street.

I was exhausted by the time I joined Kat and Ray at their table in a café right in the center of the city. Ever Greens was a vegetarian place with a vast chalkboard behind the counter and a daily rotating menu of seasonal specials. They also sold avocado toast.

"God," Kat said as I sat down, and I swear she actually winced as she looked at me, "have you slept at all?"

"Doesn't feel like it," I said dully.

"Well, you sound a lot better," Ray pointed out optimistically, "no more cold?"

"No, that's true. No more cold."

Kat leaned toward me, concern creasing the non-existent lines of her face, "Are you okay? Should you even be here?"

I'd called Karen at eight that morning, telling her I needed to take a few personal days. She'd been surprisingly cool about it, but she'd also warned me not to work too hard, somehow knowing, without me even needing to tell her, that I was in Twin Rivers.

I waved away Kat's concern, telling her I was fine, just as a waitress appeared to take our orders. I was starving, but couldn't think of a single thing I wanted to eat, so I ordered a coffee to get me started and listened as Kat and Ray gave their orders for a breakfast bowl and golden beet queen bowl respectively.

My coffee came quickly, and I sucked it down frantically. When I looked up, Kat and Ray were staring at me. "Stop it, I'm fine, really. Just tell me about the email. Do you have the name of whoever sent it yet?"

"Not yet, but she says she's the same age as Spencer, same grade. Says she knows her. You got any ideas?"

I twisted my face up, trying to think of a face, a name, "Could be anyone," I said, eventually with a shake of my head.

Kat cocked an eyebrow at me and said, "Olivia is there a chance you were a little self-involved in high school?"

"There's a strong chance of that, yes," I said smiling, because I could tell she was teasing. Their food arrived and I took the opportunity to order the same thing as Kat; I was unable to make even small, everyday decisions. The waitress gone, I proceeded to tell them about my late night/early morning jog, and Nick Green's appearance in it, as well as the reason for me even being there – my most recent phone call with the mayor.

"I don't know why I should be surprised by any of this, but I am a bit," Kat said, wiping her hands on a napkin, "doesn't it feel a little desperate? Like, shouldn't she know not to reach out to you like that? And why *you*, anyway? I'm almost offended she doesn't think she should be threatened by me and Ray."

"I'm a known quantity, I guess," I said, digging into my food, which had just been delivered.

"We have to figure out a way to get to her and Nick," Kat said in a low voice, once again leaning forward against the table, giving everything a conspiratorial air. "It all boils down to those two, I can feel it. It's like we've been unraveling this giant ball of yarn, and we've finally got down to the last few strands, but they're so knotted up together, I can't untie it yet, but I know we can. I know it."

"I'm not sure that's how yarn works," Ray said, but Kat just gave him a look and he smirked in response.

"Maybe I should just go over there," I said with a shrug.

"To her home?" Kat said, frowning.

"Or her office, maybe? She seems to spend more time there than anywhere."

"Nick would be there though," Kat pointed out. "He'll just stop us getting anywhere near her again."

"True, but didn't someone you interviewed on the podcast at the rally say she held regular office hours or something? Like a civic clinic or something?" I said, spearing a cube of roasted sweet potato with my fork.

"Yes, yes, you're right," Ray said, eyes widening as he wiped his hands on his jeans and opened up the browser on his phone. "Ah!" he exclaimed, the excited squeal eliciting a smile from both me and Kat, "She's holding one today. Brilliant."

"Today? Seriously?" Kat said, looking bemused, "it's Halloween, is she insane?"

"They're held every Wednesday it says here, look," Ray said, passing the phone under Kat's eyes.

"Well, that's pretty ideal," Kat admitted, "good idea, Olivia. What will you say to her though?" Her eyebrows pulled together in heavy thought, and I picked up my cup of coffee. The truth was, I had no idea what I was going to say to her, I just had a feeling that she was feeling rattled, and where was the harm in rattling her a little more?

43

THEN

My phone is ringing. Over and over and over again, vibrating so hard it's about to shake its way off the bathroom vanity. Tyler pulls his hand away from me, takes a step back, finally putting some air between us, letting the breath back into my lungs.

He picks up my phone and looks back over at me, eyes huge and dark in the dimly lit bathroom. Only the old school bulb lights above Jessica's mirror are on.

"Cole," Tyler says with a rasping breath. "Again. Does he ever let up?"

I swallow, take a deep breath, try to even it out, because it sounds ragged, even to me. I don't want it to. Not right now.

The knot in my abdomen has doubled, tripled, quadrupled up on itself and rests heavily against my pelvis. I look at Tyler, who's looking at me with hooded eyes, and a wicked little grin on his face, and I close my eyes before opening them again slowly.

"Liv!" The shout is coming from the stairs, and is quickly followed by the sound of footfalls.

I reach for the door handle, just as Tyler reaches for it, sliding his eyes towards me as the rough skin of his hands grazes mine, that shit-eater of a grin still plastered on his face. I push him away with my elbow and he staggers just a little, as I say lowly, "Tyler, don't," and then push the door open.

I was hoping Cole wouldn't have reached Jess's bedroom yet, but there he is, pulling up short as he watches me and Tyler stumble out of Jess's bathroom.

"Liv," Cole says heavily, his gaze flicking between me and Tyler. "What's going on?"

"Nothing," I say in a rush, "we were just talking." But when I look over at Tyler, hoping he'll back me up, all I see is him standing louche against the doorway to the bathroom, backlit and glowing, hands stuffed into his pockets, rocking back and forth on his heels. That grin's still there, and my stomach flips, twists, doubles over.

"What the fuck?" Cole says again, and this time there's a tear, a rip in his voice.

"Cole, it's not what you think," I say slowly, walking towards him with a hand up, ready to press it softly against his chest.

But he brushes it and me aside, not looking at me, staring at Tyler, "Oh, yeah? And what do I think Olivia? Is it the same thing I thought when I saw you both coming out of Tyler's room after prom?"

I grab at his arm, trying to pull him back to me, but all my words have left me because I didn't know he'd seen us then. I try to speak, but there's nothing there. I don't know how to say those words out loud. "What?" Cole says softly, looking down into my eyes, "Can't talk your way out of this one, huh Liv? What's everyone going to think of you, now that I get to tell them what a fucking whore you are?"

My hand drops from his arm, and I think about explaining, trying to explain, to get him back to me, but I'm so tired. "I'm going," I say shortly.

My eyes flick to Tyler, still in the bathroom doorway, and he flips me another grin, holding up my phone and tossing it to me

284

as he says, "You'll be needing this." His voice betrays nothing but his own ease in the world.

I'm halfway down the stairs when I hear Cole's resigned voice shout, "Liv, wait!"

And then Tyler's voice, an audible shrug, "Oh, let her go, Sampson, she's not worth it."

44

NOW

The 'citizens' surgery' as it was dubbed, wasn't held in the mayor's office, as I'd initially assumed, but at the community center by the river which had a large adventure playground right outside it. Normally I would've expected to find it covered in children and milling parents, but today, for some reason it was bare. It might have had something to do with the rain that hadn't let up since early morning, but those empty swings moving in the wind, and ghostly, gently rotating merry-go-round pricked at me.

Inside, chairs were set up in rows, as if this was a community theater production, with a long trestle table at the front. If anything, it reminded me of a press briefing, but the 'citizens' were all waiting patiently for their turn, and then going up to speak to the mayor in quiet tones. I gave my name to a roving assistant – although actually, I gave Karen's name, because I was sure the mayor would turn me away upon hearing my name, and Karen's was the that came to mind.

Upwards of an hour had passed by the time my name was called, and I watched as Mayor Washington's posture stiffened as I walked toward her, and her cold stare roved disapprovingly from me to her assistant. They conferred in whispers for a second before the assistant shot me a hurt, betrayed look and I just shrugged.

Standing in front of them now I said, "I knew you wouldn't see me if I gave my real name."

"From what I understand, you don't even go by your real name these days anyway, so what else should we have expected," the mayor said. "You are a natural deceiver, Olivia Hall."

My heartbeat picked up at her words, blood thrumming at my ears, "Bit rich, don't you think?" I asked.

I could feel the excited energy radiating off the still hovering assistant beside me, her gaze ping ponging between me and her boss as though she were at the US Open. Clearly the mayor could too, because instead of answering me, she merely said in the same, smooth tone as always, "Natalie, could you go and see to anyone else who's still waiting, please?"

"Why are you here, Olivia?" the mayor said once her assistant had dutifully disappeared. Her voice and manner were resigned. I'd thought I'd find her rattled, worried, but rather all she seemed was exhausted.

"I think we should talk. Properly this time. I think things are happening that neither one of us has control over, and I think it would be in your best interest to sit down and properly think about where all this might lead for you."

"Let me ask you a question Olivia Hall. Do you really think I could have run again for mayor four years ago, if there was even an ounce of truth to the accusations that are being aired on your tawdry little podcast? Do you know how brutal political opposition research is? It's tantamount to a public flaying of your private, personal life."

"I can think of more than one politician who's been voted into public office while covering up much worse. Or at least, just as bad."

"Yes, but they're men," she said brusquely. I thought she was going to leave it at that, as airy and dismissive as ever, but instead her face began to stretch and contort as she chewed on her bottom lip and stared up at me. "You can accuse me of using my son's death for my political gain ... I can accept that accusation, because on some level it is a correct assumption, and I have lain awake at night, being eaten alive with the guilt of it. But I assure you, Olivia, I did not aid in any kind of cover up of the true killer of my son. I have always believed your brother to be guilty."

Her worked up candidness took me aback, and I didn't have time to think of a retort before she dismissed me by standing up from her chair, and addressing those still left seated in the audience, by asking who was next.

I contemplated driving back to the motel to dry off, but the thought of that sad, dingy room which, despite being a non-smoking room, still managed to smell like the memory of a thousand smoked cigarettes, felt too desolate to contemplate. So, I headed to my favorite coffee shop, shaking water from me like an enthusiastic Labrador as I closed the door behind me. The large windows had misted up with condensation, and from the outside I hadn't been able to tell just how much they'd decorated for Halloween. The usually minimalist space had been transformed into a Halloween orgy of orange, black, and purple, and every one of the baristas was wearing a pointed witch's hat. I ordered a flat white and settled in at an empty table. I was about to get to some work emails when I realized that someone was hovering over the empty seat opposite me.

I looked up to see Morgan.

"Hi ..." I said, blinking stupidly at her. And then, "Wow," because there was absolutely no mistaking now that Morgan was pregnant.

"Oh, yeah, she really 'popped', didn't she?" she said, her hands leaping to her own belly, and cradling it affectionately in confirmation that she was referring to her unborn child.

"Oh," I said, swallowing hard, "you're having a girl, huh?"

288

"Oh, I don't actually know yet, I just really feel like she's a she, you know?" I absolutely did not know, but I nodded at her, as if I did. "Mind if I join you? Need to take a load off." she said, smiling happily at me.

"Um, sure," I said, trying to figure out exactly what was going on. Morgan had been on the podcast a few times of course, but she'd been dealing directly with Kat and Ray. We'd barely exchanged a word on my return trips to Twin Rivers, but now here she was, chummily asking to share my table with me.

"I hear you went to the citizens' surgery," she said, once she was settled in her chair.

"Yes," I said slowly, "I did."

"I had to drop something off for Mom, and her assistant told me all about it," she said in a hush-hush tone.

"Right," I said, still trying to figure out where all this was going.

"She was doing that thing where she's so mad, she can't even speak. It was like her jaw was glued stuck. Her assistant had to close the clinic down early. What did you even say to her?"

"I told her I wanted to talk to her about what really happened the night your brother died," I said.

"What do you mean, what really happened? We all know what happened," Morgan said roundly, reaching for her mug of herbal tea, and taking a small, deliberate sip.

"Oh, come on Morgan. Quit being so disingenuous. You know I don't believe Ethan killed your brother. What was Cole's reaction when he heard Kat's anonymous source talking about how he and Nick actually found Tyler the night of Jessica's party, rather than the morning after?" I asked, keeping my voice as low and slow as possible.

"Cole?" she said, and it was the first time I noticed her supposedly sweet, affable attitude toward me change in even the slightest. And I mean the slightest. She jerked away from me a little, her body stiffening practically infinitesimally, her eyes narrowing for the merest second. "Cole doesn't listen to the podcast."

"He doesn't?" I asked.

"No. And anyway, they're lying. Whoever they are, they're lying. If they were telling the truth they would've given their name, right? They'd have nothing to hide?"

"They didn't give their name, because they claim to be too scared of your mother, Morgan. Your mother and your boyfriend," I said.

"Ha!" Morgan let out nervously, staring around at the room, as her outburst shot through the otherwise quiet coffee shop.

"Doesn't that worry you?" I asked, before staring pointedly down at where the table hid her growing baby bump.

"I know what you're doing, Olivia, don't think that I don't, okay?" Morgan said, suddenly sharp, and I raised my eyebrows at her. "You're being really shitty right now, okay, and I haven't done anything to you, not really."

"Cast your mind back to ten years ago, Morgan, you might come to a different conclusion."

"My brother was dead," she hissed at me, eyes narrowed and fixed on mine, "he'd just been murdered, okay? How was I supposed to act toward you, you tell me?"

Someone pushed the door open, letting the outside in for a second, and I let her question hang in the blast of cold, October air for a beat or two before answering. "You're right," I said eventually, relenting. "I'm sorry. It was a rough time."

"Yeah, for all of us. You know, I always figured, that out of everyone, we had the most in common, could relate to each other the most. We'd both lost our brothers, right? But you didn't even try, Olivia. You didn't even try to understand what I was going through or where I was coming from. It was all about Ethan for you, the wrong that had supposedly been done to him. Well, it wasn't your brother's body they found lying in the woods that morning, it was mine. And you didn't even have the decency to send me a fucking text. Pick up the phone. We were friends. I was your captain, but no. All of that went to shit. I would have

290

found a way to understand where you were coming from if you'd just tried, even a little. If you'd come to the funeral. Sent flowers, a card. *Anything*. Because you were friends with him too, Olivia, and he died. He. *Died*. But no. It was all about you and your brother, wasn't it? I don't think you gave even a second's thought to what I was going through."

I'd never seen Morgan like this. Emotional. Indignant. Righteous. Right. I leaned back in my chair and took a few deep breaths, holding her gaze as I did so, wondering if I was allowing my surprise to be seen all over my face. "You're right," I said at last. "I didn't really think about you and what you were going through." Morgan issued a self-satisfied sound and began to wriggle around in her chair a little. "Are you okay? Is the baby …?"

"She's fine," she said shortly, "these chairs are just really fucking uncomfortable."

I raised my eyebrows. That was two 'fucking's in just over two minutes which was highly unusual for Morgan. Choosing to ignore it, I said, "Do you really think I would've been welcome at that funeral?" and Morgan finally broke away from my gaze to reluctantly stare around the room again. Her mouth moved into a sulk and she heaved a heavy sigh, before eventually shaking her head.

"Maybe not. I just really wished you'd tried, Liv. We were friends. Weren't we?"

I nodded, "Of course we were."

"So, didn't you care at all that I'd lost my brother?" she asked. It came out as a soft whisper, breaking on the word 'brother', and I wondered if she might be about to break down in tears. Somehow it was so much worse than if she'd shouted the words at me.

"I'm sorry. You're right – it just became all about Ethan for me, about saving him. I went into survivor mode."

She let out a small harrumph again, her hands fiddling with the string of her teabag, hanging over the side of her ceramic cup. "But Ethan wasn't arrested until almost a week after Tyler died, Olivia. And I didn't hear from you once."

The coffee shop was already unnaturally hushed, considering how many people were in there, but when she said that it was as if the whole world had been put on mute, I rushed to remember if that was really true. Did I not even send her a single text?

"I'm … I'm sorry, I honestly don't know what to say. I guess I didn't know what to say then, either."

Morgan's face hardened, just by a fraction, and she shook her head stiffly at me before saying, "You always knew what to say, Olivia. It was like, your gift."

"It's not as if any of us had been in that situation before though. We were just kids."

Morgan shrugged, and I felt dismissed all of a sudden. "Well. It was a long time ago now," she said, a little primly.

"I really am sorry, Morgan. I wish I'd dealt with everything differently back then," I said, watching as her eyes slid back towards me and she nodded a little in recognition. "I've been meaning to ask you a question though, if that's okay?"

Morgan's eyebrows pinched together as she said, "Yeah..?"

"Where were you that night of the party? I don't remember you being there, but I was just wondering where you were instead. I feel like you should have been there."

"I was at Veronica Butler's house, you remember her? I was going to go to Jessica's party but then Tyler and I exchanged words, nothing serious, and I decided to go to Veronica's instead," Morgan said.

"What did you and Tyler argue about?" I asked.

"I honestly can't remember, I just remember that he was being really super annoying and I decided I'd rather not spend the whole evening with him."

"Had he taken something?" I asked and Morgan shrugged again.

"I don't know. Maybe?"

"It seems weird you can't remember what you argued about that night considering it was the last time you ever saw him," I said.

"Maybe, but it's not like it was particularly unusual for us to be arguing about something or other, and it's not as if I knew at the time that he was going to die later, is it?" Morgan demanded.

I waited a second before answering, letting the question lie between us for a few beats before leaning forward and saying ever so quietly, "Morgan, are you sure you can't remember what you argued about, or do you just not want to tell me?"

Morgan closed her eyes, maybe hoping that once she opened them again, I'd be gone. She had no such luck though, as I was still determinedly staring at her when she reopened them a few seconds later. "Nick had been texting all day, that's what we were arguing about."

"Nick," I said. "Why, though? Was there ... something going on between the two of you?"

Morgan gave me a look that seemed to say *give me some credit*, and shook her head. "It was about the money. The three thousand dollars. He was trying to get me to pay it, to cover for Tyler."

"So, you knew? This whole time? That Tyler owed Nick money back then?"

"Don't look at me like that, Liv. You knew too, and never told anyone," Morgan said with a small pout.

"I told the fucking police, Morgan," I hissed at her, "they just didn't do anything about it. Did you ever mention it when you spoke to the police at all?" Morgan shook her head again, this time having the decency to look a little guilty as she did so. "Why not?" I asked. My voice was louder than I'd intended, and Morgan exchanged a look of alarm with the person sitting at the next table. She shifted in her seat, smiling pleasantly at the man with the handsomely greying beard and cowl neck sweater before answering me.

"My mom said she dealt with it," she said, practically through gritted teeth.

"Your mom," I said dully, watching as Morgan nodded her head. "So, she definitely knew about the money?"

"Yeah, of course," Morgan answered, although it sounded to me as though her voice was coming at me from a long way off.

"How?" I asked, "Did she know before Tyler died, or after?"

"I ... I don't know, actually," Morgan said. "What does it matter?"

"Because she's claiming she didn't know your brother was dead until the police told her the next morning, but we think Nick called her the night Tyler was killed."

"And you think that's when he told her about the money?" Morgan asked.

"Yes."

Morgan didn't speak for a while, but I felt as though something may have shifted slightly when she said, "Nick and my mom, they have kind of a ... weird relationship."

"You mean, like ... romantic?" I asked skeptically, trying to imagine it, and thankfully, failing.

"No! God no," Morgan said, visibly sickened by the suggestion, "nothing like that. It's just very ... ugh, I don't know how to describe it. They're close, but they don't actually like each other. It's very 'you scratch my back, I'll scratch yours', you know?"

"How well do you know Nick these days?" I asked, assuming that they would be pretty close considering he worked with her mom, and was best friends with her boyfriend. Surely, he was still practically part of the family? But Morgan took a long time to answer, and when she did, the answer surprised me as much as the pause did.

"Not well at all," she said at last, and it sounded like the words had been dragged out of her against her will.

"You don't spend much time with him and Cole, then?" I asked.

"No ... I mean, yes, I do, I suppose. But I don't know him. When I moved back home, and started dating Cole, I kind of just assumed it would be how it had always been, you know? And in a way, it was. We hung out together all the time – we still do. But it's not the same. There's this … thing, and I don't know how to describe it, except maybe it's just that Tyler isn't there anymore. You know Nick has nothing to do with his parents now? His dad died two years ago and he didn't even go to the funeral. He paid for it, but he didn't go. I just think there's something broken about him."

"What does Cole think about all this?" I asked.

"Oh, Cole won't talk about any of this with me. And they don't talk about any of it together, that's for sure. I once suggested to Cole that he and Nick talk about Tyler more – or you know, *at all*, and he completely lost his mind."

"What did he do?" I asked.

"He almost drove the car off the side of the road, I swear to God. We were coming home from somewhere, I can't remember where, but it was like this thing had just come over him, and he almost lost control of the car. It was pretty scary, to be honest."

"And that was all because you mentioned talking about Tyler?"

Morgan shifted in her seat again, and slid her gaze away from mine. I could tell she was chewing on the inside of her cheek. It was something she used to do when we were younger, a tell she had when she realized she'd said the wrong thing, or accidentally blurted out something someone or other had asked her to keep a secret. Morgan was a terrible secret keeper.

"I don't know," she said, waving her hand in an upwards direction, brushing her remarks away. "He'd probably been drinking, it probably had nothing to do with Tyler at all."

I raised my eyebrows at her, but she was determinedly not looking at me. "Morgan," I said in as quiet a voice as possible, like I was trying not to startle a skittish animal. "Morgan, did you know that Cole and Nick found Tyler's body that night?"

I watched as her eyes filled slowly with tears, but they didn't spill. Not even as she silently shook her head at me. "You listened to the podcast, right? When Spencer told Kat about what actually happened?"

"That was Spencer?" Morgan gasped. I nodded as Morgan continued to chew on the inside of her cheek before saying, "I thought it might be. I don't know why, I just really felt like it was Spencer."

"I shouldn't have told you, but I doubt it matters you know," I said. Kat probably wouldn't say the same, but she wasn't here, and hopefully would never know. "Morgan, what if … what if, Cole and Nick didn't just *find* Tyler's body that night?" I suggested.

Morgan's eyes widened, and I watched as one tear slipped out and slid down the side of her face. Her mouth was pulled into a rigid line, jaw as tight as a fist, skin pale and taut. I reached a hand across the table and touched her forearm. She flinched ever so slightly, but then relaxed and met my gaze again. "Morgan," I said, my voice low and calm, the same soothing voice I might have used with Reid, "we have to consider every possibility here. Don't we?"

"I don't … no, I can't. No, it's just not possible," she said, practically gasping the words out.

I stared at her, willing her to go where I was taking her, and then flickered my gaze at her stomach. "But what if …" I said, my voice trailing off, not quite able to give voice to the words, eyes still trained on her growing stomach.

Her hands instinctively went to cover it, and she shot me a look of pure horror. The coffee shop around us seemed to have taken on a different atmosphere. It was almost uncanny, somehow; the everyday noises, the low, background chatter, the warmth of the lighting lending everything a honey yellow glow. And there I was intimating that the father of her child might have had something to do with the death of her brother.

Morgan licked her lips, tried to control her breathing which had turned sharp and ragged. I reached across to her again, taking her hand, "Morgan, are you okay?" I said, watching as she closed her eyes, took a deep breath, and slowly nodded her head.

"I'm fine, I'm fine," she said, almost mantra-like.

"You want some water?" I asked, getting up to retrieve some from the counter when she silently nodded.

When I got back to the table, she'd opened her eyes again and her breathing seemed to have returned to normal. She took the cold glass of water, condensation misting up its sides, and gulped it down greedily. I almost expected her to smack her lips when she was done. Instead she said nothing, and I was forced to ask, "Have you ever wondered at all about Nick? Or Cole? About what they might or might not know about Tyler?"

"I've wondered about Nick, of course," she admitted. "I knew about the money, and then when he started working for my mom, it was all so … shady. But Cole? No, no, I can't think that. I can't go there."

"You know," I said slowly, "if anyone knows anything about Nick, and that night, it would be your mom."

"Really?" Morgan said, raising her eyebrows as she rubbed her stomach in soothing, concentric circles.

"Don't you think?" I asked.

"Yeah, yeah. I guess you're right," she admitted.

"Don't you want to know if she really knew about Tyler's murder before the police told her?"

"You mean, like Spencer said on the podcast?"

"Yeah. Spencer didn't stick around long enough to know for sure if your mom turned up, but if I were you, I'd want to know."

Morgan nodded thoughtfully, and then looked up at me suddenly, eyes squinting, "What do you mean, if you were me? Don't act like you're not desperate to know too, Olivia."

"Well, yeah, of course," I conceded, "but she's your mom. He was your brother." I was about to add, *'and Cole's your boyfriend,'* before deciding that Cole was the wrong button to push here.

"I suppose you're right," Morgan said, still nodding thoughtfully. "I've actually tried to convince her to speak to Kat, to go on the podcast, but that was before Spencer spoke to them, and said what she said. She'd never agree to go on it now."

"But isn't it more important now than ever? She's less than a week away from her election, and there's people out there saying she might have been involved in some way with her own son's death. Surely, she should want to address that. Even if it's not on the podcast."

"Involved with her son's death?" Morgan said, staring at me, and I inwardly cursed at my choice of words.

"Sorry, I misspoke. I don't mean that she was involved in his actual death, just that she might have … I don't know, that she might know more than she says she knows?"

Morgan didn't say anything again for a while, and I was worried that I'd lost her. "I don't know, Olivia. I just don't think my mom would be capable of keeping a secret like that. Not when it came to Tyler."

"But don't you want to know for sure?" I asked. "Just talk to her about it. You don't have to mention the podcast, or anything. Just see what she says, when you ask her what really happened the night Tyler was killed."

"And then what?" she said bluntly, "Go on the podcast and tell Kat all about it?"

"No, no, not if you don't want to. Look, I know the podcast has brought a lot of shit to the surface, but what this is really about is your brother, and mine. You're right: we do have the most in common, because we have the most to lose. So, if you talk to your mom, and you feel like you want to share it with the world, then sure, go ahead and go back on the podcast. But look, Kat's not here, and she doesn't even have to know I spoke to you today, if you don't want her to. So, you can just find out what you need to find out for yourself, and leave it at that. If that's what you're most comfortable with."

She was nodding her head slowly again, but her eyes had a far-off look I couldn't quite decipher. "Morgan? You okay?" I said, prompting her to stare back at me.

"Yeah. I'm okay. I'll … I'll talk to her tonight," she said.

"You will?" I asked, unable to hide my surprise. This was the outcome I'd been hoping for of course, but I was still a little shocked to have gotten through to her.

"Yeah. You're right. I want to know what she knows. And for how long she's known it," Morgan said. She had started rubbing her stomach again, her hands moving round and round and round. It was meant to be soothing, comforting. But in that moment it struck me more as obsessive.

45

THEN

My abdomen clenches and unclenches, clenches and unclenches, clenches and unclenches again and again. Leaning my head back against the cool wall of Jess's living room I take a deep, steadying breath before bringing my beer bottle up to meet my lips and taking a long swig. It won't help with the pain that's starting to radiate from deep within my abdomen out towards my hip bones, down into my pelvis and straight towards my knees; in fact, it'll probably make it worse, but the cool rim of the bottle pressing against my lips and the slightly sour but refreshing taste traveling down my throat calms me.

Everywhere I look people are enjoying themselves. Summer's almost over and we'll all – or at least most of us – be leaving soon, and the knowledge of that sets the party on edge a little, making everyone a little more hysterical, a little more drunk, a little more high, than usual. I wish I wasn't about to get my period, so I could enjoy it properly, but just then there's a deep, pulsing pain that tells me I need to get to the bathroom *right now*. I don't bother searching for my bag; I know there'll be tampons in Jess's bathroom, so I put my beer down and jog up the stairs, taking them two at a time.

I'm in there longer than I really need to be, relishing the quiet, the space, the time to think. But I know I've been there too long when I hear the door to Jess's room being pushed open and I go to open the bathroom door, assuming it's Jess. But to my surprise it's two male voices I hear, and something stops me from opening the door.

"Woah there, Nick," Tyler says, laughing, "what's going on here? What the fuck's got into you?"

"I need the money now Ty, I'm not kidding," I hear Nick say, strain and stress leaking from his voice.

Tyler laughs again and I hear bed springs. He must've sat down. "I'll get it to you, don't worry about it. You know I'm good for it, for fuck's sake." His voice is light and confident as always. Striding through the world on a cloud of self-assurance.

"Do I know that?" Nick demands, "because you haven't paid me in months, man, *months*, and I've been covering you so that I don't get my dick chopped off or whatever, but you're leaving next week, and I need you to pay the fuck up."

"You'll get it, brother," Tyler says, and I hear bed springs again.

"Don't 'brother' me, Ty, don't do it, I'm serious. I need the fucking money."

"Chill, dude, it's what a grand? We're all good. I've got you," Tyler says.

There's a beat where all I can hear is my own breathing as I press my ear up against the bathroom door, and for half a second I wonder if they've realized they're not alone. Tyler owes Nick a thousand dollars? But then Nick says, "It's not a grand, Ty, it's more like three, and if it's so easy for you to get it, why don't you fucking just get it and pay me back." His voice is tight, controlled, and I wonder how long he's been holding this in, how long he's waited to let this all out. "I'm out here doing everything I can just to afford community fucking college, and meanwhile you're fucking off to California next week, leaving me with three grands' worth of debt I'll never be able to pay, waiting to see if someone's gonna stop by to help me get rid of my kneecaps."

Tyler laughs, "Sorry man, but don't you think you're being a little dramatic? This isn't *The Sopranos*."

"People care about whether or not they get their money back, Tyler, whether or not they get paid. Maybe you don't understand that because Mommy and Daddy have always been there with a couple hundred bucks to hand over to you whenever you fucking ask for it, but for most people, getting paid is kind of a serious fucking deal," Nick says.

Tyler lets out another laugh, but this one sounds different, forced. I wish I could see his face, wish I could see Nick's too because I've never heard either of them talk this way before. They're as tight as can be; Tyler, Nick, and Cole have been friends since seventh grade, and I've seen them all lay into one another before, but never like this. I know from Cole that Tyler's developed a nasty little habit over the past few years. Not just party drugs, but steroids to keep him pumped up, Adderall or Ritalin to keep him going, and pretty much anything to bring him back down again when he's about to crash. I also know – just like everyone else at school – that the person to go to for such things is Nick Green, but I had no idea that by the sounds of things, Tyler hadn't been *paying*, and that he now owes him three thousand dollars. The amount winds me, it's so big: I've never even contemplated that amount of money in my life, let alone spent it, and owed it to somebody. Soon enough I'll have student loans, and student debt, just like everybody else, but right now money is the small amounts I earn from summer jobs, and the monthly allowance from my parents.

"Okay, okay, man," Tyler says eventually, his voice finally more serious. "I hear you, okay? I've got you, Nick. We'll sort this all out tomorrow. Nothing we can do about it now."

"Tonight, Ty," Nick says, his voice still tight and stretched. "I've got people to pay."

"What d'you expect me to do about it tonight, Nick?" Tyler says, sounding exasperated.

"Why don't you go home to your piggy bank, crack it open and give me everything you've got in there?" Nick says slowly.

Tyler laughs again, "Yeah, okay, I'll do that," but even I can tell through the bathroom door that he doesn't mean it. He's back to nothing-can-touch-me-Tyler, and this seems to send Nick over the edge.

"I mean it, Tyler. Tonight. Or we've got problems."

There's the sound of feet walking away, the door closing softly and then nothing. I hold my breath, hoping they've both gone, but waiting a little longer just in case. But just then my phone goes off; Cole. I've been gone too long from the party and now he's suspicious.

"Who's in there?" someone barks through the door, and I unlock it, pulling it open to reveal Tyler Washington.

46

NOW

I spent the evening with Kat and Ray having dinner at Kevin's. I was in high spirits all night, vibrating at a higher frequency than usual, the energy and urgency brought on by having convinced Morgan to talk to her mom. I kept my promise to Morgan though, and didn't say a word to Kat, putting my elevated mood down to too much Halloween candy.

But all that disappeared when I got back to the motel. Ray had stayed at Kevin's, and Kat had driven the two of us back, pulling up in front of her room, which was several doors away from mine. I said good night to her, waving her away into her room and laughing off her good natured teasing about my good mood. The walk to my own room was just several short paces, but the night was dark, pools of orange street light and flickering halogens above guest room doors my only guide.

I didn't see him until he said my name, and then suddenly there he was.

Cole.

He was getting out of a car, striding over to me. A face like thunder, eyes like two strobes of lightning in the dark night.

"What the fuck are you playing at, Olivia?" he said. It was a shout hidden inside a whisper, his voice low and quiet, masking the anger I could feel vibrating off him.

"Cole," I said, putting out a hand as if to stop him coming any closer. "What are you doing here?"

"What are *you* doing here, Liv? What the fuck are you doing here? You've got my girlfriend about to ask her mom if she covered up the death of her brother in any way, and you're asking me what I'm doing here? Are you out of your fucking mind?"

I looked behind me, checking to see if Kat was still there, stood outside her motel room, fumbling with her keys, even though I knew she wasn't.

We were alone.

"Cole, calm down."

"Calm down? Calm down? You're telling me to calm down." He lifted his arms to the sky, as if in prayer, or more likely in resignation, and barked out his laughter. "What do you think you're doing, Liv? Do you have any idea how dangerous this all is? Or has your narcissism got to the point where you actually think you're bullet proof?"

"Narcissism?" I said, "what are you even talking about?"

"You really think you're above it all, don't you? Untouchable. Well, this little podcast won't protect you for long. Not anymore, not the way you're headed."

His eyes were clamped down on mine. The features of his face had solidified in the shadowy lighting, and I was forcefully, inevitably reminded of the night Tyler died. It had been raining then too and Cole had stood over me, rainwater slipping into his eyes, soaking him to his skin, hands pressed into my upper arms. All I'd wanted then was to run away.

I wanted to do the same now.

"I don't know what you're talking about, Cole. If anyone here thinks they're above it all, it's the Washingtons," I said, and despite everything my voice sounded clear and certain through the thundering rain.

Cole shook his head at me, but his eyes still burned into mine. "You're not this clueless, I know you're not, Liv. Just get in your car, and drive home to Portland, okay? Because you're right, okay, you're totally right. The Washingtons, the mayor. These are not people you want to be messing around with. Just get out of here, and leave all this alone."

"Is that a threat, Cole?" I asked, while taking a step toward him. Shock flashed across his face, before being wiped away again almost instantly.

"A threat?" he said, through another bark of laughter. "No, it's not a fucking threat, it's just the truth."

"What do you know that I don't?" I asked. This wasn't the Cole I knew. The Cole I'd grown up with, and been in love with. At least I didn't think so.

"What do I know?" he said, throwing his hands up in despair again, "You're kidding me, right? You're the one with the freakin' investigative podcast here, Olivia. Why don't you tell me what you know." His voice had turned rich with scathing, a hard knife cutting through something soft and smooth with terrifying ease.

"Oh, don't give me that. You're having a baby with the mayor's daughter, and you were best friends with her son. You're right there in the mix with them, aren't you Cole? You and Nick. That's what this is about. You've cashed all your chips in with them, and now you're worried the house is finally going to lose."

"Well, that's a lovely little metaphor there, Olivia, but if anyone should be worried about losing, I think it's you," Cole offered through gritted teeth and a tight jaw.

I shook my head, took another step toward him, and looked him dead in the eye, as I said, "I'm not going anywhere, Cole. Not right now, at least."

"Fine," he replied shortly after some time had passed. "Just don't say I didn't warn you."

I watched as he walked away, a tall, broad shadow stalking across the dimly lit parking lot, and back into his car. I stayed watching as he pulled out onto the highway, and finally drove away.

Maybe it was Cole's friendly visit that had me once again waking up at two thirty in the morning. I could still hear the rain outside; it hadn't let up all day, and it wasn't letting up anytime soon by the sounds of things. It didn't stop me from slipping out of bed again, getting dressed, this time in leggings, a fleece, and windbreaker, all of which I'd bought at Kevin's shop the day before. I drove out to the spot by the high school as if on autopilot. When I got out the car this time I swear I could hear, from a long way off, the hollowed out whoops, cheers, laughter, and steady bass of some teenagers' Halloween party. The sound grew more distant, but no less haunting as I jogged into the woods, picking up pace as I left the streetlights behind, and slipped into the never ending darkness of the woods. I was using my cell phone's flashlight beam again, watching it wiggle and waver ahead of me as I moved steadily along the path.

A snap somewhere up ahead made my heart leap, an animal reaction that betrayed my all too human vulnerability. Taking a deep breath, I carried on, determined to reach the spot where Tyler had died, and my brother's life and mine were changed forever.

It was still raining but the woods provided enough coverage that only the occasional raindrop reached me. The sound of the rain falling through branches made for a strange soundtrack, at once comforting and alienating, and it seemed to amplify every other sound I heard, so that when a twig snapped behind me I spun around. I was too unsteady on my feet, though, not used to running along woodland tracks anymore, and I almost tripped up. In the confusion of the moment and the movement, my phone slipped from my hands, slippery with rainwater, and I heard the dull thud of it hit the ground. Its light was immediately obscured, and I was plunged into darkness, fear kicking through me as I dropped to the ground, reaching around for my phone, and finding nothing.

The sound came again and I looked up, forcing myself to think that I was just being stupid, paranoid; that if I saw anything there, it would just be the low lying figure of a small animal, possibly even a bird, high up in the trees. Instead a tall figure loomed in front of me, long and lean, and my heartbeat picked up to a breakneck speed. In the fumbling darkness, all I could hear were labored, heavy breaths, and it took me a second to realize that it was my own breathing I could hear. The figure stepped towards me, and I shuffled back on the ground, trapped like an animal, before they said,

"Liv, it's me. Nick."

I swallowed, peering blindly at him, before checking the shadow black of the woods around us; making sure he was alone.

After his appearance outside my motel earlier, I wouldn't have been surprised to find Cole standing back among the shadows too.

Feeling around on the damp ground I finally found my phone, clutching it in my hand as I stood up and swung the beam of the flashlight over Nick.

"Jesus, can you turn that off?" he said, squinting into its light and holding a hand over his eyes.

"Did you follow me here?" I demanded, turning the flashlight off and plunging us into darkness once more.

"Yeah, I saw your car. What are you doing out here? Again?" I didn't say anything immediately, and I watched as he shifted from foot to foot, before saying, "That was you I saw last night, right? Looked like you were out for a run at three thirty in the morning, except you were wearing a freaking trench coat. Had you been here then too?"

I nodded before realizing he wouldn't be able to see me, and said "Yes. I don't know why I keep coming back. I just keep thinking that if I do, maybe I'll figure it all out," I said, not sure why I was even giving him an answer. I didn't owe him anything. But something about the hidden away darkness of the woods, the not-quite animal silence of them; silken but threatening, made me want to see an ally, a friend in Nick, rather than an adversary. It was scary enough out there as it was.

"That's all long gone, Olivia. You won't be finding any answers out here, not ten years later." I didn't say anything again, and although I couldn't really pick out his face from the shadows, I could tell he was watching me carefully when he said, "Do you ever think about him? Tyler?"

"Every day," I said, and he let out a 'yeah right' snort.

"So, what … you miss him?" Nick asked, the skepticism dripping from him like the rain dripping from the trees around us.

"I don't know that I miss him, per se," I said slowly, "But I do think about how he left. And what he took away from me."

"Wow," Nick said after a short pause, "Typical Olivia, making it all about you."

"I could make it about you instead, Nick, if you really wanted," I offered.

"What the fuck is that supposed to mean?" he snapped.

"Just that I'm wondering how much more there is to this story. How much you haven't told me."

"Oh, there's plenty I haven't told you. Just like there's plenty you haven't told me, I'm guessing."

"Did the mayor really not hand you over to the police all for the sake of three thousand dollars, Nick?" I asked.

"Wait," he said, taking a step closer to me, "you really think *I* killed Tyler? And that his mother helped me cover it up? Because he owed me three grand?" He sounded confused at first, but then, I swear, he started to laugh. "Are you fucking kidding me, Olivia? I didn't have anything to do with Tyler's murder."

"You really expect anyone to believe that?" I asked. "When I left that party you and Cole were both about to beat the shit out of him, and from what I've heard, you were only just getting started."

"Yeah, well Cole had more reasons than three grand to beat the shit out of him, didn't he?" He was standing close enough that I could feel his breath now, a cool ribbon laced with a little too much beer. I wondered what he'd been doing earlier in the night. It was Halloween after all, maybe he'd stopped by a party, or maybe he'd been in one of the city's bars or breweries. Maybe he'd been drinking at home, or with colleagues. Either way, he was getting way too close, and I took a step back, blood thrumming through my veins. But the ground was uneven and of course I stumbled, and it was Nick who reached out, grabbing me by both of my shoulders in a slightly too-hard grip. He didn't let go immediately, even when I was safely standing upright. "What's wrong, Liv? Don't you like me reminding you of your past indiscretions?" he sneered at me.

"I can't recall which indiscretion it is you're referring to, Nick," I said.

"Right, because there's been so many," and Nick's laughter echoed through the woods like an animal's call. "I'm talking about you fucking Tyler in Jessica's bathroom while Cole was looking for you downstairs, Olivia."

A bird took flight, crashing through leaves and branches up into the dark rainy night above the line of the trees, and we both looked up, the almighty sound drowning out the sound of my heart. I swallowed, taking the moment for myself, and hissed, "I didn't fuck Tyler in Jess's bathroom, Nick. I didn't ever sleep with him at all."

I just about managed to cover up how much my voice was shaking with rage.

Nick shook his head, and even in the darkness, I could tell how dark and hooded his eyes were. He didn't believe me.

No surprises there, I guess. Cole hadn't believed me either.

"You used to be a better liar, Liv," Nick said, once again sneering at me through the dark, the snarl in his voice unmistakable.

"So, what are you saying?" I asked, "that you think Cole killed Tyler because he thought I was sleeping with him?"

"No! Jesus, Olivia, I don't know who killed him, okay? I just know that he was already dead when we found him," Nick said.

"So, why the call to the mayor if you weren't trying to cover your asses? Why not just get out of there and let someone else trip over the body the next morning?"

"Because I had some pretty scary fucking guys after me for that money, okay? And I'd sent Tyler off to get the money he owed me, so I figured when he didn't make it back to Jess's that they'd got to Tyler as a warning to me. So, after that there was no way I wasn't gonna pay them back, the only person I could think of who'd be able to get that kind of money for me at short notice was the mayor, and I knew she wouldn't want anyone tracing Ty's murder back to a bunch of backwoods meth makers, anyway."

"Wait, Tyler was doing *meth*?" I asked.

"No. He was a fucking monster for pills, but to give him his credit, he never did meth."

"So, who were these guys you owed money to, then?" I asked.

"They were my suppliers, Olivia. I'm surprised you haven't figured that out yet."

I stared at him. It seemed incredible to me that he was blithely admitting all this to me. The one-time town drug dealer who now worked for the mayor. But then there was something about standing there in those woods that felt both secretive and safe. A place where the truth could come out, but also never leave. Maybe this was what Catholics felt sitting in the confession box. I could barely pick out Nick's face in the dark, after all, let alone his expression, and maybe there was something about that blank darkness that made him feel at once guilty, and untouchable. To confess and be washed clean of what you're confessing to in one easy brushstroke. It was an appealing concept, a neat trick. But I wasn't about to tell him how many Hail Marys it would take to cleanse his soul of his past sins.

"And the mayor knew all this?" I asked.

"She knows everything I know. Maybe even more," Nick said, somewhat ominously.

"What does that mean?" I asked quickly.

Through the dark, I saw Nick shrug before he said, "Just that she has a way of knowing about everything, and everyone owes her something. To her, knowledge isn't just power, it's currency."

I didn't say anything at first, allowing the silence to deepen around us. The rain had stopped finally; the endless thrumming of the raindrops on the branches above us had reduced to the gentle, sporadic drip drip that comes after a seemingly endless downpour. I shouldn't have been surprised by Nick's astuteness, I suppose. He wasn't stupid after all, and he knew Mayor Washington as well as anyone by the sounds of things. Or at the very least, knew how she worked, and what made her tick.

"So, she knew Ethan had absolutely nothing to do with it?" I said softly, almost to myself really. I was thinking about what she'd said to me earlier at the community center. I wasn't sure if I'd believed her or not at the time, but she'd been pretty convincing all the same. I guess that was the point though; she was a woman who could convince almost anyone of almost anything. Guilt and disgust groped through me as I realized I really had almost believed her. She'd almost convinced me that, although she might have knowingly and willingly covered up the true nature of her son and his death, she hadn't knowingly and willingly sent the wrong man to prison for it. I should have known better. I should have recognized a lifelong liar when I saw one.

THEN

Cole arrives to walk over to Jessica's with me, a silly grin plastered all over his face.

"Are you drunk already?" I hiss at him while shrugging on a jacket in the entryway.

"No, I'm not drunk already. Just happy to see you," Cole says, laughing.

I call out a goodbye to the rest of my family and follow Cole out of the house, across the street, and onto the pathway that leads to the woods, and is the shortest route to Jess's house. It's grey and cool, about to rain, and the evergreen trees make it feel even cooler under the canopy of the woods, where Cole begins to weave and roll down the path, cartoonishly imitating the walk of a drunk person. He turns around and sees me watching him, laughing at my expression.

"You are a bit drunk, aren't you?" I say, because his energy seems off somehow, but I can't quite put my finger on how. "Where've you been all day?"

"I'm not drunk, Liv," he says again, laughing. "Speaking of though, maybe we should …" and here he dangles his water bottle in front of my face, the one he's always got filled with something other than water whenever we go out. He takes a swig and passes it over to me.

"What is it?" I ask.

"Vodka cranberry," he says.

"Ugh, no. You know I can't drink that, not since prom," I say, remembering the hot pink puke I'd vomited up all over my parents' driveway. I'd tried to blame it on Ethan, but he'd just laughed for a full fifteen minutes in response, and my parents had known I was lying.

"Your loss," Cole says, taking another swig and raising his eyebrows at me as he does so. After he's done, he waggles the bottle at me again, and I relent, peer pressure working its magic. It doesn't taste as bad as I thought it would, the dry sweetness masking the ever present shock of the vodka. It's only the after-taste that makes me think of prom, knees digging into gravel as I heaved over the driveway.

I make a face and Cole rolls his eyes before pulling me towards him and planting a wet, cranberry-scented kiss on my lips. "Cheer up, huh? You look like you're on your way to a funeral, not a party."

I sigh and ease into his arms a little, taking another drink from the bottle and smacking my lips after, in a masquerade of enjoyment. "Sorry," I say, "just feeling a bit shit."

"Why?"

"It's just finally sinking in, you know … this time next week, everything will be different, everything will be over," I say, widening my eyes at Cole as he raises his eyebrows yet again in amusement.

"Not like you to be this sentimental, Liv," he says, giving me a squeeze.

"Yeah, well. Like I said, it's finally starting to sink in."

"We'll be fine," he says to me softly, leaning over and kissing me again, "we're going to the same college, for Christ's sake. Nothing's going to change, just you wait."

314

Warmth seeps through me; from his body, from the vodka, from the reassurance, maybe from all three, but then a whistle and a whoop breaks the rustling silence of the trees and suddenly there's footsteps everywhere, a voice calling our names, and Tyler rushes towards us, barreling into us both, pushing us to the ground.

He jumps up almost instantly, letting us crawl our way back to standing as he swipes the stainless steel water bottle off the ground, and takes one long wild swig of the vodka, declaring it empty when he's done.

"What's up losers?" he asks with a grin, "You ready to party, or what?"

48

NOW

There was silence after the recording stopped and Mayor Washington raised her head to look at me, blinking slowly as she said, "What is it that you want from me, Olivia?"

I'd been at her office before even she or her assistant had arrived. I'd got there early, waiting in the chilly hallway of City Hall, hoping and praying she'd turn up before Nick did. She'd arrived at eight thirty sharp. She was sipping from a travel mug – identical to the one I'd seen Nick with at the brewery rally, her name shouting itself across the side – as she strode down the hallway peering at her cellphone as she answered emails. She didn't notice me until I stood up from the wooden bench and said her name. If my presence had surprised her, she hadn't given herself away.

I'd recorded my entire exchange with Nick the night before on my phone of course. I'd turned on the 'record' button at the same time as I turned the flashlight off. The sound quality wasn't great, but that didn't matter. No one else was ever going to hear it, and the mayor had been able to decipher the most pertinent information, just as I'd been able to when

I listened to it all back in my motel room in the early hours of the morning.

"I want you to come forward and say that you not only knowingly corrupted the crime scene where your son's body was found, but that you perverted the course of justice by lying and saying you didn't already know your son was dead when you called the police that morning. That, along with Nick Green and Cole Sampson, you concocted a story involving my brother in order to cover up the fact that not only did Tyler regularly abuse drugs, but that he owed his drug dealer three thousand dollars, and that in helping to frame my brother for his death, you not only sent an innocent man to prison, but allowed the manufacture and sale of drugs to continue in Twin Rivers and beyond. How does all that sound to you?" I asked.

"I can't do that," she said with a fluid shake of her head.

If I'd been hoping to see what Maria Washington looked like when nervous, and caught out, I was severely disappointed.

"But you admit it's all true?" I asked.

"Up to a point," she said, and I raised my eyebrows in surprise. "But this would undo everything I've ever worked towards, don't you understand that?"

"Of course, I understand that, Maria," I said, leaning forward in my seat and placing both of my hands on her antique mahogany desk. "That's exactly what I want."

"You're not a girl who looks for the bigger picture, are you Olivia?" she said.

I bristled at her use of 'girl', trying not to show how easy it was for her to get under my skin like that and said, "I think maybe the problem here is that we're looking at two quite different pictures, Mayor, not that I don't see it. Here's what I'm envisaging: I can either send this recording to a friend of mine at the Portland PD, or I can send it to a contact at the local TV news station. Or if I'm feeling really visionary, I might do both. Either way, you'll be left on the backfoot, and in all likelihood, instead of being voted in as mayor again next week, you could find yourself being arrested. How do you like that picture, Mayor?"

She didn't say anything, but she didn't avert her gaze either. It was strange, but she didn't remind me of Tyler at all in that moment. Tyler had been larger than life, and although Maria had become this towering figure in the city, she was always so controlled, so contained. Tyler had been a whirlwind, a tornado ripping through life, leaving only destruction in his wake. If Maria was anything, she was an arrow shot straight to the heart, a knife slipped between the ribs, letting you bleed out before you ever realized you'd been hurt. "I'll give you until the end of the week," I said, "if you haven't gone to the police by then, I will."

"It's Thursday, Olivia. *Tomorrow* is the end of the week; that doesn't give me much time," she said, shifting slightly in her high-backed desk chair.

"I know, and I might have given you more time, but it's the election on Tuesday, and I really think the electorate has a right to know exactly who they're voting for before they go to the polls, don't you? I'll give you until the end of business, of course, then I'll act."

The mayor's mouth pinched, her eyes narrowing almost imperceptibly as I watched her swallow. But then she seemed to pull herself together, sitting up even straighter in her chair, if that was possible. "I'm assuming Nick didn't know he was being recorded, which makes that recording illegal, which makes your threats rather hollow, Olivia."

I shrugged. "Maybe. Maybe not. It might not stand up in court, you're right, but it'll certainly do some damage in the court of public opinion. Are you really willing to take that risk?"

She didn't say anything, so I stood up, tucking my phone into the pocket of my trench coat. "Five p.m. tomorrow, Maria. That's all the time I can give you."

I didn't look back as I pulled her office door closed behind me, but I could feel the twin darts of her eyes boring into my back.

Taking my phone out of my pocket, I stood, shaking slightly as I pressed the 'stop' button on the recording again, and emailed myself the audio clipping of our conversation for safe keeping.

I spent the rest of the day in the Daily Grind, replying to emails, and doing as much work on Reid's case as I could get done remotely. My concentration was fractured though, my mind shattered from weeks of waking up too early and going to bed too late. It didn't help that so much of Reid's case reminded me of Twin Rivers, of Ethan, of what could go wrong in the heat of the moment. I added an alert to my browser so that if anything happened related to Mayor Washington, I'd know immediately. But the day grew longer, my patience grew shorter, and still nothing happened. There didn't even seem to be any new news stories covering her campaign, so I sat there, endlessly refreshing my social media feeds, waiting for the world to change.

But the world didn't change until almost eleven o'clock the next morning. I'd been awake for hours of course, with nothing but my email inbox, and some old episodes of *Parks & Recreation* for company. I'd headed across the street to the IHOP as soon as it was open, my stomach hollow and rumbling after hours of being awake without eating. It was Kat who broke the news to me, my phone practically buzzing itself off the table before I picked up the call.

"Olivia, have you seen the news?" she demanded, her voice racing down the line to me.

My laptop was open in front of me; I still had a Wi-Fi signal from the motel, but it was weak, and my internet browsing had been seriously impeded by this. I clicked on the tab open to the local news site, holding my breath and clenching my jaw as I did so.

"It was her *husband*, Liv, not her!" Kat was saying as I set eyes on the headline, "he's the one who saw Tyler's body the night of the party, after Nick called him, and helped to frame Ethan so that no one would find out how bad Tyler's drug use had gotten."

"No," I croaked, staring dumbly at the headline which read: MAYOR'S HUSBAND TURNS HIMSELF IN FOR PODCAST CRIMES.

"No," I said again, not hearing whatever it was Kat was saying down the phone to me, "no, it was her. She admitted to it. It was the mayor."

"What are you talking about, Olivia?" Kat asked. "We never knew that for sure. We had Spencer saying that Nick was about to call the mayor when she left, but what if he got through to Sandford Washington instead?"

"No," I said, still croaking in disbelief, "Nick said he called the mayor, that he saw her that night."

"What are you talking about?" Kat said, clearly confused and it took me a while to answer. I couldn't exactly explain that I had the mayor on record saying that she'd seen the body of her son that night; Kat had no idea I'd been to Maria Washington's office the morning before, that I'd set all this in motion.

I suddenly regretted giving Maria so much time to stitch a new story together. I should never have given her the opportunity to weave her own narrative through all this; she had a tendency to write herself as the hero, when in reality she was anything but. But I'd handed her the pen, and she'd written the ending that worked best for her. Should I really have been as surprised as I was?

"Liv, you still there?" Kat said.

"Yeah, yeah, I'm here, I just … what happens now?" I asked.

"Well, Ray and I are about to record an emergency bonus episode, that we'll probably drop later today, but I'm guessing your boss Karen might have a better idea about what all this means specifically for Ethan?"

"Yeah, you're right, I should probably call her," I said, still staring at the screen of my laptop. I thought I'd done everything I needed to checkmate Maria Washington, but in the end, at the last second, she'd outmaneuvered me.

"There's a press conference this afternoon, we'll see you there?"

Kat said, clearly ready to get off the phone, and get on with recording the podcast.

"Yeah, yeah, I'll see you there."

"City Hall at one," Kat said by way of a sign off and promptly hung up.

I looked up from staring dumbfounded at my computer screen, to see the waitress hovering over me. She had a slightly concerned look on her face, and I had to wonder how long I'd been staring numbly into the middle distance. I ordered another cup of coffee, even though I didn't really want it, and certainly didn't need it before my phone started to vibrate again: Georgia. Picking my phone up I saw that I'd missed a call from Daniel, and had a whole stream of messages from Samira too. My chest constricted; this was it, everything was about to change, the clouds were about to clear, my brother was going to see blue sky again, my parents were going to hug him as a free man again. My eyes burned as I stared down at my sister's name illuminated on the screen of my phone. The feeling in my chest grew even heavier, a brick wall pressing down on my heart. I touched the space bar of my laptop and the screen turned on again, the headline still screaming its lies at me. Could we ever achieve anything approaching a victory when one of the major players had removed herself from the game?

The waitress brought me my coffee, and I could feel her staring at me as I stared at the computer screen.

"Are you gonna answer that?" she asked, nodding at the phone that was still in my hand.

"Oh, yeah, right," I said distantly, pressing 'accept' and holding the phone up to my ear.

I could hear the waitress muttering as she walked away, "*Always knew that guy was hiding something.*"

I joined Kat and Ray at City Hall for the press conference at one o'clock. Both the mayor and her husband were present, although a spokesperson for them both addressed the crowd first. Morgan and Cole were standing to the side of the podium, next to her parents, but a little way off, as if trying to distance themselves from the elder Washingtons while still showing their support. I locked eyes with Cole for a second before he looked away, and despite the crowd and too-high heating, a shiver ran through me. Morgan was standing with her hands clasped just below her bump, eyes cast downward. I wondered if she'd been prepped to stand that way by someone, but probably I was being unfair; her life had been upturned once again, and she must've felt just as out of control as she had done back when Tyler died. Eventually the crowd settled and the spokesperson stepped forward. He was a man in his mid-fifties, with possibly the squarest jaw I'd ever seen in real life, and dark grey hair.

Clearing his throat before he began he said, "At nine o'clock this morning, Sandford Washington admitted in person to a representative of the Oregon State Police to obstruction of justice, and to knowingly withholding evidence in the criminal investigation into the death of his son Tyler Washington, as well as to lying to police about his own movements on the night in question. This admission was precipitated by the sustained media speculation surrounding his wife, Mayor Maria Washington over her own possible involvement in a so-called cover-up. Mr Washington has assured the police, and would like to stress here today, that his wife had absolutely no knowledge of his wrong doing, and neither did his daughter, Morgan. He would now like to say a few words on the subject."

At this, Sandford and the spokesperson swapped places. My eyes had been trained on Maria while her spokesman had been telling her lies, watching the quiver in her mouth as he spoke, staring at her hands clasping those of her husband, looking for anything that might give her away. But there was nothing; of course there wasn't. Now, I switched to Sandford, wondering why on earth he was doing any of this, what kind of agreement he and his wife had, what kind of a marriage resulted in this kind of miscarriage of justice. I thought I saw his hands shake maybe just a little as he took a piece of paper from the inside pocket of his suit jacket and smoothed it out on the lectern, but otherwise he was poised and in control. He had thick, dark eyebrows, striated with silver and the kind of stature that gave him the distinguished air we've been trained to trust, and are only just beginning to realize hides a hundred sins. How ironic that this time, he was using it to hide his wife's sins. He too cleared his throat, but the sound was reedy and insubstantial in the hush of the room, the crowd silent and heavy with anticipation.

"Like many men I have made hundreds of mistakes, but none more severe than the mistake I made amid the panic of loss on the night of August 23, 2008." He cleared his throat again, and I wondered who had written his speech, with whose words we were being lied to. "At roughly two thirty a.m. on the morning of August 24, I received a phone call from one of Tyler's friends, telling me they'd just found him unconscious in the woods. Like any father would, I rushed over to where the boys had found my son, only to find that he had already passed away. Instead of calling the authorities then and there, as I should have done, I made the reckless decision not to do so. My wife and I had long been aware of our son's use of drugs, and had done our best to both get him help, and shield him from the press, as we didn't want our otherwise good natured, and much-beloved boy to have his reputation tarnished irreparably. We were not aware however, that his prolific use of drugs had become so bad that he had become indebted to a local drug dealer. At the time of his death, in fact, Tyler owed up to three thousand dollars. My only wish is that I as a parent had made him feel safe enough to come to me to get him the help he so desperately needed in paying off this debt, and in getting free of his vicious drug habit, so that he could be the happy, healthy boy we knew and loved again," Sandford broke off to swallow, took a deep breath and cleared his throat again. His voice had started to thicken as he spoke, and I could tell that everyone else in the room was eating it up. "What I did instead is unforgivable. I placed the reputation of my family, and the position of my wife above the needs of my son. Upon hearing that Tyler owed three thousand dollars to his drug dealer, and had repeatedly refused, or been unable, to pay, I came to the conclusion that his death was the result of either a drug deal gone wrong or an act of revenge for not paying. Wanting to protect the good name and reputation of not only my beloved son, but my family, and my wife who was, and still is, mayor of this city, I took it upon myself to distance Tyler as much as possible from the true nature of his murder, and the true identity of his killer, or killers."

I pulled my gaze away from Sandford and looked around the room for the familiar shape of Nick Green, but couldn't see him anywhere. Sandford had yet to mention 'Tyler's friends' by name, and I wondered if the Washingtons were trying to keep Nick and Cole out of this confession.

"However," Sandford continued, "I want to stress that I played no part in placing Ethan Hall at the scene of Tyler's murder, and that as far as I'm aware the witness testimony of both Nick Green and Cole Sampson was true and accurate. I do not, however, believe he is my son's murderer, and by stepping forward and finally taking responsibility for my actions, I hope to also be able to help clear his name, and free him from his prison sentence. I am working with both the state police and the office of the District Attorney to expedite this process so that Ethan will be able to come home as soon as possible. I understand that neither Ethan himself, nor the Hall family will ever likely be able to forgive me, but I do hope this goes some way in helping make reparations." At this, I felt the energy in the room shift, my body stiffening as heads started to rove and people tried to find me in the crowd. Kat shuffled up next to me, so that she was standing even closer than before, but didn't say anything, and I was glad. If she'd asked me if I was okay right then, I wouldn't have been able to answer her. I knew the words that were coming out of Sandford Washington's mouth were a lie; there was a bedrock of truth to them, of that I was sure, but there was also a whole ecosystem of lies lying above that truth, and I might have been the only person in that room who realized that. My heart was beating so fast I could feel it through my clothing, and my blood felt warm in my veins. Eyes found me, the many gazes lying hot on my skin, and some people began to mutter. I didn't have to hear their words to know they were talking about me, my family, Ethan.

I wanted to leave, but couldn't.

Sandford finished up his statement, and the spokesperson stepped forward to introduce the mayor. Her gaze was hard and level as she stared out into the room, and even though I knew she wasn't, it felt like she was looking right at me, talking straight to me. She didn't have any notes with her, and when she spoke, her voice was as clear and as unyielding as her gaze.

"As you can imagine, the trials of the past 24 hours have only been surpassed by those hours, days, weeks, and months after my son Tyler was found dead just over a decade ago. As my husband has stated, I had no idea of his true involvement in finding our son's body, and no involvement in the cover-up and collusion of the true nature of his death. I will be working with the police, the District Attorney's office, and if they let me, with the Hall family to rectify this huge miscarriage of justice as quickly as possible. Once that has been done, I will then do my utmost to uncover the true identity of Tyler's killer and make sure that they are, finally, brought to justice." A chill ran through me as she said this, the steel in her voice, her eyes, her entire demeanor telling me she meant what she said, even if what she was saying wasn't the whole truth. The ability to lie, and mean it isn't one you see that often, not really. It's impressive when you recognize it.

Maria modulated her voice slightly as she wrapped up her statement. The steel was gone, replaced by a conciliatory softness. "I understand that you must have a lot of questions, but we only have time for a few, so please keep it brief."

A reporter's arm near the front of the crowd shot up into the air, and the mayor pointed at her. "Will you be withdrawing from your mayoral reelection race, Mayor Washington?" she asked.

Maria glanced towards her spokesman before answering, "No. I thought long and hard about it, but in a few days the people of Twin Rivers will get the opportunity to decide whether or not they still trust me with their city, and I will accept their decision either way. If I am reelected and there are still doubts about my eligibility, then there's always the recall process to fall back on. I believe in the democratic process, and its power to protect the people."

Kat let out a little snort next to me, and I glanced at her. Ray was on her other side, microphone out, recording every word, but he still managed to turn to Kat, rolling his eyes as he did so.

The funny thing was that they were scoffing at the one part of the mayor's speech she probably truly believed in.

I trailed Kat and Ray as we left the building. I wanted to see if I could catch Nick in the crowd, but I couldn't spot him anywhere. Was he already talking to the state police about his involvement that night? Had the mayor told him about my recording of him two nights ago in the woods? I should probably have been trying to avoid him at all costs; who knew what his reaction to all of this would be. But for some reason, I felt bound to him somehow. That woodland confessional had created a kind of steady magic I couldn't quite describe. He'd shared his truth with me under the cover of darkness and a canopy of evergreen, and I felt like that meant something. It didn't hurt that I had the recording to hold over him, should he ever feel like threatening me, of course.

Kat and Ray were already standing by their van by the time I exited the building, blinking into the weak sunlight. The rain had finally stopped, grey clouds turned white with patches of blue in between. I thought I was the last one out – I'd stood in the lobby of City Hall, waiting in vain for Nick to appear, until the whole place had emptied – but the doors creaked open behind me, and I turned to see Morgan and Cole walk through them. Morgan was staring down at her feet, her face pale, except for two red patches high up on her cheeks. She'd been crying. Cole had his arm around his girlfriend's shoulders, and was practically walking her through the doors.

Neither of them saw me immediately so I was forced to clear my throat and say, "Hey."

Both sets of eyes were on me in a flash. "Olivia," Cole practically growled, "I think it's probably for the best if you get out of here right now."

Morgan's eyes widened as he spoke and she pulled out of his grip, turning her stare of consternation on him. "Cole, what are you talking about? I think we owe Olivia an apology or two, don't you?"

"She's the reason all this is happening, Morgan!" Cole exclaimed. "If Olivia hadn't brought her fucking podcast friends into this –" here he turned his eyes on Kat and Ray standing some distance away down the street, "none of this would've happened."

"Cole," Morgan said steadily, taking a step towards him, and placing a hand on his right arm. "This is all happening because of what my dad did ten years ago, and because of those awful men who killed Tyler, whoever they were. It has nothing to do with Olivia." Cole's eyes met mine, but Morgan continued to talk, her voice low and yet still loud enough for me to hear, "Ethan, Olivia, and their family are victims in all this too, can't you see that? We have to recognize that there were two wrongs here, and it's not going to be easy to make it right again."

Cole looked down at Morgan, who was peering up at him with a serene but pleading look on her face. His voice was still cold when he said, "Funny, but I'm finding it hard to see Olivia as a victim in anything, right now."

Then it was his turn to shrug Morgan away from him as he

327

stalked down the steps to the street and walked away from us.

"Sorry," Morgan said to me, "he's having a hard time coming to terms with all this. He's always believed Ethan killed Tyler."

"Really, Morgan? You really believe that? Surely, you can see now that Cole's known all along Ethan didn't kill Tyler."

Morgan stared at me, demolished. "You're wrong," she said with a shake of her head, "he had no idea, there's no way he would do that. *Lie* like that. He couldn't have been lying to me for so long, it's just not possible."

"The distance between what we believe to be possible, and what actually is possible is vast, Morgan," I said, "I learnt that ten years ago."

Morgan didn't say anything for a while, and I was surprised to feel a soft drop of rain fall on my cheek as I waited for her response. I looked up; the sky had clouded over again, blue had been replaced with grey as we stood there and suddenly the day was gone, an early dusk falling over the autumn afternoon.

Within seconds, the rain was really coming down, and Morgan reached into her purse for an umbrella, opening it out in one seamless motion, while I just let the rain fall on me. I'd never seen Morgan without something to say, and for as long as I'd known her, she'd liked to have the last word. So, I was surprised when instead of answering me, she just gave me one tight nod goodbye, and headed off down the street in the same direction Cole had gone, her mint green umbrella a pastel colored beacon of brightness in the downpour.

Extract from transcript of Season 3 SPECIAL BONUS EPISODE of *Shadow of a Doubt*:

Kat Thomas [voiceover]: If you've been following the news, then you'll know that the father of Tyler Washington, Sandford Washington, recently turned himself into police for lying during his son's murder investigation and obstructing the course of justice. In a press conference yesterday, he admitted to finding his son's body in the early hours of August 24 and to leading the investigation away from the true identity of his son's killer or killers, who he believes to have been Tyler's drug dealer or dealers. His reasoning behind this remains somewhat unclear to me.

He claimed that he was trying to protect the reputation of his son and wife, who was then, and is now mayor of Twin Rivers, but would such concern really lead you to go so far as to cover up a key aspect of your son's murder? To lie to police during an active investigation, to perjure yourself in court, and to be part of the reason why an innocent man went to jail for ten years?

Leaving behind the elder Washington's motives for a while, I'm lucky enough to be joined by Ethan's attorney, Karen Powers, who's here to take us through what this means for Ethan and what the next couple of steps will be.

[to Karen Powers] Karen, what happens now? How soon can Ethan expect to be released from prison?

Karen Powers: Hey, Kat, thanks for having me on the podcast, and to answer the second part of that question, actually pretty soon. We're talking on Saturday November 3, the day after Sandford gave his statement to the press, but I filed for a retrial almost as soon as I heard the news yesterday. If I'm honest, there was so little evidence against Ethan in the first place, that with this new information, and Washington's confession to obstructing the investigation could lead to exoneration. I'm not sure that prosecutors would want to take their chances in court again, after all this.

KT: Especially as they'd be going up against you this time.

KP [laughs]: Thank you. Although to be serious for a second – and I hate to disrespect the work of a fellow defense attorney – your remark does touch on some of the issues around Ethan's attorney at the time of the trial, Robert Castle. So we actually have multiple strands to work with here: there's Sandford's confession, but then there's also the fact that Olivia Hall, Ethan's twin sister, told the police about overhearing Tyler and Nick Green arguing on the night he died about the money that Tyler owed Nick. Was this evidence withheld by the prosecution and police, or was Castle aware of it, and disregarded it? So, basically, did the prosecution withhold exculpatory evidence or was Ethan provided with ineffective counsel?

KT: Well, we didn't find any transcripts from Olivia's interview with Twin Rivers police when she made that accusation in Castle's files from the trial. We actually only found it after you did us a favor by finally getting hold of Ethan's police file.

KP: That's a very good point, and points towards evidence having been withheld, which, as you can imagine, is a pretty big deal.

KT: So, would that alone have been enough to file for a retrial?

KP: Actually, it probably would've been, and I was in the process of building our case around that omission from the original trial, when Sandford Washington came forward. But our lives have all been made a lot easier because there's no way a judge could deny a retrial now.

KT: And when a retrial is granted, will Ethan be released?

KP: I think we can conclude that he will be, yes. It's not always the case, because although the accused is taken back to a state of presumption of innocence with a retrial, unfortunately in this state, bail is almost never granted for anyone accused of murder. Which, in my opinion, and people are welcome to disagree with me, directly opposes that presumption of innocence, but that's a story for another day.

KT: But you think in this case, Ethan could expect to be released at the same time as being granted a retrial?

KP: Yes. I think Mr Washington's confession is really going to play a part here. This isn't just a case of prosecutors playing fast and loose with evidence, a real crime was perpetrated against Ethan Hall, and Sandford Washington is probably going to be facing obstruction of justice and perjury charges, not to mention any civil case that Ethan might eventually want to bring.

KT: Have you spoken to him about possible civil cases?

KP: We've touched on it in passing, and obviously it's not my area as I'm a criminal defense attorney, but Ethan's been robbed of ten years of his life. And not just any old ten years, but the years he would have been in college, and establishing a career for himself, possibly even a family. He's missed almost his entire twenties; he was robbed of them, and he can't get them back, but I think we can get him something.

331

49

SIX WEEKS LATER

It took a little longer than Karen anticipated, but finally there we all were, back in court, waiting to hear whether or not my brother would be granted a retrial. If he was, Karen thought there was a strong chance that the DA wouldn't even follow through with a retrial, not with all the evidence that had come to light. Ethan didn't kill Tyler Washington, and now, finally, the world knew it. Even more importantly, they believed it.

It was less than two weeks until Christmas, and winter lay like a delicate wreath over Twin Rivers. Fog filled the woods and the streets, shop windows glowed with warmth, streetlights stayed on throughout the day, and I'd woken up at a very respectable six thirty a.m. that morning. None of it would feel real until we got Ethan back home to Portland, but for now it was enough to see him standing tall next to Karen, nodding silently along as she talked in his ear. Next to me, Kevin twisted his gloves in his hands, stretching the leather, pulling and pulling on them until Ray, who was on his other side, placed his hands over Kevin's and hissed, "You're gonna ruin them if you carry on like that."

"I know, I know," Kevin practically groaned, before settling back in his seat. He'd been shifting and shuffling ever since we took our seats; memories of the last time we were all here making him shiver and shake with nerves that Ray and Kat – who was sitting behind us, next to Daniel – couldn't understand. "I just can't let myself believe it, until it actually happens, you know? I'm not going to let myself think he's free and clear, until he's actually free and clear."

Finally, we were asked to rise and the judge entered the chambers, motioning everyone to sit with a wave of his hand.

Just like every day in court ten years ago, I watched the back of Ethan's head with keen interest. His hair had been cut short, and he'd shaved off his beard. From where I was sitting, it was as if nothing had changed; as if those long, ten years had dissolved to nothing and we were all eighteen years old again. That feeling of time folding in on itself hit me again. Stretching and pulling, folding and unfurling until the past and the present blurred and broke and I couldn't tell what was what, and when was when. But then Ethan's shoulders shifted and he turned his head to the side, talking to Karen too quietly for me or anyone else to hear, and I returned with a jolt to the present day. They chatted easily together, full eye contact, obviously having built up a rapport I couldn't quite penetrate or translate. It struck me as the most grown up – the most adult – I'd ever seen Ethan. He'd always had this self-assurance as a teenager, a sense of self that was hard to rattle, but he'd still been a kid. Young and cocky, maybe, but a kid. And then, all those markers of adulthood; going to college, graduating from college, first real job, first apartment, second job, all that stuff, had been replaced by prison, where grown men are forced into an institutionalized dependency that looks and feels a lot like infantilization.

He didn't look infantilized now. He looked grown up and determined. He gave off an air of confidence that, on first glance, might have you thinking he was the defending attorney, rather than the defendant.

But then the judge started to speak, and any confusion over who Ethan was, and why we were there, disappeared.

"Your Honor," Karen said, beginning her closing statement, "the evidence against my client was only ever circumstantial. Witness testimonies placing him near the scene of the crime by witnesses who have since been proven untrustworthy. Friends of the victim who at best lied to the police, obstructed the course of justice, and committed perjury. And at worst, may have been more involved in the death of Tyler Washington than we currently know or understand —"

"Objection," called the prosecutor, standing up slowly from his chair, with all the conviction and energy of a man just given a terminal diagnosis, "calls for conjecture."

"Sustained," the judge said, his voice as clear as a bell. "Ms Powers, please stick to the facts from here on out. God knows you've got more than enough on your side."

"Of course, Your Honor, my apologies," Karen said, nodding first at the judge, and then at the prosecutor. "Ethan Hall was found guilty long before his trial began. Tried in the court of public opinion, my client was pilloried by the media, who saw him as a loner and an outlier, someone so isolated and miserable, that he'd kill the former classmate who bullied him in high school. But that is not, nor ever was, Ethan Hall. While he may not be the son of the mayor, or have had as many friends as Tyler Washington, it's clear to see from the way his family have stood by him, and fought for him all these years, that he is just as beloved as the victim was. But Ethan – and Tyler's – personality traits are neither here nor there.

"Because the fact of the matter is that we now have proof that crucial evidence was held back from Ethan Hall's defense team in discovery. Evidence that could have helped point the way forward to the real perpetrator or perpetrators of this crime. And that's before we even get to the revelations of Sandford Washington six weeks ago. Your Honor, we all know how slowly the justice system moves. We know that it could take months for Sandford Washington to be brought to trial for his crimes in this case, and we simply cannot ask my client, Ethan Hall, to spend six to eight more months in prison for a crime it's looking more and more likely will be proven he didn't commit, while we wait for Mr Washington, and anyone else involved in this crime and cover-up, to be brought to justice. Mr Hall must be granted a retrial, and should be allowed to be released into the custody and care of his parents until that retrial."

There was a long, draining pause while the judge took in Karen, and then turned his gaze on Ethan, who was still sitting stiff and straight in his chair.

"Mr Hall," the judge said finally, on a long, deep exhalation, his eyes still on Ethan. "Ethan," he said, his face softening suddenly, and I wondered whether he had children, and if so, how old they were, "it is my opinion that you have been victim to a great injustice, the first at the hands of Mr Washington, and any co-conspirators he may or may not have had, the second at the hands of the city's police department, the third by the media, and the fourth, finally, and I say with the deepest regret in my heart, at the hands of this very court and the justice system itself. Your guilt or innocence, however, is not what we are here to deliberate on. What I can do is grant you a retrial. Until then, you will be released on bail, into the custody of your parents, and with the aid of an electronic monitoring system."

There was a moment – just a flash, a millisecond – of deep, profound silence, the kind that is charged with a decade's worth of energy, and hope, and desperation, of loss, and wishing, and praying, of waiting, and waiting, and waiting; of waiting so long, you start to believe all you will ever do is wait. And then: the silence burst, seemingly at the seams, and the courtroom went from static to kinetic, from the very moment before a storm, to the moment the lightning strikes and the thunder rolls.

I watched, rooted to the spot, as my parents and Georgia rushed to him; Ethan's body still stiff but shaking as each one of them threw their arms around him. For a second his eyes slipped to mine, anchoring me further as the reality of what had just happened began to sink in, and then he buried his face between the tops of our family's heads. I could feel someone's eyes on me, and turned to see Karen gazing at me, a perplexed look on her face. I shook my head, tears finally spilling over. I realized I could barely hear anything – the moment had swallowed the room whole, muffling everything, but then Daniel placed a hand on my shoulder, leaning forward to press his face close to mine.

"Liv?" he said, "you in there? You look a little shell shocked."

"I am," I said, voice cracking.

Daniel grinned, his warmth and easiness spreading across his face, before giving me a tight hug, and telling me to go see my brother. But my mother and sister were clamped to his sides, talking over him and one another, shock and euphoria mixing to make their voices louder than usual. Karen smiled indulgently at both of them and inclined her head at me, indicating she wanted to talk.

"You okay?" she asked when I got near. Her hand gripped my right arm, and she began to vigorously rub it, as if I'd suffered an injury or hypothermia and she was trying to get the circulation going again. "Honestly, you look as blown away as Ethan does right now. You know he's the one who just escaped a prison sentence, right?"

There was laughter and teasing in her voice, but I wasn't fast enough to grab hold of it like the lifeline it was. Instead my head twisted back towards Ethan, the sun around which all of us were currently orbiting. "Kitson?" Karen said, pulling me back to earth, surprising me with the use of my fake last name. A name I might never be forced to use again.

"I know, I know, it's stupid, I just sometimes feel like everything that happens to him, happens to me too," I said, trying to keep my voice even and light.

Karen raised her eyebrows, and even though I could tell part of her wanted to make a joke, she remained serious as she said, "Well, I've never been a twin – and I thank God for that every day, frankly – but I've certainly heard weirder. This is your victory too, Olivia. You've worked yourself to the bone for this, he knows that."

"I'll never be able to even the scale though," I said, still looking at Ethan, suddenly obsessed with my brother's face, now that it was free. I looked back to Karen when she didn't answer me, and that image of perplexity was back. She rocked back on her heels, peering up at me, as if that would give her better insight. I forced a laugh at her expression and said, "It's just like what you said on the podcast; he's missed out on so much. Everything I've experienced in the last ten years, he's missed out on. You're right: he'll never get that back. He's free now, but it doesn't make up for everything else that was taken away."

"That doesn't mean it wasn't worth it," she said.

"I know," I said, nodding, "I know."

Just then, out of the corner of my eye I saw a familiar figure about to leave the courtroom, and I followed after, making my excuses to Karen.

"Spencer!" I called out, stopping her as she slipped down the front steps of the court house and almost disappeared into the mist. She turned on her heel, and slowly made her way back up to meet me.

"Congratulations, Olivia," she said, "I'm really glad Ethan's finally getting the freedom he deserves."

I nodded in response, and said, "It was nice of you to come. I didn't see you earlier."

"I slipped in a little late. I was with Reid. She wanted to come too, but she still hasn't been able to actually leave the house."

"She hasn't?" I said, unable to keep the surprise and concern out of my voice. Reid was no longer under house arrest, but after everything that had happened, she appeared to have developed fairly severe, although hopefully short-lived agoraphobia. After getting the second opinion from Karen's medical examiner stating that it would be impossible for one person – especially one of Reid's size – to have inflicted the damage done to James Asher, the prosecutors working the case had asked their own ME to examine the body again. This had led to the case being re-opened, and eventually – less than two weeks ago – the arrest of the bartender at Tin Man's, Rachel Grey's two brothers. As far as I knew, Rachel herself hadn't been arrested, but all charges against Reid had duly been dropped and the monitor around her ankle removed. But the damage had already been done.

"How's she doing?" I asked. Spencer shook her head, unable to answer, and I noticed how stretched and strained she looked. Her eyes were bloodshot, her face drawn, skin too pale. "How are *you*?" I asked in a low voice.

It took her a while to answer, but eventually Spencer said, "It's been a lot ... between Reid and this ... it's all brought up some things I've been trying to forget."

"Spencer," I said, taking a step closer to her and finally finding the courage to say out loud what I'd suspected for weeks, "did Tyler assault you in any way when we were in high school?"

Her eyes snapped to mine and then slipped away again as she swallowed something down and said, "He raped me, Olivia. He didn't assault me, he raped me."

I'd already guessed her answer, but it didn't make it any easier to hear out loud. "I'm so sorry," I said, my voice almost getting lost in its own whisper. "Is that ... is that what your non-disclosure agreement was about?"

Spencer's face was rigid, taut, but her expression was raw, undiluted even as her voice skipped and broke on her words. "I went to the police," she croaked, "did what I thought my mother would want me to do, did it so that my sister would never have to, did it even though I didn't want to, and when I got there, do you know what they did? They left me for hours in an interview room. Made me feel like the suspect. And do you know what I remember most? Feeling so cold. Just absolutely freezing. I have no idea why: It was the middle of summer. And then Maria Washington showed up. At first I couldn't figure out why. I thought maybe she was there as mayor, like it was normal for the mayor to show up at times like that, but then I realized she wasn't there as the mayor, she was there as Tyler's mother. She apologized on his behalf. Told me he was troubled, that he had his issues. That they'd been struggling with it his whole life. As if raping me was the same as disrupting the classroom. Then she asked me not to press charges. She took me through every stage of the process, pointed out how much of an uphill battle it would be to press charges against Tyler. How much more difficult it would be for me than if I just let it all alone. She quoted some statistic about how few rape charges lead to a conviction, and she made it seem as if she were right there with me, bemoaning that statistic and the state of our legal system, even as she convinced me not to press charges against her own son." Spencer shook her head, as if shaking herself out of the memory, trying to rid herself of it. Her mouth had twisted and turned as she spoke, a slash of rage drawn across her face, but she hadn't cried.

"And that's when you signed the NDA?" I asked.

"Not right then and there. She didn't have them already drawn up or anything, but that's when she mentioned that she could help me out with tuition fees for college, maybe more. And then when I eventually did sign it, I realized it meant I could never tell anyone."

"But you'd already told Reid?" I said.

"Yes. She's always known when something's wrong with me. With anyone really. She can read people even when what she's reading hasn't been written yet." Her eyes clamped on mine and I blinked back in surprise: she'd been avoiding my gaze since she started to speak, but now her eyes sparked with fire. "Did you know?" she demanded, "not about me. But did you know what Tyler was really like? What he did to people, to girls? You were friends with him, Olivia, did you know?"

"I don't think I ever knew who Tyler Washington was. Not until he died," I said.

I didn't get a moment alone with my brother until much later. We were back at my parents' house, where he'd be staying for now, although I'd left Samira there that morning so that she could create a celebratory feast, and we'd all been met by the smell of baking as we'd walked in.

There was no fog in Portland. It had been raining as we drove back into the city, the clouds low-slung, grey, and glowering, but sulfur yellow sunshine had managed to break its way through the cracks, a rainbow arcing its way over my parents' street as Daniel and I had turned into it, and now it lay molten and golden on the garden as I pushed the back doors open and stepped out onto the deck to get some air. I didn't realize anyone had followed me until Ethan spoke.

"You seem preoccupied, Liv. Everything okay?"

I turned to him and smiled. "Just taking it all in. Plus, I should be the one asking you that, shouldn't I? How surreal does all this feel?"

"You mean on a scale of one to Dali?" he asked, and I grinned.

"Yeah, you seen any melting clocks yet?"

"No, but that rainbow as we arrived felt a bit much, to be honest. Felt like the universe was playing with me."

"If I was anyone else, I'd say maybe it was just welcoming you home," I said.

"Yeah, but then you wouldn't be you," he said looking around our parents' backyard with idle interest. "Not sure this feels like home yet though."

"You'll get used it," I offered.

Ethan nodded his head slowly, and said, "If there's anything

I've learnt it's that you can get used to just about anything. If you have to."

The air seemed very still suddenly, and I realized the wind had dropped. We were both standing in a slice of hyper-yellow sunlight, and Ethan's eyes glowed gold as he turned to me and said, "Why'd you do it?"

I stared into his eyes – my eyes – and tried to figure out what he was asking me. "What do you mean? I did it for this, I did it so that you'd be free."

"No. Not why did you get me out of prison. I know why you did that. I mean, why did you kill Tyler, Olivia?"

Everything in the world stopped except my heart, which pounded at my chest as though it were trying to escape.

Everything in the world stopped as I tried to figure out how long he'd known.

50

THAT NIGHT

There's the sound of feet walking away, the door closing softly and then nothing. I hold my breath, hoping they've both gone, but waiting a little longer just in case. But just then my phone goes off; Cole.

"Who's in there?" someone barks through the door, and I unlock it, pulling it open to reveal Tyler Washington.

His face is like thunder, a sky full of storm, until he sees that it's me and the clouds pull away to reveal a brightly shining sun, the full beam of his shit-stirring grin directed at me.

"Olivia Hall," he says, stretching out my name with all the playfulness of a bored cat. "Have you been eavesdropping?" He waves a finger cartoonishly at me, pretending to be surprised, annoyed, dismayed.

I tip my head to the side and narrow my eyes at him. "I was dealing with a lady type emergency when you two barged in and started dragging on each other. What the hell's going on, Tyler? I've never heard Nick like that."

I've learnt over the years that the best way to deal with Tyler Washington is by sidestepping around him. He could do with a good punch to the face, but you're far better off coming at him from the side and taking him via subterfuge.

He rolls his eyes and lets out a pretend sigh. "Oh Nick's fine, I'll deal with it. Always cleaning up that boy's spills aren't I?" he says, and I can't help but draw my eyebrows together in disdain.

"Yeah, you're a really great friend, Ty," I quip, but he just whips that grin back at me and takes two long strides towards me, so that his fingers are now within reach of my arm and he's dragging them up and down my bare skin.

"I *am* a good friend, aren't I?" he says, eyes lowered, trailing me, as my breath slows and my heartbeat starts up.

"Tyler, don't do this," I say, trying to make my voice strong and stable, unignorable, and instead fuming at myself when it comes out tentative and torn.

He's still smiling as he pushes me back towards the bathroom and I try to duck around him, to squeeze past, but then he hears footsteps climbing up the stairs, and his hands squeeze my biceps pulling and pushing me into the bathroom as he whispers, "Shit, Nick's coming back for his pound of flesh."

The smile's still there so I know he doesn't care, not really. Doesn't take Nick and his threats, and his fear, and the sound of his hanging-by-a-thread voice as he pleaded with Tyler seriously. Tyler pushes me up against the glass door of the shower, reaching behind him to shut the bathroom door, lock it, and turn the overhead light off all in one fluid movement.

The only light now is from the classic Hollywood starlet bulbs surrounding the mirror that Jess forced her dad to install years ago. It creates a soft, unthreatening glow, rounding out Tyler's edges and emboldening him at the same time. I reach around him to flick the lock back, to open the door, but his hand reaches mine before I can unlock it, and he pins my arm to my side. Leaning over me and smiling wryly, "Brings back memories, doesn't it, Olivia?"

"What memories?" I grunt, trying to maneuver away and out from underneath him, and failing.

"What memories? What memories, she says? I'm offended, Liv. I thought we had a pretty special time on prom night."

I let out a huff of a laugh on a puff of air, "Prom? I can barely remember prom, I was so drunk, Tyler."

"Ohhh," Tyler says, the word practically a moan while he squirms his body all up along mine, pressing my back even further up against the glass of the shower, "now you've hurt my feelings. That's not very nice, Liv."

His fingers go to the button of my jeans, but mine fly there just as fast, gripping his hands tight, trying to hold them still. He's smiling down at me still, his face practically pressed against mine, breath hot and strong, full of beer and weed. The smile is a tease, barely even a taunt.

He thinks we're playing, I realize. Thinks we're flirting.

I smile back. My smile is taut and tense, but I pray he doesn't notice, and luckily for me he doesn't. Tyler never notices what he doesn't want to see.

"Tyler. Not here. Come on, anyone could find us. Cole is right downstairs," I say, trying to reason with him. I'm surprised by how firm and fair I manage to sound. My heart is beating so hard and heavy in my chest I'm sure that if I looked down, I could see it through my shirt.

"Cole's a fucking idiot," Tyler says in response, leaning his face over mine and for a tenth of a second I think he's going to kiss me, but instead he buries his face in my neck, and begins to lift the hem of my shirt, hot fingers scraping my skin, pressing into my flesh. He stops at my waist, spanning it with his hands and digs in.

Just then, my phone starts to ring, buzzing insistently at my backside. Undeterred, Tyler slips his hand into the back pocket of my jeans, pulling me even closer to him as he does so, and flipping the screen of the phone around so we can both see who's calling.

"Someone's ears were burning," he says with a low laugh before pressing the cancel button and reaching behind him to place the phone on the edge of the vanity. I try to take it from him as he does so, but he just cuts me a look, gives another low laugh and says very softly, "No, no. No interruptions."

"Tyler, come on, he's just gonna try and come find me if I don't answer him, give me the phone," I say, trying and failing to push him off me.

This whole time, my abdomen has been clenching and unclenching, a coiled rope of iron wrapping itself up inside my stomach as I breathe through the pain. All I want is to go home, take some Midol and go to bed. I push again at Tyler's chest, but my arm muscles feel too loose, as weak and unwieldy as ribbons.

But then my phone is ringing again. Over and over and over again, vibrating so hard it's about to shake its way off the bathroom vanity. Tyler pulls his hand away from me, takes a step back, finally putting some air between us, letting the breath back into my lungs.

He picks up my phone and looks back over at me, eyes huge and dark in the dimly lit bathroom.

"Cole," Tyler says with a rasping breath. "Again. Does he ever let up?"

I swallow, take a deep breath, try to even it out, because it sounds ragged, even to me. I don't want it to. Not right now.

"Liv!" The shout is coming from the stairs, and is quickly followed by the sound of footfalls.

I'm hoping Cole hasn't reached Jess's bedroom yet, but he has, pulling up short as he watches us stumble out of Jess's bathroom.

"Liv," Cole says heavily, his gaze flicking between me and Tyler. "What's going on?"

"Nothing," I say in a rush, "we were just talking."

"What the fuck?" Cole says again, and this time there's a tear, a rip in his voice.

"Cole, it's not what you think," I say slowly, walking towards him with a hand up, ready to press it softly against his chest.

But he brushes it and me aside, not looking at me, staring

at Tyler. "Oh, yeah? And what do I think Olivia? Is it the same thing I thought when I saw you both coming out of Tyler's room after prom?"

I grab at his arm, trying to pull him back to me, but all my words have left me because how can he remember something I don't remember happening? I try desperately to think back to prom night, but it is one long blur, except for the brightly lit, camera flash brightness of leaving the house, smiles plastered on our faces, and circling the hall when we first arrived, blood starting to thin with alcohol as the beat of music picked up, and strobe lights turned memories into flickering shards. The after party happened at Tyler's house. I can't remember where his parents were, I can barely remember arriving. But I do remember the morning after, acid ripping a hole in my stomach and throat as I vomited up the night before, the headache so heavy it pinned me to the ground, and the taste of fear in my mouth as I realized my underwear was ripped and I had no way of knowing why or how.

I try to speak, but there's nothing there. I don't know how to say those words out loud. "What?" Cole says softly, looking down into my eyes, "Can't talk your way out of this one, huh Liv? What's everyone going to think of you now that I get to tell them what a fucking whore you are?"

My hand drops from his arm, and I think about explaining, trying to explain, to get him back to me, but I'm just so tired.

I run down the stairs, heart beating in time to the fall of my feet. Saying goodbye to Jess, I rush around her house, trying to find everything I've left scattered around, while keeping half an ear on upstairs, trying to work out what's going on up there between Cole and Tyler. I catch sight of Nick glowering in the corner. He's standing with people, but not talking to anyone, knocking the lip of his beer bottle against his mouth.

My stomach cramps, reminding me how desperate I am to get home, and I go to the front door, pulling it open just as I hear footsteps behind me on the stairs, and Cole's voice calling my name. But now all his voice does is force me to hear the echo of him calling me a whore, and I can hardly bear to look at him as I shake my head and rush through the open door, pulling it closed behind me. He catches up with me halfway down the street, and I try to shake him off, get him away, but for some reason, now, he wants to stick around.

"I saw you with him," he says, and I want to shake him out of his stupidity, make him see the world as it really is, but I'm too tired.

"It's not what you think, Cole," I say, as if that will do anything to dissuade him from what he clearly already thinks. What can you do when someone has already made up their mind about you? Rain falls on us indiscriminately, and I feel myself begin to shiver. The night has turned cold, even though it's only August, and the raindrops are like sharp pinpricks against my skin. It's as if I can feel each and every one, and every one is an attack.

Something moves on Jess's porch, and even though he's swathed in darkness, I know it's Tyler. Watching.

I don't want to do this. Don't want a confrontation with Cole, with Tyler. Exhaustion pours through me, as heavy as the rain, and so instead I turn towards the woods, and to home.

"Olivia," Cole says again, this time more sharply, as he rushes after me down the street, spinning me around to face him again, pulling me closer to him than I expected, his face bearing down over mine so that I can taste the beer on his breath. I flash back to Jess's bathroom and cringe, flinching away from my boyfriend, as he says, "I saw you, I saw you up there with him, so don't fucking lie to me, okay?"

"It's not what you think," I say again, but this only frustrates him further.

"What do I think, Olivia?" he roars, and I try to take a step back but he won't let me, hand gripping tight around my arm.

"He ..." I look back to the porch, where the outline of a figure still stands. "He came on to me, okay? I was trying to get rid of him when you came upstairs."

"It didn't look like you were trying very hard," Cole says, the words like missiles going off inside my head.

I look down at his hand, knuckles white in the streetlight, gripping onto my arm, and something snaps because I spit out, "What, you mean like I'm not trying very hard to get away from you right now?"

Cole's eyes dart to mine, looking like I've electrocuted him, but he doesn't let go. At least not immediately. "I just want to go home, Cole," I say, tiredness clinging to my voice the way beer and drunkenness are clinging to his. "Can we talk about this tomorrow please?"

"Cole, man, just let it go, it was nothing," a voice says close to us and I jerk my head to see Tyler standing just a few feet behind Cole. Everything about him screams amused boredom.

Cole's hand finally drops from my arm and he turns slowly to look at Tyler. He's perfectly still as he says, "You need to walk away Tyler. Right the fuck now."

I don't wait to hear Tyler's response. I don't want to see how any of this turns out. I turn on my heel and walk as quickly as I can down the street, heading home the fastest way possible, past the high school, and through the woods. I can still hear their shouts as tarmac changes to gravel, and gravel to muddy earth beneath my feet, and I leave the street behind and slip into the velvet darkness of the woods.

I've only been home a few minutes, still soaking wet and shivering, when Cole starts texting me.

Come back to the party

Come on, Liv

Fine, you don't have to come back to the party but come meet me somewhere? We need to talk about what went down with Tyler

Please

I ignore them for as long as I can, but then I start to think about Cole thinking I've cheated on him with his best friend, thinking I could or would ever do that to him. The feeling of being trapped beneath Tyler's body grips me, and I have to force myself to realize and remember I'm safe at home now. That he can't hurt me now. Then I think about the word 'whore' coming out of Cole's mouth, the sound of it in his voice, suddenly so unfamiliar. Another message pings through and I pick my phone back up to read it.

Liv, I'm sorry, I'm just so sorry
I just really need to see you, I can't get my head straight.
Meet me halfway? In the woods?

It takes me a while to answer. I don't know if I want to see him. Don't know if I can bear it. But then something rolls through me, something like pride and defiance. Something that says I don't want to spend the rest of my life hiding in my room, something that pushes me up out of bed, forces me to change my clothes, and put my shoes back on, and go back out into the woods.

The entrance to the woods is just seconds away from our house, but as soon as I walk past the tree line, I know I've made a mistake. The dark is different now. Slick, thick and dangerous. It slips around me, sharp as a knife edge, a deadly rebuke. I should've stayed home, could've been safe and warm in my bed right now. Something catches my eye, just a slice of life shuddering through the dark and I start, annoyed at myself as I do, hating how much my instincts give me away. It's just an animal, I think, making its own way through the woods, but then I hear more branches snapping, leaves underfoot, and suddenly the air is heavy with breath and footsteps. Hitching breath, catching, catching, catching me.

"Cole?" I call, "is that you?"

His hand grabs my upper arm, swinging me around, tight and hard, a human tourniquet, my pumping blood straining to reach the area of blind pain. For a long second I can't speak. Can barely think. We spend our lives thinking we're being prepared for just this moment; the hand reaching out in the dark, the attacker bearing down on you, you alone, all alone, barely bearing witness. But the truth is, nothing prepares you. His eyes are a fire in the dark, two bright lamps flashing danger, warning beacons warding me off.

"Tyler?" I gasp.

The flash of his grin, the hot breath on my face.

He lets go of one of my arms, reaching into his pocket and dancing a phone in front of me. "You stole Cole's phone?" I say, and he laughs.

"Yup, just as he and Nick were beating the shit out of me. Still managed to get the upper hand didn't I?"

"You got in a fight with Nick and Cole?" I ask, and that's when I notice he has a cut lip, beginning to swell, a bruise forming on his cheekbone.

"They tried," he says with an insouciant shrug, still smiling down at me.

I try to pull my arm free of his grip, thinking I can still ease my way out of this, walk home and pretend none of it ever happened. But all that does is make him hold on tighter. He's put Cole's phone back in his pocket now, and holds on tight to me with both hands while shuffling me backwards towards the raw bark of a tree trunk.

"What do you want Tyler?" I ask through gritted teeth.

"You know what I want," he breathes, face lowering over me, and if it was any other moment, any other time, any other night, I'd roll my eyes. Instead my heart punches at my chest, a warning shot as he almost-whispers, "we've got unfinished business, Liv."

"We don't have any business, Tyler, unfinished or otherwise," I say, attempting to push him away with both my hands splayed across his abdomen.

He looks down at where they are and seems to like it. My upper arms are still gripped in his hands, restricting any movement so instead of relying on them, I lift my right knee up with

350

all the speed and energy I have, breathing with relief as it makes contact with Tyler's groin and he staggers backwards, releasing my arms from his grip.

"Jesus!" he shouts into the night, "what the fuck was that for, Liv?"

"What do you think it was for, asshole?" I raggedly shout back at him, breath short and uneven.

But I don't wait for him to answer; I'm not here to make conversation.

Neither is he.

So, I run.

I think I can outrun him. Easily even. I'm still in pain – the Midol I took at home hasn't kicked in yet – and it feels like there's a burning hot poker pushing its way through my lower back, right the way out to my hips and pelvis. My legs are also shaking with adrenaline, muscles weak and loose, but Tyler is drunk, so much drunker than me, and he's just minutes from that fight with Cole and Nick who seem to have done a number on him.

I'm wrong though.

Of course he's faster than me. Of course he catches up. He's six foot two, going to college on a partial basketball scholarship.

His hand grabs my shoulder and I'm surprised by the force of it all over again. I refuse to turn, to slow down, but there's mud on the ground, the track thick and heavy, slick and treacherous, so as I yank my shoulder away from him, the force of his response forces me to the ground.

I land in mud, my hands only just able to stutter my fall, chin landing hard on the ground, sending my teeth chattering through my head.

I try to get up but slip, my hands and arms coated in mud that weighs me down even more.

Before I can stand, Tyler is on me again. I can't tell if he fell like I did, slipping as I slipped, or if he saw me go and took his chance, but either way it doesn't matter. The extra weight of him forces my face into the ground, my mouth open in a thwarted scream that's suddenly full of mud, and twigs, and early fallen leaves. I splutter and choke on it, trying desperately to breathe, wondering if this is what drowning feels like, perversely wishing it was water pouring down my throat, not earth which sings with life, but tastes of death.

I try to wrench myself free of Tyler, crawling up and out from underneath him, mud coating my every move, but he pulls me back down, his actions frantic and jerky.

The rest of the world has stopped. I can't hear anything except our breathing which is heavy and desperate. Panting.

He jerks me around to face him so I'm lying on my back, my face is finally free of the ground, so I let out a scream that rips through the night, and shove a handful of mud in his face. He splutters and stalls, the only words discernible "fuck", and "you."

I try to slide out from underneath him again while he's distracted, but he's not distracted enough. He pulls me back underneath him, pinning me down with his thighs while his hands, which are as coated in mud as mine are, wrench open the button of my jeans and tug at the waistband. I scream out again, hitting him on the side of his head with my left hand, pushing at his face, while my other hand scrambles in the dark and the mud. I feel something heavy and solid; cool, wet rock slipping beneath my fingers as I grab hold of it and launch it against Tyler's shoulder.

He groans in pain and says something again but I don't hear it. I heave the rock again, this time connecting with his face, and the noise that erupts from Tyler sounds animal, not human. Blood falls from his nose and it looks like he's about to roll off me, to stop, when instead he grabs at both of my shoulders and shakes, throwing my body back against the rough ground again and again. There's a knot of something, of tree roots probably and they pound into my spine with every blow. My teeth shake. My brain rattles.

My hand fastens over the rock in a life-saving grip.

He throws me against the ground, again and again, as if I were nothing, and I hit him on the side of the head with the rock, again and again. Every time he forces me back to the ground, I hit him. Again and again and again and again, until he's not throwing me around anymore. But still I can't stop.

Eventually I realize it's just my wild breaths that are left.

Eventually I realize he's slumped over me, not moving.

Eventually I crawl out from underneath him, my arms too weak to push him off, my legs having to do all the work.

I don't stop to check that he's breathing.

He didn't stop and so I don't stop.

It's not until I'm almost out of the woods, having stumbled and run all that way, that I realize I'm still holding the rock. I look down at it. I can barely tell the difference between the blood and the mud, the leaves and pine needles, and the strands of hair.

I swallow. Take a deep breath. And head back into the woods.

I don't go back to Tyler's body. I take the left turn when I need to and follow the sound of the river.

Standing on its banks I almost slip and fall. My legs have never felt so weak in my life. I look down at the rock again, and for a second, in the dark, it looks as though it's fused with my hand, as though we've been forged together, human and stone. But then I throw it down into the water, letting it fall through my fingers, and listen for the splash in the dark, waiting for it to sink and be swallowed and for this whole night to be taken with it.

51

All the light has left the sky, been leeched from it, and I can barely make out Ethan's face. His eyes haven't left me the whole time, but he hasn't said a word. Without realizing it, I've begun to shiver. The day hadn't been especially cold, but now it is, and my eyes are drawn to the window into my parents' kitchen where my family and friends, everyone I love, are still gathered. Georgia is watching us through the window. We haven't turned the backyard lights on yet, but she must be curious about why we've been stood out here for so long, the evening leaving us, the night getting longer.

"How long have you known?" I say at last, swallowing down a decade of fear and lies.

"I've had my suspicions for a while," Ethan says into the dusky, darkening air. "You can't understand how much time you have to think in prison, Olivia. You just can't get away from it. Honestly, I thought for a long time that it was either Cole or Nick, or both of them. But then Cole came to visit me in prison the week before Sandford Washington made his confession."

"Cole?" I manage to croak, trying to imagine the scene playing out between the two of them.

Ethan nods his head, "Yeah, Cole. I was as shocked by his visit as you seem to be. No love lost there, right? But he was worried, you see. About you."

I swallow again, thinking back to the evening, almost two months ago, when Cole confronted me outside my motel room.

"He seemed to think we'd both lied about that night. That we'd done it for the same reasons. For you," Ethan continues. "He told me I had to stop you from doing the podcast, that he couldn't lie for you anymore, that he couldn't protect you anymore. He's having a baby with Morgan. He said that they had to be his first priority, and that if anyone could get you to stop going on with the podcast, it was me."

I nod silently, and in that silence I hear myself gasping for air, for breath. I have imagined this moment so many times over the last ten years, but it still hasn't prepared me for it.

"But you didn't tell me to stop," I say.

"No."

"No," I repeat, unable to say what I really want to say which is: why?

"Cole thought I should. He was sure this was some kamikaze mission of yours, running towards the bomb just as it goes off. But he doesn't know you like I do. He never did."

"No?" I say again.

"You're a survivor, Liv. A self-preservationist. You've never run towards a fight you didn't think you could win in your life."

I take a deep breath, gulp it down like water. "I wasn't so sure this time," I say.

Ethan's eyes are trained on me. I watch, through the gloom as they widen almost imperceptibly. The evening light has stripped both the day and my brother's eyes of any warmth they had earlier. I look at his face, take it all in, and realize I don't know it at all.

It's mine but not mine.

He is me but not me.

355

"The mayor's husband had nothing to do with it, did he?" Ethan says.

I shake my head, "No."

"He took the fall for her."

"Yes."

"Why, do you think?"

"I don't know," I say, and to my horror it comes out as a whisper.

"Not love then," he says.

I shake my head, "No. I don't think so," I say.

"You must have some theories, though?"

I can't see through his words. It's as if a brick wall has been built up between us, and every word Ethan says is muffled and blunted, impossible to decipher, to figure out. Morgan once said that my gift had always been having the right words, knowing exactly what to say. But that's not true. What I'm good at is realizing what it is people are actually saying when they speak. Maybe it's because I'm so rarely saying what I mean. A lifetime of lies, a life made out of a lie, lived as a lie, has made me into, not a lie detector exactly, but a translator at least. Because no one's ever really saying what they mean.

But not now. Not anymore. I wonder if I've ever known what Ethan is really saying, if I've just fooled myself into thinking my own deception means I can somehow detect when someone is deceiving me.

"Fear," I say, answering Ethan's question at last. "He's scared of her. Of what she's capable of."

"I can understand that," Ethan says.

"Have you ... did you –"

"Have I told anyone?" he finishes for me.

But just then, before I can answer, before he can continue, the back door opens with a squelch and I turn to see Kat backlit by the lights indoors, Ray not far behind her.

Her eyes stray to Ethan who's looking right back at her, and I watch carefully at what passes between them.

"Olivia," Kat says, moving towards me in the almost-dark, "Ethan. What's going on?"

But I can't answer her.

I can't speak.

I am locked inside my body, muscle gripping at bone, everything tensed and waiting.

From somewhere far, far away I think I can hear my brother saying my name, but it's barely audible over the sound of every lie I've ever told crashing down around me. I take a deep breath, wait for my senses to return to me, and take a step forward.

Toward what, I have no idea.

Acknowledgements

It's probably pretty obvious by now that I'm a true crime podcast junkie, and it's fair to say that this book would never have been written if I hadn't become so obsessed with them over the past few years. Needless to say, I've almost always got one on the go, but the series that most influenced the writing of this book and the concept of *Shadow of a Doubt* were *Accused*, *Up and Vanished*, *Undisclosed*, and of course, *Serial*. But while it couldn't be more different in tone to the fictional podcast in this novel, it's my love of *My Favorite Murder* that really spurred me to make a podcast central to the plot like this, so, thank you, Karen, and Georgia et al, and of course, SSDGM.

Thanks, as always, to my amazingly supportive family and friends, as well as to my agent, Devin, and editor, Kathryn, both of whom have helped whip this tricky and often headache-inducing manuscript into shape.